Praise for

New York Times bestselling author
Jeaniene Frost's
Night Huntress series

"Intense, emotional, and flat-out
fantastic... Put Jeaniene Frost on your
must-read list!"
—Lara Adrian, *New York Times*
bestselling author of *Ashes of Midnight*

"A can't-put-down masterpiece that's
sexy-hot and a thrill-ride on every page.
I'm officially addicted to the series."
—Gena Showalter,
New York Times bestselling author of
The Darkest Whisper

"Witty dialogue, a strong heroine, a
delicious hero, and enough action to make
a reader forget to sleep."
—Melissa Marr,
New York Times bestselling author of
Fragile Eternity

By Jeaniene Frost

JEANIENE FROST

First Drop Of
Crimson

AVON
An Imprint of HarperCollinsPublishers

This is a work of fiction. Names, characters, places, and incidents are products of the author's imagination or are used fictitiously and are not to be construed as real. Any resemblance to actual events, locales, organizations, or persons, living or dead, is entirely coincidental.

AVON BOOKS
An Imprint of HarperCollins*Publishers*
10 East 53rd Street
New York, New York 10022-5299

Copyright © 2010 by Jeaniene Frost
ISBN 978-0-373-60210-0
www.avonromance.com

All rights reserved. No part of this book may be used or reproduced in any manner whatsoever without written permission, except in the case of brief quotations embodied in critical articles and reviews. For information address Avon Books, an Imprint of HarperCollins Publishers.

First Avon Books mass market printing: February 2010

Avon Trademark Reg. U.S. Pat. Off. and in Other Countries, Marca Registrada, Hecho en U.S.A.

HarperCollins® is a registered trademark of HarperCollins Publishers.

Printed in the U.S.A.

If you purchased this book without a cover you should be aware that this book is stolen property. It was reported as "unsold and destroyed" to the publisher, and neither the author nor the publisher has received any payment for this "stripped book."

To Jinger.

My sister, my friend,
and the person I can vent to
or laugh with.
Glad you're in my life.

Acknowledgments

There are so many people behind my books that it's impossible to list them all, but specific mention is more than due to the following:

I have to thank God first, both for the inspiration to dream up my stories—and the determination to turn them into books.

Thanks so much to the readers of the Night Huntress series. Your encouragement and enthusiasm have been more than I ever dreamed. You make it fun for me to share my stories, and that's an amazing gift.

My agent, Nancy Yost, superbly handles the business aspects of publishing so that I have more time to concentrate on what I love most: writing. Thanks also to my editor, Erika Tsang, for her wonderful expertise in keeping me on track with my plots…and for trimming out my occasional rambling. If I had Erika edit my Acknowledgments page, it would be much more eloquent and succinct! Huge thanks go to Thomas Egner, for yet another cover that left me breathless.

Also a big shout-out to Pamela Spengler-Jaffee, Carrie Feron, Liate Stehlik, Wendy Ho, and Amanda Bergeron at Avon Books/HarperCollins, for all their efforts to get this book onto as many shelves—or electronic readers—as possible.

My husband, Matthew, deserves his own chapter of thanks, but I'll keep it brief and just say that without you, I wouldn't have much to write about the power of love. My parents, sisters, and other family continue to be my rock. I'm so fortunate to have all of you.

Melissa, you're an incredible critique partner... and an even better friend. Vicki, Ilona, and Yasmine, whether it's been words of wisdom when I'm faltering or an ear when I need to vent, you ladies have been priceless. In my mind, you're ALL kick-ass heroines.

Tage and Erin, I'm so glad for all that you do with the fan site. It's one of my most fun places online to visit. And finally, thanks to all the booksellers who've stocked me on their shelves or recommended my series to their customers. You're awesome. Consider yourselves kissed!

Prologue

New Year's Eve, one year before

Even though they were in the basement, Denise could still hear the sounds of battle outside. She didn't know what had attacked them, but they couldn't be human, not for Cat to look so scared when she'd ordered them downstairs. If she was frightened, then they should all be afraid.

Crashing noises above made Denise gasp. Randy's arm tightened around her. "It'll be okay."

His face said he believed otherwise. So did Denise. But she smiled, trying to convince her husband she believed the lie, if only to make him feel better.

His arm eased off her. "I'm going upstairs to help look for *it*."

It was the object that had drawn these creatures,

whatever they were, to this house in the middle of icy nowhere. If *it* could be found and destroyed, the attack would stop.

Five years ago, Denise wouldn't have believed in vampires, ghouls, or objects possessing supernatural powers. Now because she'd chosen to spend the New Year with her half-vampire best friend in a house filled with things the average person didn't believe in, she and Randy would probably die.

"You can't go up there, it's too dangerous," Denise protested.

"I won't go outside, but I can help look in the house."

Denise knew finding *it* was the only chance any of them had. "I'll go with you."

"Stay here. The kids are scared."

Denise looked to the faces huddled in the far corner of the basement room, eyes wide with fear. Former runaways or homeless kids who lived with the vampires, their rent paid in blood donations. The only other adult in the room was Justina, and even her normally imperious expression was tremulous.

"I'll stay," Denise said at last. "Be careful. Come right back if those things get any closer."

Randy gave her a quick kiss. "I will. Promise."

"I love you," she called out as he flung open the door.

He smiled. "Love you, too."

He went out the door and Denise locked it behind him. It was the last time she saw Randy alive.

Chapter 1

"I think Amber was murdered."

Denise gaped at her cousin. She was well into her third margarita, but she couldn't have misheard him. *Maybe we shouldn't have gone to a bar after the funeral.* Still, Paul had said he wasn't up to sitting another shiva. His mother and sister had just died within a month of each other. If getting a drink made Paul feel better, who cared what they were supposed to do?

"But the doctors said it was her heart."

"I know what they *said*," Paul growled. "The police didn't believe me, either. But the day before she died, Amber told me she thought she was being followed. She was twenty-three, Denise. Who has a heart attack at twenty-three?"

"Your mother just died of a heart attack," Denise reminded him softly. "Heart disease can be hereditary. It's rare for someone as young as Amber to have heart problems, true, but your sister was under a lot of stress—"

"No more than me now," Paul cut her off bitterly. "You saying I might be next?"

The thought was so awful Denise didn't even want to contemplate it. "I'm sure you're fine, but it wouldn't hurt to get checked out."

Paul leaned forward, glancing around before he spoke. "I think I'm being followed, too." His voice was barely a whisper.

Denise paused. For months after Randy's death, she'd thought every shadow was something sinister waiting to pounce on her. Even over a year later, she still hadn't totally managed to shake that feeling. Now her aunt and her cousin had died within a month of each other, and Paul also seemed to think death loomed right behind him. Was that a normal part of the grieving process? To feel that when death took someone close to you, it was coming after you next?

"Do you want to stay at my house for a few days?" she asked. "I could use the company."

Actually Denise preferred being alone, but Paul didn't know that. The careful investing Randy had done disappeared in the stock market crash, leaving her with just enough to bury him and to put a down payment on a new home, away from most of her family. Her parents meant well, but in their concern, they'd tried to take over her life. At work, Denise kept herself distant from her co-workers, and the seclusion had helped this past long, hard year as she dealt with Randy's death.

Still, if staying with her helped Paul through the initial shock of his double loss, she'd gladly give up her solitude.

Her cousin looked relieved. "Yeah. If that's okay."

Denise signaled for the bartender. "Of course. Let's head to my house before I have any more drinks. You've already had too many, so we'll take my car and pick up yours in the morning."

"I can drive," Paul argued.

Denise glared at him. "Not tonight."

Paul shrugged. Denise was glad he didn't fight it. She'd hate herself if Paul got in an accident after going out drinking with her. Aside from her parents, he was the closest family she had left.

She took care of the check over Paul's objections and they went out into the parking lot. After that incident three months ago, Denise made sure to park in a well-lit area as close to the bar's entrance as possible. As a further precaution, even though Paul walked with her, she kept her hand on the repellent spray dangling from her key chain. She had two of those; one filled with pepper spray, the other with silver nitrate. Humans weren't the only ones who liked to attack at night.

"The guest room is small, but there's a TV in it," Denise said as they reached her car. "You want to—"

Her voice cut off in a scream as Paul was jerked back, a man appearing out of nowhere behind him. Paul tried to scream, too, but an arm tight across his throat prevented him. The stranger's eyes seemed to burn as they looked from Denise to her cousin.

"Another one," he hissed, placing his fist across Paul's chest.

Denise screamed as loud as she could, raising her pepper spray and sending a burst of liquid in the man's face. He didn't even blink, but Paul's eyes swelled shut as some of it hit him.

"Somebody, help!" Denise shouted again, spraying until the container was empty. The man didn't even budge while Paul's face began to turn blue.

She grabbed the silver nitrate next, unloading its contents in four frantic bursts. The man did blink at that, but in apparent surprise. Then he laughed.

"Silver? How interesting."

Denise was out of weapons and the man hadn't loosened his hold by a fraction. Panicked, she balled her fists and flung herself at him—only to fall to the ground a moment later on top of her cousin.

"What's going on out there?" someone from the bar called out.

Denise glanced up. The stranger was gone. A large German shepherd sat a few feet off, its mouth open in a doggy grin. It turned around and ran when a handful of people from the bar came over to them.

"Someone call 911!" Denise exclaimed, noting with horror that Paul wasn't breathing. She placed her mouth over his, blowing hard—and began to choke as she tasted pepper spray.

Coughing and gasping, Denise saw a young man try CPR on Paul and then fall back, choking as well. She pressed her fingers to Paul's throat. Nothing.

Almost a dozen people stood over her, but none of them seemed to be reaching for their cell phones.

"Call a goddamn *ambulance*," she got out, pounding on Paul's chest and trying to blow into his mouth even though she could hardly breathe herself. "Come on, Paul! Don't do this!"

Through her blurred vision, she saw her cousin's face turning a darker shade of blue. His mouth was slack, his chest motionless under her hands. But Denise continued to pound on his chest, cupping her hands around his mouth to blow into it without her lips coming into contact with more pepper spray.

She didn't stop until the paramedics arrived, seemingly an eternity later. When they pulled her off, Paul still wasn't breathing.

"You're saying the man just...disappeared?"

The police officer couldn't quite keep the disbelief out of his tone. Denise fought the urge to slap him. She didn't know how much more she could take. She'd already had to call her family and tell them this unthinkable news, then grieved with them as they arrived at the hospital, then gave her report to the police. The one they seemed to have such trouble believing.

"As I said, when I looked up, the killer was gone."

"No one at the bar saw anyone out there, ma'am," the officer said for the third time.

Denise's temper snapped. "That's because they were inside when we were attacked. Look, the guy choked my cousin; doesn't Paul have bruises around his neck?"

The officer glanced away. "No, ma'am. The medical examiner hasn't looked at him yet, but the paramedics didn't see any signs of strangulation. They did say they found evidence of cardiac arrest..."

"He's only twenty-five years old!" Denise burst, then stopped. Ice slid up her spine. *Who has a heart attack at twenty-three?* Paul had asked just hours ago, followed up with a statement she'd summarily dismissed. *I think I'm being followed, too.*

Now Paul was dead—of an apparent heart attack. Just like Amber and Aunt Rose. Denise knew she hadn't imagined the man who'd been immune to both pepper spray and silver nitrate. The one who'd disappeared in a blink—and the big dog that had come out of nowhere.

Of course, she could relay none of this to the officer. He already looked at her like she was teetering on the crazy end of distraught. It hadn't escaped Denise's notice that when she'd been treated for pepper spray, her blood had also been taken, presumably to check her alcohol levels. She'd already been asked multiple times how much she'd drunk before leaving the bar. It was clear nothing she said, even leaving out mention of the supernatural, would be taken seriously if the medical examiner ruled that Paul had died of a heart attack.

Well, she knew people who'd believe her enough to investigate.

"Can I go home now?" Denise asked.

A flash of relief crossed the officer's face. It only made Denise want to smack him more. "Sure. I can arrange for a squad car to take you."

"I'll call a cab."

He stood, bobbing his head. "Here's my card if you remember anything else."

Denise took it only because wadding it up and throwing it at him would look questionable. "Thank you."

She waited until she was inside her house before she made the call. No need to have the taxi driver talk about how his latest fare had babbled on about a murder by a man who *might* have turned into a dog. If the police found out she'd said that, she could forget them following up on any leads she gave them, even if they did figure out this was a murder.

On the third ring, however, an automated voice intoned that the number she'd dialed had been disconnected. Denise hung up. That's right, Cat had been moving from place to place because some crazy vampire was stalking her. She had obviously changed her number, too. Was Cat still overseas? How long had it been since Denise last spoke to her? Weeks, maybe.

Next Denise tried the number she had for Bones, Cat's husband, but it, too, was disconnected. Denise dug around her house until she found an address book with the number for Cat's mother. The number was from over a year ago, so no surprise when that was also out of service.

Frustrated, Denise flung the address book on her couch. She'd been avoiding contact with the undead world, but now when she needed someone plugged into it, she didn't have anyone's current number.

There had to be *someone* she could reach. Denise scrolled through the entries in her cell phone, looking for anyone who had connections to Cat. When she was almost at the end, one name leapt out at her.

Spade. She'd saved Spade's number in her phone a few months ago, because he'd been the one to pick her up the last time she saw Cat.

Denise hesitated. Spade's sculpted features, pale skin, and penetrating stare flashed in her mind. Put Spade in a Calvin Klein ad and women would be tempted to lick the page, but Denise's memory of Spade was irrevocably tied to blood. Especially since the last time she'd seen him, he'd been splattered in it.

She shoved that aside. Someone had murdered Paul, and Spade might be her only link to reaching Cat. Denise pressed "call," praying she didn't hear that chipper monotone telling her the number was no longer in service. Three rings, four...

"Hallo?"

Denise felt light-headed with relief at hearing Spade's distinctive English accent. "Spade, it's Denise. Cat's friend," she added, thinking of how many Denises a centuries-old vampire probably knew. "I don't seem to have Cat's number and… I'm pretty sure some *thing* murdered my cousin. Maybe both cousins and my aunt, too."

It came out in a babble that sounded nuts even to her. She waited, hearing nothing but her breathing during the pause on the other line.

"This *is* Spade, isn't it?" she asked, wary. What if she'd hit the wrong number somehow?

His voice flowed back immediately. "Yes, apologies for that. Why don't you tell me what you believe you saw?"

Denise noticed his phrasing, but she was too wired to argue about it. "I saw my cousin murdered by a man who didn't even twitch when I maced him with pepper spray *and* silver nitrate. Then the next thing I saw, a big damn dog was standing where the man had been, but it ran off, and the police think my twenty-five-year-old cousin died of a heart attack instead of being strangled."

Another silence filled the line. Denise could almost picture Spade frowning as he listened. He scared her, but right now, she was more afraid of whatever had killed Paul.

"Are you still in Fort Worth?" he asked at last

"Yes. Same house as…as before." When he'd dropped her off after murdering a man in cold blood.

"Right. I'm sorry to inform you that Cat is in New Zealand. I can ring her or give you her number, but it would take a day at least for her to get to you, if not more."

Her friend and expert on all things inhuman was halfway around the world. Great.

"...but I happen to be in the States," Spade went on. "In fact, I'm in St. Louis. I could be there later today, have a look at your cousin's body."

Denise sucked in her breath, torn between wanting to find out what had killed Paul in the quickest way possible, and feeling edgy about it being Spade doing the investigating. Then she berated herself. The deaths of Paul, Amber, and her aunt meant more than her being *uncomfortable* about who was helping her.

"I'd appreciate that. My address is—"

"I remember where you live," Spade cut her off. "Expect me 'round noon."

She looked at her watch. Just over six hours. She couldn't get from St. Louis to Fort Worth that fast if her life depended on it, but if Spade said he'd be there around noon, she believed him.

"Thanks. Can you tell Cat, um, that..."

"Perhaps it's best if we don't involve Cat or Crispin just yet," Spade said, calling Bones by his human name as he always did. "They've had an awful time of it recently. No need to fret them if it's something I can handle."

Denise bit back her scoff. She knew what that translated to. *Or if she'd just imagined all this.*

"I'll see you at noon," she replied, and hung up.

The house seemed eerily quiet. Denise glanced out the windows with a shiver, telling herself the foreboding she felt was a normal reaction to her violent night. Just to be sure, however, she went through each room checking the windows and doors. All locked. Then she forced herself to shower, trying to block the images of Paul's blue-tinged face from her mind. It didn't work. Denise put on a robe and began restlessly prowling through her home once more.

If only she hadn't agreed to go out drinking with Paul, he might still be alive now. Or what if she'd immediately run into the bar for help, instead of staying in the parking lot? Could she have saved Paul, if she'd come out with a bunch of people to scare the attacker off? He'd left as soon as people responded to her screams; maybe she *could* have saved Paul, if she hadn't stood there uselessly macing his killer.

Denise was so caught up in her thoughts that she ignored the tapping sounds until they happened a third time. Then she froze. They were coming from her front door.

She left the kitchen and ran quietly up to her bedroom, pulling a Glock out of her nightstand. It was filled with silver bullets, which might only slow down a vampire, but would kill anything human. Denise walked down the stairs, straining her ears for each sound. *Yes, still there. Such an odd noise, like whimpering and scratching.*

What if it was someone trying to pick the lock? Should she call the police, or try to see what it was first? If it was just a raccoon nosing around and she called the cops, they'd *really* discount anything she said in the future.

Denise kept the gun pointed toward the sounds as she edged around to the front windows. If she angled her body just so, she could see her front door...

"What?" Denise gasped out loud.

On her porch was a little girl, something red on her outfit. She was tapping on the door in a way that looked hurt or exhausted or both. Now Denise could make out the word *help* coming from her.

Denise set down the gun and yanked open the door. The little girl's face was streaked with tears and her whole frame trembled.

"Can I come in? Daddy's hurt," the child lisped.

She picked her up, looking around for a car or any other indicator of how the little girl had gotten here.

"Come in, sweetie. What happened? Where's your daddy?" Denise crooned as she took the child inside.

The little girl smiled. "Daddy's dead," she said, her voice changing to something low and deep.

Denise's arms fell at the instant deluge of weight, horror filling her as she saw the little girl morph into the same man who'd murdered Paul. He grabbed her when she tried to run, shutting the door behind him.

"Thanks for inviting me in," he said, his hand clapping over Denise's mouth just in time to cut off her scream.

Chapter 2

Spade closed his mobile phone, mulling the conversation he'd just had. Denise MacGregor. He certainly hadn't expected to hear from her again. Now she fancied her cousin had been murdered by some sort of weredog—except weredogs or were-anything didn't exist.

There could be another explanation. Denise said she'd maced the attacker with pepper spray and silver. She could have missed him, true, but then again, perhaps she hadn't. If a vampire murdered her cousin, he could have tranced Denise into thinking she'd seen him transform into a dog—and that he hadn't been affected by the liquid silver spray. Humans' memories were so easy to alter. But if Denise *had* witnessed a vampire attack, the murderer would wonder how she'd known to use silver. He might decide to use more than glamour to make sure Denise didn't retell the tale. That was a risk Spade wasn't willing to take.

He cast a look at his bed with regret. Though he'd long ago mastered the crippling lethargy that came with sunrise, that didn't mean he relished driving to Texas now. Ah, well. It was the least he could do to ensure Crispin and Cat didn't rush back from New Zealand for what was, in all likelihood, just the emotional breakdown of a human who'd snapped from too much grief and stress.

He remembered the look Denise gave him the last time he'd seen her. Specks of blood dotted her clothes, her face had been as pale as Spade's own ivory skin, and her hazel eyes held a mixture of revulsion and fear.

Why did you have to kill him? she'd whispered.

Because of what he intended to do, Spade had replied. *No one deserves to live after that.*

She hadn't understood. Spade did, though. All too well. Humans might be more forgiving with their punishments, but Spade knew better than to show a rapist, even a potential one, any naïve mercy.

He also remembered the last thing Denise said when he'd dropped her off at her house later that night. *I'm so sick of the violence in your world.* He'd seen that look on many humans' faces, heard the same flat resonance in their voices. If Crispin weren't so busy with everything that had happened lately, he'd explain to Cat how the kindest thing to do was to erase Denise's memory of all things undead. Perhaps Spade would do that himself, if Denise had become delusional. Kindness aside, if her grasp on reality *had* slipped, it would also eliminate a liability if everything Denise knew about them was erased from her recall.

Spade filled his satchel with enough clothes for a few days and went downstairs to the garage. Once settled behind the wheel of his Porsche, he put on dark shades and then clicked open the garage door. Bloody sun was already up. Spade gave it a baleful glare as he pulled out into the dawn.

Humans. Aside from tasting delicious, they were usually more trouble than they were worth.

Denise could barely breathe. Pain seared from her chest up her right arm and seemed to spread through her whole body. Lights danced in her vision. *I'm dying...*

"Why did you spray me with silver?" a conversational voice asked.

The hand came off her face and she sucked in deep, painful breaths. Some of the burning left her chest, and her eyes focused enough to see that she was still in the foyer by her front door. Denise tried to push against the man gripping her, but she was so weak, she couldn't even raise her hands. If the stranger let go of her waist, she'd crumple to the floor.

"Answer me." A new flash of pain accompanied his demand.

Denise managed to reply even though the tightness in her chest made it hard to breathe.

"Thought you were...a vampire."

The stranger laughed. "Wrong. Insulting, too, but interesting. What do you know about vampires?"

Her gun was on the table six feet away. Denise sagged in his arms, hoping he'd let her go. Maybe if he did, she could make it to the gun.

"Answer me," the stranger said again, jerking her around to face him. His eyes burned with red highlights, but aside from that—and the faint smell coming from him, like he'd just set fire to something—he looked like a college student. His hair was a lighter brown than hers and pulled back into a ponytail. With his flared jeans and tie-dye T-shirt, he could have doubled as a young hippie.

But he wasn't human. *Red eyes.* She'd never seen that before. He wasn't a ghoul or a vampire, so what was he?

"I know vampires exist," Denise got out, breathing a little easier as that crushing pain in her chest lessened into a throbbing ache.

"Any Goth wannabe could have silver mace on a key chain and believe in vampires," the man said dismissively. "You'll have to do better than that."

Another blast of pain accompanied his statement, almost doubling Denise over. When she could see again through the pain, the man was smiling. Denise thought of this monster's face being the last thing her aunt and cousins had seen, and anger stiffened her spine.

"Vampires originated from Cain after God cursed him to forever drink blood as a reminder that he'd spilled his brother, Abel's. They're immune to crosses, wooden stakes, and sunlight. Only silver through the heart or decapitation can kill them—and decapitation is the only way to kill a ghoul. Is that good enough?" she growled.

He laughed as if delighted, letting Denise go. She fell as expected, but made sure to pitch forward, closer to the table and the gun.

"Very good. Are you someone's property?"

"No," Denise said, knowing *property* referred to humans kept by vampires for feeding purposes. Like TV dinners, only with pulses.

"Ah." The stranger's eyes gleamed. "A more romantic arrangement?"

"Hell no," Denise replied, edging closer to the table under the guise of fixing her robe back around her. She'd been naked underneath it, but modesty wasn't her goal. Reaching the gun was. No matter what this creature was, bullets might hurt it. Maybe enough to give her a chance to run away.

"Don't mention that place," the man remarked, wincing. "Brings back bad memories."

That made Denise pause. She studied the stranger more closely. Red eyes. Smelled like sulfur. Not human, vampire, or ghoul.

"Demon," she said.

He bowed. "Call me Raum."

Denise racked her brain to come up with what she knew about demons, but most of her knowledge consisted of watching *The Exorcist*. Even if she had holy water, which she didn't, would flinging it on a demon, chanting, "The power of Christ compels you!" as in the movie do any real damage?

"This Spade you were talking to on the phone before," Raum went on. "Is he a vampire, or a ghoul?"

Dread swept over her. Even though she and Spade weren't friends, she didn't want to put him in danger.

"He's human," she said.

The demon arched a brow. "But you told him what you saw, so he must know about vampires and ghouls. If you're not property or a girlfriend, what's your association with those walking corpses?"

Denise was careful not to say anything that could come back to hurt Cat. "I, um, survived a vampire attack a few years ago, so I tried to find out as much about

them as I could. Along the way, I met other people like
me. We share information. Look out for each other."

Raum considered this. "You're saying you have no
real connections to the undead world or anyone in it?"

She nodded. "That's right."

He sighed. "Then you're of no use to me."

Agony slammed into her chest, as sudden as if she'd
been shot through the heart. Amid the paralyzing pain,
Denise managed to gasp out a sentence.

"Wait! I do…have connections…"

Just as abruptly, the pain stopped. Raum smiled in
satisfaction.

"I thought you might. You know too much not to."

"What do you want from me?" Fear unlike any she'd
ever known slithered up her spine. She was at the mercy
of a demon. There was no worse position to be in.

Raum knelt next to her even as she edged back. "I'll
show you."

His hand pressed to her forehead. Light burst inside
her mind, then images followed. *Raum inside a pentagram, a red-haired man on the other side. "Give me
power like yours," the red-haired man said, "and you
can have anything you want." Raum put his hands on
the man, who fell back screaming.*

Another flash and the images changed. *Raum standing in front of the man, holding out his hand. The man
shaking his head and backing away. Raum advancing, then howling in rage as a pentagram appeared all
around him. Flames rose from the star, the bottom fell
out, and Raum disappeared from sight. Nothing but
fire for a long while, then a slew of horrifying, blood-
soaked images. Finally a sense of freedom. Then doz-*

ens more images of people dying, until at last, her aunt Rose, then Amber, Paul...and herself.

"Your ancestor Nathanial backed out of a bargain with me." Raum's voice felt like phantoms in her ear. "He managed to lock me away for quite some time, but I'm back and I want my payment."

Denise shook her head to clear the awful images from it. "How can I do anything about that?"

"Because he must be hiding with vampires or ghouls," Raum purred. "I can't go into their world, but you can. Find him for me. *Bring him to me*, and I'll leave you and the rest of his spawn alone."

The rest of his spawn. Her parents' faces flashed in Denise's mind. One of them had to be a descendant of Nathanial's, since she and her cousins obviously were, and Raum meant to kill all Nathanial's remaining family in his quest to find him.

She couldn't let that happen. "I'll find him," Denise said. *I don't know how, but I will.*

Raum traced his fingers along her arms. Her skin crawled in revulsion.

"I believe you mean that. But as extra incentive..."

His hands tightened around her while a ferocious new pain erupted inside her. She could hear herself screaming, but over that was Raum's careless laughter.

"Try not to die, will you? I've only just started."

Spade wrinkled his nose as he turned down Denise's street. Something foul reached him even through the ventilation system of his car. His eyes swept the road, expecting to see a car with a smoking engine or a roof being tarred, but there was nothing. The smell worsened as he pulled into Denise's driveway.

Spade reached into his satchel, pulling out two long silver blades that he concealed in each sleeve. Then he got out and walked up to the front door. Once there, he inhaled deeply near the frame.

The stench of sulfur filled his lungs, enough to choke him if he were human. Spade expelled his breath with a curse. Only one creature could leave such a smell in its wake.

Denise MacGregor wasn't imagining things, after all, but she might not be alive for Spade to tell her that.

He leveled the door in one kick and then burst through, rolling at once to avoid any attack. Denise was crumpled on the floor near a couch, but Spade didn't rush to check on her. He glanced around the room, assuring himself no one else was there. Nothing but the sounds of her breathing and heartbeat.

He checked every room and closet upstairs and downstairs, but found nothing. Satisfied that he wasn't walking into a trap, Spade went to check on Denise.

She was unconscious, wearing only a robe with the belt untied—and she stank of sulfur like she'd bathed in it.

Spade's lips thinned into a grim line as he peeled back the robe. He'd been prepared to find the worst, but surprisingly there were no signs of an assault. It looked as though the demon had come, knocked her out, and then left.

Spade closed her robe and smoothed away the damp mahogany hair that covered her face, shaking her lightly.

"Denise, wake up."

It took a few tries, but then her hazel eyes opened, focused on him—and widened in panic.

"Where is he? *Is he still here?*"

Spade kept a grip on her, making his voice soothing. "No one's here but me. You're all right."

Denise let out a harsh sob. "No, I'm not."

She pulled up the sleeves of her robe to expose her forearms. Spade couldn't stop his curse as he saw the star-shaped shadows marking her skin.

Denise was correct; she wasn't all right. The demon had branded her.

Spade sat on the closed lid of the loo in Denise's bathroom. She'd insisted on showering, even though he'd had to carry her up here. He'd offered to help her wash but she flatly refused. Humans. As if this was any time for him to feel voyeuristic.

He refused to leave the bathroom, though, stating he wouldn't have her death on his conscience if she slipped and broke her neck while trying to get out of the tub. Denise responded bitterly that the demon told her she was beyond mortal death after being branded. Spade wasn't sure that was true, so he'd taken her robe, leaving her with no other option but to sit on the tile floor and tug the shower door closed.

He could see her hazy outline against the smoked glass. Hear her fumble about as she went through what must have been all her soaps and shampoos. The air filled with different perfumes, overpowering the lingering scent of sulfur. Spade closed his eyes. He'd have to get Denise to a safe place soon. It was doubtful the demon would leave only to come right back, but she couldn't stay here.

"I need a towel."

Spade pulled out two, handing the bigger one through

the crack she'd opened in the shower. Once she'd wrapped it around herself, he opened the shower fully, ignoring her protest, and lifted her up, using his free hand to rub the smaller towel against her dripping hair.

"I can do this myself," she said, pushing at him weakly.

"Under normal circumstances, I don't doubt it," he replied, carrying her to her bed. "But you had a demon nearly give you fatal cardiac arrest, then force his essence through your body. No one would be on their feet after that, so quit arguing and let me help you."

She sagged against him, as if it had taken all her remaining strength to put up that last bit of fight. Spade kept his arm around her, bracing her next to him as he dried her hair with one hand and held her towel closed with the other. Her eyelids fluttered, her head tilting to rest on his arm. It left the smooth expanse of her throat mere inches from his lips.

Spade fought back a sudden urge to trace her pulse with his mouth. It had been over a day since he'd eaten, but hunger wasn't his only motivator. A muscle flexed in his jaw. He'd hoped time would eliminate the strange draw he felt toward Denise, but clearly, it was still there.

He'd first seen Denise when he went to Crispin's holiday party over a year ago. Spade walked in, and the first thing he'd noticed had been a dark-haired woman, her head thrown back in laughter over something Cat said. The woman glanced in his direction a moment later, as if she'd felt him watching her. Her full mouth was still open in mirth, but it was her direct gaze that snared his attention. That, and the unfamiliar charge that went through him as he stared.

"Who's she?" he asked Crispin.

Crispin followed Spade's gaze and let out a snort. "Sorry, mate. That's my wife's best friend."

And with those words, Denise became off-limits. She was human, and Spade had only two uses for human women—feeding or casual shagging. Since Denise was Cat's friend, indulging in either would be an insult to Crispin. Spade had stifled that odd twinge as he glanced back at her, but she'd already turned away to smile at a tawny-haired lad. It was almost a relief when Crispin told him she was also married. He truly had no reason to give her further thought.

But now Denise was widowed, wearing only a towel, and in his arms. Hard to ignore the draw he felt toward her under these circumstances.

She's not for you, Spade reminded himself sternly.

Still, no harm in noticing she was lovely. Her hair appeared darker while wet, and her complexion was roses and cream. The harsh smell of sulfur was gone, leaving her own scent of honey and jasmine to rise through the other perfumes covering it. Looking at her clad in the towel, her eyes closed and mouth slightly parted, was far more enticing than when he'd seen her naked while he'd been checking her for injuries.

Spade forced himself back into a businesslike mentality. "Let's get you dressed," he said. "Once we're somewhere safe, I'll contact Crispin. Tell him where he and Cat can collect you."

Denise's eyes snapped open. "No."

"No?" Spade repeated, surprised.

She gripped his hand with more strength than he thought her capable of. "You can't tell them. Cat will drop everything to go after Raum, but he's too strong.

I—I saw what he's capable of. I can't let her fight him, and if she knows about this, she'll try."

"Denise." Spade made his voice very reasonable. "You can't just wander around pretending you don't have demon brands on you. You have to find a way to remove them, and—"

"I know how to get them off."

Spade's brows went up. Did she now?

"The demon wants me to find an old relative of mine named Nathanial," Denise went on. "Seems Nathanial hocked his soul and then ran off without paying. The demon thinks he's hiding out with vampires or ghouls. If I find Nathanial, bring him to Raum, I get these brands off and Raum leaves the rest of my family alone."

Spade found his voice amid his amazement. "And if you don't deliver this Nathanial to the demon?"

A shudder went through Denise. "Then Raum's essence keeps growing in me…until I turn into a shape-shifter like him."

Chapter 3

Denise glanced away from the road. If she wasn't in such dire circumstances, she was sure her life would be flashing in front of her eyes. Spade drove like a bat out of hell, weaving in and out of traffic with dizzying efficiency and no regard for the speed limit. When she'd pointed out that if he kept it up, a cop would soon pull him over, Spade had only smiled and said he was hungry anyway.

She had a feeling that he wasn't kidding.

To avoid looking at the blur of cars and scenery passing by, she studied Spade instead. His hair was pure black, lifting in what looked to be a natural spike off his crown to hang in shiny waves down to his shoulders. Brows the same inky color framed burnt-amber eyes. Both were in vivid contrast to his skin, which had the beautiful crystal paleness that marked him as a vampire.

Even sitting, he was obviously very tall, but his height didn't look awkward on him as it did with some people. No, Spade towered over people around him with a straight-spined confidence, his long limbs moving with grace and precision. Deadly precision.

Memory flashed in her mind. *"You just stand by my buds while your friend and I get in this backseat,"* the grinning stranger said, grabbing Denise. In the next instant, he was on the ground, nothing but red gore where his head had been. Spade stood over him, his eyes flashing green as he kicked the man's body hard enough for it to dent the nearby car.

Then the worst memory of all. *Spade, covered in blood, pulling her away from what used to be Randy. "He's gone, Denise. I'm so sorry..."*

She looked away. Better to stare at the nausea-inducing rush of scenery than at him. After all, the whirring of cars outside the window didn't stir her memories as he did. When she was away from vampires, she could pretend Randy really *had* died in a car accident, as his family believed. But every time she was around vampires, sooner or later, memories of blood and death that she'd tried to suppress came to the surface.

And now she had no choice but to immerse herself in the last place she wanted to be—deep inside the vampire world.

"I'll need to hire someone to take me around to, you know, places where your kind hangs out," she said, mentally calculating how much cash she could get on short notice. "I'd appreciate it if you could refer me to a vampire private investigator or whatever equivalent you have."

Spade gave a look she was fast getting sick of; the kind that said he thought she was crazy.

"A vampire private investigator?" he repeated. "You're putting me on, right?"

"I know you have vampire hit men, so why wouldn't you have vampire private investigators, too?" she flared back. "I can't just run an ad with Nathanial's description on it titled 'Have you seen this soul welsher?'"

Spade's hands tightened on the steering wheel. "No, you can't," he said in a calm tone. "But vampires don't have vampire private investigators. If we want to find someone, we ask our Master to contact other Masters to see who owns this missing person. Then whatever business is sorted out between the two Masters. We have undead hit men for the times when vampires want to skip that formality and don't care about the consequences. It's unheard of for a human to contact other Master vampires in search of someone's property, which is what Nathanial would have to be. And no Master vampire with any self-respect would offer up his property so you could take him to be sacrificed."

Denise hated how casually Spade referred to humans as property. He didn't even seem to be aware that it was insulting.

"Then I'll hire a hit man and just tell him not to kill Nathanial. What will he care, if he gets paid to deliver a live person versus a dead one?"

Spade muttered something under his breath that was too fast for her to catch.

"What?" she asked, with an edge.

He stared at her long enough that she almost snapped at him to keep his eyes on the road.

"No vampire will steal another vampire's property

for a human, no matter how much quid you offer. That risks war, whereas killing some bloke with no evidence as to who did it is much simpler. You might be able to get a vampire to blow Nathanial's head off for a fee, but you won't get one to kidnap him."

Denise felt like pounding on the dashboard in frustration. There had to be someone who could help her. Who else did she know that was dead?

"I'll ask Rodney," she said with a burst of inspiration. "He's not a vampire, he's a ghoul. Rodney knows me, so maybe he'd be willing to find Nathanial without anyone knowing who did it *or* getting messed up in vampire politics."

A muscle ticked in Spade's jaw. "Rodney's dead."

Denise didn't say anything for a long moment. Her mind was too busy rejecting the idea that the sweet, funny ghoul she'd known was dead. *Decapitation is the only way to kill a ghoul*, she'd flung at Raum earlier. That knowledge made her sick now. Why, why, why would anyone murder Rodney?

"He was a good man. It's not right," was what she said after the silence stretched.

Spade grunted. "Indeed."

Denise wanted nothing more than to close her eyes and not have to think about death for a week. Or a day, or even an hour. But unless she found Nathanial, her family's deaths loomed on the horizon.

She'd have to involve Cat. Bones was a Master vampire *and* a former hit man, so he had the expertise of finding people combined with the clout in the vampire community. It was the only logical choice—except that Bones would feel honor-bound to save her, if things got too hairy and dangerous. *I already got my husband killed*, Denise thought dully. *How can I live with myself if I get my best friend's husband killed, too?*

"We should be in Springfield in a few hours," Spade said. "Once there, we'll stop at a hotel and—"

Denise sat straight up. "You."

His brows rose. "Beg your pardon?"

"You," she repeated. "You're a Master vampire. You've tracked down people in the past, Cat told me, and you don't care about me, so if things get too dangerous, you'll bail without getting yourself killed. You're the perfect person to help me find Nathanial."

Spade didn't bother giving her one of those you're-crazy looks; he swerved off the road and came to a stop on the shoulder before she even had time to worry about oncoming traffic.

"I can't drop all my responsibilities just to chase down a demon-dodging human who should never have trifled with the dark arts in the first place," he said through gritted teeth. "Sorry, Denise."

Desperation made her rash. "You're sorry? I doubt that. Yes, I know I'm asking for a huge favor, but I don't expect you to do it for me. I was *hoping* you'd do it for your friend, because you know I'll only have one place to go if you don't help me. But hey, maybe you can tell Cat, 'I'm sorry' if Bones gets killed doing what you didn't have time to. After all, it's so much easier to say you care than to prove it."

He was next to her in a blink, his face so close she couldn't focus on one distinct feature. But there was no need to see his expression. The growl in his voice told her how furious he was.

"No one knows you called me. No one knows where you are. I could have your body buried before sunset, then I wouldn't need to fret about Crispin risking himself for you. So you might not want to dare me again to prove that I care for my friend."

Spade's eyes weren't their normal cognac color. They were glowing green, blazing with intensity, and Denise didn't have to be undead to sense the power leaking off him. But still, instinct told her Spade wouldn't harm her, no matter how angry he might be with her. If it was just herself Raum had threatened, she'd take her chances alone, but her family's lives depended on convincing Spade to help her.

"Then after you bury me, you may as well find each member of my family and kill them, too," she replied. "Because that's what Raum will do unless I give him Nathanial. How many murders are you willing to commit instead of helping me?"

He leaned back, something like disbelief on his face. "Are you blackmailing me?"

Denise gave a bitter laugh. "Blackmail implies that I have something you want, but I have nothing…except the hope that I won't cause anyone else I care about to get killed. You've made it clear that humans don't mean much to you, but can't you understand that?"

Spade glanced away, looking out the window at the cars whizzing past them. Finally he jerked the gear shift out of park.

"Luckily for you, I can."

Denise had gone straight into the bathroom once they arrived at the hotel, reminding Spade he'd neglected to stop so she could use the facilities along the way. She hadn't said a word, poor girl. She was no doubt hungry as well. He heard the shower switch on and decided to order for her instead of waiting to ask her preferences. With the day she'd had, he'd be surprised if she was awake by the time the food arrived.

Spade hadn't driven straight to his house because he wanted to clear some things up before they had an audience. He'd gotten one room at the hotel, wanting to be close in case the demon somehow followed them, unlikely as that was. Still, it didn't do to let his guard down when it came to demons. Raum could attempt to ambush him and hold him hostage as incentive to get more cooperation in the undead world. Spade wouldn't put anything past a demon. It was a good thing they were so rare, or humanity would have far more to concern itself with than the occasional rogue vampire or ghoul.

He slid his shoes off, stretching as he settled himself in the overstuffed chair. This was a fine kettle he'd gotten himself into. How to find Nathanial without anyone realizing he was looking for him? If he was open about his search for him, then Spade would be the obvious suspect when Nathanial turned up missing—and he didn't fancy getting involved in *another* undead war. Not to mention, he'd have to hide the fact that Denise was with him. If word of that got 'round to Crispin, he'd instantly suspect trouble.

But no one else really knew Denise. Few had seen what Denise looked like, and of them, many were now dead. Who was to say Denise wasn't just another sweet snack he was traveling with? As long as he avoided Crispin, Cat, and the rest of their close friends, there was a chance he could find Nathanial without anyone knowing Denise was involved.

Spade didn't want to calculate the odds of that. No matter that wisdom said he needed to avoid Denise, for more than one reason, he really didn't have a choice about helping her.

The bathroom door opened and she came out, wearing a robe with the hotel's name stitched on it. Spade nodded at the closet, indicating where he'd put her bag. She retrieved some items from it and then stood there, chewing on her lip as if debating whether to speak.

Spade arched a brow. "Unlike some vampires, I can't read minds, so whatever it is, you'll have to say it out loud."

"I want you to know I intend to pay you for your time," she said, the words coming out in a rush. "And reimburse you for any expenses, like this hotel room."

First she'd manipulated him, now she'd insulted him. "No."

She blinked. "No?"

"I understand your confusion," Spade said smoothly, "since it seems you don't hear that word often, but allow me to explain. It means I'm not your employee. It means you'll need to do what I say in order for me to find your greedy relative, and it means your personal preferences in the matter aren't my concern. Quite clear now as to its definition?"

She gave him a look that could have cut steel. He noted with mild amusement that her hazel eyes seemed greener with her anger, almost like how a vampire's eyes got in the early stages before they changed color completely.

"In that case, I'm starving, so I hope this hotel has room service and a good steak," she replied with barely restrained curtness.

He let out a bark of laughter. "I already ordered something for you."

As if on cue, a knock sounded on the door. Spade got up, pausing to make sure he sensed only a human on the other side of it, then opened it. A uniformed young man gave him a mechanical smile as he pushed in the cart.

"Where would you like this, sir?"

"Right by her," Spade said, and shut the door.

He let the lad uncover the dishes and rattle off their contents to Denise, who looked surprised at the variety of items before her. Then when he turned to Spade with a politely expectant expression, Spade hit him with his gaze.

"What are you doing?" Denise gasped.

He ignored her, focused on the pulsating vein that called to him. A quick slide of his fangs into the lad's neck produced the flow of rich, nurturing blood. Spade waited before swallowing, allowing his mouth to fill from the pumping of the pulse under his lips instead of sucking, forming a seal to prevent any of those red drops from escaping.

Denise stared at him, uncertainty clear on her features. Spade glared at her, hoping she wouldn't do something foolish, like scream. She didn't, but her hand came to her mouth as if she was fighting one back.

The gnawing hunger in him eased after his fourth swallow. He drew back, catching the spare leaking drops with his tongue before closing the holes by cutting his thumb on a fang and holding it over them. In seconds, his blood healed the punctures, causing them to vanish from sight.

"You delivered the food and left. Nothing else happened," Spade said, pressing a twenty into the lad's palm.

He nodded, that artificial smile returning to his face

as the memory of what happened evaporated under the power in Spade's gaze. "Have a good evening, sir," he said.

"Thanks so much. I'll ring when she's done with the food."

Spade closed the door. Denise was still staring at him. "You bit him. You didn't even…you just *bit* him."

He shrugged. "You weren't the only one hungry."

"But…" She still seemed at a loss for words.

"You lived with Cat and Crispin for over a month; did you never see him feed?"

"He never did it in *front* of me!" Denise exclaimed, like he'd suggested something preposterous.

Spade rolled his eyes. "You'll have to get used to it, because I've no intention of starving."

Denise looked down at the cooling food on the tray. "I think I lost my appetite," she muttered.

He bit back what would have been an annoyed reply. No need to snipe at her when she'd had a truly horrible day.

"Make yourself comfortable in the bed. I'll sleep in the chair," he said, pulling off his shirt.

He was undoing his trousers when Denise's expression stopped him. Right, humans and their silly modesty. It had been a long time since he'd been around average mortals. The ones he associated with were all familiar with a vampire's lifestyle and habits. He'd have to remember what was appropriate and what wasn't.

"I dragged you into this," she said stubbornly. "I'm taking the chair."

He almost rolled his eyes again. As if he'd allow a woman to stuff herself in a chair while he was stretched out in bed. "No."

"I'd feel better if—"

"I wouldn't," he cut her off. "And I'll remind you again that since I'm helping you, the least you could do is not argue with me over every little thing."

Frustration and defiance competed on her features, but she clamped her mouth shut. *Good on you, darling. Perhaps this won't be such a burden, after all.*

"Sleep well, Denise."

Chapter 4

She awoke to the sounds of an English accent. For a moment she was confused. Had she left the TV on? Then the events of the previous, nightmarish day came back to her. *Paul, murdered. She, branded by a demon. The owner of the accent, a vampire who wanted nothing to do with her, but who was her family's only hope.*

"Ah, you're awake," Spade said, closing his cell with a click. "Ordered you breakfast, considering you didn't touch your food last night." His mouth curled in a grin. "You'll be pleased to know you slept through *my* breakfast. Perhaps now you'll be able to keep your appetite."

"You eat the room service employees every time?" Denise asked, shocked.

"Of course. But don't fret on their behalf. I always tip well."

A sharp pain in her stomach brought her attention to

the cart with the covered dishes and the mouthwatering scent wafting from it. Suddenly ravenous, Denise flung the covers back and went to the cart, flipping off the top of the container closest to her. *Pancakes*. She picked one up and stuffed it into her mouth, closing her eyes in rapture. *So good*.

It was gone too soon. She grabbed another one, too hungry to bother with syrup or silverware, and popped it in her mouth. *Mmmm. Delicious. More*.

She'd just finished the third pancake when she noticed Spade watching her. He glanced at her now-empty plate, then at the untouched silverware, and back to her.

Denise felt a flush heat her face. What was wrong with her? It hadn't been *that* long since she'd eaten.

"I, uh, was really hungry," she stammered.

His mouth quirked. "It would seem so."

As if to accentuate the point, another pain jabbed her in the stomach, followed by a rumbling, audible gurgle. Denise forced herself to arrange the napkin neatly on her lap, pick up her silverware, and cut the contents of the next container—country fried steak and eggs, her favorite!—into small pieces before taking her next bite. By that time, the rumble in her stomach had increased to almost a roar. Spade continued to watch her, that half smile still curling his mouth.

"Always enjoy seeing a woman with a healthy appetite," he said, amusement clear in his tone.

Denise quit the pretense and speared two chunks of fried steak at once, chewing them while giving Spade a glare that dared him to comment. So she was a little too hungry at the moment to eat like a bird, who cared? Maybe it had been longer than she realized since the last time she'd eaten.

"Do you have a plan for how we're going to start looking for Nathanial?" she asked after she'd finished all the steak and eggs. Would it look too piggish to move on to the next shiny container? Screw it. Who knew when they'd break for another meal?

"I do," Spade replied. "We'll start with my line. Though I don't have any blokes named Nathanial in it, who's to say your ancestor didn't change his name? You do remember what he looks like from what Raum showed you, yes?"

Denise shuddered. "Yes." As if she could forget all the horrible images Raum had forced onto her mind.

"Good. I'll hold an assembly and you can pick through my people's property. See if you recognize any of them."

"You know, it's really rude how you keep referring to humans as property. I'm human, too, remember?"

Something glinted in his gaze. "I remember it well. Which is why I'll be introducing you to my line as my newest piece of property."

Her jaw dropped. "Oh no, you won't."

He waved an elegant hand. "You don't want Crispin or Cat to find out what you're up to, so this is best disguise. I don't date humans; that's common knowledge. But I do have other uses for them, and no one would question a vampire traveling with his property. We seldom go anywhere without one or two of them along, in fact."

His expression practically dared her to argue with him. Denise paused. What if this was Spade's way of trying to get out of helping her? If she refused to go along with this charade, he could abandon her without a second thought. Maybe he wasn't as concerned about keeping Bones out of this as she'd bargained on.

"Fine," Denise forced herself to say, thinking of her parents. A little embarrassment was nothing if it ended up saving them.

Spade seemed to be waiting for her to say something else. Denise picked up her fork and began to eat the fruit salad in the next container.

"Good," he said at last. "We'll be in St. Louis later today."

Spade snapped his mobile shut. That was the last of the calls he needed to make. While it wasn't common for him to gather his people to introduce a new human as property, he'd been traveling most of the past year, so several things had piled up that needed his attention.

Denise had been very quiet the past three days. He suspected it had to do with the call she'd placed to her family, telling them she was taking off to grieve for her cousin privately. From what Spade could hear, that hadn't gone over well, though she couldn't explain that she wasn't abandoning them in their time of need, but trying to help them instead.

Still, her brooding had to stop. If Denise slipped up in her charade as his latest property in front of his people, Spade could contain the negative results. In front of another Master vampire, one who wasn't an ally? That could be deadly.

You need to get your back up, Denise, he thought. *And I know how to help.*

Spade went down to the first floor, guessing that he'd find Denise in the kitchen. She'd proven to have a voracious appetite regardless of her mood. All his residences had a cook to make sure the human members of his line were well fed. Henry, the chef for his St. Louis home, had been even busier since Spade arrived with Denise.

"Sire," Henry said to Spade.

It amused Spade to see Denise's reaction. Her back was to him, but the tightening in her shoulders was unmistakable. His title among the members of his line made Denise uncomfortable. It didn't bother Spade. After all, he'd been addressed far more formally back when he was human.

"Henry." Spade nodded at the young man before taking the seat next to Denise at the kitchen table. From the looks of her plate, she'd been eating lasagna, heavy on the garlic.

He stifled a smile. Cat had told Denise a lot about vampires, but not everything. Spade plucked a sautéed clove off her plate and ate it, making sure to grunt in feigned bliss.

"Ah, Henry, delicious. I'll take a plate myself."

"Won't that make you sick?" Denise asked in surprise.

He kept his expression blank. "I can eat solid food. I just don't prefer to most of the time."

"Not that." Denise waved a hand. "Garlic. Doesn't that make vampires sick?"

"Indeed not. That's one of the reasons I so enjoy visiting Italy. Can't swing a cat without hitting a vein seasoned full of that delicious flavor."

Spade licked his lips. Denise saw it and blanched, pushing her plate back. It was all he could do to contain his laughter.

"I have a present for you," he said, as if he hadn't noticed her reaction.

Suspicion clouded her gaze. "Why?"

She really needed to work on her acting skills. No new human in his line would use such a tone with him, especially with others around.

He rose. "Come."

"Sire, would you still like the food?" Henry asked.

Spade held out his hand to Denise. She paused. "Keep it warm for me," he said to Henry, and hardened his gaze at Denise. *Take it*, he silently told her.

She slid her hand into his. Her flesh was warm, almost feverish, except there was no glaze to her eyes that spoke of illness. No, they were bright with irritation over his little power play. Spade ignored that, clasping her hand and pulling her out of her chair. He didn't let go once she was on her feet, either, despite her tug.

"Let's go to my room, darling," he said, making sure his voice was loud and clear.

Her eyes widened. She'd slept in her own room since they arrived, because demons couldn't enter private residences, even if Raum *had* managed to follow them across several states. But it didn't do for there to be doubts among the people here as to her station with him.

To her credit, Denise didn't sputter out an indignant refusal. She pressed her lips together and let him lead her up the stairs. If he didn't know better, he'd think her temperature flared a degree in just the time it took them to get to his room.

Once inside, she shut the door and then pulled her hand away. "There are limits as to how far I'm willing to take this act."

He didn't show his irritation at her implication that he'd use the circumstances to coerce her into bed. "Name them."

From the way her mouth opened and closed, she hadn't expected that response. Finally she said, "It would take less time to list the things I *would* do."

"So list that, and I'll tell you if you need to add to it."

That challenging look was back in her eye. Spade smiled inwardly. Anger was good for her spirit. It was bad for his plan if she couldn't balance it with common sense, but time would prove if Denise was as smart as she was lovely.

"All right." She squared her shoulders, her dark hair rustling with the movement. "Obviously I'm willing to bunk with you when the circumstances call for it. I can act subservient if necessary, but don't expect it once we're alone. I can act affectionate and even kiss you to make things look real. But it stops there, and I'm not letting you drink from me."

Spade couldn't help himself. "With all that delectable garlic in your blood? I shed a tear."

Her gaze narrowed. "You're making fun of me."

He allowed himself a smile. "A little."

"Are you done?" Her chin thrust out, as did her shoulders. Spade's smile widened. If she knew how her aggressive stance made her breasts jut out even more enticingly, he rather doubted she'd keep it.

And far be it for him to say such an ungentlemanly thing out loud.

Spade pushed that thought aside, because it led to other musings best not explored. "As to your limits, they should suffice, though you need to get over your aversion to close proximity with me. Vampires are often affectionate in public with their property. If I should lean close to you, or put my arm around you, it would look odd if you jumped like you'd been stabbed."

Denise had the grace to look abashed. "Sorry. I'll work on that."

"Indeed." He couldn't keep the dryness out of his tone. "And while I'll confess it was fun watching you choke yourself on garlic the past few days, you need have no fear of me biting you."

So much relief crossed her face that he was torn between being amused and being insulted. Had she been about to invest in a silver neck brace next?

"As for things going further than kissing, you need not fret about that, either," he went on, raking her with a gaze. "I don't lack for bed partners, so I don't need to scrounge for unwilling scraps."

Her breath sucked in, those hazel eyes looking greener with her anger. It had to be a trick of the light, but again, they reminded him of a vampire's. He gave her another rake of his gaze, more slowly this time. Pity she *wasn't* a vampire. If so, he might forget Denise was under Crispin's protection. He might forget he shouldn't mix pleasure with business, and he might test whether she was over her grief for that poor bloke who was torn to pieces.

Spade took a step closer, something inside him flaring when he noticed her breathing change. It became faster, as did her heartbeat. He took another step and then her scent changed, too, that honey and jasmine fragrance growing stronger. With his next step, he was a foot away, able to feel her residual body heat from the air around her. Her eyes were wide, more brown than green now, and her mouth—full, luscious—parted ever so slightly. Would she taste like honey and jasmine if he kissed her? Or would she have a richer, darker flavor, like the depth of her spirit he caught glimpses of in her eyes?

Abruptly he spun on his heel. Denise wasn't a vampire, so there was no point wondering such things. They'd find Nathanial and give him to Raum. Then, once she had those demon marks off, she'd walk away from him, soon to be dead as all humans were.

And he wasn't going through that again.

"Your outfit for tonight is on the dresser," he said, and slammed the door behind him.

Chapter 5

Denise took a deep breath and tried to act nonchalant. It was a good thing the heat was on in this hotel, or with what she was wearing, she'd freeze.

An attendant had taken her coat as soon as Denise entered the Khorassan Ballroom with Spade. It was a huge room, fitting well over two thousand, and yet it was still almost full. The sheer size of Spade's line was staggering. Then once her coat was off, even though she was amid so many people, heads turned.

Denise raised her chin and refused to cringe. *Go on, look. You've seen more skin on a beach, it isn't that shocking.*

Except this wasn't a beach, though what she was wearing looked inspired by a bikini. Her top was a diaphanous bolero, and the matching sheer pantalets looked swiped straight from the set of *I Dream of Jeannie*.

Vampires are perverts, every last one of them, Cat

had said on many occasions. If this was standard "property" garb for an undead event, then Cat was dead right.

Denise had expected a smart-assed remark from Spade when she came downstairs in her ridiculous garb. Why wouldn't he be amused? He was the one who'd gotten this harem-girl outfit for her to wear. But he'd only glanced at her for the barest second and then handed her a coat, remarking that it was cold outside.

Of course it was. February in St. Louis wasn't supposed to be balmy. If Spade had a heart, she'd be in pants and a sweater. He wasn't scantily dressed, wearing a long black coat over a white shirt and black pants that fit him so well, they had to be custom designed. With his dark striking looks, Spade practically dripped with decadent elegance, and here she was, like a knock-off Scheherazade.

So the least he could do was take the time to appreciate how the costume he'd foisted on her looked. Or notice that she'd done her hair and makeup in a very flattering way, if she said so herself. She might be getting introduced as property, but she'd make sure people knew this property was high-end, dammit.

Yet Spade hardly looked at her then or during the twenty-minute car ride to the Chase Park Plaza hotel. He didn't speak, either, except to exchange a few words with the driver. If he hadn't opened her car door as she entered and exited the vehicle, she might have thought she'd somehow become invisible. To add insult to injury, he'd left her almost as soon as they entered this huge room. Denise had grabbed a glass of champagne from a passing waiter so she'd look occupied, instead of just standing there like a statue.

Why do you care that Spade's being cold to you? a little voice inside asked.

I don't, Denise told it.

If it was possible to hear an internal scoff, she did. She ignored it, concentrating on the people around her instead of her inner idiot. As soon as she did, however, she realized she'd made a mistake.

So many pale faces. Those quick, deliberate movements. Cool flesh all around her. Fangs everywhere. All those glowing eyes...

A familiar panic began to rise in her. Denise tried to fight it back, but it rose without pity, choking her in the memories.

"I have to get out of here," she mumbled.

Spade jerked his head around. He'd been across the room, talking to someone, leaving her surrounded by the creatures from her nightmares. *Vampires everywhere. Blood would follow. Death would follow. It always did.*

The memories thickened until they consumed her. *That awful howling getting closer. All those other screams. We're trapped, and they're coming.* Something grabbed her arm. Denise yanked back in terror, but the cold grip didn't budge.

"Let go of me," she shouted.

"What's with her?" someone muttered. Denise couldn't understand why the person sounded so clueless. Why wasn't anyone running? Didn't they realize the things coming after them couldn't be *killed*?

That grip tightened and a new one clamped across her mouth. She struggled but couldn't get free. *There's no hope. We're trapped in the basement, and they're coming. Any second, the door will burst open, a grotesque figure springing toward me. No. No. NO!*

Cold water splashed in her face. She blinked, coughing a little, and managed to hold up her hand to block most of the second icy splash.

"Stop it."

Spade loomed over her, one hand under a running faucet. She blinked once more. The front of her was soaked and she was shivering, crouched in a ball on a bathroom floor. And she had no idea how she'd gotten here.

"Not again," she moaned.

Spade turned the faucet off and knelt in front of her. "You know where you are now." It was a statement.

She rested her head on the cabinet next to her, giving it a slight bang out of sheer frustration.

"About three miles from Crazytown with my foot on the pedal, I'd say."

Spade made a noise that sounded like a sigh. "This has happened before?"

"Not for months. Not since..."

A knowing look crossed his face. "Not since you saw me kill that bloke," he finished for her. "Why didn't you tell me you suffered from post-traumatic stress disorder?"

Now that the episode had passed, she felt embarrassed. "I said it hadn't happened in a while, and wasn't that the least of my concerns when I saw you again?"

Denise held up her wrists for emphasis. The demon marks were concealed by wide silver and gold bangles, but they both knew what was under them.

"I just ruined the plan for tonight, didn't I?" she groaned. "I can't believe I let that happen."

Spade brushed her face with one of the paper towels. "If I'd been paying more attention, I would have anticipated this possibility. We'll leave now. We can sort out how to get a look at the others later."

"No." Denise took the towel from him and swiped under her eyes. Her mascara was probably everywhere. "We're here. Let's do this. I'll be okay if—this sounds so pathetic—I'll be okay as long as you don't leave me alone again. Being around all those vampires by myself just reminded me too much of—of that night. I don't know if it's possible, at this sort of thing—"

Something flashed across his face, too quick for her to translate. "I won't leave you alone." He held out his hand. "Please."

She placed her hand in his. Then she caught a glimpse of herself in the mirror.

"My makeup is *ruined*."

"Nonsense, you look beautiful. In fact, I've been propositioned on your behalf twice already."

An edge was in his voice. Denise couldn't tell if it was amusement or annoyance. She decided not to ask.

"I'm sure that'll change after my little psycho episode. It usually leaves a bad impression. That brings up a point, by the way. Aren't you worried that down the road, one of your people will say to Bones or Cat, 'Hey, I recognize the brunette. She's the nut job who belongs to Spade's line,' and then you'll be outed for your role in this?"

Spade's gaze locked with hers, his burnt-copper eyes both distant and fathomless. "No. Because we both know you have no intention of seeing anyone in the vampire world again once this is over."

Denise looked away. Her panic attacks had only

abated after she'd cut ties with Cat and anyone else who wasn't human. No way was she going back to being at the mercy of her memories, never knowing when her mind would trick her into thinking she was back at that awful ambush on New Year's Eve.

"You see what being around your kind does to me. I don't want to live like that, and I know how to make it stop."

His hand was still curled around hers, his grip cool, secure, and with an underlying strength that was utterly inhuman.

"Right, then," he said at last. "Let's see if we can't hasten that day for you."

Denise sat to his right at the ornate table in the ballroom, unaware this was the reason behind the discreet gawks she was getting. No doubt she thought those were due to how she'd screamed and blanked out from shock earlier. She didn't realize such an outburst would garner only mild intrigue among his worldly line members. A hysterical human? Who hadn't seen that before?

But what his people *hadn't* seen was a woman with a beating heart seated at his right during a formal event. Such placement indicated far higher standing than that of mere property, but his left was reserved for Alten, the most senior vampire in his line. Spade had intended for Denise to sit behind him, as was more fitting for property—even favored property. But while that would have been prudent, and likely even sufficient for her PTSD, he found he was loath to let go of her hand.

And that spelled trouble in every language he knew.

If there was a God, Nathanial would be among the people here and Spade would deliver him to the demon tonight. Spade would even put a bow on the sod and wish Raum good sup, as long as that meant Denise exited his life immediately. He could *not* afford to let himself care for a human. Not again.

Yet the cynic in him wasn't surprised that after the painstakingly long process of introducing Denise to the hundreds of people, alive and undead, in his line, she shook her head in disappointment.

"He's not here," she whispered.

Spade bit back a curse. Right. It would be too easy if he were.

Alten leaned over and handed him a CD. "Financials," he said. "I've run through the numbers. Everything seems on the up-and-up, except for Turner. He's missed his second quarterly in a row."

Spade absently continued to stroke Denise's knuckles. Her skin was still warmer than it should be. Could she have caught ill? Perhaps he shouldn't have sought to irritate her out of her depression with the ridiculously scanty togs she had on. "Mmmph," he grunted.

Alten stared at him. "For the second quarter in a row," he repeated.

Spade snapped his attention back to the other vampire. Yes, right, Turner's refusal to pay ten percent of his salary was an issue. Every vampire owed that to the Master of his line.

"Turner," he called out. "Do you have a reason for missing your tithe?"

The blond-haired vampire came through the others to stand in front of the table. He gave the proper bow, but when Spade caught Turner's scent and saw the mutiny in his expression, he heaved a mental sigh. Turner was about to brass him off something awful.

"I didn't pay my tithe because I want my freedom from your line, sire," Turner said, straightening his shoulders.

Spade eyed him, his patience dwindling by the second. "Undead just forty-four years, and you think you're ready to become Master of your own line?"

"Yes," Turner said. Then, with even more arrogance, "Release me to be my own Master. I have no wish to fight you, but if you deny my request, I will challenge you."

Stupid. Reckless. Fool.

"Overconfidence like that is exactly why you aren't ready to lead your own line yet. Your rashness would get you killed, and then all those you've created would be left without protection. That is why I deny your request for freedom, Turner, and if you follow through with your intention to challenge me, I promise you will regret it."

Out of the corner of his eye, Spade saw Denise looking back and forth between him and Turner. He glanced at her and saw her face was pale. She might not know a great deal about vampire society, but it was clear she understood that unless Turner had a sudden flash of intelligence, things were about to get bloody. That might be disastrous for the hard-fought calm she'd shown these past few hours, surrounded by far more undead people than living ones.

Spade returned his glare to Turner. Turner looked around, and then his hand went to his belt where he had a silver knife.

"I challenge you."

Very slowly, Spade let go of Denise's hand. Then he leaned in, his mouth almost brushing her ear.

"According to my laws, I must answer this. I'll have Alten wait with you in the car. This shouldn't take long."

"I'm staying."

He drew back to see her face. She was still very pale and her fingernails dug grooves into her leg, but her voice had been hard.

"That might not be wise…"

"If I feel a freak-out coming on, I'll leave, but until then, I'm staying."

Stubborn woman. Did *no one* have any sense tonight?

Spade rose, giving a sharp look to Alten. "If she wants to leave, take her to the car and wait for me there."

Alten quickly masked his surprise with a nod. People didn't decide to get up and *leave* in the middle of a duel. Especially not property. "As you wish."

If he was being logical, he'd have Alten take Denise to the car now. Instead he was inviting more speculation about Denise, both by seating her at his right and by letting her argue with him publicly. *No one has any sense tonight*, Spade thought jadedly. *Least of all me.*

He shoved that thought aside and settled his attention on Turner. He'd have to make an example out of him, else he'd be flooded with challenges from other young vampires thinking they were ready for what they couldn't handle.

Spade pulled off his shirt and set it on his chair, not taking his eyes off Turner. "Withdraw your challenge, or you'll be lucky if I let you live."

Turner shook his head. "No."

So be it, then.

Chapter 6

Denise couldn't tear her eyes away from the two vampires circling each other, even though her common sense screamed at her not to watch. She and Alten were still seated at the table, but everyone else hung back by the walls, giving Spade and Turner the majority of the room for their imminent fight. The ballroom doors were guarded and the catering staff quickly green-eyed into not noticing the abrupt change in the party atmosphere. Even being in a public hotel wouldn't stop this duel from happening. To make matters worse, Spade was weaponless while Turner had a large silver knife.

She leaned across the empty seat toward Alten. "Why isn't Spade allowed to have a weapon?" she whispered.

The vampire looked startled that she'd spoken to him, but he replied in a low voice, "He's allowed. He's just choosing not to use one."

"Why?" Denise blurted.

Dozens of heads swung her way. Even Spade paused in his predatory stride to throw her a single glare that spoke volumes.

Right. Guess it wasn't appropriate "property" behavior for her to wonder why Spade would fight unarmed against a vampire who had a big damn knife!

Something blurred, then a red slash appeared under Spade's chest. Somehow, the two vampires were now several feet away from where they'd been an instant ago and Turner's knife had a smear of red on it. Denise fought back a gasp. He'd slashed Spade too quickly for her to see it.

"Forfeit the duel and give me my freedom," Turner said, waving the knife while he began to circle again.

Spade laughed, a cold sound that was more scary than amused. "That was your best chance to kill me, but you missed it. How long do you think you'll be able to hold on to that knife until I take it from you?"

The wound on Spade's chest closed before he was finished speaking, but the smear remained. It was so vivid against the pale, muscled smoothness of his skin. Like scarlet against snow. Spade's eyes glowed with green fire, meeting Turner's equally bright gaze.

Denise couldn't stop the flood of mental images. *Glowing green eyes burning through the waning light. Vampires everywhere, blood and dirt spattering them. She slipped, landing in something dark and sticky. The stain coated the floor, widening as it led to the kitchen...*

"No," she whispered, pushing at the memories. Not now. Not here.

Alten looked at her sharply, but this time, Spade didn't deviate his attention from Turner. Another blur of limbs ended with Turner thrown onto his back, Spade standing over him holding that silver knife.

"Lose something?" Spade asked, wiggling it.

Turner had blood on him now, too, in a red X on his chest that remained even as his cuts healed. The X was directly over where his heart would be. Denise shuddered. The warning couldn't be clearer.

The memories continued to push as her. *Blood looks different in the dark. Almost black. Green light from a passing vampire's gaze shone on the large, misshapen lumps in front of her. What were those?*

Her hands went to her head, pressing against her temples as if she could physically force the memories back. *Not. Now.*

Turner lunged, nothing more than a pale streak of movement to her eyes. Spade whirled, more red appearing on Turner as if by magic. Another rush of flesh, a cry, and Turner stumbled back, clutching his stomach. Something thick and wet hit the floor.

Denise wound her hands in Spade's discarded shirt to keep from screaming and bolting out of her chair. Spade's whole hand and wrist were red, not to mention the knife, but he stood there almost casually, waiting while Turner gasped in pain, bent over.

"Hurts quite a bit, doesn't it?" Spade asked. "It's one thing to get cut up in a brawl, but another to have your guts spilled out of you. Have to be very strong to fight through that sort of pain. You're not nearly strong enough, but you want to be Master of your own line?"

"No one's…strong enough," Turner got out, straightening at last. His stomach was healed, but it had taken several seconds. Long enough for Spade to have killed him multiple times over, if he'd wanted to.

Spade's brow arched. "Is that so?" He tossed the knife at Turner's feet. "Strike the same blow, and if you can land that blade through my heart before I've recovered from it, you win your freedom."

Denise sucked in a horrified breath. Was Spade crazy? Why wasn't anyone else speaking up about what an *insane* suggestion that was?

Turner's blond head seemed to merge with Spade's black one as he leapt at him in a flurry of movement. For a few frenzied moments, their bodies were a crystal-and-red-splattered whir, until Turner fell back with the knife's hilt buried in his chest where the red X had been. Spade stood over him, one hand across his stomach, something red and squishy-looking near his feet.

"Yield, or I'll twist that knife," Spade said darkly.

Turner looked at the blade sticking out of his chest and then his head flopped back. "I withdraw my challenge," he rasped.

Denise felt an instant of overwhelming relief. Then she threw up into Spade's designer shirt.

Spade slid into the car, his coat the only thing on over his pants. Denise was waiting in the passenger seat, looking like she wished the ground would swallow her.

"I'm so sorry, I'll have your shirt dry cleaned," she said as soon as he shut the door.

He let out a short laugh. "That's quite all right. I threw it away."

"There's no way to describe tonight without using the phrase *cluster fuck*, is there?" she asked dryly.

My dear Denise, you have no idea. "It changes things," he said at last. "No one would believe you're merely my property after tonight."

Her expression flittered between sorrow and acceptance, then she forced a smile. "I understand. Thanks for all you've done. I know where not to look for Nathanial now, and that's a start. Oh, and you don't have to worry. I still won't involve Bones. I'll find another way."

Spade continued to stare at her, unblinking. This was his chance to be rid of her. He needed to take it. It was for the best.

Instead he found himself saying, "I won't leave you without help."

Gratitude flashed across her face. "I'll be so much better with whoever you refer me to. I'll act obedient, I won't puke on their clothes—"

He stifled a snort. "Good to know, since it will still be me."

"But you just said no one would believe I'm your property anymore."

They certainly wouldn't, but that wasn't her fault. It was his. He'd whisked her away when she panicked, though any self-respecting Master would have sent someone else to calm her. Then he'd clung to her hand, seated her at his right, obeyed her demand to stay for the duel, nearly gotten himself killed being distracted by her, and rushed to her side after she'd sprayed vomit into his shirt.

Indeed, there was *no* chance his people would believe she was just his property anymore.

"We'll have to play a besotted couple instead of a vampire and his property. It will require more acting on both our parts, but nothing that will violate your limits."

She looked confused. "I thought you said that would be suspicious, because you don't date humans."

"It will complicate things, but if we find Nathanial

soon, the charade could be brushed off as a passing fancy." Or passing stupidity, if he was being more accurate.

She touched his hand. Her fingers were so warm on his cooler skin. Just another reminder of her humanity.

"Thank you."

"You're welcome," Spade said tightly.

Fool, he lashed himself. He wasn't doing this out of pity, obligation, or honor, as Denise might believe. No, he'd just recommitted to helping her for the staggeringly witless reason of not wanting to let her go yet.

Even now, her scent and nearness tantalized his senses. It was the height of stupidity to be tempted by a woman he could neither bite nor shag. Perhaps for his next brilliant notion, he'd take up shaving with a chain saw.

He pushed that aside. Yes, he'd felt an unusual draw to her from the start, but it was just the circumstances that made her extra tempting. Denise was forbidden, so as a result, he wanted her. Add in danger, uncertainty, and close proximity, and it was no wonder he was lusting after her.

But nothing would come of it. Because she was a human, only a few heartbeats stood between Denise and the grave. *So fragile*, he thought, looking at her. *So easily destroyed...*

Spade glanced away. Detachment was what he now needed. Detachment, and a demon-dodging sod named Nathanial.

"Tomorrow we'll leave for New York. I know the Master of another large line we can check next."

Her fingers slid off his hand. "We'll just go from Master vampire to Master vampire, checking through their people?" Denise's tone said she thought that was akin to looking for a needle in a haystack.

"For a start. Once I've exhausted my friends' lines, we'll have to try different measures."

Ones that would be more dangerous than sifting through his allies' people, but he wouldn't expose Denise to the darker side of the vampire world again, if he could help it.

By the time they arrived back at the house, Spade felt in control again. Denise tried once or twice to speak to him during the drive, but he kept his answers short. Soon she fell silent. Once inside, he brought her up to his room—the only place anyone would expect her to sleep, after tonight's display—then went to shower without another word. When he came out, she was already asleep, curled on her side in his bed.

He gave her a final, grim look before he settled himself into a chair and closed his eyes. Sleep was what he needed. He'd feel better on the morrow.

When he fell asleep, however, he kept dreaming of Denise…only her hair was blond, her eyes were brown, and her throat had been cut from ear to ear.

Chapter 7

Denise gasped when she saw the red-haired man who waited for them in the drawing room. "You!"

Sadly, it wasn't her relative Nathanial she'd recognized. Ian blinked, obviously surprised to see her, too. Then his turquoise gaze slid to Spade and he laughed.

"When you said you were coming to see me, I thought this was going to be another boring social call, but I was wrong, wasn't I? Look at you, sneaking behind Crispin's back with his wife's best friend. I'm impressed."

Spade crossed his arms. "Don't snicker so, Ian. We're here on business, though yes, I don't want Crispin informed of it."

The sly smile stayed on Ian's lips. "Silence like that will cost you, mate."

"I have no doubt," Spade replied in an ironic tone.

Denise still couldn't believe Spade involved Ian in this. Bones's sire didn't have a good reputation on the best of days, and at his worst, he'd nearly gotten several of Cat's soldiers killed.

"Don't trust him, he'll go right to Bones and Cat," she muttered.

Ian's gaze settled on her, unoffended by the accusation. "Not if Charles makes it worth my while, poppet."

"Who's Charles?" Denise repeated, looking around. Then she remembered. Right, that's what Bones called Spade, too.

"My human name," Spade said, even though Denise figured it out.

"Don't know why you still insist on being called by that other name," Ian said, shaking his head. "I'd just as soon forget we were over prisoners, but you've chosen to remind yourself of it every day."

"Keeps me focused," Spade replied lightly.

"Prisoners?" Denise cast a look at Spade. He was a former convict? How could someone keep a vampire locked up, anyway?

"Didn't you know, poppet?" Ian purred. "It was how we met, on the voyage to the New South Wales penal colonies. Baron Charles DeMortimer here thought it was very beneath his station, being chained to common criminals like me, Crispin, and Timothy. Imagine his horror once we arrived and the overseer only addressed him by the tool he had to labor with instead of his title. Makes no sense that he insisted on being called that after he became a vampire, too."

A tick in Spade's jaw said he didn't appreciate the subject, but Denise was intrigued. She'd had no idea Spade had been both a prisoner *and* a nobleman. In a way, it explained some things. Spade reeked of danger, true, but he also never let her touch a door or car handle, streaking to open them for her. Then his insistence on sleeping in a chair despite it being his bed he was kicking himself out of, and she'd never heard him so much as raise his voice. Add that to the regal air he carried himself with, and she should have guessed that he'd come from far different circumstances than Bones.

"Aren't you interested in hearing what I'll offer in exchange for your discretion, Ian?" Spade asked, coolly changing the topic.

Ian grinned. "Of course."

"My property in the Keys you've long admired. I'll loan it to you for the next decade. That should be more than adequate to ensure your silence."

Denise let out a shocked noise that both men ignored. "Not good enough," Ian replied. "Crispin will be very angry at me if he discovers my part in whatever it is you're up to with her, so you'll have to *give* me the house to make it worth my while."

"You greedy schmuck!" Denise burst out.

Ian cast a leisurely glance in her direction. "And now my feelings are hurt. That'll cost you the boat, too."

Spade shot a look at her that had Denise clamping her mouth shut. *Greedy SCHMUCK*, she silently screamed at Ian.

"Only if I have your silence *and* cooperation by letting Denise pick through your property for a bloke that I'll leave with, no questions asked, if she finds who she's looking for."

Ian's brows went up. "Do I get to know what this person did?"

Spade's smile was more a baring of teeth. "No. You don't."

He'll never go for it, Denise thought, seeing the craftiness flit across Ian's features. But then the other vampire smiled back.

"I do love that house, Charles. Done."

Denise let out her breath, relieved and guilt-ridden at the same time. Now she could add a house and a boat to what it cost Spade to help her, all because she manipulated him. She had to find a way to pay him back, even if it meant making installments for the next thirty years.

Ian stretched. "You're welcome to start with who I've got in the house and work your way from there. I don't need to tell you how far-flung some of my people are, but I'll put the word out that they're to give you their full cooperation."

"And you won't mention you recognized the human I'm traveling with," Spade added, his voice steely.

Ian's gaze slid over Denise in a way that made her feel like she'd somehow lost all her clothes. "No, but it'll be interesting to see how long you can keep this a secret. Need a place to stay while you're in town?"

"Thank you, I've made arrangements elsewhere," Spade replied, to Denise's relief. The sooner they were away from Ian, the better. He was handsome, but there was something openly cold and ruthless about him. Without even realizing it, she found herself inching closer to Spade. *Let's look at his people and get the hell out of here.*

As if Spade had heard her mental directive, he took her hand. "Ian, if you'll direct us?"

Fifteen minutes later, Denise was cursing to herself in frustration. Out of the dozen men, human and otherwise, who lived at Ian's house, none was Nathanial. How long before Raum became impatient and started threatening her family again? Or how long before the demon marks manifested more dramatically in her? Right now, the only changes she'd noticed were an increasingly short temper and constant hunger, but she knew that was just the beginning. How long did she have before the marks turned her into the same sort of monster Raum was?

"Tell whoever you've got in the area to meet you at the Crimson Fountain tonight," Spade said to Ian as they made their way out. "It'll give us a chance to look at more of them without arousing suspicion."

Ian cast another speculative look at Denise before nodding. "I had other plans, but this situation piques my interest. I'll see you there, mate."

Denise waited until they were miles away from Ian's before she spoke. "I'm so sorry about your house. *Please*, let me reimburse you. I have a 401(k) I can tap into—"

"No." The single word was crisp. Spade didn't even look away from the road when he said it.

"But this isn't what I intended!" she exclaimed, the tension from the past several days sharpening her voice.

Spade looked at her, briefly but thoroughly. "You had no idea what this would entail when you involved me, but I did, and I agreed nonetheless."

More guilt piled onto her. This was wrong. So wrong. "What if it takes months to find him?"

She couldn't bear the thought, but the initial, naïve assumption she'd had that she could quickly find Nathanial if she just had an in with the vampire world had been shattered. Spade had thousands of people in his

line. How many other Master vampires had thousands
of people spread out all over the world?

"Then it takes months to find him," Spade replied,
no emotion in his tone. "I'm in this to the end, as I
promised."

And she might not have months before she became
a monster. Her former feeling of helplessness turned to
anger. When she did find Nathanial, she'd make him pay
for what he'd put her, her family, *and* Spade through.

Then the hatred faded, leaving a hollow fear instead.
*It's happening even now. Every day, a little more of me
gets replaced with something else.* The realization terrified her.

"Maybe tonight will be our lucky night," she said,
forcing an optimism she didn't feel into her voice.

"Perhaps," Spade agreed.

He didn't sound like he believed it, either.

Denise's knuckles were white as she clenched her
fists. The scent of her anxiety filled the cab, covering
the stale sweat, perfume, and lingering odor of vomit
in the backseat. The cab made another lurching movement into traffic, narrowly missing the car that had been
vying for the same lane. Denise paled until her skin almost matched Spade's in color.

"Could you be a bit gentler on the gas?" Spade said
to the driver. Poor girl, this was her first experience
with a New York cabbie. From Denise's expression,
she'd like it to be her last.

"What you say?" the driver replied in thickly ac-
cented English. Little wonder the man had trouble hearing him, with how loud his radio was.

Spade placed the driver's accent. *"Possa-o ir devagar guiar, por favor?"* he said, speaking louder.

The driver gave him a wide smile that revealed a lack of recent dental attention. "Oh, *fala portuguesa? Nenhum problema*," he exclaimed, easing off the accelerator.

"What language is that?" Denise asked, distracted enough to unclench her fists.

"Portuguese."

She looked impressed. "I kept meaning to learn more languages, but all I know is some Spanish left over from high school. When did you learn Portuguese?"

"When I was in Portugal," he replied, amused to see the surprise on her face.

"Oh," she said softly. "I've never been overseas. I haven't even been out of America, except for…"

Her voice trailed off and shadows settled over her expression. *For Canada*, Spade mentally finished. *Where your husband was murdered.*

"Remember your part tonight," Spade said, more to take her attention off that than out of concern over her forgetting. "I may have to leave you for a short time, but if I do, stick by Ian."

"I don't trust him," she said at once.

Spade let out a snort. "Nor should you, but he won't attempt to mesmerize you or feed from you. Since we're going to a place filled with different types of vampires, that makes him safer than anyone except me."

He didn't think there was any real chance of danger to Denise, but he wanted her on her guard nevertheless. Neither one of them brought up the other possibility— that with these circumstances, she might have another panic attack. Their best hope of finding Nathanial was to expose Denise to the largest number of undead persons and their property at a time, but while that was efficient, it was also hazardous to her emotional state.

There was a way around that, however. Spade chose his words carefully. "I know this won't be easy on you, Denise, but I could help with that. I wouldn't even need to bite you to do it. A simple suggestion for you to be calmer when you're around vampires or ghouls would—"

"Absolutely *not*." She turned her attention away from the traffic to glare at him. "Don't you dare mess with my mind. I mean it, Spade."

Stubborn woman. He shrugged. "If that's your decision."

"It is," she said, still glaring. "Promise me you won't do it."

The harsh scent of fear, anger, and mistrust swirled around her. Very slowly, Spade pulled out one of the silver knives from his coat. She went a shade paler when she saw it, but he ignored that, using the knife to slice a line in his palm.

"You know what a blood oath means to my kind, right?" he asked, holding her gaze. "By my blood, Denise, I swear I will never manipulate your mind."

A sliver of crimson clung to the blade even as the wound closed. Spade kept his hand well below the window that separated the driver's line of vision from the backseat. Only Denise could see what he'd done, and her scent changed even as the color returned to her face.

"I believe you."

Spade put the knife away, wiping the scant amount of blood onto his pants. They were dark enough that no one would notice. Well, no human would; a vampire or ghoul would smell it, but they wouldn't care.

The cab jerked to a stop. Spade handed over a twenty, then was outside opening Denise's door before she'd finished lowering her hand to tug on the handle.

"You don't need to keep doing that, I can get it," she murmured, looking embarrassed. She tucked a strand of her hair back, the color in her cheeks darkening ever so slightly.

It was such a lovely, feminine response, without the wariness she normally had with him. Though he would have done the same with any woman—no amount of time could erase the strict etiquette he'd been raised with—Spade found himself enjoying her reaction.

"Just because a lady can, doesn't mean she should," he teased, amused to see her color deepen as she glanced away. Christ, she was lovely.

He slid his gaze over her, unable to help himself. Under her coat, Denise wore a cowl-necked sweater and a long black skirt, her boots peeking out from under its hem and gloves covering her hands. The only skin visible on her was her face and neck. Spade found himself staring at her pulse with a hunger that had nothing to do with blood. What would she taste like, if he placed his mouth there?

And what would she taste like everywhere else he put his mouth?

Denise shivered, snapping his attention back to the fact that they were standing outside on a sidewalk when they should be inside looking for Nathanial.

"This way," he said, extending his arm.

She placed her hand in it with another shiver, not

meeting his gaze. A good thing, too, because his eyes had probably gone green with lust.

"What's it like in this place?" she asked, still looking away.

Spade forced his control back into place. "It's exactly what you'd think a vampire bar would be like, if you didn't believe in vampires."

That made her look at him. "Huh?"

He grunted. "You'll see."

Chapter 8

I am so overdressed, Denise thought, looking at the people inside the Crimson Fountain. The patrons had a decidedly Goth edge, with black clothes as an apparent must. She felt out of place in her blue sweater, although her skirt and boots were black, at least. Leather and vinyl also seemed to be everywhere, along with various gothic necklaces, earrings, piercings, and tattoos.

Spade led her through the dense crowd of people dancing. She was careful to look at everyone she passed, hoping one of them would be Nathanial. But she wasn't prepared for the fang-filled smile directed at her when she brushed by a dancer whose skin was as warm as her own.

Surprised, Denise touched his arm again. Warm living flesh, all right. The man's smile widened, showing more fang.

"Want to dance with the undead, beautiful?" he crooned, swaying his hips.

"But you're not a vampire."

His smile faded. "Yes I am."

Denise looked at the man, his faux fangs, and the people around him. *Exactly what you'd think a vampire bar would be like, if you didn't believe in vampires.* Spade was right. This place looked like every bad undead stereotype come to life. It even had some coffins propped up on the stage behind where the band performed.

"Excuse me," she said, brushing past him.

Spade waited for her a few feet ahead. He had a slight grin on his face. "What do you think?"

"That you have a sick sense of humor, telling Ian to bring his people here," she replied. "And that you're overdressed, too."

Spade also wasn't wearing a speck of leather or vinyl. Instead he had on a long-sleeved, creamy silk shirt and slacks that were some sort of thick, expensive-looking material. His floor-length coat only made him look more elegant. She marveled that all the leather-clad wannabes had no idea the classily dressed man was actually the creature they were imitating.

He leaned in, his mouth almost brushing her ear. "It's the perfect meeting spot. Who'd think real vampires would frequent a place like this?"

Spade didn't move back after he spoke. Denise wasn't sure if he was waiting for her to reply, but her mind was suddenly blank. His hair rested against her cheek, dark and silky, and his lips were so close to her ear that her slightest movement would connect them. He was also so tall, she couldn't see past his shoulders, and with the edges of his coat brushing around her, she felt like one step closer would result in her being swallowed up by him.

The thought was somehow tempting.

Denise jerked back, confusion, guilt, and fear competing in her. Was her reckless train of thought due to the growing demon essence within her? The inhuman in her drawn to the inhuman in him? Had to be. Spade was a vampire, the same creature that promoted panic attacks in her, and besides that, Randy had been dead for only a year...

Spade stared at her until Denise had to look away. His gaze was too knowing, too intense. From the corner of her eye, it almost looked like he'd taken a deep breath, but of course that was impossible. Vampires didn't need to breathe.

"Ian's this way," he said, turning around. His voice sounded lower. Throatier.

She followed him, keeping her eyes on his shoulders as he maneuvered through the crowd.

Ian was seated in an open booth, two women on either side of him. Denise felt her former angst melt away, replaced with incredulity. Even in a room full of people pretending to be vampires, Ian stood out.

Black boots with crisscrossing chains adorned his legs, the same color as the leather pants that dipped low on his hips. And aside from the studded slave collar Ian wore around his neck and the studs pierced through his nipples, that was all he had on.

Ian grinned at her, trailing a pale hand down his chest. "Luscious, aren't I, poppet? Go on, stare. I don't mind."

Denise tore her gaze away, but not because she'd

been transfixed in admiration. Sure, Ian had an abdomen that could double as a washboard and his face was eerily handsome, but he also had *monster* written all over him. Couldn't those women sense the menace oozing off him? If she'd met Ian in an alley, she'd run like hell, no matter how much beautiful skin he showed.

"You look like a Dracula porn movie reject," she managed.

Spade laughed, but Ian winced. "Let's not speak of him. Like the devil, Vlad might appear if we do."

The word *devil* sobered her. That's right, she wasn't here to focus on Spade, or Ian, or anything except searching for Nathanial. Her family's lives depended on it, and so did her humanity.

As if in response, her stomach let out a growl, even though it had been only three hours since she'd eaten. Ian raised a brow, hearing it even over the pumping music. Spade glanced down at her, hearing it as well, then gestured at Ian's booth.

"Wait here whilst I see if there's anything for you to eat."

A slow smile lit Ian's face. Denise didn't want to be left with him, but insisting on following after Spade sounded too clingy. The brunette to Ian's left scooted over, making a space for Denise. She sat, concentrating on searching the faces of the men in the club, not the vampire to her right. Or the one on his way to the bar.

"How amusing," Ian drawled.

Denise didn't look at him as she replied. "What?"

"Charles, going to fetch you food as though he were a servant," Ian replied. "Master vampires don't do that, poppet. Makes me wonder even more about the two of you."

Denise glanced over, noticing that neither of the women reclined on Ian seemed to care about him saying *vampire*. Maybe they were humans who belonged to him. Or maybe he'd tranced them into not caring.

"We're, ah…he's…it's none of your business."

What had she been about to do, tell Ian Spade was with her only because she'd coerced him? Or how it was demonic essence that had turned her into a compulsive overeater? It had to be. Normally when she was stressed, she ate less, not more. Besides, if this wasn't something supernatural, she'd have put on ten pounds this past week.

"He's only being polite. You should look the word up," Denise settled on.

Ian snorted. "And angels fly out of my arse when I fart. All his chivalrous tendencies aside, I haven't seen Charles this attentive with a human in almost a hundred and fifty years."

Denise was still shaking her head over Ian's crude imagery when the rest of what he said penetrated.

"What human was he attentive with a hundred and fifty years ago?"

Even as she asked it, she wished she hadn't. For one, it was none of *her* business, and for another, she was starting to sound like a vampire, with "human" this and "human" that. She had to get away from this world. Back to hers, where there were nothing but humans to distinguish between.

Ian's eyes gleamed. "Hasn't he told you about her yet?"

She couldn't help herself. "Her who?"

"Ah, ah." Ian tsked. "That's not my tale to tell, poppet."

"Then you shouldn't have brought it up," she snapped, her temper blistering in an instant.

Both of Ian's brows went up. Denise fought for control. This wasn't she. It was the damn demon marks. She had to focus on priorities. It didn't matter what happened with Spade and some woman a century ago.

To distract herself from the inexplicable rage still simmering in her, she turned to the brunette at her right.

"Sorry, Ian didn't introduce us. I'm Denise. Nice to meet you."

No fewer than eighty of Ian's people passed through the Crimson Fountain's door. An impressive number, considering Ian summoned them only earlier this afternoon. In addition to that, Spade counted several vampires not of Ian's line, plus more than a few ghouls, and dozens of humans with a distinct undead scent that marked them as someone's property.

But Denise hadn't recognized her relative among any of them. By three a.m., the scent of weariness and dejection coming from her was palpable.

"We'll be leaving shortly," Spade told her.

Denise nodded, her head propped up on her hand, her shoulders slumped.

"You did very well tonight," he added, trying to lighten her mood even as he cursed himself. He wasn't here to be a bloody cheerleader, after all. Still, the iron will Denise had exhibited, pushing back the PTSD he could tell had risen more than once, impressed him. Denise was a better survivor than she gave herself credit for. With time, she'd be able to defeat her anxiety around vampires and ghouls entirely.

But she doesn't want to, he reminded himself. Once

Denise had those marks off, she'd have no need to, because she'd never willingly associate with a vampire or ghoul again.

The thought soured his mood. He stood. "I need to feed before we leave. Stay here with Ian."

He didn't wait for her response, but grimly headed for the dance floor. Even at this late hour, it was crowded enough that he could have his pick of people to feed from. The Crimson Fountain didn't close until dawn, still a few hours away.

Spade tore his thoughts away from Denise and concentrated on the moving feast before him. A young woman didn't wait for him to make his decision. She sidled over, smiling as she snake-hipped to the music in front of him.

"Hello, gorgeous," she crooned.

Spade raked her with a gaze. Human and healthy; she'd do. He wasn't feeling particular at the moment.

He let her lead him deeper amid the other dancers, smiling back as he pulled her to him, fitting his body along the length of hers. She gasped when he began to move, swaying and bending her in time to the pulsing rhythm. Lust reeked off her, and she gave him a seductive look as she began to unbutton his shirt, trailing her hands down his flesh once it hung open.

Spade allowed her to explore for another minute. Then he spun her around, her warm back heating his chest, her pulse—so close to his mouth—jumping with excitement. She rubbed, catlike, against him, letting out a moan as he brushed her hair back and nuzzled her neck. He kept dancing as he held her, unconcerned about letting his fangs show in this crowd, or in bending his head to her throat. Anyone watching would think it was an act, the same pantomime that had been played out countless times tonight. And she'd never know it had been the real thing once he was done mesmerizing her.

Right before he sank his teeth into her neck, however, a sharp whistle jerked his head up. Ian stood next to the railing over the dance floor, gesturing almost lazily toward the exit.

"Thought you'd want to know. Denise just ran off."

Chapter 9

Her heart pounded and panic vibrated just below the surface. Denise increased her pace, wishing she could somehow outrun her feelings. The worst part was, this had nothing to do with her PTSD.

She couldn't help but watch as Spade stalked off to the dance floor, contemplating the people on it the same way a predator eyed a herd. Then that black-haired woman sashayed up, almost dry-humping the air in front of him. And he'd gone with her. Started to *move* in a way that the word *dancing* didn't even begin to describe. Denise's mouth had gone dry and her palms started to sweat. As the buttons came off Spade's shirt and his pale, hard flesh was revealed in the fluorescent lighting, her pulse began to thump, too. His corded muscles rippled with each new bend and sway he made, that aura of dangerousness replaced with raw, blistering sensuality instead.

And when he'd spun the woman around, his black hair sliding forward to cover his face as he bent to her throat, pure, adulterated heat had slammed into Denise. It was so fierce, so unexpected, and so overwhelming that she'd trembled in her seat—only to be shaken out of her trance at Ian's low chuckle.

"You're full of surprises, aren't you, poppet?"

From the expression on Ian's face, he knew exactly what she'd been feeling—and what had inspired it.

So she'd run like hell. Better Spade think she was crazy than realize the truth, as Ian had.

Some fuzzy part of her recognized that the places she passed seemed to blur together. She had no idea where she was going. *Away* was good enough right now. At this hour, traffic was light enough that she didn't need to pause before crossing the streets, or maybe she didn't care about causing cars to slam on their brakes. Such tall buildings, narrow streets, and endless concrete. It felt like she was in a maze that was slowly closing in on her. Even the night's sky was only visible in small slits between the buildings looming above.

An iron grip closed around her elbow. Denise jerked away, but that grip didn't budge. Instead she was swept up against a hard, tall body, her feet swinging in the air with how rapidly she'd been grabbed.

"Let go!" she gasped.

Spade's face was very close. He'd left his jacket back at the club and obviously hadn't stopped to button up his shirt, either, because his muscled, bare chest pressed against her sweater.

"You're all right, Denise," he said firmly. "Nothing's coming after you. You're safe."

Of course. Spade thought she was in the midst of

another panic attack. That was partly true, only for a different reason.

"I'm okay now. I just…needed to get away from there," she said, her breath coming in pants.

Spade's eyes narrowed and he relaxed his grip, but didn't let her go. Denise tried to slow her breathing, praying her previous bout of lust wouldn't raise its head again.

"I see."

He still hadn't let her go. Denise wiggled experimentally. His grip loosened more, but his arms stayed where they were.

Denise cast about for something, anything, to distract her from what being in Spade's embrace felt like. "This city is so stifling. It's just buildings, more buildings, and more buildings. Isn't there anything *alive* around here?"

His lips curled even as she groaned at her choice of words. "I meant alive, like trees and grass—"

"I know what you meant," he cut her off, still with that half smile. "In fact, you ran in the right direction, if that's what you're seeking. Come."

His arms finally dropped from around her, but he placed a light hand on her back. Denise walked next to him, torn between the urge to tell him to button up his shirt and her own enjoyment at catching glimpses of his bare chest.

"Aren't you cold?" she asked at last. She was. She'd left her coat back at the Crimson Fountain. Thankfully, her sweater was thick and she hadn't taken off her long gloves. Couldn't risk someone seeing the demon brands on her, after all.

"Not really," Spade replied. "Vampires don't react to cold like humans do. I can feel the cold, of course, but it doesn't cause the same sensation in me. I'd say we should go back to fetch your coat, but we're more than halfway to the hotel already."

Denise glanced at the next street sign—and gasped. A shiver of a different nature ran up her spine.

"How far did I run?"

Spade's expression was both hard and pitying at the same time. "'Round a dozen blocks."

She shouldn't be able to run that far in the scant minutes that had elapsed. An Olympic runner would have a hard time doing it, and she was no Olympic runner. Raum's brands were manifesting even more than she'd realized.

"Oh shit," Denise whispered.

Spade didn't respond with any useless, comforting clichés, for which she was grateful. She'd heard enough of those well-meaning phrases after Randy died. Why couldn't people acknowledge that occasionally, life just sucked? Didn't they realize that sometimes silence was more comforting than the most sincere expression of sympathy or attempt at showing the deeper meaning behind it all?

Up ahead, the horizon of buildings broke and a vast expanse of open space and trees met her gaze.

"Central Park," Spade said, nudging her forward. Denise hadn't even noticed that she'd stopped. "Our hotel is right down the next street, in fact, so not far if you get too cold. With all the snow, you can't see everything that's still living in the park, but it's there."

Denise smiled, some of the anxiety leaking from her. "It's perfect."

She let Spade lead her into the park, marveling that she didn't feel the slightest bit afraid. Under normal circumstances, it would be the height of stupidity to wander through here in the dark, wee hours of the morning. Still, there was nothing normal about having a vampire at her side and demon marks on her skin. *Potential muggers beware*, she thought wryly. Spade hadn't gotten his dinner before. He'd probably eat the first person who approached them in a threatening manner.

"How old were you when you died?" she asked, going off the path in favor of walking in the snow. Spade followed behind her, his steps sounding so much surer than hers in the dark.

"Thirty."

Denise sighed. "I'll be twenty-eight on my next birthday."

"I'll be two hundred and fifty-seven on my next birthday," Spade replied, an edge of something she couldn't name in his voice.

Giving him another once-over, Denise couldn't help but laugh.

"You look pretty good for such an old man."

He grinned, his smile a white, wicked flash in the night. "Flattery will get you everywhere, darling."

She had to turn away quickly, because if she didn't, her gaze would linger too long on all the evidence of her statement. Spade *did* look good. Too good, especially with his shirt blowing behind him, showing a chest that looked like carved moonlight. His long black hair also rustled in the breeze, taking turns hiding or revealing his face, but it wasn't hard for her to see his eyes. Their depths glowed with green specks, drawing her gaze even though she knew it was dangerous to keep looking.

Denise sat down, pretending to draw something in the snow, ignoring the cold seeping in through her long skirt. She had on tights and knee-high boots underneath her skirt, but that wasn't enough to protect her from the freezing earth. Still, better to shiver from contact with the snow than reveal the tremble that had swept through her while she'd stared at Spade. *This isn't you*, she reminded herself. *It's just the demon marks.*

The crunching of snow announced that Spade was walking over to her. Denise didn't glance at him. She felt her heart speeding up and cursed herself for it.

"Denise."

Spade's voice was lower, and he drew her name out in a way that made her heart speed up even more. Still, she kept her attention on the random pattern she'd drawn, even when she felt him kneel down next to her.

It's just the demon marks, just the demon marks...

His hand slid across her back. Shivers rippled through her that had nothing to do with the cold. Then Spade's shoulder brushed hers, followed by his leg touching her thigh as he moved even closer.

Everywhere he grazed her, her flesh felt like it was vibrating. Denise kept her head bent, her hair covering her face, hand quivering as she continued to blindly trace her fingers through the snow.

It's just the demon marks, just the demon marks!

Spade brushed her hair back with a light, caressing stroke. She wished his fingers felt lifeless and cold, but they didn't. They felt strong, supple, and knowing. Like he realized exactly how she was reacting to his touch.

"Denise..."

His voice was so deep, and the breath he'd used saying her name touched her cheek in its own caress. Denise closed her eyes. Everything in her wanted to turn toward Spade and abandon the last, thin thread of con-

trol she had. The need surging inside her *had* to be from
the demon marks. She'd never felt such a strong pull
toward anyone before, even Randy...

Randy. Murdered because she'd thought it would be
fun to spend New Year's Eve with vampires. And now
here she was, a scant fourteen months later, about to
throw herself into a vampire's arms.

No. She wouldn't let herself.

"You must be hungry." Guilt and grief had thrown
a much-needed bucket of ice water on her emotions. "I
interrupted your dinner by running off, so let me make
that up to you."

Denise flipped her hair back, able to meet Spade's
eyes without the same shivery need as before. She had
to stop thinking of him in any way except a vampire—
and she would not *let* herself be lulled into another false
sense of security about what the vampire world entailed.
Having Spade bite her was the surest way to remind her
of what he was; a vampire who lived in a world filled
with blood and death.

Spade's eyes were all green, lighting up his face with
a hazy emerald glow. Denise didn't want to know if
they'd been that way before her offer, because she knew
what else could have drawn such a response.

"You want me to bite you?" he asked, low and rough.
"Just days ago, you were stuffing yourself full of garlic
trying to prevent that very thing."

"You've made it clear that you won't let me pay you
back any of the money you've lost helping me, so giving you blood is the least I can do, right?"

Denise kept her gaze challenging as she tilted her
neck. It would hurt being bitten. She knew that from
experience. It was how Denise had met Cat, when Cat

rescued her from a vampire trying to drink her to death. A little pain now would go a long way toward reminding her of why she needed to stay away from Spade—and all the undead—once she found Nathanial.

Spade's voice was very soft. "Get up and walk away from me, Denise, or I will take you up on your offer."

His gaze pinned hers, that green glow penetrating. She knew he wasn't using his power on her, because her mind felt clear, but she was drawn in nonetheless.

She had to end this bewildering attraction she felt for him. Now, before it got any stronger. If she was lucky, she'd have a PTSD attack on the spot.

"Go ahead, vampire," she replied, equally soft.

Spade's mouth was on her throat before the last word left her.

Her skin was so hot, even in the frigid air. He'd intended to bite her quickly, to give her what she was looking for—repugnance. He knew that was her goal when desperation and anger replaced the intoxicating fragrance of desire coming from her.

That desire had almost been Spade's undoing. He'd gotten the first hint of it at the club when he'd whispered in her ear, but it vanished so fast, he hadn't been sure. He was sure a few minutes ago. Denise's scent and the way she reacted to his touch confirmed it, razing his willpower and drawing him to her even though his common sense warned him to stop.

Then her angry offer to let him feed from her, motivated by an obvious wish to see him as nothing more than a beast. He'd almost thrown it back in her face, but then realized she was right. It was the perfect solution. Let her be repelled by him. Do them both worlds of good.

But now, feeling her pulse vibrating under his mouth, he couldn't be rough with her. Couldn't do anything but slide his lips over her skin until that stiffness in her limbs was replaced with a different sort of tension. Couldn't stop himself from inhaling her honey and jasmine scent, salted by her residual anger, but deepening as his hand wound in her hair. He pressed her closer, opening his mouth to flick his tongue across her throat.

Ah, darling, you taste just how I thought you would. Dark, lush, and sweet.

He continued to trail his mouth over her neck, searching out where she was the most sensitive. Not there, though that resulted in a delicious shiver running through her. Not there, but it made her uncurl her hands from the clenched fists she'd held at her sides. His tongue flicked out again, probing a new spot—and Denise gasped, arching against him. *Yes. There.*

Spade closed his eyes, absorbing her scent with another deep breath. Then he slid his fangs into her neck, relishing her shudder of pleasure as the venom they contained merged with her flesh, erasing the sting of breaking her skin and producing a false, pleasant sensation of heat.

As soon as he swallowed her blood, however, he knew something was wrong. But it was too late. As if he were a vampire rising undead for the first time, Spade couldn't stop himself from swallowing again. And again, and again.

Chapter 10

Denise wrapped her arms around Spade, lost in sensations she never expected. Each new, deep suction sent pleasure stabbing through her, followed by cascading waves of heat. Her earlier cold was only a memory. Now she burned from the inside out, her earlier reservations forgotten, twisting against Spade in a combination of need and bliss.

He yanked her closer, then rolled on top of her when even that proximity didn't seem to be enough. Denise's gasp turned into a moan at the feel of him pressing her down with a wonderful, hungry urgency. His hips aligned with hers at his next suction. Then he rubbed against her, the hard bulge in his pants sensually grinding between her legs.

The resulting heat in her loins exceeded the fire running through her veins. She dug her nails into his back at the next twist from his hips, rocking with him to feel more of that incredible friction. A sweet dizziness filled her as he drew more strongly on her neck, holding her in a grip she couldn't break—and didn't want to.

"Spade," she whispered, her eyes fluttering, the treetops and stars blinking in and out of her vision.

He tore his mouth from her throat, somehow crouched several feet from her in the next instant. The sudden absence of his weight and that luscious feel of his body pressing into hers left her confused. She reached out to him, only to have his growl stop her.

"Stay away."

His eyes were blazing green while blood dripped from his mouth. She reached for her neck. A slow trickle met her fingers. It throbbed with the same demanding ache she felt between her legs.

"Is something wrong…?"

He started toward her, and then flung himself backward so hard, he hit a tree. It tilted with an ominous creak.

"Run," Spade said tightly. "Run away from me right now, or I will drink you to death."

The feral hunger in his gaze finally penetrated through her haze of dizziness and lust. She managed to get to her feet, still holding her neck and feeling the wetness between her fingers. Spade's eyes were transfixed there, his mouth pulling back in a snarl that revealed fangs so long and sharp, his face looked more animal than man.

"Go."

She turned and staggered away. Soon she was back on the path, heading in what she hoped was the same direction they'd entered from. The hotel was on the next street, Spade had said.

A crashing noise directed her gaze up. It was dark, but she could make out something big jumping impossibly high up from tree to tree. Was Spade following her? A sick fear lurched in her stomach, covering the sensual warmth that had so recently filled her. Was he *hunting* her?

"Faster," his unmistakable voice snarled.

Denise ignored her lingering dizziness and ran for all she was worth, bursting through the same part of the park she recognized as where they'd entered from. She glanced around wildly, hearing more branches snap above her. Then she ran toward what she hoped was the street Spade had pointed to earlier.

A dash across the street revealed the sign she'd been looking for. The Plaza. Denise fumbled in her skirt pocket, glad she'd stuck her room key in there instead of her coat at the beginning of the night, and ducked inside the ornate doors. She kept her head down, holding her hair over the bloodstained spot on her neck, and made it into the elevators without any of the employees calling the police. The early hour probably helped; the few people Denise passed looked sleepy when she glanced at them.

By the time the elevator opened on her floor, that previous, heated need was gone and she was disgusted with herself. She'd practically begged Spade to take her right there in the snow. Was that why he'd been thrown into a feeding frenzy? Had her lust-crazed reaction pushed him past the normal control a vampire had? And what was wrong with her, responding like some sort of nympho from a *vampire* bite? Yes, it had been well over a year since she'd had sex, but that didn't explain the intensity of her reaction.

Denise was still lashing herself when she closed the door to her room. She leaned against it in weariness—and then wrinkled her nose. What was that smell?

Raum rounded the corner of the bedroom. "Hello."

The demon was at the door before she could yank it back open, the sulfur scent emanating from him almost choking her.

Raum smiled. "Alone at last."

Spade used the last of his willpower to make sure Denise made it into the hotel. When he saw her stumble through the glass doors, he couldn't hold back the effects of her blood anymore. The dark magic in it, instantly addictive, merged his reality with hallucinations and the present with the past.

Spade fell from the tree, barely registering the impact of the ground. *Naked branches waved in the wind as he and Crispin rode past, following the grooves the carriage made in the dirty snow. They were from earlier that morning at the most. Spade leaned forward, urging his horse faster.*

He rolled on the ground, hearing his own guttural moans as he tried to push the memories back. *No. I don't want to see that again. Not again.*

He got to his feet and began to run. The trees morphed and seemed to reach for him, their branches turning into skeletons that bent down and swiped him as he passed. Then the trees grew thicker, transforming into the Argonne forest from that day a century and a half ago.

"No," Spade said, gritting his teeth. He ran faster,

stumbling over the large rocks he somehow hadn't seen that jutted out of the earth. This wasn't real. It wasn't *real*.

Or was it? What if he *was* back there? What if it wasn't too late to save her?

"Giselda," he shouted. "I'm coming!"

Crispin spotted the wheel first, turned on its side off the lip of the road. For a moment Spade was relieved. Her carriage had suffered a mishap, that's why Giselda had been delayed. But then he smelled it. The scent of blood and death.

Spade bounded off his horse, streaking toward the carriage without even touching the ground, not caring that he was flying for the first time.

Crispin flew faster, grabbing him from behind and wrestling him to the ground. "Don't, mate. Let me go instead."

Spade flung him off, his hand going to his knife when Crispin started toward him once more.

"Touch me again and I'll kill you," he growled, whirling and running in the direction where Giselda's scent was the strongest—and where other harsh, vile scents intertwined with hers.

He didn't pause to check on the footman sprawled in a heap at the edge of the woods. A scrap of material clung to the thorny bush just beyond the footman. Spade dashed into the woods, following the reeking scents, seized with terror as he saw the multiple footprints in the mud and snow. She'd run, but she'd been chased.

The torn-up spot of earth he came upon next brought him skidding to a stop. It stank of sweat, blood, terror, and lust. Rage exploded in him as he saw pieces of a woman's pantalets strewn about, the circling imprint of boots, then a larger impression of a body pressed into the earth, blood and other stains at the center of it.

Spade swung around, following the trailing scent of blood until he came to a large splatter at the crest of a hill. Everything in him tightened as he looked down the steep incline.

A redheaded woman was crumpled at the bottom, her dress half ripped off, her bruised body twisted and motionless. For a split second Spade felt overwhelming relief. It wasn't Giselda; her hair was blond. Perhaps this poor lass had been traveling with her—

Realization crashed through him in the next instant. He flung himself down the ravine, a cry tearing out of him when he turned the woman over. Giselda's frozen, pain-ravaged face stared back at him, her hair red from the blood soaked into it, her throat sliced open to the bone.

"You lied to me," Raum said, tutting with the sort of disapproval one would use on a child. "You told me Spade was human, yet that's a vampire you were rolling around in the snow with, calling by that name."

Denise glanced at the door, hoping that Spade would somehow magically appear. But there was only the demon in front of her, his light brown hair in a ponytail again, wearing an Ozzy Osborne T-shirt over his jeans.

"How did you find me?" Had Raum been following them the entire time? He'd obviously been spying on them in the park, at least.

Raum cocked a brow. "You didn't think I'd let you loose without a leash, did you? These"—he grasped her arms and the brands under her gloves—"have many uses. I would have called on you before, but the vampire was always there. Glad he's finally gone. Got a bit too excited drinking from you, hmm?"

Denise was too scared to be embarrassed over what the demon had seen. "You haven't done anything to my family, have you?" *Please, no.*

"I will," Raum said bluntly. "It's been a week. What progress do you have to report?"

"It's not as easy as I thought it would be," Denise began.

Raum released her. "Off to kill your father," he said in a cheery tone, reaching for the door handle.

"Wait!" Denise grabbed him, panic welling in her. "I'll find Nathanial soon, I promise! *Please* don't do that."

The demon considered her, a little smile still hovering over his lips. "I do so enjoy begging. It would be even more fun if you were covered in blood when you were doing it—but there's some here, isn't there?"

Raum yanked her head to the side with a fistful of hair, sniffing deeply near her neck.

"You stink like vampire. Is this how you repay my generosity? I offer you and your family a reprieve, but you squander your time feeding vampires instead of finding Nathanial. I'm beginning to question your usefulness."

Denise blinked back tears from the twisting grip Raum had on her. She'd probably be missing a hunk of her hair when he let go.

"What do you think the vampire wanted in exchange for his help?" she lied, thinking fast. "We're close. We have a good lead and we're closing in on Nathanial. I just need a little more time."

Raum let go of her. As she'd anticipated, he had several strands of her hair still wound around his fingers.

"An extension," he mused. "And you want me *not* to kill any of your family during this extension, I suppose?"

"That's right. Please," she added, hatred burning inside her at his delight over her anguish.

"But I have to punish you for your slowness," Raum said, as though that were the only logical conclusion. "Still, I'm in a good mood, so I'll give you a choice. Pick which family member you want to die. It can be anyone, even a second or third cousin. Or I'll increase the effect in those brands."

Denise glanced down at her wrists. She couldn't see the marks, but they seemed to throb in Raum's presence. She wanted nothing more than to get his foul stamp off her, not amplify it, but what he'd offered her was no choice at all.

Denise took her gloves off and then slid her hands into Raum's grip. "Go ahead."

He grinned. "Are you certain? This will hurt."

She braced herself even as she met his gaze. "I wouldn't expect anything less."

Raum's hands closed over her wrists. Denise promised herself she wouldn't scream, but once he started, it was impossible not to.

Spade heard the voices as if from a long way off.

"...body of a white male, late twenties to early thirties, no identification," a female intoned. "Preliminary cause of death appears to be a stab wound. The knife is still embedded in the victim's throat..."

Bollocks, Spade thought, listening to the multiple

heartbeats and the shambling of feet around him. He must have passed out and been taken for a corpse. From the sounds of it, there were too many witnesses for him to get up, thank them for their time, and get the hell away, either.

Now that he was conscious, the silver burned in his neck and his head banged with a truly awful clamoring. The pain from the silver he expected; the headache was a mystery. *It's a hangover*, he realized in amazement, noting how sluggish and ill the rest of him felt as well. *Thought I'd experienced the last of those when I was human.*

But at least his mind was clear, painful as the banging in his head might be. Denise's blood had caused him to hallucinate for who knew how long, until it occurred to him that he had to purge himself of the poison in him. That's when he'd taken a knife to his throat, wedging the blade in and willing his blood to flow out of the wound. Only when he'd drained himself to a trickle had he felt the worst of the hallucinations leave him, but apparently that was also when he passed out.

And now he was being photographed, printed, and processed as a murder victim. Why couldn't the citizens of New York go back to not caring when they stumbled across a body? Everyone had to be such a Good Samaritan nowadays.

It took another hour of him lying there, waiting for the coppers to finish with him, until Spade was zipped inside a body bag and wheeled into an ambulance. He waited until the ambulance was well away from the park before ripping the heavy plastic with a fang and pulling it open.

"Jesus!"

A white-faced paramedic stared at him, shock and horror competing on his face. Spade yanked the knife out of his throat, tucked it into his trousers, and gave the lad a cool smile.

"Not nearly, mate."

The ambulance swerved as the driver stared back at him with equal shock. Spade rolled his eyes. Poor bloke would wreck if he wasn't careful.

"Watch the road," he said, letting power leak out of his gaze. "You didn't see me get up. You don't know what happened to me."

"Don't know," the paramedics mumbled in unison.

Spade climbed into the front and then went out of the side door, not bothering to tell them to stop first. A quick leap into traffic and then he was back on the sidewalk, heading for the Plaza. He was anxious to return to Denise. He'd taken quite a lot of blood from her while in the initial throes of its druglike effects. She'd looked stable when she made it to the hotel, but what if she'd gone into shock since then?

The strange looks from the people he passed reminded him that he was covered in blood and missing his shirt. Right, that would draw too much attention. Spade ducked into the nearest alcove and then grabbed the next person walking past.

"Quiet," he said, glaring at the young woman with his gaze lit up. "Give me your coat."

She handed it over without another word. Spade put it on. It was several sizes too small. Still, it covered what it needed to and he wouldn't be wearing it long.

"Off you go," Spade told her.

He made it to the Plaza as quickly as he could without revealing his supernatural speed. Once inside, though, he ignored the elevators in favor of the stairwell. One clear shot upward had him flying past the different floors in a blur, arriving at nineteen in seconds.

The stench of sulfur drifted to him as soon as he opened the stairwell door. A demon had been on this floor.

Spade flew the rest of the way, not caring now who might see him. He crashed through his hotel room and rolled when he hit the carpet, the same silver knife that had been in his throat now gripped in his hand.

"Denise?" he called out. "Denise!"

She appeared in the bedroom doorway, blood still staining her neck, her face even paler than his normally was.

"You're back," she said, swaying.

Spade caught her before she hit the floor.

Chapter 11

Denise's eyes fluttered open. Spade leaned over her, a deep frown creasing his face. Blood covered the front of him and even clumped in his hair. Considering what had happened the last time she'd been this close to him, she should have been concerned about his proximity to her throat. But right now, she couldn't summon the strength to worry about being bitten.

"You look like hell," she murmured.

Spade didn't smile. "What did he do to you?"

She didn't want to talk about it. She'd thought it was agonizing the first time Raum forced his essence into her, but this last occasion made her realize what the word *pain* really meant. The hotel had sent security to her room. She'd had to lie and say she twisted her ankle—as if that would explain several minutes of screaming. What they'd heard, anyway. Raum had covered her mouth after he got bored listening to it,

"What did he do?" Spade repeated, more emphatically this time.

Denise closed her eyes. "He upped the dosage on the marks," she said, trying to keep the horror of remembrance out of her voice. "He wasn't happy with my progress."

Spade muttered something low and fierce, too rapidly for her to catch. "Shouldn't have stayed at a hotel," he finished with. "Should have picked a private home where demons couldn't enter. I didn't think he'd follow us here, but he's obviously smarter than I realized. We're leaving, Denise, just as soon as we get cleaned up."

"Doesn't matter where we go." It was so exhausting to talk. She'd stayed awake only out of concern over where Spade was. When he didn't come back at dawn, she'd been worried that something happened to him. Now her energy was totally depleted. What Raum did felt like it almost killed her.

"What do you mean?" A light shake made her open her eyes. "Come on, you can't sleep yet."

It took all her effort to wave her wrist at Spade. "He can track me through the brands. So it doesn't matter where we go. He'll find me."

Spade didn't say anything. Denise closed her eyes again. It felt like she'd only shut them for a second, but then the splash of warm water jolted them open.

She was in the shower. Clasped in Spade's arms, it looked like. And he'd taken her boots off and was now peeling off her skirt.

"What?" she managed.

"I have to get your blood off both of us," he said grimly. "It's not safe otherwise."

If she didn't feel like she'd been run over by a truck, she would have protested. But right now, as long as she didn't have to move, she didn't care what Spade did.

His hand cupped around her forehead, then more water ran down her neck. Denise closed her eyes.

"Sorry."

It came out in a whisper. Spade turned them, and the stream from the shower ran over her stomach next. He must have gotten her sweater off, too, from the feel of it. Was her bra still on? An exhausted glance down revealed it was. So was her underwear.

"What are you sorry for?"

Her face was in the crook of his throat, so his voice vibrated against her. Maybe it was because she was still only half conscious, because she answered with the truth.

"How I acted when you bit me. Didn't mean to. Didn't know it would make it hard for you to stop—"

"Christ, is that what you think happened?" Denise felt his hand brush her face. "It wasn't you; it was your blood. The essence from Raum's brands turned it into a sort of drug for vampires, it seems. I felt the effects as soon as I swallowed; but what's in your blood is so powerful, I couldn't stop. I've heard of altered blood being sold on the black market to young, stupid vampires seeking a thrill, but I didn't realize..."

Spade's voice trailed off. Then he shook her until her eyes opened. The intensity on his face was enough to wake her all the way up.

"What?"

"That's it, Denise. Your blood changed after Raum branded you. That's how we'll track Nathanial. Through his blood."

* * *

Spade strode into Ian's parlor without waiting for the butler to announce him.

"Who would I go to if I were looking for some Red Dragon?"

Ian clicked off his telly with a snort. "I say, Charles, you've *truly* turned over a new leaf since you started shagging this one, haven't you?"

"Don't speak of her that way," Spade growled at once.

Denise looked pleased that he'd corrected Ian's rudeness, but Ian's slow smile confirmed he knew the real reason behind Spade's response. He cursed himself for his possessive reaction. It was one thing to act as though Denise were his while they were in public. Quite another to *feel* that way, however, Spade felt like he was in quicksand when it came to his emotions for Denise. The more he struggled, the deeper he sank.

"Curiouser and curiouser," Ian drawled.

Spade gave Ian a single glare.

"Looking for some Red Dragon, you say?" Ian replied, his arched brow saying he'd drop the matter... for now.

"I don't remember talking about a dragon," Denise whispered.

Spade glanced down at her. *"Chasing the Dragon is an expression for seeking a narcotic high. Vampires call their drug Red Dragon, because it's only through tainted blood that we can be affected by a chemical stimulant."*

Though now he knew the stimulant in Red Dragon wasn't chemical at all. The vampires who sought it out either didn't care what ingredient in it gave them the high, or knew not to ponder it publicly. Consuming or selling Red Dragon was against vampire law. After all, hallucinating, out-of-control vampires threatened the secrecy of the race, and nothing was of more concern to the undead world than keeping their existence a secret.

Denise had no idea how dangerous her blood was. If the Law Guardians found out she was a walking drug, they wouldn't give her the chance to find Nathanial and have the brands taken off. They'd kill her without a moment's hesitation. And if the suppliers of Red Dragon discovered Denise was another source for their illicit, highly expensive trade, they'd turn her existence into a living hell.

A muscle ticked in Spade's jaw. Damned if he'd allow either to happen.

"Can't say I have any," Ian went on, with a shake of his head. "Very hard to come by, of course. I tried it once. It was fun for 'round an hour, but then it gave me the most rotten dreams plus a headache the next day—a bloody headache! Why would you want to trifle with that poison, Charles?"

"I have my reasons," Spade replied.

Denise glanced at her feet, shuffling uneasily, but not saying a word. Smart lass. He'd trust Ian with many things, but not this.

Ian's clear turquoise gaze considered him. Spade kept his face impassive. If Ian couldn't direct him to a source, he'd go to someone else who could. Red Dragon might be rare and illegal, but there were ways to find it. There were ways to find anything, if one was prepared to look hard enough.

"I'll tell you who I got mine from," Ian said at last. "Can't promise the bloke is still dealing it; that was a few years ago. In any event, his name's Black Jack, and at the time, he frequented the high-stakes games at the Belaggio."

"The Belaggio in Vegas?" Spade clarified.

Ian shrugged. "It is Sin City, after all."

That muscle ticked in Spade's jaw again. "So it is. That offer of a room still open, mate?"

"Why?" Denise blurted.

Spade took her hand and gave it a light squeeze, but Ian just laughed.

"Don't care for me, poppet? I suppose it's those wretched stories Cat must have told about me. Women do like to exaggerate."

"You're saying you *didn't* try to blackmail Cat into having sex with you by threatening to kill some of her soldiers?" Denise asked, ignoring Spade's tightening grip on her hand.

Ian's smile was shameless. "Ah, that? Yes, I did that."

Denise's hand seemed to get warmer while her scent sharpened with anger. "That's more than enough reason not to like you."

"Denise." Spade turned her to face him. "Trust me on this."

She shot another mutinous glare at Ian, but nodded.

Glad she wouldn't argue further, even though Ian had been deliberately baiting her, Spade pressed a kiss to Denise's forehead. As soon as his lips touched her skin, however, she froze. So did he.

Kissing her felt like such a natural thing to do, he hadn't even thought before acting on the impulse. But now the memory of the last time his mouth had been on her flashed across his mind.

Spade couldn't stop the flare of heat inside him. Some of Denise's response could be rationalized as the normal reaction any human would have to a carefully placed vampire bite. Not all of it. Not even half of it. Despite her aversion to the vampire world, her PTSD, and the grief that still shadowed her for her slain husband, Denise wanted him.

And despite her humanity, the growing danger she was in, and his own common sense, he wanted her, too. So badly it burned.

Spade's lips slowly left her skin, her heat still lingering on them. When he caught the deepening fragrance blossoming from her, it was all he could do not to press them to her mouth.

"Will you be needing that room *now*?" Ian asked with heavy irony.

Denise wasn't amused by Ian's comment. She spun around and walked away.

"Second floor, third door on your left. Springy mattress, too," Ian called out.

Spade crossed over to Ian in a blink, stopping himself just in time, though his hands were still curled into fists.

"Were you about to *strike* me, Charles?" Ian asked, disbelief replacing the amusement on his face.

Spade relaxed his hands. He'd never acted in such a way over a human in all the centuries he'd known Ian. In truth, he'd never acted such a way over anyone, vampire or human. He had to get control of himself when it came to Denise. The situations they'd be in to track Nathanial wouldn't allow for witless, possessive responses like this.

"I know it's your nature to act this way, Ian, but try to curb it when you're around Denise," Spade managed to say in a very calm tone.

Ian stood, his movements slow and deliberate, then he placed his hands on Spade's shoulders.

"I don't know what's going on between you two, but it's starting to concern me. Sneaking behind your best mate's back. Seeking out Red Dragon. Your temper snapping over any perceived slight to her. Have a pause, mate. This isn't like you."

No, it wasn't, and Spade knew it. But he couldn't pause. Time was running out in more ways than one.

"Don't fret about me," he replied, touching Ian's hands briefly before stepping away. "I know what I'm doing."

He started toward the direction Denise had gone—which was out the front door, not up the stairs to the room with the springy mattress—when Ian's voice chased after him.

"I'm starting to doubt that, Charles."

Spade didn't respond. He was starting to doubt it, too.

Denise rubbed the brands underneath her long sleeves. Amid her embarrassment, confusion, and frustration, she was also *starving*. Damn Raum and Nathanial. If not for them, her cousins and aunt would still be alive. She'd be home, trying to rebuild her life in as normal a way as she could. Not here, outside this monstrosity of a house owned by an undead asshole. She'd been so careful to stay away from the other, dark world, yet none of her precautions seemed to have made a difference, because here she was, cursing one vampire while inexorably drawn to the other.

Spade had to know she was attracted to him. Cat told her vampires could smell emotions in humans, like anger, deception, fear—or desire. Spade wouldn't have even needed undead senses back in the park, but she hoped he was too drugged to fully register what happened. Now she'd ruined any chance of Spade passing that off as something misremembered. What was wrong with her? He'd told her to expect casual displays of affection as part of their act. She hoped Spade thought she was just going for an Academy Award with her response to his kiss on her forehead.

Denise rubbed the brands again, wishing she could scrape them off and be done with it. Not that it would do any good. Raum's essence would still be pumped through her with every beat of her heart. These brands were only her "leash," or his form of a demonic LoJack. If Nathanial was similarly branded—and based on the images Raum showed her, he was—why did the demon need her at all? Why couldn't he just track Nathanial the same way he'd tracked her?

She turned to resume her pacing…and collided with Spade. He'd come outside without her hearing it, and she, so distracted, had walked right into him.

Spade steadied her with a cool hand on each arm. His tiger-colored gaze was hooded. He opened his mouth, then paused, like he had something unpleasant to say and was choosing his words.

Denise was so anxious to cut off a humiliating discussion about her earlier reaction to him that she babbled the first thing that came to mind.

"What if Nathanial's blocking Raum? Nathanial has these, too"—she held out her wrists—"but Raum needs me to find him. That doesn't make sense, unless Nathanial discovered a way to negate the marks, even if it was only enough to throw Raum off his tail."

Whatever Spade had been about to say, that succeeded in distracting him. He frowned, his eyes raking over her covered wrists.

"You're right. Or Raum is lying about being able to track you through them and he's just following us instead. The possibility changes what I had planned, but it's worth investigating."

Denise wondered what the old plan had been. What if Spade was about to say he couldn't continue helping her? That her obvious attraction made it too awkward, or that his rejections would get colder due to necessity? He must think she was a special sort of stupid with how she kept coming on to him even though he'd made it clear that this was just business for him. Yes, Spade had responded in the park, but he'd also been half crazed from the effects in her blood. Add that to the general perverted nature of vampires, and Denise expected Spade would've acted the same way even if she'd been a sheep.

She *should* let him walk away. She'd manipulated him into something that had already cost him a great deal, both in time and in money. How could she continue to use him, even if it was for a good cause? She wasn't any better than Raum or her soul-selling relative.

Denise straightened. "This is turning into a lot more than you agreed to and it's not fair. It wasn't fair to begin with, but I was so scared then, I—I wasn't thinking. I am now, though, and I can't let you keep helping me."

He looked at her like she'd lost her mind. "You think you can walk away and handle this on your own?"

"I know a lot more than I did to begin with, and maybe…maybe I could even hire Ian to help me," she added, hating the idea but willing to try anything to let

Spade off the hook. "He proved to be for sale with the whole property-for-silence thing before, and—"

"You couldn't afford Ian's loyalty," Spade cut her off. "And if I hadn't been his close friend for centuries, neither could I. We've been over this before, Denise. I'm not just your best option; I'm your only option."

Frustration boiled in her. "I already promised I wouldn't go to Bones. You didn't want to help me to begin with, so good news, I've come to my senses and you're free."

Spade moved closer until he towered over her, green blazing from his eyes.

"You haven't come to your senses—you've lost them entirely, which is why I'm going to ignore everything you just said."

"Don't patronize me," she snapped.

His brow arched. "I'm being practical. You lost a good deal of blood and then Raum had at you again. It stands to reason those two events would leave your wits less than...optimal."

Denise's anger gave way to rage, fueled by all the other emotions she wouldn't let herself express.

"Fuck you," she spat. "I'm not asking you, I'm *telling* you I'm leaving, and you're not following me. Period."

Spade's eyes glinted dangerously. "Try it. See how far you get."

She balled her fists—only to feel pain jabbing her in the palms. Startled, Denise glanced at her hands. And screamed.

Yellowed, daggerlike nails protruded from impossibly long fingers, their sharp, hideous points leaving bloody half moons on her palms. They weren't her hands. They were the hands of a monster.

Chapter 12

For a second, Spade just stared at Denise's hands. He'd never seen such a thing before, not in all his centuries. Then the panicked, horrified expression on her face snapped him into action.

He yanked his coat off, wrapping her hands in them, catching the spare drops of blood that dripped out after those gruesome nails punctured her skin. He couldn't risk anyone coming across her blood and finding out it was a drug. Then he swept Denise up in his arms. She was still staring at her hands even though they were now bundled in his coat. Her whole body trembled and harsh gasps came out of her. She was in shock, he realized. Little wonder; the sight of her hands had shocked *him*, and they weren't sprouting from the ends of his arms.

Spade carried her inside, whispering soothing nonsense more to distract her than in any belief that what he said would make her feel better. *Second floor, third door on the left*, Ian had said. Spade took the stairs three at a time and went into the third room he came to, kicking it closed. Then he sat on the bed, holding Denise, still whispering a string of comforting promises he had no idea if he'd be able to keep.

He was glad when she burst into tears, because it meant the shock had worn off. He'd been worried this last thing might break Denise. There was only so much one person could take, after all, and it had just been last week he thought she'd snapped from stress, *before* he knew about her demon brands and the threat to her family. Christ, if he were Denise, he'd weep, too. And possibly stake himself.

Spade held her tighter, leaning back on the bed, pulling the blanket around them since she was still shivering. He shifted to curl his body closer around hers. Her head was tucked against his chest, hiding her face, and her shoulders shook with sobs she was now trying to choke back.

He wished he could do something more for her than the pitiful comfort he was providing. Had he helped her at all since she came to him? It didn't feel like it, and her hands certainly seemed to be damning evidence of his failure. What part of Denise would pay next if he continued to fail, warped into monstrosity by the demon's essence continuing to grow inside her?

I won't let that happen, Spade promised himself, his arms tightening around her. Her wretched relative Nathanial had found a way to defeat Raum for several generations. Spade was a centuries-old Master vampire; he'd be *damned* if he'd fall short where a human had succeeded.

"It will be all right," he told Denise, and meant it this time.

She made what sounded like a gasping snort. "You've got a delusional sense of optimism, you know that?"

Brave, lovely, stubborn Denise, making a joke when she should be senseless with horror over her circumstances. Spade laughed even as something clicked in his heart that he knew would be permanent. This wasn't just lust he felt. It went so much deeper than that.

"It's my secret shame," he told her, brushing his lips across her hair and not caring that it shouldn't feel as right as it did.

She sighed, a choppy, hoarse sound. Her previous shaking had faded to a recurring shiver and her sobs had been replaced with a slight hiccup. Spade marveled that it was less than ten minutes since she'd first seen her hands. Bloody *strong* woman.

"That's one coat, two shirts, a house, and a boat I've cost you," she muttered. "God, Spade, save yourself. Walk away."

He leaned back against the high headboard, still keeping his arms around her. "No."

"This isn't your −"

"Could you argue with me later, darling? I'm rather knackered now."

So saying, he closed his eyes, silently willing her not to keep battling him—and not to get up, either. He wanted to keep holding her like this. It was the source of the most contentment he'd felt in over a century, though he'd also told the truth about being tired. The sun was high and he hadn't slept aside from a couple of hours knocked unconscious from blood loss and drugs. Denise also had to be exhausted. She hadn't slept at all after he'd drained her blood and then Raum performed his evil workings on her.

She didn't say anything. Spade waited, inwardly tense even though his limbs were loose. She still had her face tucked against his chest, her mahogany-colored hair spilling across him, her hands still wrapped in his coat under the blanket. The minutes began to tick by, but she remained quiet, and she didn't try to leave. Gradually, her breathing lost the congested irregularity from her previous tears to become slow and even.

He didn't fully relax until he knew she was asleep. Then he allowed himself to drift off, one arm still wrapped around her, his other hand cupping her head to his chest.

Denise stretched, yawning, her eyes still closed. The big, hard body next to hers shifted, pulling her closer while murmuring something unintelligible. She wrapped herself around him before her slowly returning consciousness took note of the situation.

You're in bed with Spade.

Denise's eyes flew open. Spade's face was only inches away, his arms encircling her, his legs tangled in hers. That was the good news. The bad news was that her breasts were pressed against his chest and his thigh rested between her legs, snug against her crotch. She couldn't be closer to him unless they were welded together, and the tangle of blankets around them said they'd been like this for a while.

Spade was still asleep. Even though her heart began to thump at their intimate proximity, she couldn't help but take a moment to stare. His hair was so black against his pale skin, several long locks falling over his cheek.

His brows were equally dark and thick, curving over closed eyes that were framed by sooty, long lashes. His nose was a straight bridge between two high cheek-bones, his mouth full enough to be sexy, and strong enough to be nothing but masculine.

Denise remembered what those firm, supple lips felt like pressed to her forehead. Then how his mouth had felt when he'd trailed it over her neck so sensually and thoroughly before he'd bitten her, and a long-denied ache began to throb within her. She was seized with an overwhelming desire to kiss him, to know what those lips would feel like against her mouth.

Spade's eyes opened, startling her, because not a muscle on him had moved before in warning. Denise jerked back guiltily, afraid he'd know either from her scent or from her expression what she'd been thinking, but his arms hardened, preventing her escape. She was caught between hoping he'd let her go and hoping he wouldn't as she stared at him, trapped inside the circle of his arms. Spade's eyes began to fill up green. His lips parted, showing the tips of fangs…and it only made the throbbing heat inside her grow.

Did he want her, too? Or were those signs of hunger of a different nature? After all, how could he want a demonically deformed human—

Denise gasped as her gaze settled on her hands, freed from Spade's coat sometime while she'd slept. Gone were the hideously long fingers and clawlike nails. They were *hers* again. Normal.

"Spade, look!" she exclaimed, waving her hands between them.

His eyes turned back to their natural tiger-colored shade and he let her go, sitting up to examine her hands.

"It's as if nothing ever happened to them," he said musingly, turning them over in his grip.

Relief flooded through her so completely, she almost felt dizzy. A wide smile broke across her face. She wasn't a monster. Not yet. There was still time to save her family *and* herself.

And at the same time, her stomach let out a yowl that extended into an ominous-sounding roar. Spade's brow lifted and his mouth twitched.

"Perhaps it's time to get you something to eat."

An hour later, Denise cleared her third plate, ignoring Ian, who watched her with a sort of mystified fascination.

"Where do you put it?" he finally asked, his turquoise gaze sliding over her. "Or are you one of those lasses who vomits?"

She shot him a glare, but didn't answer. Maybe one day, she'd ask Spade how he ever came to be friends with someone like Ian. If Ian had another side in addition to *rude schmuck*, she hadn't seen it yet.

Still, even he couldn't ruin her mood. She looked at her hands again as she took another forkful of food. She'd never thought the sight of them, with her right finger slightly crooked from being broken as a child and her nails perpetually chewed off, would make her so happy.

Spade came back into the kitchen. He'd been booking their flight and rental car, though they'd still stay tonight at Ian's. With her improved mood, that didn't even bother her anymore.

"Ah, and here's Baron DeMortimer again," Ian said, twirling his wineglass. Something thick and red was in it. Denise had been telling herself it was wine so as not to be grossed out.

Spade's mouth tightened at the mention of his former title. "We're set to leave in the morning," he told Denise.

She glanced at the window. Ian didn't have a clock nearby, but it was very dark out. Morning could only be a few hours away.

Ian winced. "Traveling so close to dawn? You must be in quite the hurry to find your illicit drug."

That note of challenge was in his voice. Denise ignored it. Ian was fishing for information, but he wasn't going to get it from her.

Spade ignored it, too. He went to the seat next to her, sitting with an effortless grace that looked like his body somehow poured itself into the chair. His fingers idly tapped on the edge of the counter while his dark eyes watched her.

"Finished?"

Denise glanced down. Oh, so her plate was empty again—and a fourth one really would be pushing it.

"Yes."

She rinsed it and put it in the dishwasher, gritting her teeth at Ian's comment that he had *other* humans who could do that. But she didn't snap back a caustic reply, reminding herself that they were leaving soon and Ian would only enjoy her display of temper anyway.

It wasn't until Spade closed the bedroom door behind him that Denise concerned herself with what the next few hours might bring, with the two of them alone in a room and her attraction to Spade growing more obvious by the minute.

Randy. Thinking of him made her feel both wistful and guilty. She still loved Randy, still missed him, but somehow Spade had gotten under her skin in a way she didn't seem to be able to hide. Yes, it had been a long time since she'd had sex, but Spade wasn't the first attractive man she'd been around. Why was he the one who stirred her so intensely? Why did she feel so drawn to him, both physically *and* emotionally?

Denise's heart started to race. What if Spade wanted her, too? If the other times he'd stared at her with heat in his eyes, it hadn't been bloodlust? Spade disdained relationships with humans, but he admitted to having sex with them. Could she do that? Sleep with a vampire who thought her humanity made her unworthy of anything more than casual sex? The idea was insulting.

And yet could she say no if Spade started to touch her the way he had in the park? To kiss more than her throat with that knowing, passionate mouth? She'd had a hard time controlling her cravings lately when it came to food. Would *this* craving prove more powerful than her pride, how she missed Randy, and her intention to leave everything supernatural behind once she got these brands off?

Denise didn't want to find out. "I think the food upset my stomach," she lied, and rushed to the safety of the bathroom.

Spade waited until they were well into their flight before he told Denise about their change in plans. She'd been antsy enough once she saw they weren't flying commercial, but a twin-engine prop plane instead. No need to upset her with the rest of the itinerary before she needed to know about it.

"We're not going to Vegas. We're going to your parents' house in Virginia," he told her.

Denise looked stunned. "Why?"

"They're your closest family, and I don't fancy taking Raum at his word that he won't kill one of them in an attempt to motivate you to greater speed. Demons aren't trustworthy, to say the least."

"But we can't tell my parents about this. My parents aren't in the best of health, not to mention they know nothing about vampires, demons, or anything paranormal."

Spade waved a hand. "Nor shall they. You'll introduce me as your new beau and tell them the good news that you're sending them on a cruise."

Denise simply stared at him for a second. "My parents are Jewish, and my aunt and cousins just died within a few weeks of each other. They're not going to go on a cruise; they'll barely be done sitting shiva!"

"They'll go once I'm done changing their minds—and before you protest, what is more important? Their lives, or your aversion to me using mind control on them?"

Her mouth opened and closed, as if she was about to start several arguments but then discarded each one. Spade watched in amusement despite the seriousness of the topic. She looked quite fetching that way.

"All right," she said finally. "I don't like it, but you're right. Their safety is more important."

One potential argument averted, now on to what would *really* upset her.

"In case Raum isn't following you through your brands, it's important we throw him off from tracking us the normal way," Spade said, unclipping his seat belt. "Which is why we won't be on this plane when it lands."

"What?" Denise gasped, looking around in sudden

agitation. "No way. I'm afraid of heights. If you think I can strap on a parachute and go skydiving, you're crazy. I'll puke and then pass out before I can even pull the cord."

Spade didn't say anything, but the look on his face—and the lack of any parachutes on the plane—must have clued her in.

"Oh *hell* no," she said, whitening.

"It's the best way to find out if Raum is lying about the brands," Spade replied, unclipping her seat belt even though she smacked at his hands. "I've already tranced the pilots into believing we were on the plane the whole time and then disembarked with them in Vegas. And you don't have to fret about pulling a cord with me."

Denise didn't look comforted in the least. "You're out of your mind! Splattering on the ground won't kill *you*, sure, but I'll be nothing more than a stain wherever I land!"

"I won't let you splatter," he said, picking her up when she clung to the seat in refusal. "We have to do it now; we're flying over the right area."

"This is too much," she argued as he dragged her over to the door, sliding it open and bracing them both in the sudden vacuum of wind. "Don't do this, Spade, don't do this—"

"Hang on to me and close your eyes," he replied, settling his arms around her.

Denise cursed him, but she grabbed him with the hold of the damned. The co-pilot stood, ready to close the door behind them and then forget about their jump, just as Spade had instilled in him earlier.

Spade looked at the hazy ground below them, seeking the natural landmark that would confirm their location. Denise's heart hammered against his chest, her scent of fear enveloping him and her breathing so accelerated, he wished she hadn't made him swear a blood oath against trancing her.

Once he found what he was looking for, Spade pulled Denise tighter to him and jumped out of the plane.

Chapter 13

The air rushed past Denise too fast for her to suck enough of it in to scream. It felt like all her organs rose within her, making her earlier threat about puking a real possibility. The whooshing speed and endless emptiness beneath her was terrifying. If she could have crawled inside Spade's skin to cling tighter to him, she would have. Only the feel of Spade's arms around her, hard and steady, kept her from passing out.

Then some of that nauseating lift in her guts began to ease and the roar of wind became less deafening. Now she could breathe enough to scream, so she did, in longer and longer peals.

Over that, she heard Spade speaking. "We're fine, no need to scream. You could even open your eyes now, if you like."

She did, looking down—and then squeezed them

shut with another shriek. Spade had them zipping through the air parallel to the ground, still so high that cars looked small in contrast. Was he *crazy*, telling her to look at that?

"How much longer?" she managed to grit out.

"Just a few more seconds."

Even freaked as she was, it didn't escape Denise's notice that Spade sounded amused. *Sure, laugh at the human who can't fly, Mr. Master Vampire.* Just wait until they got on the ground.

After what seemed like hours, Denise felt a small jerk, and then Spade said, "See? We're here and you're perfectly safe."

She tilted her head down and opened her eyes a slit. Their shoes, surrounded by grass, met her gaze. Beautiful, solid, wonderfully *flat* grass. Spade let her slide from his arms, but it took a few moments before the shaking left her limbs enough for her to stand on her own.

As soon as she did, she shoved him away hard enough to make him take a step backward. "How dare you laugh at me on the way down!"

Spade held out a conciliatory hand, but that amused expression didn't quite leave his face.

"Now, Denise—"

"Don't you 'Denise' me," she snapped. "I don't care how old, powerful, or strong you are. If you ever do something like that again, I'll stab you in the heart. Son of a bitch, I can't believe you threw me out of a *plane*!"

Spade still looked like he was fighting back his laughter. "I didn't throw you out. I jumped with you. Very different."

She wanted to smack him, but the small part of her

that wasn't still crouched in an inner ball over their recent free fall recognized the logic behind his actions. No way could Raum track her in a normal way, with Spade winging them several thousand feet off the ground after leaping from a plane. Denise had known vampires could fly, but she hadn't realized the extent of that ability. She'd just thought they could do short little spurts off the ground. Not double as a helicopter with fangs.

"Now where?" she said, trying to calm her still-slamming heartbeat.

"To your parents' house, of course. I've had a car left for us over by the monument. Then we'll be off to my home."

"Your home in St. Louis?"

Spade smiled. "No, Denise. My home in England."

Almost twenty-four hours later, Spade saw the familiar high hedges that encircled the perimeter of his property in Durham. He nudged Denise beside him. Although she'd stayed awake for the entire flight from Virginia to England—flying a commercial jet, much to her preference—she'd finally fallen asleep on the car ride from the airport. Alten drove, so Spade would have settled her more comfortably in his lap, but she'd insisted she wasn't tired right up until she nodded off.

"We're here," he told Denise.

She blinked…and then her eyes widened as they pulled into the driveway.

"This is your house?" she asked.

Spade heard the shock in her voice and suppressed his grin. His estate properties used to be much larger, but as he traveled so much, he'd sold off several acres in the past century and just kept his manor home for sentimental reasons. The main house was considered average-sized in his youth, but it would look sprawling by modern standards. The first segment was built in the early sixteen hundreds, and then different generations of DeMortimers added to it for the next two hundred years. It changed hands in the early eighteen hundreds when Spade was a new vampire in Australia, but once he reclaimed it in the mid eighteen fifties, he'd added two new wings. Then he'd renovated it every few decades or so. The result was a mixture of gothic architecture and modern convenience.

Denise swung her gaze back to Spade. "You must be *filthy* rich."

He shrugged. "I inherited it, at first. Lost everything when I was sent to New South Wales, of course, but over time, I managed to get it back."

She still seemed unable to reconcile him with the manor they were pulling up to.

"I thought barons were a smaller class of aristocracy. Guess I remembered my history wrong."

"Barony was indeed the lowest level in the rank of nobility back in my time, but baron was also a courtesy title given to the oldest son. My father was the Earl of Ashcroft, the title I inherited after his death. But by then I was a vampire, so I never felt right about using earl as my title. That was intended for a living son, something I no longer was."

Spade couldn't stop the memories from thickening his voice. The last time he'd seen his father was in the jailer's cell, shortly before being sent off to the colonies. His father hadn't said anything to him. He'd stood there, his once proud frame hunched, and cried. Not in shame at the fate of his only son being transported due to debts that couldn't be repaid, but in guilt.

Denise was silent for another minute. Then she said, "I don't want to know what that house looked like that you gave to Ian because of me. No wonder you keep telling me you won't let me pay you back. I probably couldn't, even if I gave you every cent I had."

Spade jerked his memories back from the past. "Will you stop fretting about that? Ian will likely offer it to me in a wager over something in the next few years, then I'll win it back. Or he'll want a favor and he'll swap it in return for my assistance. Its loss isn't permanent."

She gave him a watery smile. "You'd tell me that even if it wasn't true, wouldn't you?"

Yes, he would, not that he'd admit that. "Nonsense. That's just how vampires are. If you want something, it has a price, but then it comes back 'round again."

Alten stopped the car at the front of the house, leaping out to get their bags from the boot. Denise looked away.

"You've never asked me to pay a price," she almost whispered.

Spade felt something tighten in him as he stared at her profile. *Oh, I want many things from you, Denise. Too many to tell you about right now.*

"You're not a vampire," was all he said.

Alten opened his door. "If you will?"

Spade got out and extended his hand to Denise. She took it, then let go self-consciously once she was out of the car.

He walked her to the front door, which was opened by his smiling housekeeper, Emma. Then he let Denise know the last bit of the plan.

"I'm leaving now. Alten will stay with you for the next few days."

Denise's mouth dropped. "You're leaving?" she repeated. "Where? Why?"

Spade leaned in, lowering his voice. "Don't leave the house under any circumstances, and no matter what, do not invite *anyone* in."

She still had that look of surprise on her face, but underneath that was something else. Hurt.

"Are you coming back?"

Frustration competed with another, deeper emotion in him. Did she really think he'd flown her all the way here just to abandon her? Didn't she know him enough by now to realize he wouldn't do that?

"Yes, I'm coming back," he said, his voice rough

Then he did what he'd wanted to do for longer than he'd admit. He pulled her close, tilting her head back and covering her mouth with his. Denise's surprised intake of breath parted her lips, and he slid his tongue along them. They tasted even better than her skin had, and when he delved deeper, stroking her tongue with his and learning the curves of her mouth, her taste there was like red wine—dark, heady, and sweet. Absent the drugging effects of her blood, but somehow just as potent to him.

Spade let her go and spun around. If he didn't stop now, he'd be carrying her straight to his bed, and that wouldn't do for the rest of his plans.

He got into the car and drove away, leaving Denise staring after him.

Denise gave Alten a pointed look as she shut her bathroom door. If she hadn't insisted that there were some places the vampire couldn't follow her, he'd have taken up a perch right on the countertop while she peed.

According to Alten, Spade had given instructions for her not to be left alone while he was gone. At all. Thus she had a constant shadow in either Alten or Emma, except in the bathroom—and Denise was beginning to fake the need for trips there just to grab a few minutes of privacy.

Her feelings swung in a pendulum. One part of her was irritated that Spade had arranged for round-the-clock protection. If he was that worried about something happening to her, then where was he? The other part was touched that he took her safety so seriously—though was that because of his friendship with Bones and Cat, or another reason?

Wondering about his motivations made for an emotional Mad Hatter ride, and her moods were already out of whack from her period arriving two days ago. Why had Spade kissed her before he left? To keep up appearances to Emma and Alten that she was his girlfriend? It was traditional for couples to kiss each other goodbye, after all, and they were posing as a couple. Nothing about that kiss should have struck her as unusual, except she couldn't stop thinking about it.

Had Spade been only faking? That kiss didn't *feel* fake. It was skillful, demanding, intense, and...promising. Like Spade was giving her a glimpse of what it would be like in bed with him. Or was it just the practiced kiss of someone with hundreds of years' experience and it meant no more to Spade than the other acting he'd done in front of his people?

And the most frightening question: Which did she want it to be?

Denise ran the water so Alten wouldn't guess that she'd just snuck in there to get away from him. Wondering whether she wanted Spade to be acting or not played hell on her emotions. She'd tried to think of Spade in a detached way the past several days, but it hadn't worked.

If she were honest, she'd admit she felt a powerful draw even the first time she'd seen him at Cat's party. Denise had been chatting with Cat when she suddenly felt compelled to glance up. A stranger lounged in the doorway, his black hair dusted with snowflakes and his intense gaze lasered on her. As she stared at him, the weirdest shiver rippled through Denise, like something important was about to happen. But then Randy called her name and Denise snapped back to reality, shaking off her bewildering reaction to the dark stranger.

Now, over a year later, that strange pull hadn't gone away. If anything, it was stronger. Despite how she didn't want to be involved with the vampire world, a big part of her wanted to be involved with one vampire in particular.

As quickly as that thought surfaced, however, guilt followed. Already Randy was no longer the last person to kiss her. Yes, Denise knew that eventually Randy wouldn't be the last person to make love to her, either. But wasn't it too soon to be thinking about someone else, and especially a *vampire*? It was a vampire war that had gotten Randy killed, so in a way, she'd be sleeping with the enemy.

But it was really you *who got him killed*, her guilt mocked her. *You didn't just drag him to a house filled with vampires; you also let Randy leave the basement during the battle while you stayed safe below.*

Denise hurled the soap across the room, glad that it didn't hit anything except the tub. If she found Nathanial and got the brands off, she could keep more people she loved from dying because of her. She could return to hiding from the vampire world and all the emotions Spade stirred up in her, but she couldn't hide from the real guilty party in Randy's death: herself.

In the next moment, Alten burst through the door, his fangs out, his eyes streetlight green, and a large knife in his hand.

"What's wrong?" he growled, stalking around the bathroom. "I heard a commotion."

Her heart, which had instantly started to hammer, now began to slow. "Nothing's wrong. I threw some soap, that's all. Look at what you did to the *door.*"

Shards of wood now littered the floor where Alten had busted the lock. His gaze fell on the soap, dented and resting near the Jacuzzi-sized tub.

"Oh," he said. "Sorry. It sounded like you were in danger."

Denise's face burned. At least she'd been standing fully clothed instead of squatting on the toilet with her pants down.

"Can you, uh, please leave now?"

Alten placed the door back over the frame, leaving himself on the outside.

"I'll fix it once you're through," he said, as calmly as though something very strange hadn't just happened.

Denise didn't say anything. She glared at her wrists, always covered with long-sleeved shirts. She couldn't afford to keep waiting for Spade, and neither could her family. Her parent's cruise lasted three weeks, and five days of that had already been spent with her doing *nothing.*

If Spade didn't come back in the next day or so, she'd have to start looking for Nathanial without him.

Denise had just started on her after-lunch, predinner meal when Alten cocked his head to the side.

"Someone's here," he said. "I hear a car."

Her fork clattered to her plate. She jumped up, ignoring Alten's admonishment to let Emma see who it was first, and almost ran to the front of the house. It took a minute, due to its massive size and the fact that the kitchen was on the second floor near the back Still, Denise couldn't rationalize having Emma set the dining room table when she was the only one eating solid food.

Emma had beaten her to the door. The salt-and-pepper-haired vampire smiled at Denise before looking again down the long driveway.

"It's Spade," Emma said.

Denise shaded her eyes against the last rays of the setting sun, which shone directly behind the car rounding the final curve. She couldn't see who was in it, with the growing dark and the tinted windows, but she'd take Emma at her word. If Denise didn't think it would look too clingy, she'd be waiting on the driveway instead of in the doorway—but dammit, it had been five days! Five days with no call, no word, and no looking for Nathanial while she was locked up in the equivalent of a gilded Alcatraz. She had every intention of giving Spade a piece of her mind for this.

The car stopped and Spade got out, looking as suave and heart-stoppingly handsome as usual. He smiled at her as he approached, his dark brow cocked.

"Aren't you going to invite me into my own home, Denise?"

She opened her mouth—and was knocked to the side. Stunned, Denise looked up to see Emma—sweet, petite, soft-spoken Emma—baring her fangs.

"Get away from here," Emma hissed.

That was when Denise noticed the smell, acrid and wafting faintly from the doorway. Spade's teeth bared in his own snarl while the skin on his face seemed to melt until it reformed into Raum's features.

"Let me in," Raum said, each word a furious growl.

Emma slammed the door, cutting off Denise's vision of Raum's rage-filled face. Alten pulled her to her feet without once deviating his gaze from Emma's.

"Send up the flares," Alten said.

Emma ran off in the direction of the main hall. Denise looked around, waiting for Raum to appear any moment. Oddly enough, he didn't. Outside, an unearthly howl seemed to rattle the windows. It was enough to make Denise's heart kick into a higher gear while the brands on her wrists felt like they were igniting.

Alten took her arm. The vampire's skin was cool through the sleeve of her blouse, his grip light but unwavering.

"Don't worry. That's a corporeal demon out there, so he can't come in unless someone invites him."

"I thought that was just a vampire myth," Denise replied shakily, absorbing this information. That must be why Raum disguised himself as a little girl when he first went to her house, and she'd invited him inside. Carried him, even. "Now what? We can't just wait and hope he goes away."

Alten didn't have a chance to reply. Several *booms* went off, sounding like they were all around the house.

Outside, Raum screamed, so high and loud that Denise covered her ears.

"Salt bombs," Alten said in satisfaction. "I always heard salt burned demons. Guess that's true."

"I know you can hear me, Denise," Raum roared from outside a minute later. "Let me in *right now* or I'll kill every last person related to you! I know where your family is. You can't hide them from me!"

Denise started forward, but Alten's grip turned to steel. "He's lying," he said flatly. "Demons always lie."

She chewed her lip, torn. What if Raum wasn't lying? What if standing here was the same cowardly complacency she'd shown with Randy that night, and it would result in the same lethal consequences? And what was Spade thinking, booby-trapping his house with bombs custom-tailored for a demon? They obviously hadn't succeeded in killing Raum. They'd just pissed him off into a frenzy that might result in her parents' deaths.

Outside, Raum continued with his screaming threats. Denise was getting more desperate. Before, she'd had an agreement with the demon. Now it looked like all bets were off.

"I have to go out to him," Denise said, tugging on her arm. "I have to tell him I'm still going to give him what he wants."

Alten didn't budge. "You're not going out there."

"You don't know what our deal was!" Denise shouted, yanking harder on her arm. "I won't let you get my family killed!"

Alten didn't argue with her. He just clapped one hand over her mouth and picked her up with the other, carrying her, kicking, up the stairs. She could still hear Raum shouting about all the horrible, torturous ways he'd kill her parents unless Denise let him in. She couldn't, though. She couldn't even speak.

"I'm sorry, but I can't risk you doing anything unwise," Alten said, ignoring Denise's muffled, furious grunts against his hand.

Almost thirty minutes later, Raum abruptly went silent. Denise heard the screech of car brakes, then the sound of the front door flinging open.

Spade filled the door frame in the next few moments. His black hair was tousled, as if he'd been running, and his eyes were bright green. He nodded to Alten, who finally took his hand off Denise's mouth and his arm from around her waist.

She shoved Alten aside and then went up to Spade, slapping him across the face as hard as she could.

"What have you done?"

Chapter 14

It wasn't the slap that angered Spade. As soon as he saw Denise gagged and restrained by Alten, he rather felt he had it coming. He wasn't even concerned about her striking him in front of Alten. Alten presumed Denise to be his girlfriend, so a lovers' spat wasn't cause for leadership concerns within his line. But what made rage shoot through Spade was the strength behind her blow—strength no human should have. And the sting across his face was combined with the scent of his own blood.

A glance confirmed it; her hands had transformed, curved claws replacing her nails and her fingers twisted into something like talons.

Bloody demon would pay for what he'd done to her.

Quickly, before Alten noticed, Spade pushed Denise onto the bed and clasped her hands above her, hiding them between the pillows as his body pinned hers.

"Leave," he told him. "Keep watch on our guests."

Alten left, wisely shutting the door behind him.

Denise had gasped when he'd flattened her on the bed, then the scent of her anger rose and her flesh felt like it was scalding him. He hadn't been imagining it before, Spade noted grimly. Her temperature *did* rise when she was upset, and right now, she was furious.

"Get *off* me, Spade. I mean it—"

He released her hands and rolled off her, putting a finger to his lips in the universal gesture for silence. Then he nodded at her hands.

Her face whitened when she saw them.

"I couldn't let him see," Spade said, so low she might not hear him.

She did, because she nodded once. Her gaze brightened and then she looked away from her hands, as if she couldn't bear the sight of them.

"Denise." Spade gently took her deformed hands into his grip, ignoring her attempts to pull free. "It might not be permanent. It wasn't last time."

She blinked rapidly and then her face hardened. "It doesn't matter. What does matter is what you've done to Raum. He'll never leave my family alone now. You've pissed him off too much."

Spade got up and went over to the telly, switching it on and turning the volume up very loud. The demon had left at the first sight of him, which was noteworthy. The salt bombs must have wounded Raum enough for him to run from a fight with a Master vampire, which Spade would have relished. Still, Spade didn't want to risk Raum overhearing what he had to say to Denise, if the demon still lurked nearby.

He sat back on the bed, leaning close to Denise so

she could hear him above the blaring telly and trying very hard to ignore the headiness of her scent that said she had her monthlies.

"We know now that Raum wasn't lying about tracking you through the brands," Spade said. "Which means he would have followed you if you'd gone with me. Since that was a possibility, I left you here, both to see if the demon found you, and to keep Raum from finding out what I was doing."

"Your plan better be amazing, or after those salt bombs, my family's as good as dead if Raum finds them," Denise said, fear and anger still sharpening her tone.

He met her gaze, wanting her to see the intentness in his. "We now know Raum is a corporeal demon, not merely a possessed human. A corporeal demon can't enter a private residence unless invited, can't move around in the daytime, and can be injured by salt. A possessed human being piloted by a demon can go wherever he pleases, whenever he pleases, and has no aversion to salt."

"Is that a good thing about Raum, or a bad thing?" she asked.

In point of fact, it was a bad thing, because a possessed human would be much easier to dispose of, but Spade wasn't about to inform her of that.

"Before you can kill your enemy, you have to know what your enemy *is*," Spade replied, choosing his words. "Now we know what Raum is, which means we're one step closer to killing him. As for your parents, they're in the middle of the ocean. Raum wouldn't want to be anywhere near all that salt water, even if he did know where they were, which he doesn't, or he'd have taunted you with their exact location."

Denise chewed on her lip, reaching out to brush her hair back and then pausing in disgust when she caught a glimpse of her hands. She wound them in the bedspread without a word, though, and met his gaze without that former shine in her eyes.

"They can't cruise forever, Spade, and Raum can still track me whenever he wants. I get that you needed to know what sort of demon he was, but unless I never see my parents again, they'll be in horrible danger whenever I'm around them. You should have discussed this with me instead of deciding we weren't looking for Nathanial and we were going after Raum instead."

His brow arched. "We're still going to find Nathanial, but once we do, we'll be in a position of strength to deal with Raum. Not dependent on his goodwill that he won't kill you despite you fulfilling your promise."

He couldn't risk that. His time away from her had served several purposes; discovering the truth about her brands, determining the type of demon Raum was, and confirming how Spade felt about her without her presence clouding his judgment. All three of those questions had now been indisputably answered. Denise was more than a situational fancy. She was special. When he was with her, she stirred things in him that he hadn't felt in a century and a half, and it had started from the first moment he laid eyes on her. As for Denise being human, well...she wouldn't remain that way, if he had anything to say about it.

So after Raum took the brands off, Spade intended to kill him.

The fact that no one he knew had any inkling of

how to *kill* a corporeal demon was something he wasn't about to share with Denise. If Spade couldn't discover any concrete information on demon dispatchment, he'd start with decapitation and work his way down from there.

"When we find Nathanial, I want you to leave," Denise said softly. "Raum will know you set the salt bombs. He'll want revenge, and if he can track me, he'll know the second we find Nathanial. Then he'll probably try to kill you. He won't need you anymore."

Raum wouldn't need Denise anymore, either, and she knew that as well as he did. Even if the demon didn't have a grudge against her—and Spade doubted that, after today—Raum could kill her just for amusement.

"I have a plan for that as well," he said.

Her hazel eyes narrowed. "What?"

If Alten or Emma thought it was strange that she came downstairs with towels wrapped around her hands, neither one of them gave any indication. Denise hoped that just as before, her hands would transform back to normal. Otherwise, she'd have to find a more practical solution for keeping them covered aside from Spade's monogrammed towels.

She prayed it wasn't permanent, and for more reasons than just anyone seeing how monstrous they looked. If it was permanent, even if they did defeat Raum, there went her hope of one day being a mother. How could she cradle a child without fear that claws would slice into her baby's skin? How could she even risk getting pregnant, if she had demon essence inside her?

The sight of the two strange people in the front hall jerked Denise from her depressed musings. One was a blond woman who stood near the fireplace, seeming to admire its huge size. Even though she was tall, if she'd decided to walk into it, she would have easily fit. The other was a young man with a closely shaved head and tattoos covering his arms like sleeves.

Spade nodded at them. "Denise, this is Francine and Chad."

"Nice to meet you," Denise said, walking toward them. Out of habit, she started to extend her hand, then flushed and dropped it to her side.

They cast pointed glances at her towels, but didn't comment. Once again, Denise cursed Raum, the brands, and her long-lost relative for starting this whole mess.

"Very nice to meet you, too," Francine said. Chad echoed that while giving Denise a once-over that made her feel like a woman instead of a walking monstrosity. Then Chad glanced at Spade, blanched a little at whatever Spade's expression was, and cleared his throat.

"Do you want to wait, or should we get started now?"

"Let's get started," Spade replied. "Emma, please draw all the curtains. Alten, bring Mr. Higgins's case, and then turn on every telly and radio in the house. Loud."

The housekeeper didn't go to the windows, but instead took a remote control and began pressing buttons. The drapes began to close. *Mechanically controlled,* Denise thought, shaking her head. Her mother would love that, let alone all the other expensive upgrades Spade's house contained.

Alten carried a suitcase into the room and left it at Chad's feet. Spade nodded at Emma and Alten, who took that as their cue to leave.

While the TV and other devices began to blare from

every room, Chad opened the hard-sided suitcase and started pulling items out of it. Denise couldn't help but peer curiously over his shoulder. The interior of the case was custom, because the larger pieces came out of their own padded, contoured cradles. Chad began to lay objects on a shiny steel tray. One looked like an oddly shaped power drill, then a package containing several long metal sticks, mini dark bottles, a cord, some sort of pedal, a razor, a squirt bottle, surgical gloves, something that resembled a square surge protector, and was that a *watercolor* set?

"I think it's time to be very specific about your plan," Denise said.

Spade sat on the couch, indicating the place next to him. She sat as well, but stiffly, putting her wrapped hands in her lap.

"Chad and Francine are demonologists," Spade said, keeping his voice low. Denise didn't think it was possible Raum could overhear anything with all the other noise, even if he was still nearby. "They're also vampires, so they've been studying demons and people affected by them for quite a while. Such a long while, in fact, that they're the ones who once helped a bloke with demon marks on his forearms…"

Denise sucked in her breath. *Nathanial*.

"…which is why I had to leave you here. If the demon could track you through those brands, then someone, somewhere, had to know how to negate them. So I needed time to track down the best experts on demonology, and I needed to do that without your demon being able to follow me," Spade continued, his gaze steady.

She'd been right. Nathanial *did* manage to have the marks negated—at least enough that they weren't used to track him anymore, and possibly enough that the marks didn't continue to turn Nathanial into a monster. It made sense. If Nathanial had transformed wholly into some sort of beast, that would've made him a lot easier to find. People tended to notice a monster among them, even jaded people like vampires and ghouls.

Denise was so excited that she threw her arms around Spade, freaky towel-covered hands and all. She thought he'd left her for no reason, but he'd been out finding the people who'd helped Nathanial give Raum the boot. Maybe there was hope for her family *and* her, after all.

"Spade," she choked, unable to find the words to tell him how grateful she was.

His hands slid across her back, and then slowly, he pushed her away.

"You don't owe me anything," he said, as something flashed across his face. "I don't need reimbursement or gratitude to see this through to the end. I made a promise. There's nothing more required from you for me to keep it."

Denise sat back, stung. Was this Spade's way of reminding her that things were strictly business between them, so she should lay off the looks and the hot flashes?

"Right," she said, scooting back farther away from him on the couch. Then the numb composure that had seen her through Randy's funeral and the months of dealing with PTSD came to the rescue, blanketing her hurt. Spade was doing her and her family an incredible favor. She wouldn't spend however much longer it took sulking over being rejected. He might not want her gratitude, but he was going to get it, *and* her cooperation.

"What do I need to do?" she asked, proud her voice was even and calm.

Spade gave her a look she couldn't read. "Chad's going to tattoo you."

Of all his possible replies, *that* one she didn't expect. "Come again?"

"To simplify the explanation, brands are essentially permanent symbols representing a demon's power," Francine said, coming over to sit by Denise. "What we're going to do is cover them with our own permanent symbols of power. These symbols will deflect the demon's tie with you, or at least mute it to levels that the demon shouldn't be able to strengthen—unless you come into contact with him again and he rebrands you. So don't do that."

Denise couldn't stop her bark of laughter. "I don't plan to."

Chad was still arranging things, but he still spoke even though he didn't glance up. "You can get preventive symbols, too. The ones on my arms are protection spells. Did them when I was human. They kept stray, noncorporeal demons from being able to possess me. You want any of those?"

This was so much to take in. "Do I need them?"

"I doubt it," Francine replied. "Demon possession is rare, and it's done by lesser demons trying to cross over. Most people never come into contact with demons, but when we were human, we needed them. When you fight demons, they fight back."

Denise gulped. Considering how enraged Raum had been earlier, that wasn't a comforting thought.

"Just another few minutes," Chad said. "Then we'll get you marked up."

Chad began mixing various packets of powders with the contents of a few of the small bottles, frowning at the wet, black mass in the dish.

"We'll have to test you before we begin the tattoos," he said. "Take off those towels and give me your arm."

"No."

Spade said it before Denise could begin to sputter out a refusal. His dark gaze was unreadable.

"The towels stay on. You'll need to work around them," he continued.

Chad looked like he wanted to argue, but Francine shrugged. "As long as the brands don't reach into her hands, that should be fine," she said.

"It's not proper procedure," Chad muttered.

Francine smiled at Denise. "Artists are always a bit temperamental, and Chad was an artist before he became a demonologist or a vampire."

Denise smiled back at the woman, a little tentatively. Francine had such a warm, welcoming vibe about her. It made her occupation—and her being a vampire—seem so at odds with her personality.

Or was it? Francine was the first demonologist Denise had met, and in truth, she hadn't known *that* many vampires. There was the one who tried to eat her when she met Cat, of course, and Cat herself was half vampire. Then Bones, Spade, Ian, Ian's sire Mencheres, Tate, a bunch of guards she never exchanged a real hello with…and now Emma, Alten, Francine, and Chad.

Less than a dozen, she realized. Not many to form an opinion about the entire species from, if she was being fair. But still, that New Year's Eve, she'd seen how ugly the undead world could get.

"Denise."

Spade said her name like it hadn't been the first time. "Sorry," she said, giving her head a small shake. "What do you need me to do again?"

"Sit on the floor and put your arm on the table, sleeves up," Chad said.

Denise sat, trying to roll up the sleeve of her right arm while being careful that the towels didn't fall off. Trying to get a grip on anything with her clawed hands bundled up was difficult, to say the least. After a second, Spade just tugged her sleeve up for her. Chad and Francine exchanged a glance, but didn't say anything.

Chad looked over the exposed brand, whistling low. "It's deep," he said at last, tracing the star-shaped markings on her skin. "We'll need to shave you and sterilize the area," Chad went on, soaping and then shaving her inner forearm with a few quick, thorough swipes. After a spritz from the bottle next to him, he picked up one of those metal chopsticks with sharpened ends. Next Chad dipped the end of it in the panel that looked like a child's watercolor set, but was actually the place to hold ink, it appeared. Then Chad poked her in the middle of her branded forearm hard enough to break her skin.

It pinched, but not bad. More like one of those finger-prick blood tests. Francine and Chad were staring very intently at her, though, as a drop of her blood mixed with the dark ink...and then the blackness faded to crimson.

"We have a problem," Chad muttered.

Chapter 15

"What problem?" Denise and Spade asked at the same time.

Chad swiped at the drop of her blood, bringing it toward his mouth—and then his arm was gripped in Spade's hand.

"If you taste her blood," Spade said, very quietly, "I'll kill you."

Francine stood up at that. "You have a very good reputation, but I won't tolerate threats—"

"There will be no threats, as long as he doesn't try to taste her blood again," Spade cut her off, his tone pleasant and lethal at the same time.

"Just like the other vampire," Chad said, shaking his head.

Denise leaned forward. "What other vampire?"

Spade wiped her blood off Chad's finger, then with

an arched brow, squirted it with the solution from the bottle and wiped it again.

"The vampire that was with that human, the one who had the brands like yours," Chad replied, sounding a little annoyed. "He freaked over us not tasting the human's blood. I'd forgotten about it until just now."

Spade met her gaze, but Denise already knew not to say anything. Still, inside, she hummed with excitement. It verified that the vampire who brought Nathanial to Chad and Francine all those years ago obviously knew Nathanial's blood had been turned into a drug from the brands. Just like hers. Tracking Nathanial through the Red Dragon trade would work. It had to.

"Remember the bloke's name?" Spade asked.

Both Chad and Francine shook their heads. "He was a young vampire at the time. That's all I remember," Chad said.

"Must have been his property," Spade said, dismissing it as if it were nothing. "Not polite to try and feed from someone's property, even a drop."

He didn't trust them knowing. Denise felt a shiver of fear. She'd been so focused on the brands turning her into a monster, she hadn't dwelled on how their *other* side effect might be dangerous. Spade might not want anything to do with the drugging effects of her blood, but others would. *Red Dragon* was the substance vampires bought to get high, and here Denise had it running all through her veins.

"As I said, we have a problem," Chad continued. "Her blood overpowered the mixture in the ink, which means anything we'd tattoo over her brands would be worthless. We need to increase the dosage in the ink. A lot."

"Okay, so do it," Denise said. "Do whatever you did with my...with that other human who had brands like this."

"It will burn," Francine said in a sympathetic tone.

If it would keep Raum from tracking her and possibly stop her from warping into a monster, it could burn like hell and she'd still do it.

"That's okay. Let's just get it over with," Denise replied steadily.

Francine patted her. "Chad, use the Jerusalem salt," she said, her tone becoming brisk and businesslike.

Chad picked a small bottle out of his suitcase and gave Spade a meaningful look. "This changes the price."

Denise cringed in guilt even as Spade snapped, "Let that be the last mention you make of price in front of her."

"Chad," Francine said in a lightly chastising way. Then she smiled at Spade. "My apologies. We'll settle such matters once everything is complete. The important thing is to get our lovely girl here taken care of."

"Quite," Spade said, still with an edge in his voice.

Denise wanted the ground to swallow her, but she refused to let her embarrassment show. *I don't care what Spade says, I'm going to find a way to repay him*, she promised herself.

"What's Jerusalem salt?" she asked, to change the subject.

"Salt is a natural weapon against demons. Jerusalem salt is even more powerful, because it's drawn from the place where all the major religions of the world converge. Then it's specially milled there and mixed with, well, with things I can't tell you," Francine finished with a smile. "But it should work to cover the power in your brands."

"Ready," Chad said a minute later. He dipped another metal stick into his new ink creation, then jabbed the tip into Denise's forearm.

Fire sizzled up her arm, so unexpected and intense, Denise couldn't stop from crying out and jerking her arm back. They'd said it would hurt, but she hadn't been prepared for this kind of agony. It was just as bad as when Raum had branded her.

"Turning black," Chad said in satisfaction, staring at the drop of blood that pearled on her arm. Then his gaze flicked to Spade. "You'll need to hold her down while we do the tattooing."

Denise tried to push her attention past the flaming pain in her arm. It didn't even seem possible that it had come from a wound so small, it was little more than a needle prick.

"How much tattooing? A few outlines?" she asked.

Her hope was dashed by Chad's reply. "I'll be filling in a pattern over both your arms. It will take a few hours."

She shuddered as Chad got out that odd-looking power drill that she now knew was the tattoo machine. Hours, being held down while she experienced the same sort of pain that had almost driven her mad when Raum inflicted it on her for a mere few minutes. Denise thought she'd throw up, but there was no other choice.

"I'm going to need a drink first," she said, inhaling deeply. Maybe a whole bottle. Or a concussion. Anything to numb the pain.

"Denise." Spade knelt beside her, intensity lurking in his gaze. "You made me swear a blood oath, but you can release me from it. Let me ease this for you. You don't need to feel a thing."

She was confused for a second, but then his meaning clicked. "No. I don't want you controlling my mind."

"And I don't want to hold you down while you're in agony for hours," Spade replied flatly. "If you hadn't made me swear by my blood not to mesmerize you, I wouldn't even ask."

She turned to Francine. "The other guy with the brands like mine, did he handle it on his own? Or did he have the vampire with him mind-trick him?"

Francine's expression was guarded. "He couldn't be mesmerized. The vampire tried, but it didn't work."

Because of the effect of the brands, Denise realized with a sinking feeling. The inhumanity in Nathanial had grown to a point where even a vampire's power couldn't breach it.

"The vampire with him was young, you said, and I am a Master," Spade replied. "I can do it."

He had total confidence in his voice. Denise wavered. It wasn't just the pain she feared, although the burn in her arm still throbbed enough for that fear to be very real. Even if the logical part of her realized it was for a necessary cause, being held down while she was, in essence, tortured for hours by a vampire would bring on a PTSD attack as surely as she breathed. Even now, that familiar-feeling panic was rising in her. It seemed inevitable that she would lose control of her mind one way or the other, either in a flashback of that horrible night, or from the pull of Spade's eyes.

"Trust me, Denise," he said, very softly.

She took a deep breath. The idea of giving up control of her mind was something she fiercely hated. Already her PTSD had cost her enough of that. But…she did trust him. As odd as it was, she trusted Spade more than anyone else in her life right now. Besides, she'd wanted to show Spade her gratitude. Well, keeping him from needing to restrain her for hours while she had a severe panic attack seemed like the least she could do.

"All right."

Spade smiled, and the sight of it distracted her from everything else for a second. He was handsome even with his normal guarded expression, but when he smiled, he was breathtaking. Pity he didn't smile more often.

His eyes changed, becoming green in the next instant. Denise's first instinct was to look away, because she knew this would be different from every other time she'd seen them this way, but she didn't. She stared right into his gaze as their color flared even brighter.

"I can feel you resisting me." His voice sounded deeper. Almost vibrating. "Let me in, Denise. It's all right. You'll be safe…"

Her eyelids suddenly felt heavier. Spade was still talking, but his words became indistinct, blurring together. Her vision narrowed until it seemed like all she could see was the beautiful emerald blaze from his eyes. Their powerful glow wasn't frightening anymore. They were so lovely…

She blinked. Spade's face was still right in front of hers, his expression intense. Resignation rose in her.

"It's not working," she said, steeling herself for what was to come.

A smile eased across Spade's face. "You're finished."

Denise looked at her arms. Intricate patterns covered the brands from her wrists to her elbows, like black lace stitched into her skin. There was no pain, not even a twinge. Francine and Chad were gone, but she was in front of the fireplace with her arms stretched across the table, something like Vaseline spread on them.

"Wow, you're *good*," Denise breathed.

Spade's laugh held an undercurrent of wickedness. "You have no idea."

That was when she also noticed the towels were off and her hands were back to normal. Tears sprang into her eyes. *Had this cured her?*

"Do you think it's gone? All of it?" With her whole heart, she hoped the demon's essence inside her had been driven out.

Spade sobered. "I tasted a drop of your blood before I took you out of the trance. It's still altered."

Disappointment coursed through her, but she pushed it back. "Maybe it won't get worse now. Then when I deliver Nathanial, it'll all be gone."

And you can walk away, she silently added to Spade. They'd both be able to go back to what their lives were before this mess. Somehow, the thought wasn't as comforting as it used to be.

Chapter 16

Spade opened the door to the Cherry Suite, pleased to see Denise's reaction. Her eyes widened as she walked inside, looking around at the floor-to-ceiling windows, the plush red living room with its circle of couches, the dining room with its extravagant orange bar, and the two large bedrooms. The suite was easy to see at a glance, even with its size. The four rooms were cordoned off by curtains instead of doors, and the curtains were all open.

The butler deposited their bags, leaving after Spade assured him that they didn't need their clothes put away for them.

"This is *amazing*," Denise said after a few minutes. Then that familiar guilty look flashed in her eyes. "It must be so expensive."

"If it wouldn't have been a betrayal of your trust,

when I had you under my gaze, I would've compelled you to never again fret over my finances," Spade replied in amusement. "I'm supposed to be here looking for illicit entertainment at any price, remember? It wouldn't do for me to skimp on my accommodations."

"No one will accuse you of skimping when they see this place," Denise murmured, walking into the guest room with its oversized Jacuzzi bathtub and enormous round leather canopy bed.

In truth, Spade didn't intend to bring anyone else back to their suite, but he wouldn't tell Denise that. She'd be aghast if she knew he'd chosen this suite because he wanted her surrounded with over-the-top opulence during her first trip to Vegas, even if it was under trying circumstances.

And Denise would really be aghast if she knew the only thing he *had* been tempted to implant in her mind was the desire not to return to her human life after they found Nathanial. He hadn't done it, though. What he wanted from her couldn't be achieved by cheating, or he'd never know if it was real.

"What would you like from room service?" he asked, not bothering to ask if she was hungry. Of course she was.

"A hamburger, extra fries, chicken soup, crackers, and chocolate cake," Denise called out at once, heading into the master bedroom.

And I intend to have a nice long drink from whoever brings it, Spade mentally added. After the flight overseas, then the deliberate zigzagging flights across the country designed to throw off any demon trying to follow them, it had been two days since they left his house in England. They'd either been on flights, in taxis, or in airports the entire time, so he hadn't had a proper meal. He hadn't wanted to leave Denise alone long enough to find one—and airports were so heavily recorded today.

Denise poked her head out of the bedroom, a shy look on her face.

"I was going to take a shower, but it's, um, there's not a separate bathroom area. The shower's out in the open and it's all glass, so...just don't come in until I'm done, okay?"

Spade hid his grin. He'd known about the open, clear-glass shower in the center of the bedroom when he reserved this suite. In fact, he had chosen it specifically for that reason. Some things he wasn't above cheating on.

"Of course. You may also want to catch a nap after you eat. We won't be going to the Belaggio until closer to midnight."

She sighed but nodded, and pulled the curtains to the bedroom all the way shut. Spade was tired and jet-lagged as well, which meant Denise had to be exhausted since she didn't have the advantage of being a Master vampire.

Though she wasn't just a human anymore. Spade wondered how much of that she noticed and chose not to talk about, and how much she was unaware of. He'd quickly realized Denise's voracious appetite combined with her inability to gain weight was related to her marks. Her temperature, always a few degrees hotter than a normal human, spiked when she was angry. Then her speed that night when she ran from the club. The bite marks on her neck that healed completely within a day. The tattoos. Denise's skin should have been scabbed for days after such extensive work, but after an hour or two of redness, it returned to being smooth as silk, healing even faster than her neck had.

He also noticed she'd manifested the changes in her hands only when she was very angry. Then after she calmed down, her hands returned to normal. Denise hadn't had an incident since England. That could be from the tattoos keeping Raum's essence from growing in her...or it could be because she'd hadn't gotten extremely angry since then.

Spade didn't plan for her to lose her temper any time soon, either. He intended to show Denise there was more to being with a vampire than what she'd seen that awful New Year's Eve. Then she could finally conquer her fears of the undead world—and join it.

He'd lost the woman he loved before, but he wouldn't let himself lose Denise. Once he found her wretched relative and forced Raum to take the brands off Denise, he'd make her a vampire. Then death couldn't steal her from him as it had stolen Giselda.

And one way to ease her reservations over the undead world was to show her the pleasures of it. Denise already wanted him, conflicted though she might be. Spade intended to show her that their attraction couldn't be ignored anymore. It would be the gentlemanly thing to give her more time to come to terms with her feelings for him, but he didn't have time. They were closing in on Nathanial, and once they found him, his time was up.

So, if the quickest way to defeat her reservations about the undead world was through her attraction to him, he'd exploit that weakness with relish. Soon she'd be finished with her monthlies—not that it would bother him under normal circumstances, but her blood was too dangerous now—and he'd be able to complete his seduction.

Soon, darling, he promised her, hearing the shower turn on and imagining the water dripping down her bare skin. *Very soon*.

Denise felt like her senses were on overload. First, the unimaginable hotel suite. Then the drive to the Strip, seeing those lights growing ever closer, until it felt like they were driving into the mouth of a glittering behemoth. Spade had the limo drop them off a couple of blocks from the Belaggio to walk the rest of the way. Denise didn't know if that was for some sort of security precaution, so the driver didn't know where they were bound, or because he wanted to enjoy the sights.

They were certainly amazing. All the neon lights, crowds, noise, and the vibe along the Strip sent an almost palpable message that inhibitions didn't apply here. *A playground for grown-ups*, she'd heard Vegas called, and the dazzling display of entertainment options, even at midnight, seemed to agree.

"What do you think?" Spade asked as they entered the Belaggio.

Denise shook her head. "Ask me later, when I'm less overwhelmed."

He gave her one of those sly smiles she'd come to enjoy far more than she should. If not for the seriousness of their objective tonight, she'd feel like she was on a date. A very, very extravagant date. Aside from their accommodations, Spade insisted on buying her a new dress, shoes, purse, and jewelry—all without letting her see any of the prices. It was her costume for tonight, he'd said with another of those grins. Granted, her new outfit was far more in line with Spade's Armani shirt and tailored pants. Hell, his watch probably cost more than her entire ensemble.

Yet Spade wore his clothes and accessories with elegant diffidence, without the superior attitude that usually accompanied someone with his bank account. Denise had dated a few rich guys before Randy, but most of them had seemed so impressed with themselves, they weren't interested in her except for sex or arm decoration. Spade, even under these pretend circumstances, was attentive and charming. Add that to his odd combination of gallantry, ruthlessness, and loyalty, and Denise's feelings were running well beyond physical attraction.

If only he wasn't a vampire, she thought. Then she gave herself a mental slap. If Spade wasn't a vampire, she wouldn't be here with him, because she'd needed a vampire's help to find Nathanial. She had to stop getting caught up in the illusion and focus on reality.

Spade led her past the entrance with the medley of slot machines, craps tables, and blackjack dealers to the back of the casino labeled Club Privé. Denise was amazed how the atmosphere seemed to change from gleeful hedonism to stylish avarice within the space of a few dozen feet.

After a polite exchange with the hostess, they went inside the gold-and-mulberry decorated room. It had several booths, servers hovering in attendance, and at least two games already in progress.

Spade gestured to the bar. "Order me a scotch, please. Won't be a moment."

Denise glanced at the window discreetly located in the corner. "You just don't want me to see how much money you're exchanging for chips, or I'll have a heart attack, right?"

He laughed. "Clever girl. But it's not all on your account. I find I'm feeling lucky tonight."

She could have read so much into that last sentence, accompanied as it was by a sinful curl to his mouth, but that was a road best left untraveled.

"I'll get your drink," Denise managed. And one for herself. A stiff one.

A few minutes later, Spade came back carrying a tray of different-colored chips. Denise had already finished her scotch, but decided against another one. As was customary for the date of anyone gambling, she'd be on her feet for a while tonight, standing behind Spade as he played. No need to invite swaying with too much alcohol.

Spade took her arm and then handed his drink to a waitress who seemed to appear by magic.

"Bring that to the table for me, would you? And keep them coming."

Spade pretended to study his hand in front of him, though he'd had his cards memorized at first glance. He was really concentrating on Madox, the player opposite him. The oil executive was good at hiding his tells, but he was still human. His pulse might remain admirably steady and he managed not to sweat, but his scent betrayed him. When he went all in on this hand, Madox's scent turned into a mixture of musk and rotten orange. Just like every other time he'd bluffed.

Madox's eyelids drifted lower, like he was bored enough to fall asleep while he waited to see if Spade folded or not.

Spade let out an extended sigh, as if wrestling with the decision. "What to do?" he mused out loud.

Behind him, he could feel Denise's tension increase until her aura almost crackled with anxiety. Her jasmine and honey scent had soured as well in the past two hours, watching him lose hand after hand. She didn't know he was losing deliberately to bait the other players. He hadn't told her because he needed her reaction to be genuine or it would have roused suspicion in the observant gamblers.

But to her credit, Denise remained silent, even though she must be inwardly screaming at him to fold his hand. Poor girl. With her conscience needled over every pound he spent, she must be ill at the quid he'd turned over to his opponents thus far.

Madox's overripe citrus scent increased, but he didn't so much as twitch as he waited for Spade to fold or call.

"Sod it, I'll go out with a bang," Spade declared, sliding his remaining chips into the center of the table. "I'm in."

Denise took in an audible breath. Madox smiled and flipped his cards up.

"Two pair, hearts. And you, Mr. Mortimer?"

Spade laid his cards on the table with a wolfish grin. "Straight flush, spades."

Acrid disappointment wafted off Madox. The onlookers around the table clapped as Spade claimed the large pile of chips. Out of the corner of his eye, he saw Denise sag a little, her grip on the back of his chair lessening.

Spade turned, taking Denise's hand and kissing it. "There, darling. Told you I felt lucky tonight."

She let out a little snort, giving his hand a quick

squeeze. Then Spade felt the energy in the room shift, filling with the unmistakable vibe of an undead. Spade let go of Denise's hand and turned casually toward the source.

A vampire met his gaze; either his power was cloaked as Spade's was, or he was a lower-level Master. Judging by appearance, he'd been in his thirties when he was changed. His hair was dark brown, slicked back in a style best left in the seventies, and his outfit was an expensive mistake.

From the way the waitresses greeted him, he was also a familiar sight. Spade inclined his head in acknowledgment, and then returned his attention to lining his chips back up in his tray. He would come over. The vampire had to be curious to meet the man who just fleeced one of the regulars.

"Evenin'," the vampire said, taking the seat Madox had just vacated. "Looks like you're short a player."

Spade made mental notes about the other vampire. *Faint Southern accent. Probably younger than me in undead years, but not by too much.* "We certainly are. I do hope you join us. I find I've got a second wind despite the late hour."

Behind him, Denise's scent changed. She must have recognized the newcomer as not being human, too. Spade didn't look away from the man's ice-blue eyes, waiting. If the vampire didn't want him in what he might consider his territory, now would be the time to make that known.

But the vampire just smiled. "I'd swear it was still early with how I feel. Deal me in, Jackie, and Sam, bring me a tray. My usual amount."

The dealer shuffled the cards while the manager pro-

duced a tray of chips. *Two hundred thousand*, Spade
noted. Very respectable for a "usual" amount.

"I'm Henry," Spade said, using the name his room
was registered under.

"BJ," the vampire replied, reaching out to take the
cards expertly flung in front of him.

Spade took his as well, not letting any reaction show
as he observed the pale fingers that wrapped around
those cards. BJ's left pinky finger was missing, but
on his right, he had a thick gold ring with "21" emblazoned in diamonds.

This had to be Black Jack. *Ian, mate, I owe you one.*

Spade leaned back, sliding his arm around Denise's
waist. "You don't mind waiting for a while longer, do
you, darling?"

Her body was more tense than normal and her feet
had to be sore, standing there for two hours in high
heels, but Denise didn't hesitate in her reply.

"Not at all. I love to see you play."

Spade almost laughed. With her frugal tendencies,
Denise couldn't despise this more, but her tone was
steady and confident. She even leaned down, brushing
her lips across his throat.

"Maybe we could find something else to do after
we're done here, because I'm not tired, either."

Her voice was raspy and seductive at the same time,
a low purr that seemed to rub him from the inside out.
He'd only heard it that way once before, when she'd
moaned his name in Central Park as he drank from her.
Combined with the silky, heated feel of lips on his skin,
it was enough to make him pause when he was supposed
to ante up in the new game. Spade wanted to hear her
voice like that again. When they were in bed together.

Black Jack's eyes flicked with interest to Denise. Spade saw it and stopped himself before he bared his fangs in instinctive possessiveness. Instead he tossed in a few chips and ran his hand along Denise's side one more time, meeting the vampire's gaze in challenge. *Mine.*

Black Jack's lips curled and he tilted his head in acknowledgment. One of the strongest vampire urges was territorialism. No vampire would tolerate someone ogling his property—unless that property was being offered. Denise, Spade had clearly indicated, was not.

"King high, first bet to BJ," the dealer said.

Spade forced himself to relax. The goal was to put Black Jack at ease, not to threaten him over a simple glance. He'd forgotten how falling for someone affected him—the absence of normal control, the emotional highs and lows. It was more consuming than even the most potent dose of Red Dragon, in his opinion.

"Come on, mate, give me more luck," Spade said to the dealer as cards were passed out.

He could have sent the same request to Fate about Denise.

Chapter 17

When Spade stood up, announcing wryly that he was done for the night, Denise was so relieved she could have cheered. If she had to watch him gamble away any more staggering amounts of money, she'd throw up. BJ, the vampire she desperately hoped was Black Jack, had beaten Spade three times in a row, the last one clearing out all Spade's chips. While she understood he had to appear as a high roller with a limitless budget, she also wanted to shake Spade. Couldn't he be a *little* smarter about his betting? Who went all in with only a full house consisting of threes and twos?

"Where you headed now?" BJ asked, lazily gathering up his winnings.

Spade turned to her, his hands sliding down her back. "Still not tired?"

It was four in the morning and she was about to pass

out on her feet, but she nodded. "Night's not over until the sun's up."

"I couldn't agree more." Spade pulled her closer, leaning down to give her ear a light nip that made gooseflesh break out on her arms. "Except I'd rather spend the remaining hours in bed with you."

With his hands still tracing her back, their bodies close enough to slow dance, and his mouth hovering over her ear as he spoke, Denise thought the erotic shiver that ran through her was understandable. At least her reaction would look authentic to BJ, that was for sure.

"Don't you want to, um, have a little fun first?" Wasn't the goal to pump BJ for information, if he was indeed Black Jack?

Spade's laugh was a seductive caress. "Indeed. It's called foreplay."

Either Spade had to think she was the greatest actress ever, or he'd know the sudden race to her pulse and the low clench in her belly had nothing to do with BJ watching them.

"BJ, good to make your acquaintance," Spade said next, still holding her close. "Perhaps I'll see you tomorrow. I'll be back to recoup my losses."

"Well, then, I'll see you here," BJ drawled.

Denise's back was to BJ, so he couldn't see her expression, but she frowned at Spade. Why were they leaving? Wasn't this the guy?

"Come on, darling," Spade said, kissing her lightly on the lips.

Spade led her out of the club and toward the entrance. Even at this hour, the casino was still fairly busy.

It wasn't until after the hotel limo picked them up

and they were in the private elevators of the Red Rock that Denise asked the question she'd been wondering for half an hour.

"Wasn't that him?"

Spade gave her a knowing look as the elevator re-opened on their floor. "Oh, it was, no question."

"Well?" she prodded. "Then why did we leave?"

He held open the door to the suite, waiting until they were inside and he'd done a quick sweep of the place to answer.

"Because now our friend is curious, comfortable, and happy at the prospect of relieving me of more quid when we next meet," Spade replied.

"You should never have gone all in on that last hand," Denise muttered.

He chuckled. "My poor dear. You'll have nightmares over that for days, won't you?"

Denise shot him an exhausted look as she set her new shawl neatly on the red couch. Spade sauntered over, none of her weariness in his gait.

"Casinos love rich losers. I couldn't have them asking me to leave after a run of luck that was too good to be true. Now Black Jack believes me to be a bad gambler, which is what I want him to think."

Denise admired his coolly logical strategy even as she winced over what it had cost him. She hoped Spade recovered some of his losses tomorrow night, or she'd have to give him *all* of her 401(k).

"I'm washing my face and then passing out," she announced. "Which bed do you want?"

"I'll take the guest room. Have some things to look up on my mobile first, so if you hear the shower later, it's only me."

Denise didn't think anything short of clanging cymbals could wake her once she hit the bed, but about half an hour later, she'd just drifted off when she knew she wasn't alone in the bedroom.

She kept herself perfectly still, listening to the slow slide of Spade's zipper being drawn down on his pants, the brush of fabric against skin as he drew his shirt off, and then the sounds of him gathering up his discarded clothes. Suddenly that bone-deep lethargy was gone and she felt very awake. Imagining Spade so close, totally naked, made her eyelids almost burn to open

The shower came on, that cascade of water dulling the soft sounds Spade made. Where was he now? He moved so quietly, he could be right in front of her and she wouldn't know it. What if she opened her eyes and Spade was right there, close enough to touch?

Denise couldn't help it; her eyes slit open. Nothing in front of her. A soft click on the other side of the room was the shower door opening, she guessed. That was confirmed when she heard it again, the cadence of the water changing as Spade moved under the spray.

The water will steam the glass opaque, Denise reasoned. *You won't be able to see anything. In fact, it's probably steamed up now...*

As quietly as she could, she rolled over, keeping her face half concealed by the pillow.

The light in the shower illuminated Spade's bare, gorgeous flesh. The glass wasn't fogged. It didn't even look like it was there, giving her an uninterrupted view of him under the cascade of water. The sight made her lick her lips before she could stop herself.

Then Denise shut her eyes. *Congratulations, you're officially a Peeping Tom*. She should be ashamed, spy-

ing on Spade like that. If she had any dignity, she'd roll
back over and face the wall. Now.

She opened her eyes again. Spade's back was to her,
suds sluicing down his broad shoulders like sea foam.
His hair was so black against the paleness of his skin,
long strands separating under the streams of water.
Those suds slid farther down his back, chased by spray,
gathering at his waist and then dragging down the hard
globes of his ass.

Denise snapped her eyes shut. Took a deep breath
and promised that she would *not* open them again. This
wasn't right. It was an invasion of Spade's privacy, a
violation of his trust, a—

She opened her eyes, smothering a gasp. Spade's
hands caressed down his chest, more of those suds
covering them. His head was back, eyes closed, water
splashing onto his face and sluicing down to clear away
the suds even as he lathered more across his skin.

She'd seen a few attractive naked men in her life, but
none of them came close to Spade. Every inch of his
body was taut with perfectly proportioned muscles, like
he'd been carved by an expert sculptor and then magically transformed into life. His height only emphasized
his stunning physique with those long, powerful legs,
rippled sinews crisscrossing his back, arms and chest
flexing as he shampooed his hair next.

Stop looking. Right now.

She stared as Spade washed his hair, then turned to
rinse the lather out, giving Denise another view of the
jaw-dropping exquisiteness of his ass. Her heart started
to pound while an answering throb took up cadence
far lower. She knew she had to shut her eyes, but she
couldn't seem to do it. Spade pivoted again, this time

facing her. Denise flinched guiltily, but his eyes were still closed against the suds trailing down his face. She let her gaze travel down the grooves of his chest, past his stomach, following the thin dark line of hair that flared when it met his groin...

Her mouth went dry while another part of her flamed with heat. Dimly she was aware that her heart was now hammering, but she couldn't look away. Spade's hands slid down his stomach, a wealth of suds in them, to close around the flesh crowned by that patch of dark hair.

Stop looking, stop looking!

Spade soaped the length of himself with a slow thoroughness, his flesh beginning to lengthen and thicken under his hands. Denise's gaze was welded despite her common sense howling at her to look away. She swallowed, that throb inside her doubling in intensity while heat spread through her. Was he getting hard as a natural reaction to touching himself while he washed? Or was he thinking of someone? Maybe even...her?

What if Spade caught her looking right now, but instead of being upset at her spying, beckoned her to join him?

Frustration finally snapped Denise's eyes shut. She wasn't done with her period yet, so even if her fantasy came true and Spade *did* invite her to join him, she couldn't. And even if she could, she shouldn't.

It wasn't fair. The first man since Randy who stirred her emotionally and physically was a vampire who thought humans were only good for eating and screwing, probably in that order. She'd already sacrificed her pride by accepting that she was nothing more than a costly thorn in Spade's side until they found Raum. The least she could do was avoid total humiliation by more rejection from him—or worse, being fucked out of pity.

Denise hugged the pillow and rolled to face the wall, burying her face in it. Once this was over, she'd be okay. She'd go home, spend time with her family, and her infatuation with Spade would go away. Everything faded with time. Even, it seemed, her wild grief over Randy's death and the PTSD that used to strike every time she was around a vampire.

The shower shut off after a few more minutes. By that time, Denise's heart settled into a slower rhythm and that gnawing hunger inside her quieted to a dull ache.

See? she told herself grimly. *Everything fades with time.*

When Spade went into Club Privé with Denise the next evening, Black Jack was already there. It was just after eleven. Spade smiled inwardly. *Not chancing missing me, were you, mate?*

"Hallo, all," Spade said genially once he'd gotten his tray of chips. "I'm here to win back what I lost last night."

Everyone chuckled except Madox, the oil executive Spade had cleaned out. He gave Spade a single baleful look and then folded his hand.

"I'm done for the night," he announced.

"Still mad at him for calling your bluff, Madox?" Black Jack smirked. "Got to win and lose like a man, pardner."

"Redneck trash," Madox muttered under his breath.

Black Jack just laughed and slid Madox's chair out

with his foot. "Siddown, Henry. You're more fun than old Oil Slick, anyway."

Spade sat, Denise standing behind him. Personally, he thought it was a poor house rule that she couldn't sit next to him, but with luck, they wouldn't be here too long.

BJ glanced up at Denise, nodded, then resumed his attention to the game. The other two players who'd since folded were less respectful in their evaluation. If the gray-haired bloke stared any harder at Denise's cleavage, Spade would find a way to eat him before the clock struck midnight.

She did look exceptionally lovely in her strapless red dress with long white gloves. Her mahogany hair was up, leaving her neck enticingly bare and highlighting the diamond and ruby earrings he'd told her were costume.

If Spade had his preference, he'd be on a real date with Denise elsewhere, instead of making her stand here watching him play with this pack of sods. Still, tonight should bring him one step closer to that, if all went well.

Black Jack won the hand and then Spade was dealt in. He let the other players beat him in every round, until his chip supply had dwindled to less than half of what it started as. Then Spade sighed with mock resignation.

"Think I'll chase my entertainment elsewhere, BJ, mate, any recommendations on where I can find some red-hot fun?"

His carefully chosen words struck the right chord. Although Black Jack's face remained impassive, he folded his hand when, by Spade's card-counting calculations, he had three of a kind in queens.

"Think I'm gettin' bored of poker, too," BJ said. "Wait up, Henry. I might know something you'll enjoy."

Spade cashed out his remaining chips and waited while Black Jack did the same.

"Chasing some red-hot fun, huh?" Black Jack remarked as they headed out of the Belaggio.

"Indeed. Preferably the kind that'll make the rest of my night with her even more enjoyable."

Spade kissed Denise's neck as he said it, savoring the shiver that went through her. He couldn't wait until he could kiss her and she'd know it wasn't part of an act.

"Let's try Drai's," Black Jack said. "I'm there more than I'm at the Belaggio nowadays. Crowd's more compatible for me."

Black Jack glanced at Denise as he said that last sentence. Spade grunted. "No need for pretense. She knows what we are."

"Ah." The vampire smiled at Denise, fangs peeking out of his upper lip. "What's your name, gorgeous? Henry here's only ever called you darling."

Noticed that, did you? Spade thought coolly, but before he could reply with a fake name, Denise answered.

"My name's Cherry."

Spade stifled his grin at Denise's choice of the name of their suite. Black Jack glanced at her again before meeting Spade's gaze.

"So, who do you belong to?"

Spade smiled pleasantly. "Myself."

BJ laughed. "No shit. You don't feel like a Master, if you don't mind my sayin'."

"The Master of my line was killed several years back. Didn't give me a choice about being on my own. And you?"

"Mine doesn't like me to reveal who he is," Black Jack replied, his expression daring Spade to challenge that.

With Black Jack's occupation, Spade wasn't surprised. "That's quite all right. I don't need to know all your secrets…just one."

The vampire's brow arched. "And that one is?"

"Whether or not BJ stands for Black Jack, the person my mate Ian told me about," Spade replied.

The other vampire came to a halt. Spade waited, his arm still around Denise, ignoring the crowds pushing by the three of them.

"And what did Ian say?" Black Jack asked, his voice hardening.

Spade shrugged. "He told me if I had something very rare, something I'm interested in selling, that you were the one to see."

Denise shot a glance at Spade, but Black Jack laughed and started walking again. "You don't have anything to sell that I don't have better of. Guaranteed."

"Care to place a wager on that?" Spade asked mildly.

Interest flashed across Black Jack's face before he masked it. "What do you wanna bet?"

"All the money I lost to you that I've got higher-quality Red Dragon than the best you have to offer."

Now Denise really gave him a questioning glance, but Spade just squeezed her waist, silently telling her not to say anything.

"We'll talk more when we're in Drai's," Black Jack said. "Too many cars out here."

Spade shrugged. "Lead the way, mate."

Chapter 18

Denise pursed her lips as they went down the stairs of the Bombay Coast hotel. Drai's was underground, of course. What better environment than a black-and-red lacquered basement-turned-nightclub to discuss selling her blood? She didn't know what Spade's plan was, but she didn't like it.

And when Denise got a good look at the people in Drai's, she *really* didn't like it. Almost a third of them were vampires. Their pale skin and too-graceful movements gave them away compared to the other patrons, even in the very low lighting.

She shuddered. Underground in a place filled with the undead. Possibly the drug-addicted undead, and here she was, with a narcotic fountain running through her veins. Oh yeah, a PTSD attack couldn't be too far off.

"Let's get a drink," Black Jack said.

Denise wasn't drinking anything here. It would probably come spiked with supernatural roofies, but when they got to the bar, she ordered a scotch to look polite. She hoped Black Jack wouldn't notice the level of liquid in her glass never went down.

Spade sipped his own scotch and exchanged absolutely pointless pleasantries with Black Jack for about ten minutes. It was enough to make Denise grind her teeth in frustration, which didn't help the panicked, claustrophobic feelings already rising in her. *So many pale faces. Cool flesh all around her. Blood would follow. Death would follow. It always did.*

Black Jack gave her a suspicious look. "You all right, missy? You smell awful nervous."

Denise tried harder to push back the memories, but they came faster than even her improved willpower could deal with. *We're trapped. That terrible howling. All those screams. Something wet and thick on the kitchen floor...*

"I don't think I can do this," she mumbled.

Spade began rubbing her shoulders with firm, soothing strokes. "There, darling, just relax. You'll get your fix soon."

Denise concentrated on the feel of his hands—strong, cool, and steady. They were her anchor while she kept trying to pull her mind out of the deadly quicksand of memories. *It's all right. You're not there. You're not trapped. You're here, and Spade won't let anything happen to you.*

"What's she hurtin' for?" Black Jack asked.

"OxyContin," Spade replied shortly. "Forgot it back at the hotel. Don't bother about it, she'll be fine."

"I might have some," Black Jack replied, and smiled.

Even in Denise's state with reality battling memory, she noted his smile was like a shark's—all teeth, no humor.

"Yes, why don't we see what you've got?" Spade drew out meaningfully.

"Come to my office."

They followed Black Jack to a door in the back. It led to another flight of stairs, possibly a service entrance or a fire escape, from the looks of it. At the bottom was a short hallway with three doors. Black Jack took the first one on the left, holding it open so they could go inside, still grinning in that predatory way.

The last thing Denise wanted to do was go farther underground to a smaller space with even fewer exits, but she had no choice. She was breathing harder by the time she sat on the animal print sofa, and her heart was racing. Spade pulled her into his lap as if it was normal for them to sit that way, his strong fingers continuing to knead her neck and shoulders.

Denise clung to the feel of his hands as she pushed at her panic. *It's okay. You're safe…and this has got to be the* ugliest *couch ever.*

"So you think you have some Red Dragon to sell, huh?" Black Jack drawled. "Ante it up, then."

Spade leaned forward. "Not so fast. I said what I had was better than anything you had, but you haven't given me a sample yet to prove that, have you?"

Black Jack grunted. "If I hadn't already pocketed a lot of your money, I'd swear you were just lookin' for a free handout. You have yours with you?"

Denise tensed, but Spade didn't hesitate. "Yes."

"Alrighty, then." Black Jack opened a lower drawer on his desk, ruffled through it for a few seconds, and then pulled out a tiny dark vial. He handed it to Spade.

"This is top-shelf Dragon, ten CCs. Goes for a grand at friend prices. If you have anything half as good, I'll cover your losses from the past two nights. If not, you pay me twice. Agreed?"

"Agreed."

Spade took it with one hand, still using the other to trace firm patterns across her shoulders. Denise almost held her breath as he popped the top on the vial and then tilted it to his mouth. What was he doing? Wouldn't that make him insane with hunger, as it had before?

Spade closed his eyes, swallowing. Her heart began to thump when he set the vial down and opened them. They were bright green…and fixated on her neck.

Then he turned to Black Jack. "You sell that shite for a grand? That's bloody robbery, in the most literal sense."

Black Jack's eyes went green as well. "Now you're insulting my business, pardner, and I don't take kindly to that."

"You'd take kindly to the idea of quadrupling your profits, wouldn't you?" Spade shot back. His hand slid down from Denise's shoulders to her arm. "Hand me a knife and I'll show you what I mean."

Her eyes widened. He couldn't intend to give him her blood, could he?

Black Jack looked both intrigued and annoyed as he pulled out what looked like a silver switchblade from his jacket. Spade flicked it open one-handed and then pricked her upper arm, tightening his grip when she would have pulled away.

"Don't," he said in an uncompromising tone.

Denise froze, but not because she was afraid of Spade doing anything to her if she refused. If he was so insistent on this course of action, he had to have a reason. *I trust you*, Denise thought, meeting his gaze and then relaxing her arm.

Spade held the knife, slanted, against the cut he'd just made. A drop of crimson pearled onto the blade. Spade took the knife away and then offered it to Black Jack.

"Taste."

The vampire laughed. "Is this some kind of joke?"

Spade didn't blink. "Do I look like I'm laughing?"

Black Jack gave another amused snort and then took the knife, licking the tip where her blood stained it.

As soon as he swallowed, his eyes widened, and then he bolted out of his chair.

"Ho-lee shit!" he shouted. He was around the desk in a blink, but Spade was standing, too, blocking his path to Denise.

"No more. Too much will make you lose control, and I can't risk her safety for obvious reasons."

Part of Denise was still battling against the horrible memories from New Year's Eve. The other part was telling her to run like hell. But still she waited, trusting that Spade had a plan that didn't involve selling her *blood* to this asshole.

"She's a source," Black Jack said almost reverently, staring at Denise in a way that made her want to hide. "And she's a woman! A *beautiful* woman. Good Christ, boy, do you know how much fuckin' *money* we're going to make off her?"

Spade smiled coldly. "I haven't decided if I want to partner with you yet. So far, you've only shown me that you're a peddler of inferior goods. How do I know you'll be able to provide the sort of protection that would be necessary to keep her away from the Law Guardians, or any other meddling vampire trying to stop the trade?"

Anger made its way through Denise's other emotions, covering her panic. She knew Spade was faking, but Black Jack meant it when he was talking about her like she wasn't even a person.

Black Jack threw up his hands. "Do you know how rare sources are? There's only one, to my knowledge, so we have to dilute his blood seven ways from Sunday to stretch it and still keep him alive. That's why the Red Dragon you tasted is like puke compared to her blood. But another source…and a woman…" The vampire shuddered in what looked like ecstasy.

"What's the bonus of my being a woman?" Denise couldn't help but ask. "I mean, blood is blood."

Black Jack opened his mouth and then shut it. "We'll talk more about details later, but you have nothin' to worry about."

"We won't talk at all if you don't start impressing me with your connections," Spade replied inexorably. "So far I haven't heard any. Perhaps I should go to the other peddler Ian told me about."

It clicked then what Spade was doing. Denise saw the logic of his strategy even as she wanted to run away from the looks Black Jack kept giving her.

"There might be other sellers, but none like me." Black Jack leaned against his desk, smiling cockily. "My Master is Web. You'll have heard of him, and he has direct access to the people who started the Red Dragon trade. Connections don't get higher than that."

Spade snorted. "Nice story, but where's the proof? Anyone could say they're one of Web's. I could claim it myself to someone who wouldn't know better."

Now Black Jack looked frustrated. "What proof do you want? You'll meet him once I tell him about this. Believe me, he'll want to collect her personally."

"Ring him. Right now. Let me hear his voice. Otherwise, I walk out with her and find someone else to partner with."

Black Jack didn't like being threatened; it was clear from the fury that crossed over his expression. But just as quickly, his face smoothed into another smile.

"No problem."

He picked up the phone on his desk and dialed, whistling. "Give me Web," Black Jack said to whoever answered. After a few minutes of waiting, his smile widened.

"Master. I have the *best* news for you—"

Spade's hand shot out, grabbing the phone. Black Jack went to snatch it back, but stopped at the glare Spade gave him.

"What is it?" Denise heard an annoyed voice bark from the phone. Then, "Black Jack? Can you hear me?"

"I hear you just fine," Black Jack said, almost whooping. "And so does my new pardner, Henry—"

Spade clicked the phone off and then, to Denise's surprise, ripped the base from the wall. Black Jack's whoop turned into a curse.

"What the fuck you'd do that for?"

Spade handed Denise his own cell from his jacket. "Go up to the main hotel entrance and call for our ride. I'll meet you there."

Glad to get out of this drug-infested vampire underground, Denise snatched Spade's phone and headed for the door.

Black Jack immediately tried to block her, but Spade

was faster, grabbing him by the collar. "No, mate, we have some further business to discuss whilst she gets the car."

The other vampire relaxed, letting out a snicker that made Denise's skin crawl. "Right. See you soon, sweetie."

"Yeah, sure," Denise muttered.

She made her way up the metal staircase to Drai's main room, then up the nicer staircase that led to the ground floor of the Barbary Coast hotel. The hotel driver answered on the first ring—a perk of staying in a penthouse, she assumed. She'd just given their pick-up instructions and clicked the phone shut when a cold premonition slid up her spine.

Spade had never before sent her off by herself to get the car. He was militant in his chivalry, not to mention his protectiveness. Yet he'd just sent her unaccompanied through two floors of vampires with a shallow cut on her arm. Something wasn't right.

Denise swung around and practically ran back into the hotel. She darted past the people and raced down the stairs. A few heads turned in Drai's when she continued with her frantic pace, but she ignored them, focusing on getting down that last staircase to Spade. Right as she reached the narrow hallway, Black Jack's door burst open and Spade appeared. His jacket was ripped, he had blood on his shirt, and there was a red-smeared silver knife in his hand.

Denise didn't need to see the inside of the room to figure it out. "You killed him," she whispered.

Spade put the knife in his jacket, giving her a frustrated look. "You weren't supposed to be here."

Denise stared at Spade, taking in the lethal aura coiling around him. Her growing emotions had blinded her, but nothing had changed. Spade was a vampire, so he lived in a world dominated by violence. *Blood will follow. Death will follow. It always does.*

She opened her mouth to voice her repugnance at what he'd done, but Spade grabbed her, moving so fast everything blurred. Shouts sounded behind them, doors banged, there were popping noises, and Spade shoved her head against his chest, cutting off her vision. Then, a few frenzied moments later, that nauseating lift of her stomach followed by a whooshing everywhere told her they were flying.

Chapter 19

Spade set them down in the desert several miles from the shining lights of the Strip. Denise pushed him away as soon as her feet touched the ground. He let her stomp off without trying to stop her.

"Do you understand I had no choice?" he said, following behind her.

She tossed a snort over her shoulder. "Right. Because with your world, death is the only choice. No other option exists."

He flexed his jaw when she stumbled over a dip in the sand she couldn't see, but he didn't try to steady her. She'd only smack his hands away.

"Black Jack had no intention of letting me leave that room alive. Did you notice the gunfire behind us, or the other vampires rushing the room? He'd summoned them, and not to welcome me as his new partner."

She paused at that, but then kept walking. Spade didn't point out that she had no idea where she was going. He reckoned she realized that herself.

"You sent me away so I wouldn't know you were going to kill him."

"Yes."

She finally quit walking. Spade stayed back several paces, giving Denise her space.

"What was he so excited to talk to you alone about?"

Rage coursed through him at the memory, sharpening his tone. "He was mostly stalling until his mates showed up with weapons, but he talked about all the quid we'd make with package deals on you."

Denise might not be able to make out his features in the blackness around them, but he could see hers, and her expression hardened.

"What sort of package deals?"

"Selling shagging and biting at the same time," Spade replied bluntly. "That's why he was so pleased that you were a beautiful woman. The opportunity of an unfiltered taste of Red Dragon combined with sex would go for top dollar—and be very addictive, he wagered."

Giselda's ravaged, blood-drained body flashed in his mind. The idea of Denise going through something similar, and for decades or more, almost made Spade's control snap. Even if he hadn't needed to kill Black Jack out of defense, he would have slaughtered him anyway just for intending such a fate for Denise.

She rubbed her arms, reminding Spade how chilly it was during the early morning hours in the desert. He took off his jacket and slid it around her shoulders, but she jerked away.

"It's got blood all over it."

"Better his than yours," he countered, but took his jacket back. *Stubborn woman.* Ah, well. They shouldn't need to be out here much longer. Just long enough to make sure they hadn't been followed. None of the vampires Black Jack summoned felt like Masters, so they shouldn't be able to fly, but he didn't want to take any chances.

"I get now why you had to kill Black Jack," Denise said after a few silent minutes. "But I can't lie and say I'm okay with how murder seems to be the most common solution whenever there's a problem with vampires and ghouls."

"And humans," Spade replied at once. "You only need to watch the telly to see murder on the news every night. Violence isn't something the undead have a monopoly on. You could avoid vampires and ghouls for the rest of your life, but you'd still live in a world filled with violence."

"There's less violence in my world compared to yours," she insisted.

Spade sighed. "No, darling. There are only different reasons for it."

"Randy *died* because I brought him into your world. He'd be alive today if I hadn't exposed him to it!"

Her scent was splintered with pain, her voice choked with grief, guilt, and rage. Emotions Spade knew all too well.

"As I recall, Randy and Crispin were friends for six months before you even met him. Randy was already in this world before you knew him."

She turned away, but not before Spade saw the shine of tears in her eyes.

"It's my fault he died. I let him go upstairs alone, okay? I let him go by himself because I was a coward. If I'd gone with him, I could have watched his back. I could have *warned* him, given him a chance to run away—"

Spade grabbed her shoulders, holding them in a firm grip. "Seventeen vampires and ghouls died during that attack, some of them Masters. Those creatures were too strong, too fast. If you'd have gone up with Randy, you wouldn't have saved him. You would have only died with him."

Denise didn't try to push him away. She just stood there, head down, breath coming in ragged sniffs.

"Then that's what I should have done. Randy died trying to save me. I should have done the same for him."

"You stayed below because you were smart. He died because he was foolish," Spade replied, ignoring her gasp at his pitiless analysis. Now he turned her around to face him. "He shouldn't have left your side. That's where he belonged. Not in the middle of a bloody zombie attack no human would have walked away from. Randy made the wrong decision and he died for it. That's how it goes. It's not fair, but life in either world isn't fair, is it?"

"How could you understand? You've never lost the person you loved because you just *stood* there," she said in a broken tone.

He laughed, long and bittersweet. No, he'd lost Giselda because he hadn't been fast enough. If he'd left a few hours sooner that morning, he would have been able to save her. And if she'd listened to him, she would never have been on that dangerous road in the first place. So close to the fighting, the area had been rife with deserters from Napoleon's army. He'd sent word to Giselda to wait so he could escort her to the chalet. She'd wanted to surprise him. Just one bad, well-intentioned decision, but it resulted in her rape and murder.

No, life wasn't fair in any world, human or otherwise.

"You have no idea how much I *do* understand."

She looked at him sharply, as if she were about to demand he elaborate. Spade waited. He never talked about Giselda, but he would to Denise, if she asked.

But she didn't question him further. She lowered her head, silently braced against the chill. Withdrawing into her shame just as he'd done all the years of the past long, lonely century and a half.

Comfort wouldn't help her. Neither would his pity. Only one thing had helped him pull back from the guilt and the grief.

"If you had that night to relive, would you still stay in the basement?"

Denise's head snapped up. "No. Not in a million years."

"Then you're no longer the same person," Spade said, his voice empty of emotion. "You've already proved that by taking more of the demon's essence instead of sacrificing one of your relatives. The woman before me is not the same one from that New Year's Eve. She might have failed, but *you* won't fail, will you?"

Denise stared at him, something hard and resolute growing in her eyes. "You bet I won't."

His admiration for her increased. It had taken him over a decade to have that same strength of will after his loss. Denise managed it in just over a year. Fresh determination coursed through him. He had to make her his. The battle to win her might be long, but was too important to surrender just because it wouldn't be easy.

"Are we going back to the hotel now?" Denise asked, her tears gone.

"We're not going back to the hotel. In fact, we'll be leaving Nevada shortly."

She frowned. "But the fake ID you got me and all the rest of our stuff is back in the hotel."

"I arranged to have our things packed up after we left, and I have both our identifications in my pocket."

Denise gave him a cynical look. "You had this whole thing orchestrated down to the last detail, didn't you?"

Not every detail, else you wouldn't have discovered me killing Black Jack. "I try to anticipate," was all Spade said.

She drew in a deep breath. "And now we go after Web?"

"Now we go after Web."

My new aliases are really racking up the frequent flyer miles, Denise thought as they exited the gangway of yet another plane. She'd flown more in the past two weeks than she had in the previous five years. Web, Spade said, was rumored to live in Monaco, so they were back overseas again. She didn't know what Spade intended to do once he found Web—ring the vampire's doorbell and ask if he could take the source of his supernatural drug trade? Or just kill everyone he came across until the last person standing was her elusive relative Nathanial?

She hadn't wanted to ask, to be truthful, because she already felt like a hypocrite. Here she'd judged Spade for killing Black Jack, but he'd only done it on her be-

half. Anyone else he killed during this hunt for Nathanial would be on her behalf, too. By the time this was
over, her hands would be just as bloody as his, no matter how she kept avowing her hatred of violence. That
knowledge made Denise's emotions range from guilt,
to frustration, to fear. She was just as much of a killer
as Spade was, and it would only get worse if they were
lucky. What if they couldn't find Web at all?

Or what if the next time Spade was in a fight to the
death, he wasn't the one who walked away from it?

That thought had been festering in Denise through
the past two days of flights and hotel stays. The full
breadth of how dangerous retrieving Nathanial would
be, even if they could find him, had been underscored
by Black Jack's reaction to her blood. Spade initially
hadn't wanted to take on the responsibility of looking
for Nathanial because he might be another vampire's
property. Now they knew it was so much worse than
that. Nathanial wasn't just property; he was the sole
source of a highly lucrative drug trade, so whoever had
him wouldn't hesitate to kill to keep him. How could
she ask Spade to keep trying to find Nathanial? Once
he did, Spade's chances were about as grim as Randy's
had been when he went up the stairs of that house on
New Year's Eve.

In many ways, she was right back where she had
been that night: huddled away from the danger, while
someone else faced the monsters. She was through with
that. Spade was right; she wasn't the same person she'd
been before. If it was only her life on the line, she'd
quit looking for Nathanial and just keep running from
Raum, living—and dying—with the demon brands. But
Raum wouldn't stop looking for Nathanial, and he'd

murder every last member of her family trying to find him. If she stayed on this course, she might get Spade killed. If she didn't, she was condemning her entire family to death—all because an ancestor wanted supernatural power and sought it from a demon.

Whoever you are, Nathanial, Denise thought for the hundredth time, *I hate your guts.*

Spade collected their bags and they headed toward the airport exit. Once outside, Denise was surprised to see Alten and another person, presumably a vampire, leaning against a parked car.

"Spade," Alten said, smiling as he came forward.

Spade gave him a brief hug, handing their bags to the other man. Definitely a vampire, Denise decided, seeing him take all of them with one hand as if they weren't as heavy as she knew they were.

"Nice to see you again, Denise," Alten said, turning to her next.

"You, too," she replied, and meant it, having forgiven him for the whole bound-and-gagged thing the prior week when Raum came calling.

Spade opened the car door and Denise piled gratefully into the backseat. As long as wherever they were headed had a bed—hell, a floor—she'd be in heaven. It was never possible to get any real sleep on a plane. Their brief stints at hotels the past two days between flights had been more to shower and have Spade make his calls in private than to get any sleep. She was so tired; she'd be happy to fall asleep in the trunk, if she could fit around the luggage.

Spade introduced the blond vampire as Bootleg, making Denise wonder if he'd been changed over dur-

ing Prohibition. Most vampires seemed to pick the odd-
est nicknames. She had yet to meet a John or a Sue.

"Everything is set for tonight," Alten said when they
pulled away.

"Excellent," Spade replied, but Denise almost
groaned out loud, sensing her plans for getting more
than a couple of hours of uninterrupted sleep had just
been demolished.

She shoved back her disappointment. Spade probably
wanted to sleep, too. And not spend all his time, money,
and safety running around because of *her*.

"What's going on tonight?" she asked, glad her voice
was calm instead of whiny.

Either her acting skills sucked or he could sense how
exhausted she was, because Spade gave her a sympathetic glance. "Sorry, but tonight was the only evening
we were sure he could attend. You can catch a nap beforehand, though."

"Who? *Him?*" she asked meaningfully, not wanting to say Web's name in case their search for him was
something Bootleg and Alten weren't aware of.

"Indeed, Web will be there," Spade replied, squeezing her hand out of sight of Alten or Bootleg, who were
in the front seat. "We'll want his formal approval if we
intend to move to Monaco permanently, darling. It's
such a small island. I wouldn't want to be at odds with
any important locals."

That was the angle he was playing? A courteous,
meet-the-neighbors approach? Oh sure, it might be all
fangs and fruitcake welcome baskets at first, but then
the danger to Spade and the killings would follow if
Web *did* have Nathanial with him.

And Denise couldn't live with that.

Now wasn't the time to discuss it, though. Not with another two sets of undead ears in the car. She settled herself back into the seat, closing her eyes against the bright sunlight streaming in through the tinted windows. Her weariness was making her like a vampire; she would have turned the sun off like an annoying lamp, if she could.

Spade slid across the seat, folding her against his chest. Denise tensed for an instant, but then reminded herself of how she'd act if she really were in a relationship with him, as Alten and Bootleg believed. So she relaxed, settling herself against him with one arm around his lean stomach and the other behind his back, her head resting on his chest. His arms encircled her, hands lightly stroking her back, and she felt his chin rest on top of her head.

Deep contentment coursed through her. It wasn't just enjoyment stemming from her being tired and now situated in a far more comfortable position; it was the sense of *rightness* she felt in Spade's arms. Like she was where she was supposed to be, close to the only person she wanted to be with. It didn't even seem possible that a short time ago, she'd feared Spade.

Or maybe she hadn't. Maybe her panic attacks around vampires had been the only thing preventing her from focusing on the very real, very intense connection she felt to Spade. He understood her better than she understood herself at times. When Spade looked at her, she felt like she wasn't the broken, pitiful, helpless widow others saw. Spade saw a woman with a scarred past who had the strength to go on despite her loss. And more and more, Denise didn't look at Spade and see a vampire in a violent world—she saw a man who had the courage to take whatever life threw at him and come out on top.

She saw someone she wanted a future with.

The intensity of her emotions was shocking, but Denise was too tired to dwell on all the obstacles that made her feelings moot. She didn't have to worry about that now. Right now, she could sit here and soak up that wonderful sense of belonging, of caring, of *rightness*. After all the horror, grief, and pain of the past year plus, she needed this.

Then later, she'd do what had to be done.

Chapter 20

Spade stood over Denise. Her beautiful face was so peaceful in sleep, absent the worry, strain, and guilt that normally shadowed it. He loathed waking her, knowing she'd been running on sheer willpower for the past several days. She hadn't even stirred when he'd carried her from the car up to this room, placing her in bed. But he couldn't wait any longer.

"Denise." He couldn't resist touching her face and then drifting his hand down her neck. Her skin was like molten satin, the feel of it as addicting as her blood. "Denise, wake up."

Her eyes opened, an entrancing mixture of brown and green fixing on him. She blinked and then smiled sleepily.

"Hey. Are we here?"

"For four hours now," he replied, his mouth twitching as she glanced around, surprise stamped on her fea-

tures when she realized she was in a bedroom instead
of the car she'd fallen asleep in.

"Wow. I must have really passed out." Denise shook
her head, sitting up and running a hand through her
thick dark hair to push it out of her face. Her stomach
woke up next, judging from the howl it let out that had
her flushing faintly.

Spade moved aside, revealing the table beside him
that had several covered dishes on it.

"Hamburger with lettuce, tomato, pickle, and
ketchup, extra fries, plus chicken soup, crackers, and
chocolate cake."

Her eyes widened and then she laughed. "You remembered exactly what I like. God, Spade, I think I love you."

It was said in jest, but the tightness in his chest at
hearing those words struck him like a blow. He already
knew he cared for Denise far more than he'd cared for
anyone in a very long time, but at that moment, he realized how serious it had become. *I'm in love with you.
I never thought that would happen to me again—and
especially with a human.*

She *had* to let him change her into a vampire. He
couldn't bear losing her to her fragile human mortality, where death could pounce even under the most be-
nign of circumstances. As a human, she could choke
on a bite of that hamburger and be lost to him forever,
for pity's sake. There was no way he could tolerate her
remaining human, and if she cared for him as he believed she did, she'd want to change over so they could
be together for centuries at least. Not mere decades.

Denise cleared her throat, looking away, her honeyed jasmine scent turning tarter with discomfort over
her previous quip. Far more discomfort than she should

feel, unless she also knew there was more between them than friendly affection, necessity, or lust.

"I need to talk to you," she said, pretending to study the painting on the opposite wall. "It's important, and I don't want anyone to overhear it."

Anticipation surged in him. Was she about to admit that she cared for him? Had she realized their worlds were equally dangerous and there was no more cruelty in his versus hers?

Bloody hell, if she did, he'd cancel the party and spend the rest of the evening in bed with her, sod how Web or any of the other undead guests might be offended. He could always smooth things over with them later, but he'd be damned if he would turn Denise away were she to declare her feelings for him.

He crossed the room, shutting the door and then turning on the telly loud enough to make her feel comfortable that they wouldn't be overheard. Then he sat on the edge of the bed, fighting not to do anything to startle her. Like tearing her clothes off so he could feel her scorching, silky skin all over him.

"What is it?" he asked, not a hint of his internal struggle in his voice.

She took a deep breath. "I'm calling it off, everything. Whatever you were intending tonight with Web, looking for Nathanial, all of it."

Frustration covered his desire in a blink. "Not *this* again. I've told you a dozen times; I'm not letting you go after Nathanial on your own."

"I'm not intending to go after him at all," she said, defiance and resignation competing in her voice. "You're right, I couldn't begin to find him without a vampire's help, and no vampire but Bones would be crazy enough

to help me, aside from you. We both know I can't get
Bones involved because of Cat, but if you continue to
look for Nathanial, you're going to get killed, and I
can't... I can't live with that."

He stared at her in amazement. "What about your
family?"

She bit her lip. "They'll have to hide with me. There's
not that many of them left; my parents, my cousin Felic-
ity, her fiancé, and a few second cousins. I hate doing
that to them, but Bones has people all over the world.
He could set it up where we'd stay with one of them,
like other humans do, only without the blood exchange.
He could even trance them so they wouldn't know their
lives were in danger, or be miserable, feeling like they
were imprisoned on the far edge of the world..."

Her voice cracked at that last part, but after another
deep breath, it was steady again.

"No one has to get killed this way. You don't have to
risk your life. It's the only logical solution."

Spade took her hands, always covered with long gloves
to hide the tattoos and the brands underneath them.

"Then you'll never get these off, Denise. You won't
ever be human again, and you have no idea how long
you'll live this way, because the brands have obviously
given Nathanial an abnormally long lifespan."

She met his gaze. "I can stand that, but I can't stand
for you to keep risking your life for me. If I let you get
killed, I'd feel like more of a monster than these brands
would ever make me."

Triumph flared in him. If she'd sacrifice her humanity in order to keep him safe, she had to care for him as
deeply as he cared for her. And in that case, she *had* to
be willing to become a vampire once he returned Na-

thanial to the demon and she got those brands off. After all, that was an infinitely better prospect than being a demon-branded shape-shifter.

He reached out to caress her face, savoring how her scent changed from determined anxiety to something far richer. Then, slowly, his hand curled around the back of her neck. Her heartbeat sped up as he leaned in, closing the distance between them, his mouth parting in anticipation of the sweetness of her lips.

A bang on the door had Denise jumping back even as Spade turned around with a curse.

"Go. Away." A threatening growl any intelligent person would heed.

"Sire, my apologies, but you have an urgent call," Alten said.

"Someone better be dying," Spade muttered, vaulting up to open the door.

Alten held out his mobile phone mutely. Spade took it, barking, "What?" into the receiver.

"Why haven't you been returning my calls?" Crispin asked coolly.

Denise was still reeling from that almost-kiss when Spade turned to her, covering his cell with his hand.

"I need to take this," he said, and walked out.

She stared at the empty doorway for a second, stupefied. Had she just imagined the intensity of that moment? Had the emotions on Spade's face as he bent toward her really been there, or had her feelings only cast an illusion of what she *wanted* to see? That must have been it. Spade sure hadn't looked anything but aloof when he walked out like nothing had—almost—happened between them.

Disgusted, Denise went over to the tray and began eating. Her stomach didn't care that she'd just been left hanging; it still growled and gurgled demandingly. She thought about spending the rest of what might be a very long life like this—hiding from Raum, her body no longer recognizable to her in many ways, outcast from her world and not accepted into any other.

Was this how Cat felt, being a half vampire, not really fitting into the human world or the vampire one? If it was, it sucked.

Of course, Cat actually had *useful* powers. All Denise had from her new abnormalities was an insatiable appetite and the occasional hand deformity. *Villains of the world, beware! I can eat you under the table AND gross you out with my monster paws!*

She shoved her plate away after eating the fries and the chocolate cake. Having a pity party was useless. She had to start moving on with her life, such as it was. First she'd get cleaned up. A shower would at least take care of her hygiene needs. Then she'd thank Spade for everything he'd done and call Cat, explaining to her friend that she needed her family in the vampire version of a witness protection program. Even though she'd been a horrible friend to her recently, Cat would help her. She and Bones were good people like that.

And Spade could get on with *his* life, without her risking it or turning it upside down anymore. It was the right thing to do all around.

Spade left Denise's room and kept walking all the way down the stairs and out the front door before he replied.

"Hallo, mate. Sorry for the lack of response. Been a bit busy, I'm afraid."

"Indeed." The single word had the same emphasis as if it had been *bollocks*.

Spade waited, not about to start saying anything that would sound defensive or raise Crispin's suspicions. Either Crispin knew something or he didn't. If he didn't, Spade wouldn't make it easy on him to find anything out, but neither would he lie to his best friend, if he could avoid it.

"Don't you have something you want to tell me, Charles?" Crispin asked after the silence lengthened.

Spade almost smiled. "Certainly don't." That was the unvarnished truth.

"Right." Spade could almost picture Crispin's face hardening. "Why don't I help you out? You can start by telling me what you're up to with Denise MacGregor."

Ian must have said something. No one else had recognized Denise except for him, untrustworthy sod.

"It's nothing you need concern yourself with," Spade replied in the same cool tone Crispin had used.

A snort. "We must have a bad connection, because you didn't just tell me not to concern myself with my wife's best friend, did you?"

Spade closed his eyes at the open challenge Crispin threw down. "I know you feel protective toward Denise because of her friendship with Cat, but she's not one of your people," Spade replied carefully, each word measured. "You'd need to have bitten or bedded Denise for that, and you've done neither. So with all the affection I have for you, Crispin, I say again, *this doesn't concern you*."

Now the snort on the other line held a tone of amazement. "Bloody hell, Charles, what's gotten into you? I

didn't believe Ian when he said you were acting barmy, but now you've more than proved him correct."

Better Crispin believe he'd lost his mind with lust than discover what was really going on. He was close to finding Nathanial. He could feel it.

"You're not going to be reasonable, are you?" Crispin said, anger sharpening his tone when Spade didn't answer.

"If by reasonable you mean asking your permission before I consort with a willing woman, then you're right. I'm not going to be reasonable," Spade replied.

"Put Denise on the phone. Let me hear from her that she's choosing to be with you for no other reason than enjoyment of your company," Crispin said curtly.

Considering his last conversation with Denise, Spade wasn't about to put her on the phone until he talked some sense into her.

"She's indisposed at the moment. I'll have her ring you later."

Crispin's tone went from cool to icy. "You realize you're leaving me no choice but to assume you're hiding something."

"It's unfortunate you feel that way. I'd talk more about it, but I have to go now. Oh, one more thing." Spade made no attempt to lessen the anger in his voice as he went on. "Tell Ian I'm keeping the house."

He clicked his mobile shut, cutting off whatever Crispin's reply might have been. So much for canceling the party to have a romantic evening with Denise. He had even less time to find Nathanial now that Crispin knew something was amiss. Still, best mate or no, he wouldn't let Crispin interfere out of a mistaken sense of responsibility.

Denise was his, as Crispin would soon find out.

Chapter 21

After a nice long shower, Denise came down the stairs. On the first floor, several people she'd never seen before scurried around, preparing things for whatever event Spade had scheduled tonight, she guessed. Now Spade could consider it her going-away party, because she intended to be on the first plane tomorrow, headed to wherever Bones and Cat were. All she needed was the number where to reach them, but for that, she needed Spade, and this Mediterranean house was as big as it was beautiful.

"Have you seen Spade?" she asked one of the people who passed by.

"Who?" the young man asked, balancing an overflow-ing tray and giving Denise a look that said it was heavy.

"Never mind," she murmured. With Spade's hearing, ~ really wanted to find him, she could just yell out his name. Even amid all the commotion and the rest of the people talking, he'd hear her. Still, that seemed rude in the extreme, so she settled for looking through the first floor of the house. It was gorgeous, with marble throughout, huge windows overlooking a harbor in the distance, crystal chandeliers throwing elegant sparkles in the light, high ceilings, and archways leading to more fabulously decorated rooms.

But for all its beauty, there was no tall and dark vampire amid the pale, tasteful decor. Denise didn't want to bother anyone else by asking for him, so she went outside. If the car they'd arrived in was there, she'd know Spade was still here, somewhere.

There were several cars in the long driveway. Delivery vehicles, it looked like. The cynic in Denise was shaking her head at all the food and spirits being carted in. This was a vampire party, after all. They ate from arteries, not hors d'oeuvre trays.

After a quick search of the grounds that revealed only exotic flowers, plants, and a few really nice statuettes, Denise went back inside. The activity seemed to have kicked up in the last twenty minutes, judging from the increased bustle of people.

"Denise!"

She turned in relief at Spade's voice, but that faded when she saw him. He strode toward her, brows drawn together, handsome face wearing a thunderous expression.

"Why would you wander off without telling me?" he almost snapped.

She bristled. "Since I'm not a child, I don't consider walking around outside as 'wandering off.' And I was looking for *you*, by the way."

The tightness left his face. "Didn't mean to bark at you. Just got worried when no one seemed to know where you were. Come on, you need to get ready. There's not much time."

He took her arm, gently propelling her back up the stairs. Denise didn't reply until they were back in her room, even though with all the noise in the house now, she doubted anyone would hear her except Spade.

"I told you before; there's no need for you to have this party. If it's too late to call it off, I understand, but I don't even need to come downstairs. You can just eat, drink, and be merry without me. We don't need to worry about looking for Nathanial anymore."

Spade rolled his eyes. Actually rolled them. "If you think I'd let you martyr yourself on my behalf, then you don't know me. And you should know me enough by now to at least know that."

"Oh, but I'm the type of person who should let you get killed, or at best, kill a bunch of people for me?" she flared. "Things changed. Neither of us knew what Nathanial was involved in when this started. Even when we found out, I didn't fully understand all the implications behind it, but I get it now, and I said it's over."

He stared at her as if contemplating whether she meant it. Denise didn't blink. She wasn't making a fake offer just to assuage her conscience later. She would *not* let another man she cared about die because of her.

"You're right, it is too late to cancel this evening," he finally said. "And it would look odd if I didn't greet my guests with my lover at my side, since I invited them to meet us both specifically You don't know vampire etiquette, but that would be considered quite rude. Might even cause issues for me later."

Her bullshit alert was going off, but Spade's expression was bland, offering her nothing. Maybe a no-show tonight from Spade's supposed girlfriend *would* ruffle feathers.

The knowledge that after tomorrow, she'd never see Spade again was like a kick to the gut. Despite her best intentions, she'd gotten in way over her head emotionally with Spade. Why oh why was Spade the only man to inspire feelings in her she thought had died with Randy?

"All right," Denise said at last. "One more act, if it'll help."

He smiled, something glinting in his gaze. "Oh, it will indeed."

Spade stood in the alcove on the first floor, concealed by shadows, watching Denise as she came down the stairs. *Ravishing*, he thought, taking in the dark lavender gown hugging her upper arms while leaving her shoulders bare, the deep décolleté, fitted waist, and full skirt swaying with her steps. It was late eighteenth century, modernized with a zipper instead of multiple tiny buttons, and made of the finest Italian silk. With the diamond and amethyst necklace, matching earrings, amethyst-studded clips securing her hair, and the long, white gloves that came to Denise's elbows, she looked like a queen.

He stepped out of the shadows when she reached the bottom, taking her gloved hand and kissing it. "You're incredibly beautiful."

She flushed. "Thank you." Then she laughed. "I'm getting a flashback of that scene in *Titanic* with Leonardo DiCaprio and Kate Winslet at the grand staircase, but considering the ending, I guess that's not a good omen."

Spade drew his mouth away from her hand, but didn't let it go. "Not to worry. The only icebergs here are tiny ones served in glasses."

Her eyes roved over him in obvious enjoyment of his matching eighteenth-century attire, but then skidded away when he caught her gaze. An invisible wall seemed to be erected around her even though he still held her hand.

"So, what's the agenda for tonight?" she asked in a businesslike manner, squaring her shoulders.

Take stock of Web. See who his associates are. Have you naked in my arms before sunrise. "Just appear madly enamored of me, and that should suffice."

She smiled almost bleakly as she tucked her hand in his arm. "Will do."

Spade wondered at her abrupt switch in mood. Was she still cross with him for snapping at her earlier when he couldn't find her? Or was she glum because she believed she was destined to be chained forever to her brands? That must be it, he decided, giving her a sideways look. Soon enough she'd realize he had no intention of resigning her to such a fate.

"We'll greet our guests as they arrive, and then it will be the usual drinking, dancing, and socializing you'd expect from any party. Even though I don't expect unpleasantries, try not to be without me or Alten near you."

As if summoned, Alten appeared, wearing a modern version of a tuxedo and a white mask around his eyes.

Denise let out a small laugh. "What's with the mask?"

Spade pulled out a lavender and crystal creation with combs to anchor in her hair. "This is a masquerade ball, didn't I tell you?"

"No, you didn't," she said, taking the mask and turning it over in her hands. "The whole outfit is so pretty. Who am I supposed to be?"

"Marie Antoinette. And I'm King Louis XVI."

She gave him a pensive look. "They were both executed."

Spade leaned down, brushing his mouth near her ear. "I have no intention of letting history repeat itself with us, darling."

And he didn't. Denise would *not* suffer the same fate Giselda had by an untimely death. He'd keep her safe. This time, he wouldn't fail.

Denise took a step back, putting more distance between them, her smile a little forced as she focused on Alten.

"And who are you supposed to be?"

Alten grinned, bowing deeply to Denise. "Casanova, of course."

Denise tried to remember names by matching them with their masks, but she quickly realized that with so many people, she'd never get them all straight. For an impromptu ball, Spade had sure managed to fill a room. Or several rooms, to be more accurate.

The only person aside from Spade and Alten that Denise knew she wouldn't forget was Web. He'd almost glided into the house, a tall man with a jet and crystal mask covering tawny hair and a face that was handsome, from what Denise could see of it. His costume was also black, with crystals tastefully accenting the edges of his sleeves, shoulders, coat, and pants. After Spade made introductions and she'd accepted his compliment on her dress, she asked him about his costume.

"A cosmic black hole," Web explained, his mouth

lifting in a smile that was polite and challenging at the same time.

Something deadly and unstoppable; of course Web had chosen that to meet his potential new vampire neighbor. She supposed coming as the largest cock of the keep would have been too obvious a statement.

"How fascinating," Denise said. She even sounded sincere.

The woman with Web, whom Denise pegged as a vampire simply because *no one* could breathe in a dress that tight, didn't look pleased when Web announced that he hoped Denise saved him a dance. Spade had laughed and said he'd try to let her away from him long enough, but underneath the smoothness of his voice, he didn't sound pleased about it, either.

As the evening wore on, Denise kept reminding herself not to focus on Web and who was with him, and not to keep searching for Nathanial's face under every partial mask of every male in the room. What was the point? She'd made her decision to quit looking for Nathanial. And then tomorrow she was leaving, never to see Spade again unless he happened to drop in on Cat and Bones while she was also around. That thought actually bothered her more than being branded for the rest of her life. Despite knowing better, she'd let herself fall for him. It took the eve of her departure for her to truly realize how much he'd come to mean to her. How could she fake being a happy couple when her already-battered heart felt like it was breaking again?

Tonight couldn't end soon enough.

At least the food was delicious. Plus there was so much of it, even Denise was stuffed after her second helping. The party was spread out over the entire ground floor and the second floor, where the ballroom was. After seeing several vampires stop by one of the parlor rooms upstairs, then come out with notably pinker complexions, Denise realized Spade offered a different sort of buffet up there. She wondered if he had special humans lined up as snacks, or if there was just a plasma version of the champagne fountain that flowed downstairs. She decided not to find out.

Alten sat next to Denise, since for the past hour, Spade had been sweeping around the room exchanging pleasantries with Monaco's undead elite. She knew it was useless torture, but she kept looking for him among the crowd, his dark head so easy to spot since he was taller than almost everyone in the room. Spade looked stunning in his vintage formal wear, a complicated knot like a silk waterfall at his neck, resplendent embroidered navy coat, matching pants, waist sword, and knee-high boots.

Wow had been her first thought on seeing him dressed that way, followed immediately by *Don't drool.* Even now, watching him, Denise couldn't help but lick her lips.

"Denise."

She blinked, returning her attention to Alten. "Sorry, what?"

His mouth quirked when he followed her gaze to Spade. "I asked if you were enjoying your filet mignon."

"Oh yes. Delicious," she replied automatically, and took another bite.

"Good. Enjoy it while you still can."

That turned Denise's attention fully to him. Had Spade told Alten that she was leaving tomorrow? "Why do you say that?"

He shrugged. "Food doesn't taste the same after you turn into a vampire."

Denise almost choked on her steak. Alten instantly began clapping her on the back, but she waved him off, swallowing her bite and then taking a hefty sip of champagne.

"Why would you think I'd do that?" she managed, voice still a little hoarse from the steak nearly lodging in her throat.

Even with the white mask covering half of Alten's face, she could see his expression was dumbfounded.

"Because you're with Spade," he replied, his tone signifying that this should have been obvious to her.

"So?" Denise said, and then remembered that no, she wasn't really with Spade, which made the whole topic moot.

Before Alten could reply, Spade swept up to their table, his mouth set in a tight line.

"Have better care next time," Spade said sharply to Alten before bending down to encircle her from behind. "All right, darling?" he murmured, kissing the back of her neck.

It's only an act, Denise reminded herself. "I'm fine— and it's not *his* fault I didn't chew my food before swallowing."

Spade exchanged a glance with Alten that she couldn't read. Then he rose, holding out his hand.

"Come, dance with me."

With her fragile emotional state over him, Denise didn't want to, but considering their charade, it would look odd if she refused. She nodded, letting him draw her to her feet.

Chapter 22

When they arrived at the ballroom, Spade took Denise's gloved hand in his, the other placed at her waist.

"Do you know how to waltz?" he asked, bending low more for the enjoyment of feeling her skin so close to his lips than out of concern for anyone overhearing his question.

"Yes. I—*we*—took lessons before my wedding," she replied.

A flicker of grief passed over Denise's face before it was gone, replaced by a veiled anticipation that had nothing to do with memories of her slain husband when Spade pulled her closer.

"I was taught when I was a boy. Every nobleman's son was expected to know how to waltz, to ride, to shoot, and to tend to their estate." Spade led her along to the sedate music as he spoke, giving her time to find the rhythm and relax into the steps.

"It's so hard to imagine you as a child." Her mask did nothing to hide the frank inquisitiveness in her expression. "What was it like, back then?"

"The setting was different." He gave her a jaded smile. "But people don't change, not even over the course of millennia. When I was a boy, everything was titles, estates, and royal favor. Today it's degrees, jobs, and retirement portfolios. The motivation remains the same, however; caring for those who belong to you. Protecting them from harm. Trying to carve out a little happiness. It was that way then and it is that way now."

Denise didn't say anything for several moments. Spade studied her, not bothering to hide the intentness in his gaze. Her hair was up, but stray curls had been left deliberately trailing in places, swinging to the music as they moved. Her mask covered from her eyebrows to the top of her nose, curving around her cheekbones and leaving the lower half of her face bare. She licked her lower lip in contemplation, not knowing how that simple gesture inflamed him.

"And you met Bones on the ship to the penal colonies." Her voice lowered. "Can I ask what you were in jail for, if it's not too personal?"

In fact it was very personal. So much that not even Crispin knew the whole story behind it.

"My father was a good man. Stern, perhaps, but that was common for the time. Yet he had a weakness: He couldn't stop gambling. Today he'd be called an addict, but back then, it was seen as lack of sound judgment. He'd run deeply into debt by the time I was twenty-five. I was his only son, his heir, which meant I couldn't take to the sea or the military to garner funds to repay his debts. So I did the only thing I could—I married an heiress."

Denise stopped dancing. "You're *married*?" she blurted.

Several heads turned and Denise flushed. Spade bit back his laughter.

"When I was human, darling. She's been dead these past centuries."

The vampires around them resumed their dancing. Marriage in undead terms was far more rigid than a human marriage. He'd be risking Denise's life if he were married by vampire law. The punishment for anyone committing adultery with a vampire's spouse was death without reprisal, should the wronged spouse choose to exercise his or her right. With their very long lives, no wonder marriage was an uncommon state for vampires. Humans had enough trouble with marriage when it was only a half-century commitment at best.

Denise's cheeks were still darker than her makeup accounted for. Spade didn't mind her outburst; it pleased him. If she wasn't jealous at the idea that he might be married, then she didn't care for him as he wanted her to.

"You married someone for her money?" Denise whispered, disapproval clear in her tone.

He leaned down. "She married me for my title," he whispered back. "It was mercenary the whole way 'round, I assure you."

"Did you love her?"

As soon as Denise asked the question, she sucked in a breath, looking away. It was clear she regretted it.

He didn't, for the same reason her jealousy had pleased him. "No, nor she me," he replied evenly. "Madeline wanted to increase her station at court and I made no secret about needing her money. It was a mutually beneficial arrangement."

And a miserable one, as many arranged marriages were at the time. "Still, despite Madeline's fat coffers, it was only a matter of time until my father was in debt once more."

The years made it possible for Spade to recount the rest without emotion staining his tone.

"He hid it from me, at first. Explained away the letters from his acquaintances or the mutterings at court. But then when he indebted himself to the Duke of Warwick over a game of whist, and he couldn't pay, the duke complained to the king."

And since his father had also gotten caught bedding the lovely young duchess, Warwick had been in no mood for mercy. He'd rounded up every courtier his father owed, whipped them into a frenzy, and then implored the king for justice on behalf of all of them.

"They came for my father at night, taking him away to Newgate, where he'd rot until every last farthing was repaid," Spade said. "Warwick knew my father wouldn't live long enough for me to find a way to repay his debts. Even young, strong prisoners died all the time at Newgate. He'd done it not to jail him, but to kill him."

"I can't believe he could be jailed over *debts*," Denise gasped.

Spade let out a wry chuckle, turning her in time to the music. "Indeed, one of the things different back then was that there was no declaring bankruptcy and going on with your life, especially if you incurred royal ire. My family's estate was seized by the crown, Madeline left me since my title was now worthless, and my father grew ever sicker in jail. So I went to the duke to offer him a bargain: Transfer my father's debt to me."

The memory of that day still scalded; Warwick laughing at him, taunting him that soon he'd be burying his father, and then finally demanding that Spade beg for him to transfer the debt. Spade had done it, accepting the humiliation to secure his father's life, not realizing that ultimately Warwick agreed only because he knew this would hurt his father more. It had. His father drank himself to death less than two years after Spade's deportation.

"But you knew you'd go to jail…"

"Denise." Spade held her gaze. "I had nothing left to lose but my freedom, and I knew after a time, I'd get that back. Yet my father would have surely died in prison. What choice did I have?"

He knew that she of all people would understand, considering how Denise had endangered herself for her family these past few weeks. It was yet another thing they had in common.

She sighed. "So that's why you were sent to jail."

"Didn't expect my sentence to be different than my father's, but Warwick thought it would be grand fun to convince the king that I would be more useful to the crown sent to the New South Wales colonies than just sitting in prison. And on the voyage there is where I met Crispin, Ian, and Timothy."

"And became friends." Her voice was soft.

"Not at first." Spade raised a brow. "Me, the future Earl of Ashcroft, chained to common miscreants who'd no doubt earned every moment of their sentences? I didn't deign to even speak to them for days."

Denise smiled at his deliberately haughty tone. "What broke the ice?"

"After several days of enduring my silent disdain, Ian began to bait me. Said I must have been the bastard son of a fishmonger born with no tongue, or some such. Finally I informed them all rather snootily that I was Baron Charles Thomas DeMortimer, a nobleman and not deserving of my circumstances. I thought Crispin had been sleeping, but at that, he opened one eye and said, 'DeMortimer, aye? Blue bedchamber, purple drapes, bloody what were you thinking with all those peacock feathers everywhere?'"

It took Denise a second, but then her eyes widened. "Your wife was one of the women who hired Bones back when he was a gigolo?"

Spade laughed. "I was terribly insulted at the time, but the voyage was too horrible to concern myself with that for long. We nearly died on the way to the colonies. Once there, we nearly died again under the overseer. We only had each other to depend on, and I grew to care for them as if they were family."

"Whatever happened to Timothy? I don't think I ever saw him around Bones or Cat."

"He went on sabbatical a long time ago, searching for proof that Cain, father of all vampires, was still alive. In truth, I suspect somewhere along the way, Timothy was killed. None of us have heard from him in over eighty years."

She looked wistful. "I'm sorry to hear that, but at least you, Ian, and Bones stayed friends all these years."

"Sometimes good comes out of even terrible circumstances," Spade said quietly.

Denise looked away. She thought he was referring

to Randy, but Spade would be the last person to spout nonsense about looking for the good out of the murder of a loved one. He meant the demon brands that had led Denise to him. They'd both lost loved ones for no other reason than life being cruel at times, but despite that, perhaps they could find happiness again, with each other.

Spade tensed, feeling the encroaching power even before the light tap on his shoulder.

"May I cut in?" Web asked pleasantly.

Denise fixed a polite smile on her face as Spade relinquished his hold on her and she stepped into Web's arms. He wasn't as tall as Spade, so she didn't need to look up very far to meet his cool cobalt gaze.

"Are you enjoying yourself this evening?" Denise asked, playing her part as the polite hostess.

"It's been interesting," Web replied. A smile twisted his lips. "It's not every day a noted Master vampire abruptly decides to move next door...with his human girlfriend."

Even though she had no intention of pursuing Nathanial anymore, Denise wasn't about to let Web harbor any suspicions over Spade's claim. After all, lovers broke up all the time. Her leaving tomorrow didn't have to be seen as anything but another relationship gone sour.

"What's not to love about Monaco?" Denise asked with as much of a shrug as she could manage while waltzing. "And everyone starts out as human before they become something else," she added with a slanted glance upward.

Web chuckled in a way that didn't ease her tension. "You're quick, aren't you? Now I'm even more intrigued."

That was going in the opposite direction than she'd intended. Okay, one shallow, uninteresting female, coming up.

"I just love your girlfriend's purse," Denise said with the proper amount of feminine gushing. "Is it Versace? Versace's my favorite. Oh, well, maybe Gucci, too, but they haven't had anything really *good* come out lately, you know? And oh, you *have* to tell me where she got her shoes from. Mine are Escada, but you know, I really think I should have gotten Stuart Weitzman instead. They're a much better bargain considering what these cost…"

A glazed look descended over Web's half-covered face as Denise went on about the inadequacies of different designers, ticking off her list of bests and worsts for purses, shoes, and dresses. By the time the music ended and Spade walked up, Web almost shoved her back into his arms.

"A pleasure," he managed before stalking away.

Spade whirled Denise around so that his back was to Web, a devilish smile curling his mouth as he led her deeper amid the other dancers.

"That was brilliant," he whispered, so close to her ear any observer would think he was just nuzzling her.

She smiled, pleased at the compliment. "I didn't even get a chance to talk about my most and least favorite jewelers," she teased, her voice also just a whisper.

Spade laughed, brushing his mouth across her neck. "Tell me. I promise to be fascinated."

Denise couldn't stop the tremor that went through

her at the feel of his lips on her skin. *It's only an act*, she reminded herself.

Her body disagreed. Heat rose up inside her as Spade lingered, his mouth alternately brushing or hovering over her skin. His one hand still grasped hers in the proper waltz fashion, but his other caressed her back instead of staying at her waist, pressing her much closer than the formal dance dictated.

Denise cleared her throat, mindful of all the people who might be watching.

"Stop, dear. We have guests, so you can't follow through," she said, her voice breathier from his mouth sliding up her neck to her cheek.

"Oh?" His voice was a low growl. "I can if I take you upstairs."

The instant clench in her loins made her gasp. *It's only an act, dammit!*

"We have guests," she repeated, her voice rougher than her charade dictated.

"They'll manage." Two words, full of promise.

Denise drew back, forcing a smile to her lips. No matter how Spade was affecting her, his actions and this offer weren't real. Spade was pretending, same as actors around the world did for movie love scenes every day.

"Really, don't be such a tease. You know we can't leave yet," she said, this time managing to sound affectionate and chiding at the same time. Just as a normal girlfriend would under the circumstances.

Spade's eyes changed from tiger brown to green in an instant. "I never tease," he replied, each word emphasized. Then he swept her up in his arms, striding off the dance floor.

Chapter 23

Spade ignored Denise's stunned whisper to put her down. "I thank you for coming, ladies and gentlemen," he called out. "Even though I take my leave of you, please, stay as long as you wish. I look forward to seeing all of you again soon."

Denise felt her face flame as Spade carried her past the people in the ballroom as nonchalantly as if what he was doing wasn't outrageous. The knowing laughter by a few of the vampires they passed didn't help her growing embarrassment, either. It was one thing for Spade to act affectionate; *another* to publicly carry her off in a feigned burst of passion.

The only reason she quit arguing was that she caught Web's speculative look out of the corner of her eye as Spade swept past him. Web was too dangerous to let him become suspicious. After all, Spade had killed

Web's dealer, Black Jack, only a few days ago. Web had to wonder who'd done it, and he'd already expressed skepticism at Spade moving in next door with his shockingly alive girlfriend.

Denise kept her mouth shut the whole way up the flight of stairs to the third floor. She didn't say anything even when Spade carried her into the bedroom, kicking the door closed behind him. When he set her down, though, she immediately shoved him back, giving him an annoyed look as she crossed the room to turn on the television. Loudly.

"That was over the top," she hissed, surprised to see Spade right behind her when she turned around. He'd somehow already taken off his mask, sword, and jacket, and was now untying the complicated, elegant knot at his throat.

She swallowed hard. Maybe the costume had been uncomfortable?

"I disagree," Spade replied, drawing the knot free before unbuttoning his shirt so quickly, his hand was only a blur. His eyes were still emerald-green, locking with hers in a way that made her breath catch.

You've seen him take off his shirt before, don't read anything into it, Denise scolded herself, stepping to the side to walk past him.

His arm shot out, bracing against the wall unit and blocking her path. What sort of game was he playing?

"Spade—"

She didn't get the rest of the sentence out, because suddenly his mouth was on her neck, lips and tongue probing her pulse to send a luscious shiver through her. His arm remained where it was, an open barrier she could escape, if she wanted to.

Denise took in a shuddering breath, forcing back the heat that raced below her belly. "Stop it. I'm not like you. That sort of thing affects me even if I know it's fake."

A low laugh sounded in her ear. "It's supposed to affect you," Spade said, biting her earlobe gently. "And at no time have I ever touched you where it's been anything but real."

He drew her mask off as he spoke, his other hand still braced against the wall unit. Two light tugs and her earrings were removed, then Spade took out the combs holding up her hair.

Denise froze, her emotions in a death match with the desire sweeping through her. What had changed his mind about her, she didn't know, but Spade's intentions were clear. She could have him now, and oh, *she wanted him.* Her body almost trembled with need, especially with Spade's mouth continuing its sultry path down her neck.

But no matter how much she wanted him, she was leaving tomorrow. Was this Spade's going-away present?

"Stop," Denise said, her voice quiet but sharp. "Yes, you're affecting me, but I'm not into mercy screws, casual sex, *or* one-night stands."

She expected anger, laughter, or a shrug before he turned away, but Spade drew off his shirt instead.

"Did you hear me?" Denise asked, trying not to stare at his pale, muscular chest or that hard, flat stomach with its narrow line of black hair disappearing into his pants.

A brow arched before he bent to tug off his boots.

"I did indeed, but none of those apply, so I'm not concerned."

God, he'd be naked soon. A memory of what he'd looked like in the shower made her fists clench. That throb in her loins increased until it was so strong, Spade had to hear it.

He was beside her again in the next heartbeat, his hands caressing her face, lips so close to hers she could almost taste them.

"There's nothing casual about my feelings for you, Denise," he whispered. His voice deepened. "And I have no intention of letting you go anywhere tomorrow, or the next day, or the next."

His mouth covered hers, swallowing her gasp as he pulled her to him. Spade's tongue probed past her lips in sensual demand, making heat scorch up her spine. She opened her mouth, groaning at the sensual flicks of his tongue combined with the hard feel of his body pressed along hers.

A sliver of fear shot through her when she felt his fangs lengthen, their sharpness grazing her tongue as she explored his mouth. What if they nicked her and he was thrown into a bloodlust again? She hadn't even tried to stop him when he drank her before; it had felt too good. If Spade inadvertently drew her blood while they were making love, he might lose control and end up killing her—and she might not even notice until she woke up dead.

"Wait," she said, turning her head away from his deep, drugging kisses.

He stopped, one hand still tangled in her hair while a cooler draft on her back let her know the other had been unzipping her dress. "Too fast?" he muttered thickly.

The blazing heat in his gaze almost made Denise throw caution to the winds and not voice her concern, but it *was* a matter of life and death. "Your fangs. Can't you make them…go away so you don't accidentally bite me?"

Spade's laugh was soft and wicked. "Oh, I have every intention of biting you, but don't fret; I won't break your skin."

"What?" she gasped, but he just laughed again. That cool draft increased as he picked her up, her dress somehow in a heap on the floor next to his pants. Denise blinked. How had he gotten their clothes off so fast?

Her breath caught as she felt the softness of the bed at her back in the next instant. Spade crouched over her, completely naked, so large and so gorgeous, she could only stare. His body was even more muscular up close, his shoulders wide enough that they cut off her view of the rest of the room. Denise traced her hands down his arms, feeling the thick, corded muscles tighten as he leaned down to kiss her again.

She opened her mouth, relishing the skillful thrust of his tongue as it teased and stroked along hers. His fingers slid down her arm, catching the edge of her glove before pulling it down, bit by bit, until it was off. Then he repeated the action with her other glove. When her arms were bare, Spade drew back. His hair fell over his face, eyes glittering through the black strands as he slowly kissed each of her forearms, tracing his lips and his tongue over the intricate tattoos that covered her brands.

The erotic feel of his mouth was enough to make her almost close her eyes in bliss, but that would have cut off her view of the magnificent male poised over her.

In that moment, his gaze flashing emerald, fangs extending from his upper teeth, pale, powerful body absolutely still except for his caressing mouth, Spade had never looked more inhuman—or sensual.

A wild, primal hunger filled her. Denise didn't just want to make love to him. She wanted to devour him.

She slid down, pulling him on top of her. Spade balanced his weight, pressing her against the bed without crushing her. He kissed her, letting out a groan when she opened her legs and rubbed herself against the long, thick length of him.

"Do that again," he rasped.

The pressure at her core inflamed her, sending waves of need crashing through her. Denise arched against him once more, letting out a choked moan as Spade undulated his hips. His pelvis rubbed again her clitoris in a deep caress, the heavy length of him pushing against the barrier of her underwear.

What had started out as a sweet ache in her loins turned feverish. She ran her hands down Spade's back to his hips, digging her nails into those rounded muscles and pressing him closer in greedy demand.

Denise tore her mouth away from his. "Now," she whispered raggedly, arching against him, crying out in pleasure at the friction, but also in frustration at the material that prevented him from being inside her.

Spade yanked down her bustier, and it came apart in his hand. He tossed it away, his mouth closing over her nipple and sucking so firmly, Denise was sure his fangs would pierce it. Then she quit caring about that at the bombardment of pleasure shooting from her breast, making that throb inside her almost unbearable. She twisted underneath him, her hand descending between them to pull aside her panties, but Spade caught it. He drew both her wrists over her head, holding them with one hand, using the other to pull her underwear down her legs so slowly, Denise was sweating by the time it cleared her ankles.

"Don't tease me," she moaned.

Spade gave her breast a last lick before moving up to slant his mouth over hers, spreading her legs farther apart with his knees.

"I told you, darling—I don't tease," he said when he broke away, Denise gasping in a breath after his long, passionate kiss.

That gasp turned into a rising moan as Spade's mouth descended between her legs. His tongue raked her flesh, licking and probing where that throbbing ache was the strongest. Heat engulfed her, filling her veins with honeyed flames as that wet, flexible pressure alternated between flicking her clitoris to delving inside her depths. She arched, writhing in wordless demand to feel more. Spade yanked her closer, pulling her leg around his back, his tongue moving in firm, ceaseless strokes.

The ever-tightening bands of ecstasy inside her were about to snap. As her last coherent thought, Denise sank her hands into Spade's shoulders and pulled at him, hard, sliding down at the same time.

"Now," she almost shouted.

He was on top of her in the next moment, his mouth stealing her breath with a richly flavored kiss, his hand holding her thigh as he lowered his hips. The first hard breach of his flesh into hers made her loins contract with an almost painful pleasure. The second, deeper thrust had her moaning into his mouth at the thick feel of him stretching her inner flesh. The third stroke buried him fully inside her, and when he undulated his pelvis against her at the same time, the fullness combined with erotic pressure made pleasure burst within her.

Denise cried out at the climax rippling through her, sending rapturous contractions through her loins. Another deep grind of Spade's body intensified those ripples, prolonging them while that hungry ache inside her changed to sweet, glowing satisfaction.

She didn't realize she'd closed her eyes until she opened them to see Spade's blazing green gaze. His hair fell around his face in black waves and his expression was sheer lustful intentness as he watched the last tremors of orgasm shake her.

"I want to feel that again," he said, his tone darkly resonant.

Denise slid her hands from his back to tangle in his hair. "You first."

His lips curled as he slowly drew out of her. "I love your voice this way," he murmured, kissing her jaw while her nerve endings shivered with anticipation at that hard length entering her again. "Such a throaty purr, so enticing…say something else."

He thrust into her as he spoke, a long, languid stroke that made her moan instead of speak. Just as before, his hips flexed right when he was deepest inside her, rubbing against her most sensitive spot even as that fullness felt almost overwhelming.

"Spade…yes…"

She couldn't manage to say more, even *think* more. Her hands crept down his back, feeling his muscles bunch as another long thrust and rock of his hips made her mind go numb and her body come alive. She curled her legs around him, gasping as he moved even deeper, wanting more though she wasn't sure she could stand it.

"Ah, darling, you're burning me in the sweetest way," he muttered, hooking her knee under his arm to hold her lower body tighter to him. Another thrust closed her eyes at the building pressure inside her, returning with amazing swiftness after her recent release. The combination of those deep, seeking thrusts and that erotic massaging of her clitoris had her rocking against Spade in blind need.

He kissed her, plundering her mouth with the same passion that had her straining toward him. Denise slid her tongue between his fangs to suck his, consumed by the taste and feel of him. His arms were a pale cage around her, his weight pinning her to the mattress, hips meting out incredible pleasure with each mind-blowing thrust.

She started to whimper, her hands alternately clenching or raking down his back. The hard rhythm inside her was too much, not enough, and *so good* all at the same time.

"Please," she moaned against his mouth.

Spade pulled away, drawing her other knee under his arm and holding both of them in a firm grip. He shifted so her hips lifted, and when he thrust forward, the hard length of him pushed even deeper inside her. She cried out, the fullness too intense but somehow addictive, that sensual grinding almost constant in this position.

She couldn't reach his mouth, but his chest brushed her lips. Denise kissed it, savoring the hardness and the roping muscles moving underneath that smooth pale skin. She caught his nipple in her mouth, sucking, aroused even more by his groan in response.

Those hard strokes inside her increased in pace, inflaming her. She sucked harder, pinching his other nipple. His grip tightened.

"More." A hoarse command punctuated by a deep roll of his hips that almost made stars appear in her vision.

Denise divided her attention between his nipples, sucking, licking, and biting each of them. Her mind began to whirl as Spade kept increasing the rhythm of his thrusts. Pleasure narrowed her consciousness until she felt like her world consisted of nothing but this bed and the two of them. That inner tension kept growing, twisting and clenching her body tighter around him while her pulse seemed to thunder out of control.

"Come with me, come with me now," she gasped, feeling the pressure about to burst inside her.

Everything tilted in the next second, then she was on top of Spade. He was still inside her, and when she pressed against him, he moved with rapid, forceful strokes that rocked her backward in ecstasy. Spade sat up, one arm pressing her hips to his, the other balancing her. His mouth latched on to her breast, kissing it before catching the nipple with his teeth and biting it.

Denise would have cried out a warning, but she couldn't think. She wasn't even controlling their rhythm. Though she was on top, Spade had her locked in a sensual grip while he moved faster and more erotically than any human possibly could. She held on to his arms, her head thrown back, lost in the sensations spreading from her loins to her entire body.

The pleasure inside ruptured right before she heard Spade let out a guttural moan. Then another, powerful shudder mixed with the internal spasms reverberating through her. Denise clung to him, shaking with the remains of her orgasm and the continued throb of his.

Chapter 24

Spade lay on his back, Denise sleeping within the circle of his arms. Her honeyed jasmine scent mixed with his, creating a muskier, lush fragrance that he occasionally breathed in. It was *their* scent, sharpened by passion, and with each breath, he savored it.

She's truly mine now.

The possessiveness he felt had nothing to do with being a vampire. Yes, under vampiric law, Denise was his the moment he bit her, if he chose to claim her as such. But this was different. It was the sort of bone-deep emotion that made him want to hold her tighter with one hand—and draw a sword against the world with the other.

It also made him want to wake her up so he could take her again, even though he knew she needed more than the five hours' sleep that had been sufficient for him. He watched the steady rise and fall of her breasts, the diamond and amethyst necklace still sparkling between them. Denise had the blankets pulled up to her waist, but Spade hadn't needed them. Not with the smoldering heat of her body alongside his.

The memory of how incredible it felt inside her had Spade rolling onto his side, facing her. Maybe he'd wake her, take her just once, and then let her fall back asleep afterward...

Sounds of a car pulling into his driveway made him snap into alert. All the guests had left, so it couldn't be a late chauffeur picking up a lingering partygoer, and he wasn't expecting anyone.

He slipped out of bed without disturbing Denise, yanking on his pants and shirt from the previous evening. The sword he put back in the loop on his belt in case this was an uninvited ghoul, but the rest of the knives he grabbed were silver.

Then the car stopped and a door slammed. Spade felt waves of power emanating from the exterior of the house, growing in increasing currents that marked the identity of the person outside as a Master vampire.

Power he recognized all too well.

"Bloody hell," Spade muttered, taking off the knives and sword.

He was already down the last flight of stairs when Alten opened the door. "Bones," Alten said, surprise in his voice.

Crispin saw him rounding the corner and his brow arched. "Going to invite me in, Charles?" he asked crisply.

Even though the power crackling around him was familiar, the scent was familiar, and the annoyed expression on Crispin's face was more than familiar, Spade paused. Hotels and other public places might be fair game, but a demon couldn't come inside a home unless invited. Had Raum somehow found them, and vastly improved his disguise?

"Sire?" Alten asked, flicking his gaze between them.

"You arrived without invitation, you can walk through that door without invitation," Spade replied, tensing.

Crispin snorted in disbelief as he brushed past Alten. Some of the stiffness left Spade as he saw his friend easily clear the threshold.

"If we hadn't been mates for over two centuries, I'd be tempted to knock you on your arse," Crispin said. "What has gotten *into* you, Charles?"

"Got here right quickly, didn't you?" Spade said, walking toward the less formal living room at the back of the house. He didn't look behind him to see if Crispin followed; he'd come this far, he wouldn't stop now.

"If you were trying to hide, you did a bloody poor job of it by hosting a large party under your name," Crispin replied. "Word gets around about that, especially word that you're relocating here with your new human lover."

"Whiskey?" Spade asked, ignoring that.

"Of course."

Spade filled a crystal glass from the decanter in the living room, handing it to Crispin. His friend took it, still eyeing him in that annoyed, bemused way, but at least he'd come alone. Cat would have stormed up the stairs to search every room for Denise, impatient woman that she was.

"Sit," Spade said, indicating the sofa.

If he was anyone else, he knew Crispin would have

refused. Perhaps pulled a weapon and demanded whatever it was he'd come for, but Crispin curled himself into the sofa as languidly as if he'd arrived only to relax.

"You reek of Denise," he remarked in a conversational tone.

Spade's mouth tightened. "That's none of your concern."

"I grow very weary of you telling me that," Crispin said, his tone sharpening. "Shall we quit the pretense and just get straight to why you've taken up with my wife's best friend behind my back? What sort of trouble is Denise in, and *why* didn't you bring it to my attention when you discovered it?"

Crispin was too smart for his own good, but Spade made one last attempt at evasiveness.

"What makes you think Denise is with me for suspicious reasons? She's a beautiful woman, I'm an attractive-enough bloke, we get on..." Spade dangled the rest of the sentence with a shrug.

"Bollocks," Crispin said, brown eyes narrowing. "We both know you avoid relationships with human women, and we *both* know that a demon was in Denise's house before she suddenly showed up at your side as your devoted lover."

Crispin must have gone to her home and smelled Raum there. Bloody man was *too* smart for his own good.

"Not to mention Denise decided to shun all things vampire the last time I was around her," Crispin went on. "I heard it in her thoughts. So even if a demon dropped by to say hallo and nothing else happened, Denise isn't with you out of a sudden desire to join the vampire ranks, so why don't you quit the shite and tell

me what's going on. If you don't, I'...
her mind the moment I see her."

Damn Crispin's new telepathic skill...
deed pluck all the details from Denise's ...
as she woke up.

"Before I tell you anything, I must first inform you
that whatever her initial reasons for seeking me out,
things are serious between Denise and me," Spade said.
Then his voice hardened. "You're not leaving with her,
Crispin, unless it's over my dried, withered corpse."

Both of his friend's brows shot up, and then Crispin
let out a bark of amazed laughter.

"Lucifer's bouncing balls, *that's* why you're acting
like a nutter! You've gone and fallen in love with her.
Bloody hell, if I didn't see it on your face myself, I
wouldn't believe it."

Crispin was off the couch in the next moment, slapping him on the back. "This is cause for celebration!
And no small relief for me as well. I had to force my
wife to let me speak with you alone. She fretted that
Denise had somehow gotten into trouble and you were
holding her against her will."

Spade was momentarily speechless. Was it that obvious how he felt about Denise, or did Crispin just know
him too well?

"I'm quite pleased for Denise, too," Crispin went on,
his grin fading a bit. "She was broken up very badly
after Randy's death, and then her miscarriage—"

"Miscarriage?" Spade interrupted, gripping Crispin's shoulders.

The smile wiped completely from his friend's face.
"Didn't she tell you? Denise miscarried a few weeks
after Randy's murder. Doctors reckoned it was grief

stress. Afterward, she moved out of my home and I heard in her thoughts that she intended to pull away from our world. She ceased calling my wife or returning her calls the past couple months, so I figured she'd made the final break."

Spade closed his eyes. Denise didn't just have guilt over her association with vampires for her husband's death; she had it for her unborn child's, too.

"No, she didn't tell me."

Denise cared for him, yes, but with such a loss, would she be willing to relinquish her chance at motherhood forever for him? Vampires couldn't impregnate humans. Cat had been the rarest fluke as a half-breed, and even then, her father had been undead by days only. Not centuries, as Spade was.

Crispin must have read some of that from his face, too. "Does Denise feel the same way about you?"

Spade opened his eyes. "I don't know."

Denise stretched, rolling over. No one was on the other side of the bed, which she was used to, but then her eyes snapped open when she remembered *this* time, someone was supposed to be.

She sat up, looking around the room. It was large, yes, but a glance still told her Spade wasn't in it.

It's not unusual for him to be up before you, she reminded herself to cover that flutter of nervousness in her stomach. *How long did he even stay?* an insidious inner voice promptly asked. *For all you know, he left right after you fell asleep.*

She looked at the bed. The covers weren't mussed where Spade would have slept. Her stomach plummeted. Maybe Spade did leave right afterward. Maybe she'd misconstrued what he'd said last night about this not being casual.

Or maybe she was being an idiot and Spade had just slept without messing his side of the bed and was now getting breakfast.

Hope battled with insecurity. She hadn't dealt with this potentially awkward morning-after situation before. With Randy, the only other man she'd slept with this quickly, she knew how he felt beforehand. The other three guys, she'd dated for a while before sex came into the picture, so relationship parameters had been firmly established. Spade had said his feelings for her weren't casual, but in the harsh light of day, that could mean many things, and a relationship wasn't necessarily one of them.

Well, one thing she wouldn't do was sit in bed and stew until Spade came back. Denise got up and went into the bathroom. Any situation was better faced with an empty bladder, a clean body, and a lack of morning breath.

After Denise emerged from the bathroom twenty minutes later, though, the sight that met her eyes made her heart twist. Spade was in the bedroom, fully dressed, sitting on the couch, and he wasn't alone.

When Bones's dark brown gaze met hers, Denise almost burst into tears. Spade had called him to come get her. He'd even arranged for Bones to be here when she woke up, so there would be no messy scene. God, last night *had* been a one-nighter mercy fuck.

"Denise—" Spade began.

"No," she cut him off, holding up her hand. "Save it. Just give me a few minutes, Bones, and then I'll be ready to leave."

She wasn't looking at Spade anymore, but Bones's face registered amazement. "You want to leave with me?"

"I told you, she's not going anywhere," Spade snarled. Then it was impossible for Denise to ignore him, because he was right in front of her, gripping her arms. "What the devil has gotten into you?"

She laughed at that, a high-pitched, mirthless sound. "What the devil? Oh, good one, Spade. Har har! Well, it's nothing you need to worry about anymore, is it? Thanks for your time. *All* your time, but really, the farewell fuck was unnecessary. A vibrator can last all night, too, vampire."

Bones cleared his throat tactfully. "Need a moment alone, mate?"

"It appears so," Spade replied in an icy tone, his eyes glittering emerald.

"Don't," Denise said sharply when Bones got up. "I'm sure you'll tell him all about it anyway, Spade. But then again, when Cat finds out, I hope she sticks something silver in you where the sun doesn't shine!"

Spade's grip lessened. "You think I rang Crispin to come get you. That's why you're acting this way."

"Why else is he suddenly here?" Denise demanded, horrified to feel tears well up in her eyes.

Spade leaned very close, his hands now stroking her face. "I didn't ring him, I promise. He showed up uninvited, but it doesn't matter. I told you before, you're not going anywhere. You're staying with me, where you belong."

He kissed her, slow and searching, until the tears dried from her eyes and warmth spread through her. Even so, that warmth was followed by fear. Her feelings for Spade weren't just a combination of lust, gratitude, and friendship. She'd fallen for him. Hard. That was more than proved by her out-of-control reaction when she thought he'd called Bones to whisk her away. She was in way over her head emotionally, and she wasn't sure she was ready.

"Bugger, what do you have on your arms?" a surprised voice asked.

Denise froze. Spade pulled away, revealing that Bones was right behind them. He stared at her bare forearms, revealed when the robe sleeves fell back after she'd wrapped them around Spade's neck.

"Telly," Spade said.

Bones went across the room and flicked on the television, still set to blaring from last night. Then Bones came back and held out his hand.

Denise glanced at Spade. He nodded once, and she slid her hand into Bones's cool grip, palm up. Bones looked at the tattoos closely, then a slight hiss escaped him.

"Brands." One word, almost inaudible to Denise with the blasting TV, even though Bones was less than a foot away. He took her other hand and his frown deepened.

"You should *not* have hidden this from me, Charles. Or you," Bones added to Denise.

"Mate," Spade said softly. "You don't even know the half of it."

Denise tensed when Spade reached behind him and took a knife off the dresser. She knew what he intended, and it wasn't the tiny prick of pain that made her flinch when he pierced the tip into her palm. Then Spade smeared the single drop onto his finger and held it out to Bones.

"Don't say a word," Spade ordered in a dark tone.

With an arched brow, Bones took his friend's finger and popped it into his mouth. Immediately his eyes changed to green and he jumped back, knocking Spade's hand away.

"Christ Almighty!"

"Don't say it." From Spade, with more vehemence.

The look Bones gave Denise made her tainted blood run cold. It was shocked, calculating…and pitying.

"Bloody hell," was all he said.

Denise couldn't stop her ironic laugh. "Yeah. That's it exactly."

Chapter 25

Spade squinted in the afternoon sunlight at the boat heading straight for them. Long, crimson hair came into view at the bow, and he relaxed. Cat and Crispin.

Crispin's presence combined with the power Spade felt from Web last night, plus the several Master vampires Web brought with him, might have mandated that Spade let Crispin know what was in Denise's blood. Still, Spade didn't trust discussing it where it might be overheard, which meant the whole of Monaco. Who knew how many of Web's people lurked about, seeking gossip to report back to him?

But out here on the Mediterranean, with loud music playing and more than a mile between his boat and the closest one to it, it was as safe as it could be.

Denise came up from below deck, her gaze passing over his sleeveless shirt. "You need more sunscreen again."

"Looking for an excuse to fondle me?" he teased. "No need, darling. I want you to."

She smiled as she came closer. "Why wouldn't I look for any excuse to touch you? You've got the most amazing body I've ever seen."

He was glad the physique that had been frozen into permanence when he toiled the fields as a convict was pleasing to her. Once his lean, muscled frame was considered a stigma of the lower classes, but times had changed, and Denise was a modern woman.

"You know," Denise said, rubbing more sunblock onto his arms and shoulders, "if Web does have people monitoring us, he's not going to believe we're out here because you had a sudden urge to get a tan."

Her hands were so soft, and even warmer than the sun on him with the cool breeze. "Vampires don't tan. Without UV protection, we get sunburned, heal, and just repeat the process over and over."

She gave him a pensive look. "Then Web will know you're up to something."

"He'll suspect it," Spade agreed. "But he won't know what, and taking a boating trip is less suspicious than abruptly leaving town."

"I don't know why you told Bones after we'd both decided to keep him out of this," she muttered.

Spade set the bottle of sunblock down and folded his arms around her. "Crispin knew a demon had been in your home. He knew you were avoiding the vampire world, and he knew I normally don't take up with humans. Once he found me, he wouldn't have stopped digging until I told him the truth—and we might need his help, as it were."

Denise took in a deep breath, her scent peppering

with anxiety. "You have no intention of giving up looking for Nathanial, do you?"

"No," he said softly. "No matter if I successfully hid you and your family from Raum, as long as those brands change your blood into what it is now, you're not safe, and I won't accept that."

He could feel her jaw grind against his chest. "I won't let you get killed because of me," Denise said.

"I've no intention of getting killed. I've never had more to live for."

Spade pulled back to look in her eyes, tempted to tell Denise exactly how he felt about her, but he paused. Crispin's boat would be here in minutes. He'd rather not declare himself and then immediately have to change the subject, particularly if she returned his sentiments.

No, this wasn't the proper time.

Denise saw the boat approaching and sighed. "There's Cat. Wow, I haven't seen her in months."

The speedboat pulled alongside theirs moments later. Cat had a huge grin on her face as she jumped across, not waiting for Crispin to tie the mooring line.

"Denise!" she exclaimed, grabbing her in a hug.

Denise looked surprised at Cat's greeting. "I thought you'd be mad at me," she said, voice choked either from emotion, or Cat forgetting her strength and squeezing her too hard.

"Of course not." Cat gave Denise another squeeze and then her gray gaze lasered on Spade. "I'm mad at *you*," she said clearly.

Crispin caught his eye and shrugged, as if to say, *What did you expect?*

"Don't be mad at Spade, I made him promise not to tell you guys," Denise said at once. Then her hazel eyes brightened. "I've really missed you, Cat. I know it's my fault, but..."

"Don't." Cat hugged her again. "I understood, believe me," she whispered.

A hazy apparition appeared over Cat's shoulder, growing more solid until the translucent form of a man in his forties appeared.

"Fabian," Spade greeted the ghost that Cat had, in a fashion, adopted. "How goes it?"

"Ugh," the ghost replied, shivering. "I hate to travel over water. There's nothing for me to anchor to."

Denise looked around. "Who are you talking to, Spade?"

"That's my friend Fabian, but, um, you can't see him because he's a ghost," Cat explained in an apologetic way.

Denise looked around anyway, her eyes wide. Spade was amused until another thatch of red hair caught his eye as a third person emerged from inside the speedboat.

"Hallo, mate," Ian said, giving Spade a cheery wave.

Spade felt a smile stretch his lips. "Ian!" he exclaimed in an equally cheerful voice. Then he jumped across the boat and punched him hard enough to send Ian catapulting into the ocean.

Denise gasped. Cat hid a grin. Crispin just rolled his eyes. "Was that necessary?"

"Certainly was," Spade replied coldly.

Ian treaded water, looking not the slightest bit surprised. "All right, you got that out of your system. Can I get back in the boat without you striking me again? Or should I stay out here enjoying the marine life?"

"Why don't you swim around until you find a shark?

Then you can discuss how much the two of you have in common," Spade shot back.

"He was only concerned for you," Crispin said.

"Indeed? Then he should have grown a conscience on someone else's broken trust," Spade replied shortly.

Ian swam over to the edge of the other boat, avoiding the speedboat where Spade still stood. His lips curled when he saw Ian vault up beside Crispin, Cat, and Denise. *You can hide behind them, but I'll still get to you.*

The ghost wisely moved aside. Ian looked around before speaking. "You were acting crazed, Charles. Mooning over a human, snapping at anyone who looked at her cross-eyed. Whispering about blackmail and marks. Seeking out Red Dragon. Killing the person I told you sold it—yes, I heard Black Jack ended up murdered. Why wouldn't I bloody be concerned?"

"Then you should have come to me," Spade gritted out, judging if he could knock Crispin away from Ian without Denise being jarred in the process.

Ian gave Spade an unfathomable look. "I did. You refused to trust me."

"For *good reason*, else Crispin wouldn't be here," Spade replied with a disbelieving snort.

"Um, guys…" Cat began.

"I know I'm a rotten bastard, but there are four people in the world I'd never see come to harm, even at the cost of my own life," Ian said in a steady voice, turquoise gaze clear. "Two of them are here, yet neither of them trusts me. Believe me, even ruthless sods like me can be hurt by that."

"Yet you do lie, Ian, and you do manipulate, even the two of us," Crispin said quietly.

"Over little, *insignificant* things. Never over something that could mean your lives. Blimey, Crispin, you humiliated me over Cat, yet did I seek revenge? No. I went to bloody war for you less than a year later. I'll own what I am, but don't label me what I'm not when it comes to either of you."

"You know I don't like the man, but he has a point," Cat said, shaking her head. "He was there for Bones when I never thought he'd be, and it did end up almost getting him killed a few times."

"Thanks so much for the accolades, Reaper," Ian replied in a caustic tone.

Spade thought back over his long history with Ian. It had been thorny from their first meeting on the convict ship to when Ian had him changed into a vampire by calling in a favor, despite Spade not wanting that. Over the next centuries, there had been countless other incidents when Ian was as likely to bite the hand Spade extended to him as take it, but whenever things were truly dire… Ian hadn't betrayed him. He was right about that.

Denise caught his eye. "If you insist we keep going after Nathanial, we're going to need all the help we can get," she said.

Spade gave Ian a measured stare. "If you betray me on what I'm about to tell you, it will likely get me killed. And if it doesn't, I *will* find you, and I will kill you."

Ian shrugged. "Acceptable terms, mate."

Spade looked at Denise again. Her dark brown hair mixed with Cat's crimson strands in the wind, and for a second, seeing that flash of red by Denise's face brought the memory of Giselda's blood-soaked, lifeless image. *Not Denise*, he promised himself. *Not this time.*

"The source of Web's Red Dragon industry is probably a demon-marked bloke named Nathanial. I'm stealing Nathanial away from Web in order to give him back to the demon that marked him, and I need to do that before anyone realizes Denise is now a source, too."

Denise tried not to think about the last time she was in a house with Spade and Cat under perilous circumstances—not to mention, there was a *ghost* here, too. She was already rattled enough without those awful memories turning this into a PTSD attack. For the umpteenth time, she looked at the clock. Almost two a.m. *What was keeping Ian? Or Bones?*

"Don't you want something to eat?" Spade asked, squeezing her hand.

Her stomach let out a yowl of the affirmative, but with how tense she was, Denise was afraid if she ate anything, it might come back up.

"No, I'm fine."

Cat was clearly wired, too. She'd wanted to go with Bones, but he said it was better if she stayed back. Not because he was worried about her, but the sight of Cat would arouse too much suspicion. Alone, with his power cloaked, he had a chance at not being recognized as he lurked around the streets by Web's property. With Cat, those odds diminished.

And Cat couldn't read minds like Bones could to pick up if Ian was in any danger as he crashed Web's house under the pretense of being in the neighborhood. It was plausible that Ian had come to Monaco to see Spade, and Ian knew Web from a few shady dealings in the past. Denise questioned the wisdom of Ian doing reconnaissance at Web's house, but he brushed it off.

"Web knows I'm a scoundrel," Ian had said with a slanted grin. "He won't think anything of *me* asking for an illegal substance, whereas Charles or Crispin would make him right nervous. But who'd ever confuse me with an honorable man?"

He had a good point.

"Gotta say, I'm getting hungry myself," Cat remarked, standing up to pace.

"Oh, Spade has a ton of food left over from the party," Denise said, stopping at the look Cat gave her. "What?"

"Crap, I forgot you don't know…" Cat began.

"What?" Denise asked with more emphasis.

Cat's gray eyes turned green. That was nothing unusual; it was a mark of her half-vampire side that Denise had seen countless times. But then Cat opened her mouth in a sheepish smile to reveal two upper fangs that had never been there before.

"Holy shit," Denise breathed. "You did it. You actually did it."

"A few months ago," Cat said, those fangs retracting until just her normal teeth showed again. "At first things were too crazy for me to tell you about it, but then…"

Denise looked away. Yeah. Then she wasn't taking Cat's calls. "I'm sorry," she mumbled.

"It's all right, I knew you needed time," Cat replied softly. She gave Spade a harder look. "You'd better be good to her."

"Or you'll shove something silver in me where the sun doesn't shine?" Spade asked, grinning at Denise.

She looked away in embarrassment at the threat she'd hurled at him just this morning, but Cat nodded.

"You've got it, buddy."

"And same to you with Crispin, Reaper," Spade replied in a mild tone.

Denise stifled her snort. As if Spade's chivalry would allow him to do anything to a woman. The harshest punishment she could imagine him dishing out to Cat would be refusing to open a door for her.

"Shh," Spade said suddenly. His eyes narrowed. "I hear something."

Denise strained her ears, but came up with nothing. Cat cocked her head and then threw Spade an incredulous glance.

"Is that *singing*?"

Spade let out a snort. "Appears so."

Denise still couldn't hear anything, to her frustration. Again she cursed her brands for not giving her any useful abilities. Finally, after a solid five minutes, she caught the sound drifting from outside.

"*…I am the very model of a modern Major-General…*"

Ian's voice, loud and off tune. Denise blinked. "Is that code?"

Spade shook his head with disgust. "No. It's *Pirates of Penzance*."

Bones soundlessly came through the door a moment later, startling her. "He's so bloody pissed, he can hardly walk," he announced.

Denise knew enough English slang by now to know that didn't mean Ian was mad, and there was only one thing that could inebriate a vampire. Had Nathanial been in Web's house? Or had Ian gotten the Red Dragon from a vial, as Black Jack distributed it?

"*I'm very good at integral and differential calculus,*" Ian continued to sing, interrupted by a crash and then, "Where'd that bloody statue come from? Er, imitation anyway. *I know the scientific names of beings animalculous...*"

After more stumbling noises, the operetta-singing vampire appeared. Ian's eyes were bloodshot, he had a smear of dirt on his face, and his shirt was buttoned up wrong.

"Hallo, all!" Ian announced cheerfully. "That was a *capital* evening."

"Ian, mate, you look a bit worse for wear," Spade gritted out, glaring at him. "Let's get you tucked into bed before you break anything else."

"I know our mythic history, King Arthur's and Sir Caradoc's," Ian singsonged.

Cat looked at Bones and let out a grunt. "Useless," she muttered.

Spade grabbed Ian, hissing something in his ear Denise didn't hear. Whatever it was, Ian laughed. "Charles, mate, you fret too much. I'm a grown man, I am, and I can blood my handle."

"Handle your blood?" Bones offered dryly.

Ian grinned. "Exactly."

Denise sighed. It was clear they weren't getting any information out of Ian tonight. She, Bones, and Cat followed as Spade supported Ian, almost carrying him up the stairs to then dump him on the bed in a guest room.

"Before you go, mate, turn on the telly. Something raunchy, too. Think I'll rub one off before I sleep."

"God, you're disgusting," Cat grumbled. Denise agreed.

To her surprise, Bones went across the bedroom, flipped through the channels, and stopped on something pornographic, turning it up. Moans, cries, and groans filled the room.

Ian sat up like a puppet yanked into action. "He's got someone there with Dragon in his blood," he said low, the slur considerably less in his words. "Couldn't tell if he matched your description, poppet, because they had him covered up except for his thighs, arse, and cock. Too bad you didn't describe one of *those*, or I'd know straightaway if this was your bloke."

Denise's mouth dropped, both in surprise at Ian's abrupt recovery, and hearing the condition in which Web had the man who might be Nathanial.

Spade didn't look surprised by either. His mouth was set in a grim line. "Package deals," he muttered, throwing a glance in her direction.

Denise's stomach heaved, making her glad she hadn't eaten before. She looked at Ian in horror. *He hadn't, had he…?*

"I say, look at the melons on *that* lass," Ian exclaimed, his gaze now on the TV. "And hung like a stallion, he is."

"Focus, mate," Spade muttered.

Ian gave Spade a lopsided smile that told Denise he might not be as affected as he'd pretended, but what he'd imbibed had left its mark.

"Didn't bugger the bloke against his will, of course, so I took a swallow from his thigh and that was all. Cost a fancy bit of quid for a direct taste, too, versus the bottled, mixed version Web sells."

Denise shuddered. It would have been her exposed in that helpless and humiliating position for any vampire to bite or rape, if Black Jack had taken her to Web as he'd planned.

"How secure is the room he's in?" Bones asked, absorbing everything without a change in expression.

Ian's gaze wandered back to the TV before it snapped to Bones. "Hmm? Ah, very secure. Practically a bloomin' dungeon, though more posh. Web blindfolded me so I don't know which door we went through, but it's in the basement. Five vampires in the room, one of them a Master. At least seven more Masters in the house, plus Web. And a bloody lot of silver weapons."

"He blindfolded you? Must not have trusted you as much as you thought he would," Spade mused.

"Everyone acted like it was normal procedure. Foxed me at first how readily Web admitted to having a source at his home, but he must reckon only his people know how rare sources are. If not for her, none of us would know what caused the bloke to have Red Dragon in his veins, right? Other vampires must reckon it's a chemical Web makes and just injects random humans with." Ian paused to shake his head. "Web *is* rattled about you moving in next door, however…and is this room spinning, or is it me?"

"It's you, now continue," Spade said shortly.

"Web kept going on about why you would up and leave your ancestral home. Did I know what you were about? Who was the woman with you? Right stuck on it, he was. He's goosed enough that he might move that source of his soon."

"Bugger," Spade swore. He met Bones's gaze. "It'll have to be now."

"Now?" Denise blurted, forgetting to whisper.

Spade came over to her and smoothed his hand across her shoulders. "Dawn will be here in a few hours so they'll be winding down, off their guard as much as they're going to be. To wait would be riskier."

It's too soon! Denise wanted to cry out, but she

pressed her lips together and nodded. She'd never feel comfortable letting Spade walk into that situation, and if it was safer now, better now than later.

"They have cameras outside the house, alarms, probably the same inside as well," Bones noted. "It won't be a surprise attack, mate. Do you have any other vampires here strong enough and trustworthy enough to join us?"

Spade nodded. "One."

Chapter 26

Spade strapped on the remainder of his silver knives. Crispin, Cat, Ian, and Alten did the same. The metal tucked away in leg- and armband sheaths or lining the holsters on their backs were the only flashes of color on their all-black ensembles. Fabian carried no weapons, of course, but he was going, too. He might not be able to fight, but the ghost would serve a huge benefit in another way.

Spade felt a surge of gratitude watching them. Crispin's loyalty was endless, as Cat's presence was testimony to. Crispin hated putting her in danger, not that his wife needed coddling. Ian, now that he'd drained the Red Dragon out of himself and drunk deeply of human blood to replenish that loss, was as lethally focused as ever. As for Alten, Spade hadn't even needed to explain the circumstances before his friend agreed to help. Spade was grateful for that day eighty years ago when he'd changed Alten over. Alten would make a fine Master of his own line, whenever he chose to leave.

Nathanial's tainted blood made attacking Web both easier and more difficult. On the plus side, Spade didn't have to worry about the law against stealing another vampire's property. Who would Web complain to? Not the Law Guardians, who'd slaughter Web the moment they found out what he had been doing with Nathanial. Web couldn't risk telling other vampires, either, out of concern that one of them would report his activities.

In the negative column, Web wouldn't easily let the source of his million-dollar industry flee out the door. Web was a powerful Master vampire. In addition to him, Ian had also reported eight other Master vampires in the home, plus other undead guards. The best way to ensure they got Nathanial out alive was a quick, brutal attack. Dawn would see blood spilled; of that, Spade had no doubt.

Which was why he had sent Denise half an hour ago to the docks. She'd wanted to go with them, insisting her presence was necessary because she was the only one who knew what Nathanial looked like. Spade countered that should there be more than one Dragon-blooded bloke inside, they'd grab him, too, but it made no sense for Denise to storm the house just to make an identification. He didn't want to scare her by stressing how dangerous this was for them, strong vampires all, to attack a Master vampire's well-guarded home. For all they knew, Web might have fortified his house with booby traps. So have Denise, still mostly human, go with them? She'd be killed or get him killed protecting her. Or both.

Spade sought to soothe her by saying he'd need her to man the escape boat they'd rendezvous to, but Denise saw through the lie, because she'd turned away in frustration. Selfishly, Spade hoped this was another reason Denise would welcome changing over once her brands were off. Being a vampire did have some drawbacks, but those were vastly overshadowed by the benefits, in his opinion.

"Fabian's presence will be priceless for searches and warnings, but if things get dicey, Cat, that new pyrokinesis power of yours will be quite useful, too," Spade said, strapping on a final knife.

She grimaced. "Yeah, about that… I don't have it anymore."

Ian's brows rose. "Only a few months ago, you exploded an entire house *and* a Master vampire's head right off his shoulders. You're saying that ability's gone?"

Cat looked at her hands and sighed. "Because I was a half-breed before changing over, Fate thought it was funny to make me feed off vampire blood instead of human blood. I absorb power from undead blood whenever I drink—and sometimes, that means any special powers the vampire has, too. Kinda like normal vampires absorb life from human blood when they drink. But just as vampires need to keep feeding regularly to sustain the life in them, the power I absorb feeding from vampires fades with time. So the pyrokinesis I absorbed after drinking from Vlad was only temporary. All my hands are good for now is throwing knives. Or doubling as sparklers."

Spade digested that. "If that's not common knowledge, we might still be able to use it to our advantage.

The threat of you being pyrokinetic might be enough to sway matters, even if you're not any longer."

"You want me to *bluff* if things get dicey?" she asked in disbelief.

He shrugged. "If we're in that much trouble, what's to lose by trying?"

Crispin snorted grimly. "Let's hope we don't find ourselves in that much trouble, mate."

"Agreed," Ian muttered.

Spade glanced at the clock. Almost three a.m. It was time.

"Remember, the human has to be taken alive," he said. Then his voice hardened. "But everyone else can die."

Denise grumbled under her breath as she, Bootleg, and another vampire named Lyceum reached the Font-vieille pier. How stupid did Spade think she was? Oh sure, he was counting on *her* to have the boat at the proper coordinates of the Mediterranean. That was why he'd sent two other vampires along with her.

"You smell angry," Bootleg remarked conversationally.

"How stupid does he think I *am*?" Denise blurted, out loud this time. "Oh sure, I'm so *necessary* here. Except for the part where I don't even know how to drive a boat!"

Lyceum didn't quite stifle his laugh. "I don't know what they're doing, *chéri*, and if Spade didn't tell me, it's dangerous. You didn't really expect him to bring you? You're a *human*."

The vampire said it in the same way he might have said with the word *moron*. Denise's fists clenched. Vampire elitism when it came to humans was as rampant as it was infuriating.

"Humanity doesn't equal inferiority," she got out. "And you don't leave your only witness behind when you're looking for the perpetrator."

"You do if there might be danger," Bootleg said with a shrug. "Especially since it's you."

Denise glanced at him with curiosity and annoyance. Was she considered extra helpless as a human female, or had Spade told Bootleg what was in her blood? "Why especially me?"

"Because of Giselda," Bootleg replied.

"So true," Lyceum chimed in.

Denise felt like they were speaking another language. "Who or what is Giselda?"

The two vampires exchanged a look that stopped Denise in her tracks. "Don't you even think of holding back, or I'll… I'll tell Spade you let me get away from you," she improvised. "And that I got mugged," she added for good measure.

Cries of *"Mon Dieu!"* and "That's not fair!" echoed immediately from the two vampires.

"I'm a crazy human female, you know I'll do it," Denise warned them, her internal alert system telling her that this was important.

Lyceum gave Bootleg a dirty look. "You brought her up. You tell her."

Something like a sigh came out of Bootleg. "Giselda was Spade's lover during the Franco-Prussian war. He intended to marry her, except she was still human. You have to be a vampire to be married to one, and Giselda resisted changing over."

Lyceum muttered something in French that made

Bootleg nod. Denise didn't need it translated to guess it was something derogatory about Giselda's choice.

"And?" she prompted, premonition sliding up her spine.

"Spade was called away by his sire to assist in some dispute. He didn't take Giselda in case war broke out between his sire and the other Master. She was to stay in her chateau. But weeks later, when Spade sent word that all was well and he'd be returning soon, Giselda decided to go to him instead. She sent a messenger ahead to announce her arrival."

Bootleg cast a sideways glance at Denise that made her want to smack him in impatience. "Go *on*," she said.

"On the way, her carriage had a mishap or it was attacked, I don't know which. I do know Giselda was gang-raped by a group of French deserters—either before or after they killed her," Bootleg summarized bluntly. "Spade went looking for her when she didn't arrive at the time her message described. He found her body in the woods."

Denise felt ill even as several things clicked into place. *Why did you have to kill him?* she'd asked Spade months ago, standing over the body of her attacker in the parking lot. *Because of what he intended to do. No one deserves to live after that.* And Ian's comment, *I haven't seen Charles this attentive with a human in almost a hundred and fifty years… Hasn't he told you about her yet?* Then last week in Nevada, *You have no idea how much I do understand…*

Spade did know the horror of discovering the broken body of someone he loved, just as she did. It was the worst, most helpless, most heartbreaking, rage-inducing feeling in the world.

Was that why Spade never dated humans? They really did have a lot in common. Spade shunned relationships with humans because of Giselda, and Denise had avoided the undead world because of Randy. How ironic they'd been drawn to each other despite these reservations.

"Chéri, don't cry," Lyceum said softly. "That was a long time ago."

Denise brushed her cheek, only realizing then that it was wet. "Sorry. I just… I know what it's like," she finished, wiping her other cheek.

"We're glad you came along," Bootleg said, smiling at her. "It's good to see Spade happy again. Why, I'll bet he'll be doing cartwheels once you change into a vampire."

For the second time, Denise stopped in her tracks.

"What makes you think I'll be doing *that*?"

Web's house was on the edge of Monte Carlo and La Rousse. He'd picked the highest point as far as topography, no doubt for defensive reasons more than aesthetic ones. It did make the Greek-style architecture look impressive, rising up from the rocky hill with tastefully hidden spotlights shining on the different foliage and the house, but Spade knew those spotlights were also security. They kept all access to the house well lit, making Spade deduce that Web had human as well as vampire guards. A vampire wouldn't need the spotlights to see everything.

"From what I heard in the humans' minds who live here, food is delivered on a regular basis to a man secured in the cellar. The stairway is accessible through a hidden door in the walk-in freezer," Crispin whispered.

"Fabian, find the freezer and check there first. Ian, do you remember passing through something cold before you were taken to the human?"

"No, but where the bloke is during the day when he'd be fed is likely different than where they'd have him to entertain guests."

"Good point," Alten replied.

"I'll search for it," Fabian promised.

The ghost streaked off toward the house, passing right through trees and then, finally, the exterior.

Even if Web's guards were startled to see Fabian, they wouldn't realize he was a scout and not just a stray spook looking for a new place to haunt. Most vampires never mixed with ghosts. Cat, of course, hadn't let that stop her from befriending one and making him part of her family.

Spade glanced at the sky. "Less than two hours until dawn. With luck, Fabian will find him quickly and we can be in and out before they marshal a significant defense."

Cat glanced at the sky, too, but with trepidation. Being a new vampire, she was still susceptible to the pull of the dawn. Once the sun rose, she'd be too lethargic to fight, but Spade didn't intend for them to be there when the sun rose. If they were, then they'd be captured. Or dead.

After several tense minutes, Fabian's hazy form appeared in the doorway of Web's house. The ghost wordlessly gave a thumbs-up signal.

Ian grinned at Spade. "All right, mate. Let's have some fun."

Spade returned Ian's smile with savage anticipation. "Indeed."

The five vampires rose, Spade and Crispin at the front, and charged toward the house.

Alarms tripped, both visual and audible, when they were fifty yards from the house. Spade wasn't concerned; he'd expected that. When the first swarm of guards, human and inhuman, appeared and began firing at them, he threw two of his silver grenades. So did Crispin. Then the five of them hit the ground right before the explosions sent silver shards ripping through Web's guards.

The screams were music to his ears. He volleyed two more grenades through the window to clear the scrambling he heard inside, smashing through right after those satisfying twin booms.

"Kitchen, last room on the left," he heard Fabian shout. Then another series of booms went off.

Spade didn't turn around to see what was happening. For one, nothing but an exorcism could harm the ghost, and for another, all four of his friends were strong, capable fighters. All Spade's attention was focused on one thing: Find the source, and pray it was Nathanial.

He sped through the opulent rooms and hallways, his feet barely brushing the ground. When he neared the kitchen, a quartet of silver blades speared him in the chest right before Spade saw the two vampires crouched behind a door. They came out, crowing in victory, but Spade just yanked the knives from his chest and sent them sailing at the hearts of their owners. The blades landed with multiple thuds and cries of pain.

I'm wearing a Kevlar vest. You're not, Spade thought coldly, pausing to give the blades a rough twist before leaping past the fallen vampires.

More crashing and explosions sounded at the front

of the house. Alten, Ian, Cat, and Crispin were taking the brunt of the attack to draw attention away from him, Fabian running interface to warn them of each new danger. Still, they could only be successful at that for so long.

Even through the other sounds, Spade heard stealthy noises ahead that let him know the kitchen wasn't empty. When he reached it, he threw in his second-to-last silver grenade before rolling inside after the detonation. The three vampires wounded on the tile met a quick, rough death at the end of his knife.

But despite his rapid, thorough search of the kitchen, there was no walk-in freezer. Just a regular one with no door behind it, as Spade discovered when he ripped it from the wall.

A series of loud pops followed by heavy thuds in his back had Spade spinning around, snatching the human guard who tried to run after shooting him in the back.

"Where's the walk-in freezer?" he snarled.

The man just bleated in terror. Spade snapped his arm and twisted it, ignoring the instant high-pitched scream. "Freezer," Spade repeated before gripping the man's other arm in open threat.

"Th-this way," the guard got out between heaving sobs, pointing.

Spade dragged him in that direction, ducking to avoid another volley of silver and flinging his own blades in response. He was running low on knives, but he couldn't risk using his last silver grenade. Not yet.

The guard led him to the pantry and then pointed at an inner door with his unbroken arm. Understanding dawned. The pantry was the last door on the left *in the kitchen*, and that's where the freezer door was located.

Spade yanked at the subtly designed handle made to look like just another shelf and the door swung open. He ducked immediately, but the guard wasn't as fast. A flurry of knives landed on the man. He was dead before he hit the floor.

Spade vaulted forward on his belly, slicing into every bit of flesh he made contact with as he made his way into the freezer. Hard forms landed on him in a pile. Spade kept an unyielding grip on the knives in his hands, ignoring the pain from the stabs where his vest didn't cover him, and slashed out with relentless purpose. It was so small in the freezer; his attackers had no room to maneuver out of the way, and no protective gear over their hearts like Spade had. After a frenzied minute filled with ceaseless hacking, Spade rose, blood spattering him and the vampire guards dead at his feet.

He kicked them out of the way, looking around the small room. There wasn't a visible exit aside from the place he'd entered, but this had to be the way. Fabian had said so, and those vampires weren't here to guard frozen chunks of meat. Spade shoved hard at each of the walls, feeling a surge of triumph when the third one gave. He pushed harder and it fell open completely, revealing a narrow staircase.

Spade quickly recovered as many knives from his attackers as he could before shoving them in his sheaths and descending down the stairs. At the bottom, another door beckoned. He tensed. If a trap waited for him, it was behind that door. But in all probability, so was the person he sought.

He kicked open the door and dove into the room.

Chapter 27

Denise chewed on what was left of her fingernails as she looked up at the sky. Was it lighter? Or was that a trick of her mind?

Spade had said he'd be here by dawn. She didn't have a watch, or she would have been obsessively checking the time. Bootleg claimed not to have one, either. Lyceum, who drove a second boat nearby, said the same. Denise didn't believe either of them. *How could no one know the time?* she silently fumed, chewing her nails and staring at the sky once more. It was definitely lightening. Her stomach clenched. *Where were they?*

"Why don't you go below and relax?" Bootleg offered. "There's a nice bed in the main stateroom…"

He stopped at the glare Denise threw him. Sure, she could relax at a time like this, wondering if her lover and her friends were alive or dead. Didn't he realize nothing short of a concussion could make her even close her eyes? *You should have* insisted *on going with them*, Denise lashed herself for the dozenth time. Yet here she was, safe while everyone she cared about was in danger. *Again.*

"*Mon ami*," Lyceum said sharply. "Incoming."

Both vampires stared at the purplish sky. Denise did as well, but she couldn't see anything aside from the softly winking stars. She gripped the railing at the side of the boat. Was it Spade and the others? Or someone more sinister?

A whoosh above her head was the only warning she had before something big thudded behind her. Denise whirled around with a little scream—and then was swept up a hard embrace.

"Miss me, darling?" an English voice asked.

She didn't have a chance to gasp out a reply before Spade's mouth claimed hers in a bruising kiss. He picked her up, making their heads almost even in height. His mouth opened, stealing her moan of relief as she ran her hands over him. *Safe. Solid. Whole.* She couldn't ask for more.

"I have a present for you," he murmured once he broke off the kiss and set her down.

Denise looked behind Spade, more relief crashing through her at the sight of Cat and Bones, bloody but upright, Alten, Ian, and another auburn-haired man...

She froze, that face bringing back the rush of mental images. *Raum inside a pentagram, a red-haired man on the other side. "Give me power like yours," the red-haired man said, "and you can have anything you want."*

And now here he was, in the flesh.

"Nathanial," she whispered.

His head jerked in her direction, hazel eyes widening. "You know my name."

"Thank bloody Christ this is the right bloke. Wicked difficult getting the sod," Ian muttered, shoving him away.

"I'll take him below," Cat said, catching Nathanial before he fell.

"Wait, who are you people? Why did you take me? How do you know my name?" Nathanial demanded hoarsely.

Denise was struck speechless. When she first saw him, she'd been overwhelmed by relief. Despite the incredible odds, Nathanial was here, so her ordeal with the brands was almost over! But face-to-face with her infamous relative, she was suddenly uncertain. Should she treat him like a prisoner? Give him a piece of her mind for everything Raum had done to her and her family? Rub it in that she was returning him to the demon who'd branded both of them? If only he didn't seem so fearful—and hopeful. If Nathanial had acted like the greedy, heartless figure from her imaginings, this would be so much easier.

"Take him below, now," Spade told Cat.

Then he turned Denise away from the sight of Cat leading her relative below. "I smell the remorse starting to waft from you, but you've done nothing wrong," Spade said low. "That man made his bed. It's merely time for him to lie in it, and if the situation were reversed, he'd offer up your lovely arse to Raum without a moment's pause."

The cold logic made her feel better, pushing away her twinge of guilt. Spade was right. Nathanial willingly made his deal with Raum. He hadn't been forced as she had. He might look harmless now, but he was just like any other criminal; not sorry about committing the crime, just sorry about doing the time. Spade had just risked his life to get Nathanial. So had Cat and everyone else. She wouldn't let herself repay them by moping about it.

"Let's get moving," Bones stated. "Ian, you, Alten, Bootleg, and Fabian go in Lyceum's boat. Head east. We'll head west. If Web seeks to chase us, he'll have two trails to follow versus one. We'll meet back up in Vienna."

Ian jumped over into the other boat, giving them a jaunty wave. "My compliments on an entertaining evening, everyone!"

"Mates." Spade's voice was thicker. "Thank you."

"Yes, thanks, to all of you," Denise said with heartfelt sincerity.

The rest of them said their goodbyes and then Lyceum sped his boat off in the opposite direction that Bones aimed theirs. Denise watched until the other boat was no more than a speck on the ever-lightening horizon, then she turned to Spade.

"I'm so relieved you're all right. I was so worried."

Denise stepped back from Spade to sweep her gaze over him, inwardly cringing at the rips in his clothes along with the crimson spatters. He hadn't just risked his life; he'd also killed for her today.

"Is Web...?"

"Still living, sadly," Spade replied with a shrug. "No matter. He won't risk open war when he can't declare a reason for it."

"You look knackered, Denise," Bones called out from

the upper deck where the helm was located. "Should take her below to get some rest, Charles."

A slow smile spread across Spade's face. "What a brilliant idea," he murmured, dipping to slide his mouth over her neck.

The tremor that went through her was more than a physical reaction. Denise wanted Spade to make love to her, but that wasn't all she wanted. She also wanted to wake up with him, talk to him, laugh with him, and fall asleep with him. The intensity of her feelings shook her. Spade had become so important to her so soon. What if he didn't feel the same way about her?

And then there was that *other* matter...

"You might want to shower first," Denise said, shivering at the flick of his tongue under her ear. "I'd offer to join you, but it's so small, you might not even fit."

A low laugh tickled her. "You can always watch... again."

She was confused, then understanding bloomed about that night in Vegas. "You *knew*?"

Another laugh, infinitely more wicked. "I wanted you to watch, so I stomped around the room to wake you before I got into the shower. Didn't you wonder why the light was on? It wasn't for me, I can see in the dark. And then I kept the water cold so the glass wouldn't fog."

"With your body, that should count as entrapment," Denise muttered, feeling her face heat.

"No, darling." His voice was husky. "It's seduction, and I have no qualms about that. I intend to seduce you every chance I get."

He drew away, letting his hands slide from her grip. "I'll be taking that shower now." His brow rose with meaning. "And I'll leave the door open."

Desire rose in Denise, covering her shyness over Bones and Cat being well within listening range.

"Give me a few minutes," she said, mentally planning a quick freshening up. *Breath mints, powder, and lipstick in my purse, camisole in my bag.*

Green swirled with the cognac in his gaze. "I'll see you there."

Spade went below the deck, drawing off his shirt and the Kevlar vest before disappearing into the minuscule bathroom. Denise glanced up at the helm. Bones didn't once look away from the grayish sky ahead, even though he had to hear every word between them. *I don't care*, Denise decided, crossing the deck to the storage unit under the chair where she'd left her purse. It would be nothing Bones hadn't heard before.

She'd pulled back the cushioned seat and was fishing around the life jackets for her purse when a violent blast of movement came from below deck. One moment, Denise was holding her purse; the next, she was on her back, looking up at a tawny-haired vampire she recognized even without his mask.

Before she could blink, a knife hilt appeared in Web's chest as if by magic. Denise felt a moment of relief when Web dropped to his knees, but then an iron grip closed over her and she was jerked to her feet.

"Drop your knives," Web commanded, his arm around her throat cutting off her breath while something sharp jabbed her in the stomach.

Bones and Spade were in front of them, silver knives gripped in their hands. After exchanging a glance, they lowered their weapons onto the deck.

Another vampire dropped out of the sky in front of

Denise, smirking as he gathered up the weapons and then stood close to Web.

"Smart idea with the Kevlar," Web commented. "That's why I'm late. I have the docks under video surveillance, so I knew where to look for you, but I had to get my own vest first…and how thoughtful that you've taken off yours."

"Let her go," Spade said, rage blistering off each word.

A snort at her back. "Not likely."

"You know if you harm her, there'll be nothing to stop us from ripping you to pieces," Bones said in a calm tone. "Release her, and I promise you can fly off unharmed the same way you came."

Web gave an ugly laugh. "Not without what you stole from me. Give me Nathanial, then when I leave, I'll have Canine drop this bitch off a couple miles in the water. You can fish her out, if she means that much to you."

"You're not going anywhere with her," Spade said, voice vibrating with hatred.

"I have the hostage, so I make the rules," Web hissed.

Pain slammed into Denise's stomach in the next instant, so intense and overwhelming, she couldn't even breathe to scream. Then the only sound that came out of her was an agonized gasp.

Spade snarled and charged forward, but through the sudden haze in Denise's vision, she saw Bones yank him back.

"One more move and I'll spill her guts onto this deck," Web's voice said near her ear while another blast of pain in her belly had her almost passing out. "You give me Nathanial *now* and you can heal her in time for her to live. If you don't, she dies."

Canine snickered. Spade had quit fighting Bones and was staring at both of them with a fiery emerald gaze.

"If she dies, you will forever wish to join her in death, except I won't let you."

Denise knew she shouldn't, but she glanced down at the source of the white-hot agony. Web had a knife jammed in her stomach, blood pouring out of her onto the deck, each twitch of his hand sending new streams of that awful throbbing deeper inside her.

The blood pooling at her feet brought a surge of images into her mind. *So many glowing eyes. Cool flesh all around her. Blood will follow. Death will follow. It always does.*

But this time, instead of the paralyzing panic her memories normally instilled, Denise felt the strangest wave of anger blasting through her, growing along with the pain in intensity.

"Get that out of me."

Denise didn't recognize her own voice. It was low and feral, like nothing that had come from her throat before.

"Shut up," Web said, sounding surprised that she'd spoken at all. "I'm losing patience. Bring me Nathanial, or I spill more of her blood."

Cat slowly came up from the lower interior of the boat, Nathanial in front of her. When she was almost within spitting distance of Web, she stopped.

"Have your boy come get him and then you all can leave. But if you try to take Denise, or you do anything else to her, I'm going to fry you where you stand," Cat growled. Her hands turned blue, orange sparks starting to drip from them.

"You stop that or I'll kill her!" Web ordered, something sharp digging into her neck next. *He has two knives*, Denise realized. *One at my throat and one in my stomach.*

Instinctively she touched the lower wound, feeling the coldness in Web's grip on the handle and the warmth of her blood spilling through her fingers. Another wave of dizziness overcame her, followed by a nauseating fresh rush of pain.

Then she saw Spade's face, anguish competing with the rage in his expression, and it was his pain that snapped something within her.

"Let go of me."

Except it didn't come out as words. It was a garbled snarl that made Bones's eyes widen in amazement. That feeling of wildness grew in Denise until it was stronger than even her pain.

"Oh my God," Nathanial whispered.

Denise let go of her stomach to seize the arms that held the knives to her, savagely tearing at them with her hands. At the same instant, Spade lunged, hurtling into both of them.

Chapter 28

Spade knocked Web to the deck, his sole focus on preventing those knives from slashing across Denise's throat or disemboweling her. Terror gave him greater speed as he wrenched the knives away from Web and then flung them into the ocean.

Web staggered back, the hunk torn out of his arms by Denise's claws healing before his gaze. Her hands had changed moments before she attacked him, stretching into those monsterlike talons that punched through her gloves while her eyes slanted at an unnatural angle.

"Kitten, secure Nathanial," Spade heard Bones shout, but it barely registered. Bloodlust competed with a screaming violence within him. He needed to get Denise below to heal her. He needed to rip every limb off Web's body.

His decision was made when he saw the blood still

gushing out of Denise's stomach. Spade swung her up, kicking Web hard enough to knock him against the bow, but left him there while he hurried to take her below.

Denise fought him, snarls coming from her throat and her beautiful hazel eyes filling up with red. Spade jumped down into the interior hallway that led to the bedrooms, tearing his wrist open with his fangs.

"Drink," he ordered, holding his bleeding wrist to her mouth.

Denise tried to turn her head away, but Spade forced the drops of his blood into her mouth. She swallowed, grimacing. When his wrist healed, Spade bit it open again, this time to drip his blood directly over the stab wound in her stomach.

Even as that awful gash began to heal, Denise gasped, those noises continuing to come out of her throat instead of words. Spade went into the stateroom, setting her on the bed and watching her in rising panic. Her injury had healed; why did it seem like she was getting worse?

"Denise, look at me. Tell me what's wrong," he urged.

Her eyes were all red now, slanting at those impossible angles, and her clawed hands ripped at his wrists to knock him away. Harsh, unintelligible sounds came from her, growing in volume as her struggles increased.

"Crispin!" Spade shouted. Maybe Denise needed stronger blood than his. Could Web's knives have somehow been poisoned?

It was Cat who came barreling into the bedroom. Spade ignored her gasp when she saw Denise, not sparing her a glance.

"Get Crispin," he snapped.

Denise began to writhe, the noises from her sounding more frantic. Spade had never seen anything like this before. What was wrong with her?

"I told you, I can *help*," a voice said from behind Cat.

Spade swung around, his gaze narrowing when he saw it was Nathanial. "What's wrong with her?"

"She's like me," Nathanial whispered. "The brands... she's too far gone to stop it now."

"Make sense or I'll snap your bloody spine," Spade barked, terror seizing him at hearing "too far gone." No. She couldn't be.

"Move aside," Nathanial said.

Spade gave him a look that promised a long, horrible death if he did anything to harm her, but Denise's convulsive jerking made him willing to let the lad try whatever he thought could help.

"What's her name? Denise?" Nathanial asked.

"Yes." One word, clipped.

"Hold her, but not too tight. Let her move. Just don't let her get away."

Spade complied, moving behind Denise to wrap her loosely in his arms, ignoring her clawed nails scoring into his flesh.

Crispin appeared behind Cat in the narrow passageway. "What is it?"

"I don't know," Spade said tightly. "She's...not well."

"I killed the other vampire, but Web got away. We need to leave. He'll have more people on the way soon, if not already," Crispin said with a grim glance at Denise.

"You can't move her yet, you don't understand!" Nathanial exclaimed.

Crispin lasered a glare on him. "Did I ask for your opinion?"

"Argue with him later, I need his help now," Spade ground out. "Find another way, Crispin. Buy us time."

His friend wordlessly went topside. The boat lurched moments later as Crispin gunned the engines.

Nathanial knelt in front of her. "Denise, I know you can hear me," he began in a strong, clear voice. "You're panicking because you feel like you're being pulled inside out, but you'll be all right. You got too upset and it triggered the change. You're too far into it to stop, but you *can* control it."

"What the bloody hell are you on about?" Spade demanded. "If you're making this up, I'll—"

"Don't bother with threats, there's nothing you can do to me that hasn't been done," Nathanial replied bleakly before his tone hardened. "I've been through this before. You haven't, so be quiet and do as I say."

Cat looked almost as shocked by that bold statement as she was by Denise's altered hands and eyes, but she didn't say anything. Spade decided to follow her example. He clamped his mouth shut.

Nathanial returned his attention to Denise, who was twisting and moaning in that guttural, bone-chilling way.

"Listen to me, Denise," he commanded, moving closer. "If you don't control what you change into, your mind will pick whatever scares you the most, and I'm guessing it'll be something that ends up killing everyone on this boat. So focus on what I'm saying to you. Stop struggling."

Denise's horrible moans didn't stop, but her attempts to break free from Spade did. He felt a flare of hope. She understood what the lad was saying to her, even enough to act on it. Whatever was happening, her consciousness hadn't been buried beyond reach underneath it.

"Good. See? You're in control enough to force your body into doing what you want. You've fed the demon essence too much to stop the change, but it won't be permanent. Do you understand, Denise? You'll be okay."

Something like a sob came out of her. Spade's heart twisted hearing it.

"I want you to think of something small, something harmless," Nathanial went on. "Something that couldn't hurt anyone. Focus on that. See it in your mind. Don't think about anything else, just that…"

Denise's entire body shuddered, then unbelievably, Spade felt her bones start to shrink under his hands. Her skin rippled around her frame as if it were water, folding into itself and contracting along with the rest of her.

"Oh. My. God." Cat's voice, mirroring the shock he felt.

"You're all right," Nathanial said, never losing that confidence in his tone even though Spade felt like his world was tilting out from under him. "You're doing good. You're controlling it. Keep focusing on that small, harmless image. Don't let it out of your mind for a second…"

Denise continued to shrink until her clothes covered most of what Spade could see of her. He was frozen, unable to move or speak, watching as the woman he loved seemed to vanish in front of his eyes.

"You're doing good," Nathanial chanted.

If Spade could still talk, he'd have told the lad he'd lost his bloody mind, calling anything about what was happening "good." But he could only stare as there was a final shuddering underneath the pile of clothes that, minutes ago, Denise had worn, but now covered…whatever was left of her.

Cat recovered faster than Spade did. "Where is she?" Then louder. "Where the *hell* did Denise go?"

With a hiss, a mahogany-colored cat shot out from beneath the clothes, darting at once to hide in the corner.

"There she is," Nathanial said calmly.

Spade stood in the security line at the airport in Vienna, gripping a pet carrier in one hand and Nathanial's shoulder in the other. Crispin and Cat were right behind Nathanial. Cat looked normal, but Spade knew it was taking all her concentration to function this early into the morning.

"Will you be checking your pet with your luggage, or upgrading to first class to board it with you?" the ticketing employee asked.

A strangled noise escaped Cat. Spade clenched his jaw. "Upgrading," he bit out.

Inside the carrier, a loud hiss followed by a series of angry scratching sounds made the employee glance up.

"I'll need proof of current vaccinations," she said.

Spade leaned forward until their faces were only a foot apart, green flashing from his eyes.

"You've got the proof, now hurry along," he growled.

A glazed look settled over her gaze but her fingers flew across the keyboard. In moments, Spade had his ticket—and his papers to fly with an animal. *Nathanial better be right about this being only temporary*, Spade thought, fighting the urge to kill someone just as an outlet for the frustration seething in him.

"It'll be okay," Nathanial said, as if reading his mind. "As soon as she's relaxed, she'll change back."

The cat—*Denise*—was anything but relaxed now. She'd hissed and clawed at anything that came near her, until Spade had to scruff her in order to fly away from the boat with her. Now, of course, they needed to use a more traditional form of flying to get to a safe place. Anywhere within a hundred miles of Monaco was too close to Web and his people for Spade's comfort.

He waited another ten minutes until everyone had their tickets, needing to briefly green-eye the employee again for Ian's fake ID to pass as Nathanial. It wasn't such a stretch; both men were of similar height, hair color, and age in human appearance, but no sense risking a security delay when there was a way around it. The lad had been very cooperative since Spade told him tersely that he'd captured him to help Denise. That was true, after all. Just not how the bloke realized.

Once on board the plane to Bucharest, however, Spade's icy composure began to crack. The woman he loved was in a cat carrier at his feet, and he had only the word of a shiftless, demon-dodging sod that it wasn't permanent. Denise's hands changed back, Spade reminded himself, but it was poor comfort. Mild hand deformity was nothing compared to this.

"Does this flight have meal service?" Nathanial asked the attendant before his seat belt was even on.

"Shut it," Spade ground out, longing to strangle him. If not for him, Denise wouldn't be a hundred pounds lighter and covered in *fur*.

"But I have to eat," Nathanial said, "Stress, pain, fear, hunger, horniness…all those things, if left to build, will trigger the change. I'm already stressed worrying about Web showing up and I'm guessing I can't get a blow job anytime soon, so I have to calm my hunger cravings, at least."

Crispin leaned forward in his seat behind them. "You're telling me Web's kept you shagged, fed, relaxed, and happy, all while siphoning your blood off to sell?" he asked low, his voice dripping with sarcasm. "Bollocks."

Nathanial turned around, his face hardening from its normal, almost boyish expression.

"No. He kept me fucked whether I wanted it or not, drained to the point of constant weakness, and nothing close to relaxed. But I'm assuming with how *he* acts, he cares enough about her not to treat her that way."

"You realize if you're not telling us how to really get Denise back, you'll have a very short, awful life," Cat said with quiet steel in her tone.

Spade agreed, but just in case the lad was telling the truth, he didn't want Nathanial rattled. Having him shift into Cain-knew-what on an airplane would be disastrous.

"Now's not the time for this discussion," he said to both of them. Then, to Nathanial, "I'll see if there's anything here you can eat."

Two hours and all the available snacks on the plane later, they landed in Bucharest. England would be the first place Web looked for them, and America was too far, but Spade's sire had a home here that was well fortified, secluded, and familiar.

Ian waited outside the airport in the arrivals lane after they collected their bags. He looked at them and his brows rose.

"Where's Denise? And what are you doing with a

bloody *cat*, Charles? Some sort of mascot for our dear Reaper here?"

"Not another word," Spade snapped, getting into the car and seating the carrier on his lap.

"Ian, trust me—don't," Crispin said before he threw their bags into the boot. Then he climbed in the back, seating Nathanial between them. Cat got in front, tapping her fingers on the dashboard.

"Let's go, Ian," she called out impatiently, no doubt still tired even though she'd slept most of the way on the plane.

"I assume someone will tell me what's going on sooner or later," Ian remarked as he slid into the driver's seat. "Until then, it's a bit rude to treat me like a nosy chauffeur, all things considered."

Spade's temper snapped. "You want to know where Denise is?" He held up the carrier so the hissing feline was visible in the rearview mirror. *"Here she is! Now drive the car, Ian, or get the fuck out so I can."*

Ian drove, not saying anything else all the way to the house.

As soon as the car came to a stop, Spade got out, yanking Nathanial with him. Alten and Fabian had come out to greet them, but he strode by without a word, heading for the bedroom he'd stayed in months ago when he'd been here to help Crispin. Once there, he shut the door and then rounded on Nathanial.

"All right. How do I bring her back?"

The russet-haired man walked around the room, bending low and checking the corners, under the bed, the windows, and even the bathroom. It took all of Spade's control not to start beating him when he didn't answer.

"What the bloody hell are you doing?"

"Checking for places where she could sneak out," Nathanial answered. "An open window, a crawl space under the cabinet…you want to spend your night looking for your lost kitty girlfriend inside the walls or on the property?"

Spade clenched his fists but kept his voice calm. "All right. If you're quite finished with that, now what?"

Nathanial, were he smart, would hear the lethal threat behind those two last words and produce speedy results, but he shrugged.

"Get some tuna and a bowl of cream."

Spade had him against the wall dangling by his throat in the next instant. Only the knowledge that he needed Nathanial, if Denise did transform back, kept Spade from killing him on the spot.

"Take care what you choose to say next, because you will pay for it in blood if it's another ill-conceived quip."

"I'm being serious," Nathanial said with emphasis on each word. His hazel gaze was steady. "You've got a terrified woman stuck in an unfamiliar form who's been carted around in a small box for hours. She's hungry. Thirsty. Probably claustrophobic, too, which would explain why she's been hissing and scratching at the cage nonstop. Let her out. Let her eat something, drink something, settle down a little. And then you're going to *pet* her until she's really relaxed."

That murderous urge was almost overpowering, making a fine tremor run through Spade's body. His fangs pressed against his lips in silent demand to bury into Nathanial's throat and rip.

"All right," Spade said, once his fury died down

enough for him to talk. "But if you're putting me on, you'll be the next one in that carrier. In pieces. Alten!"

A few moments later, the door opened. "Yes?"

"Ask the kitchen to send up some tuna fish or chicken, plus a bowl of cream. Right away."

Alten blinked but didn't question the directive. It wasn't five minutes before he was back, reeking tuna on a plate and a saucer filled to the brim with cream. This time, though, Cat and Crispin came with him. They filed in the room silently, shutting the door behind them.

Spade set the containers of tuna and cream on the floor and then opened the door of the carrier.

A blur of fur burst free with a yowl, running around the perimeter of the room in a mad dash before darting under the bed. Spade felt his heart sink at the distinctly feline response. Was there nothing of Denise left in the animal hiding beneath the bed?

"Just wait," Nathanial said.

After a tense couple of minutes, a mahogany-colored head slid out from under the bed. Hissing at the room in general, the cat came out all the way and went straight to the tuna dish, devouring the smelly banquet. Then the kitty lapped at the bowl of cream until its dark sides began to swell.

"Get her now," Nathanial instructed.

Spade snatched up the cat before it could dart back under the bed. Immediately tiny claws scored his hands, but he ignored that, looking at the bundle of fur with a mix of hope and despair. Could Denise really come back from this? She said she'd seen Raum transform into a dog and back without any ill effects, but he was a demon, and she was still—mostly—human.

At least, she used to be.

"Don't let her loose. Get her as comfortable as possible, and start petting her."

Crispin muttered something Spade didn't want to decipher. With a clenched jaw, he settled himself on the bed with the now-growling kitty, holding it in place with one hand and stroking its fur with the other.

Four sets of rapt eyes watched his every move. After a minute, Spade was tense enough to growl along with the cat.

"Give me the room," he said.

Crispin took Nathanial's arm. "Come with me, mate. I'll show you to your accommodations," he said before drawing him away.

Spade almost smiled at that, imagining where Crispin would put him. The rest of them filed out, Cat shutting the door with a pensive last look at them.

The kitty continued to growl in that low, extended manner, punctuated every so often by a hiss and a twist to get free. Spade loosened his grip to where the cat could wiggle, but not escape, still stroking those dark brown ears.

"Denise," he said low. "If you can hear me, I very much need you to come back. Don't resign me to the fate of being one of those crusty old vampires who only live with their pets."

I'm talking to a bloomin' kitty, it occurred to him. He might as well dig a hole and cover himself up with his grave dirt now.

But he didn't stop, because he needed to believe Denise understood what he was saying, even if that wasn't true.

"Come now, darling, I can think of far better ways to spend time in bed with you than this," he continued in a low voice. "You make a right fetching feline, but really, there are limits to the things I'm willing to try."

The cat stopped growling, though its tail kept up its restless twitching. Spade didn't know if that was a positive sign, but he kept talking.

"We have everything we need to move forward, darling, except you. Come back, Denise. We'll return Nathanial to Raum, get those brands off your arms, and continue on with our lives. Do you know the first thing I want to do, when you have your brands off?"

A softer noise began to emanate from the cat. After a second, Spade realized it was purring.

"I'll take you somewhere very posh," he went on. "I can picture the dress you'll wear: black silk, thin straps, deep neckline—and no gloves. You'll have a wonderful dinner, and then we'll dance until you're knackered... but not too knackered, because when we get home, I'm going to make love to you. I'll go slow, taking my time over every inch of your flesh, until your voice turns into that delicious, throaty sound that inflames me. And then, afterward, I'll hold you until you fall asleep..."

A strong current rippled over the kitty's body. Spade quit talking, watching in amazement as the bundle beneath his hands grew. Another rippling shudder, then another, and another. Skin seemed to erupt from the cat's form, stretching, growing, and widening in a cataclysm of limbs, flesh, and bone that happened almost faster than his eyes could track. In the space of a few incredible seconds, a woman's naked body replaced the cat curled across his lap, her hair a dark veil across her face.

Spade didn't move, afraid his slightest gesture would cause her to magically disappear again.

"Denise."

A shaking hand brushed her hair back, and then Denise's lovely hazel gaze met his.

"Spade," she said, her voice scratchy and rough.

Then she jumped off the bed, staggered, and ran into the bathroom.

Chapter 29

"Denise, honey, are you okay? Please let me in," Cat urged.

Denise stayed on the floor, pressed as far into the corner as she could manage, and only answered because she knew if she didn't, Cat would break in.

"I'm fine," she gritted out. "I just want to be alone for a while."

She'd repeated the same phrase to Spade twenty minutes ago, after she'd finished shaking and running her hands all over her body to verify that, yes, she was indeed completely back to herself. Words couldn't explain the horrible panic she'd felt while turned into something else, not able to communicate in any manner aside from growls and hisses.

Before, on the boat, she'd had a twinge of guilt about turning Nathanial over to Raum. Now, if the demon were in front of her, she'd thrust Nathanial into Raum's arms without the slightest hesitation. Not to save her family, or because Nathanial had made a bargain, or out of gratitude for what Spade had gone through to get him. No, she'd do it so she'd never have to worry about her body becoming a foreign prison again.

"Denise." Spade's voice, rich and deep. "Open the door."

No way. He'd seen her as an animal. Her new lover had carted her around in a pet carrier, for crying out loud! What the hell was she supposed to say to him after that?

Even now, the memory of being trapped in that tiny container made her break out into a sweat. She'd always hated small, tight spaces. Being shoved into one while knowing she wasn't even human at the time had almost snapped her sanity completely.

She just *had* to look at Cat and get a bright idea to change into her namesake. Why couldn't she have thought about something *else* small and harmless? Something human?

Denise's stomach clenched and she burped, the taste of tuna following. That's right, she'd eaten out of a bowl on the floor because just half an hour ago, she'd been an animal. Bile rose in her throat with merciless swiftness. She scrambled to the toilet, making it just in time and retching until her throat burned.

A hard, cracking noise jerked her head up. Spade came into the bathroom, the door handle hanging off its perch. Denise yanked a towel over herself, her shame deepening. First Spade saw her eating from a bowl as an animal, now he saw her crouched naked over a toilet hurling her guts out.

"Please get out," she moaned.

He knelt next to her. "What's wrong? Are you ill?"

An almost hysterical laugh escaped her. "What's wrong? Are you *serious*?"

Cool hands slid across her arms. Denise flinched back, but the wall behind her prevented her from avoiding his touch.

"Don't," she said sharply.

One glance had shown that Spade was his usual handsome, impeccable self, wearing pressed pants and a crisp shirt, his scent a heady, natural cologne. In contrast, here she was, wearing only a towel, sweat-covered, and stinking like tuna vomit.

Denise began to struggle when Spade pulled her into his arms, but it was just as futile as her attempts to get away when she was covered in fur. How could he bear to touch her like this, let alone be in the same room with her? If she could avoid her*self*, she would.

"You don't need to try to make this better, okay? Just please, Spade, leave me alone."

"This isn't about you," he responded, tightening his arms around her when she would have squirmed away. *"I need this. Right now, I need it more than I've ever needed anything, including blood."*

She didn't say anything, torn between wanting to believe that and thinking he was lying just to make her feel better. And she did feel better in his arms. Oh, so much better! Like there was hope and reason in her world, instead of just the quicksand deterioration of both her body and her soul.

"You *scruffed* me."

It came out without thought. Considering everything that had happened, that should have been the last thing on her mind.

Something brushed across her head that felt like his lips. "My apologies, darling."

"How can you call me that?" Denise asked in a whisper. "If there was ever a good cause for breaking up with someone, turning into a four-legged creature is *it*."

"I'm a vampire. My closest friends are vampires and ghouls, and there's a ghost floating right outside this room. I've dealt with demons, black magic, wraiths, and zombies in the past two years alone, so I'm afraid your shape-shifting isn't going to send me fleeing away in fear."

Denise was silent for a moment. Then, "When you put it like that…you sound like a sicko."

Laughter shook his chest. "I can accept that."

Some of the crushing weight of her self-disgust lifted, but shame still swirled inside her. "Yeah, well, I'm a coward."

Spade eased away until he could look at her, a frown creasing his face. "Why would you say that?"

She wanted to avoid his gaze, but that would be even more proof of her statement, so Denise looked right into his eyes as she spoke.

"Because even though part of me thinks it's murder, I'm going to give Nathanial to Raum. Not just to save my family, but to save my own ass."

"Of course we're giving Nathanial to Raum," Spade replied, waving a hand in dismissal. "You're not offering up an innocent to settle your own debt. *That* would make you a coward, rather like Nathanial's been, letting his descendants pay for him skipping out on Raum. Don't tell me the sod didn't know others would pay for it, either. You don't renege on a deal with a demon and expect no consequences."

Spade turned her around until she fully faced him, his eyes flashing with green highlights. "And even if you begged me not to, I would still see Nathanial delivered to Raum. You're not a coward, Denise. You actually don't have a choice."

She was too emotionally wired to talk about Nathanial anymore. "I need to shower—and brush my teeth. Ugh, I'm never eating tuna *or* drinking milk again."

"Fine by me, but you need to eat something else, and soon."

Memory of Nathanial's voice rang in her mind. *Stress, pain, fear, hunger, horniness…all those things, if left to build, will trigger the change.* Denise thought back to the times her hands had morphed. Nathanial was right; she'd been a combination of hungry, angry, horny, and stressed. Guess being stressed, hungry, then getting *stabbed* and seeing Spade's reaction to it had blown through whatever defenses the tattoos had given her against Raum's essence.

Well, she certainly never intended to repeat that set of circumstances. A shiver went through Denise, her hand sliding beneath the towel to again feel the reassuring smoothness of her stomach. *No fur, no gushing wound.* She intended to keep it that way.

Spade drew her to her feet, but didn't leave. Denise cleared her throat, feeling her cheeks warm.

"Ah, could you give me some privacy? I need to use the litter box."

His lips twitched at her bad pun, then he kissed her hand. "I'll go find something for you to wear."

"What happened to the clothes in my suitcase?"

"They're at the bottom of the Mediterranean with the boat."

Oh. She hadn't remembered much of what happened right after leaving the boat, more preoccupied with terror over suddenly being an animal.

Denise gave Spade a wry smile. "Just put the sunken boat on my tab." She might be girlfriend number ten-thousand-and-one to Spade, but so far, she'd probably proved to be the most expensive.

"Stop fretting about things like that. I'm not." Spade kissed her other hand. "I'll see you soon."

He left, closing the door. Denise glanced at the dangling, useless handle and then her reflection. *Any situation is better faced with an empty bladder and a clean body,* she reminded herself. *Oh, and a lack of tuna-vomit breath.*

After Spade laid some clothes out on the bed for Denise—and threw away the remnants of milk and tuna—he found Crispin in the drawing room, sipping a whiskey and swirling the liquid around in silent contemplation.

"Where's Nathanial?" Spade asked.

"In one of the new vampire holding cells in the basement. Best place for him. He'd have to shift into vapor to escape that, not that he has any intention of trying to run away." Crispin set down his glass with a sardonic snort. "He thinks you're his bloody hero."

Spade sat across from him. "He said that? Or you heard it in his thoughts?"

"His thoughts," Crispin replied. "Bloke reckons you stole him away from Web to get his help in controlling the demon essence in Denise. He has no idea he's to be exchanged for the removal of that essence."

Spade digested that without a hint of sympathy. He'd do far worse than sacrifice one unworthy sod who'd signed away his own fate to save Denise from the destructiveness of those brands.

"We need to keep him away from Denise as much as possible. She's already begun to feel guilty over the matter."

"Agreed. When do you intend to summon the demon?"

Spade's mouth twisted. "Like to do it straightaway, except there's the small matter of my not knowing how to kill Raum. I don't fancy trusting the demon at his word that he'll release Denise instead of simply killing her, once he has Nathanial back."

Crispin gave him a shrewd look. "Your lad in the basement might prove useful for that. If he thinks you mean to destroy Raum, I wager he'd be more than forthcoming with any information he has to assist that."

Spade would wager that, too, but he had no intention of destroying Raum unless it was a last resort. He wanted the brands off Denise. Not to kill Raum on sight, dooming her to forever carrying the demon's marks.

"Cat's sleeping?" he asked absently.

Crispin nodded. "Once she knew Denise was safely back, she couldn't hold out any longer."

Ian sauntered in, his turquoise gaze flicking over the two of them before he settled himself into a chair.

"Wretched unfair, it is," he remarked. "Of the three of us, I'm the one who's always collected the rare and unusual, yet you two managed to snag the world's most unusual women. First you, Crispin, with the only living half-breed, who then turned into an even more unusual vampire. And now you, Charles, have bagged a shape-shifter. Thought you were joking when you said Denise was the kitty. I'm simply green with jealousy."

"Denise won't be a shape-shifter for long," Spade said sharply. "And once she has those brands off, I don't intend for her to remain human, either."

Even as the words left his mouth, the hairs on Spade's neck stood on end. Crispin's expression turning grim only confirmed it. Slowly, Spade turned around to meet Denise's shocked gaze.

"Bootleg and Lyceum were right. You really *do* expect me to turn into a vampire." Her voice was incredulous. "Why would you think I'd do that?"

Bones and Ian left the room without a word. Denise barely noticed them, concentrating on Spade's face, hoping he'd tell her she had misunderstood what he meant.

But he didn't. Instead his expression darkened as he rose. "Why would I think you'd do that?" he repeated. "Why *wouldn't* I, now that we're together? You didn't truly believe I'd be content to allow you to remain human, did you?"

Denise felt betrayal welling up in her. He'd just decided she'd change her species without even *talking* to her about it? She'd been willing to fight her PTSD and stay in the vampire world, just to be with him. But no matter how sweet he acted toward her, he'd never gotten past his prejudice against her being a human. She'd thought Spade accepted her for who she was, but all along, it hadn't been good enough.

"I have always been clear about the fact that if I got

these brands off, I was going back to being a normal human. That hasn't changed."

Spade was in front of her in a blink, his hands gripping almost painfully into her shoulders.

"You were willing to sacrifice your humanity to protect my life, yet you're not willing to sacrifice it for our relationship?" He let out a cruel laugh. "And here I believed you when you said you weren't interested in a casual shag, but clearly that's all I am to you."

Denise shoved at him, but it didn't even make him flinch. "I shouldn't need to change into a vampire to be good enough for a relationship with you!"

"Fancy being a ghoul instead? Fine, choose that," he flared.

She gaped at him. Did he really despise humans this much?

"I'm not going to change my *species* just to be worthy of a relationship with you," Denise got out, anger seeping over the hurt of his rejection. "If I'm not good enough for you as I am, then we're through."

Spade's eyes went green and fangs jutted out from his teeth. "So be it. I wish you joy of your short life."

He spun on his heel and strode out, his preternatural grace and speed emphasizing that the differences between them were insurmountable. Denise heard the front door slam seconds later. Only when she was sure that Spade had left the house did she finally allow her tears to fall.

Chapter 30

"That was impressively inept of you."

Spade cursed but kept walking through the dense forest that bordered the house, not deigning to respond to Ian.

The crunching sounds of leaves continued behind him. "If I were a betting man, I'd wager the lass is in tears right now," Ian went on.

Spade's jaw clenched. "Not bloody likely. She's the one who just threw me away, not the reverse."

"Hmm. I suppose. If you've resigned yourself to things being over between you two, then I think I'll wander back to the house and see if the fetching little shape-shifter is in need of any comfort—"

Spade had Ian against a tree when a knowing laugh made him drop his hands.

"Indeed, right finished with her, you are," Ian taunted him.

He forced himself to step back from Ian, cursing that he'd so easily fallen into that one.

"It doesn't matter that I still feel for her. She's as good as dead as a human, and I'm not going through that again."

The knowledge burned like silver in his heart. *Lovely, brave, stubborn Denise.* Rotting in a grave within a few fleeting decades—if she was lucky. Sooner, if she wasn't. He couldn't tolerate that. It had nearly destroyed him with Giselda.

"Your problem is you're too bloody honorable for your own good," Ian said. "Were I you, I'd change Denise over regardless of her objection."

Spade let out a cold laugh. "Mate, I know that better than anyone."

Ian shrugged. "Yes, you and Crispin would, wouldn't you?"

He stopped and gave a hard look at the vampire opposite him. Ian stared back, unapologetic, uncompromising. The same stare Ian had given him over two hundred and twenty years ago, when he'd been responsible for Spade being turned into a vampire. Ian might not have sired him, being too weakened after changing Crispin, but Spade was turned because Ian asked for a favor, ignoring that Spade hadn't wanted it.

For several long, merciless seconds, Spade considered that. He'd eventually forgiven Ian, after all. So had Crispin. True, Denise might hate him for a hundred years if he changed her despite her objections, but at least she'd be alive to hate him. Not feeding worms beneath the earth.

But could he truly do that to her? Pretend to accept her humanity, and then snatch it away from her as soon as those brands were off? If he did, how could she ever trust him again? He and Crispin forgave Ian, yes, but the nature of their relationship had been very different as betrayed friends versus a betrayed lover.

Or what if Denise didn't realize it was a betrayal? She'd proved susceptible to the power of his gaze before. He could plant the idea in her mind to welcome changing over. She'd never even remember that it hadn't come from her…

With a violent curse, Spade shook his head and began walking again. "No. I'll have something real with Denise, or nothing at all."

"Fool," Ian called after him.

He clenched his jaw again. That might be true, but it was his decision all the same.

The knock on the bedroom door made Denise's heart leap. "Come in," she called out at once.

That brief hope was extinguished when Bones entered instead of Spade. "Even if I couldn't read your thoughts, your scent of disappointment is overpowering," Bones noted.

Denise flopped back in the bed. She'd been trying with no success to sleep in the hours since Spade stormed out. Had he left for good? He might have. Bones and Cat could more than handle giving Nathanial over to Raum.

"Of course Charles didn't leave for good," Bones said, taking the chair near the bed. "He's brassed off quite a bit, but he'll be back by dawn at the latest."

"You know, I never realized how intrusive your mind-reading skills were," Denise said dryly. "Can't you switch to another channel or something?"

"Don't you realize how much Charles cares for you?"

Denise scoffed. "You can't care for what you don't respect, and Spade has *no* respect for humans."

"That's not true. Charles does respect humans. He's just avoided caring for any human again because humans always die," Bones said softly.

"Vampires die all the time, too," Denise countered. "There's no such thing as immortality, no matter the species."

"Vampires can't die from the passage of time, diseases, or accidents. No one can protect himself against every form of death, but death is so much closer to humans than vampires or ghouls. What happened with Web obviously inflated Charles's fear of your mortality to the level that had him storming out when you rejected the notion of ever turning into a vampire."

"But I don't *want* to be a vampire," Denise said, frustrated. "Why is that such an unreasonable thing for Spade to understand?"

"Because it means he'll bury you one day," Bones replied. "One day soon, to a vampire's way of thinking. It's not the same as a normal relationship, where there's a chance that your life spans will be similar. With a human, an early death is guaranteed. If the situation were reversed, would you be content to let Charles die, if you could prevent it? Don't you remember what you said when you found Randy's body? You screamed at me to fix him. It was too late, but if it wasn't, you would have demanded that I do whatever was necessary to ensure that you and Randy could still be together."

Memory sliced ruthlessly across her mind. *Vampires everywhere, blood and dirt spattering them. She slipped, landing in something dark and sticky. The stain*

*coated the floor, widening as it led to the kitchen. Green
light from a passing vampire's gaze shone on the large,
misshapen lumps in front of her. What were those?*

*Her stunned gaze diagnosed the shapes and she
gagged. Pieces of a person were all around her. The
glow of another vampire's gaze reflected off something
shiny on the small clump next to her leg. It was a hand,
with a familiar gold and silver wedding band on it...*

"You're right," Denise acknowledged, her voice
husky with remembered grief. "I would have done anything to keep us together."

Bones raised a brow. "So now you must ask yourself,
do you feel the same way about Charles?"

Spade strode through the front doors of the mansion
the same way he'd entered them yesterday—speaking to
no one and heading straight to one place. This time, it
wasn't upstairs to the bedroom. It was downstairs, past
the basement that was the living quarters of the half-
dozen humans who were permanent residents here, to
the guarded entrance of the cellar. The vampire standing at attention opened the door without a word, letting
Spade into the narrow concrete reinforced hallway that
had only two doors on opposite ends. The walls were
so thick around those two rooms, Spade couldn't hear
a heartbeat to know which one Nathanial was in.

He was in the first one Spade checked, asleep on the
narrow cot. The room was bare of most amenities, as it
was a holding cell for brand-new vampires. A vampire
took anywhere from a few days to a week to master the
overwhelming hunger that would cause him or her to
kill any human around. That was why these rooms were
perfect to hold the shape-shifter. No matter what form

Nathanial might take, he wouldn't be able to breach the walls that had been built to withstand even a rampaging new vampire.

But Nathanial hadn't changed from his normal form. Just in case, though, Spade closed the door behind him. It sealed with automatic locks. He'd need the intercom to inform the guard when to let him out.

"Wake up," he said, giving the man a shake.

Nathanial lunged in a flurry of movement that had Spade pinning him against the wall with his fangs out, fury coursing through him at the attempted sneak attack. But once Nathanial's eyes fully focused on Spade, the strength left his limbs.

"Oh, it's you," Nathanial said, slumping. "You startled me."

Spade shoved Nathanial back on the cot. "Am I to believe that was an accident?" he asked with heavy sarcasm.

Those hazel eyes that were far too similar to Denise's stared up at him. "You don't know what normally happens when someone pounces on me while I'm asleep. I've learned to wake up fighting."

Spade could imagine what. *Package deals*. He still couldn't bring himself to pity the man. Not after what Nathanial had cost Denise—and now him—but it did make Spade enjoy the memory of slaughtering Web's guards more. *No one deserves to live after that*.

"You couldn't be more safe from me when it comes to that," Spade responded. "I'm here to learn everything you know about killing demons."

Nathanial smiled at that, making his face look even more boyish. He must have been quite young when he'd struck that deal with Raum. Twenty? Twenty-one?

"Now there's a subject I like to talk about," Nathanial said with obvious relish. "Just stab one in the eyes with that knife. Instant death."

"What knife? A silver knife?"

The color drained from Nathanial's face. "When you got me, you didn't get the *knife*, too?"

"What. Knife," Spade bit out, his temper already stretched to the breaking point.

Nathanial shot up with a moan, his movements far faster than a human's should be. "How could you not know about the knife? You knew about me! You knew what I was, what the girl was, and how it happened. How could you not know about the fucking knife?"

Spade swatted him almost casually, sending Nathanial crashing back onto the cot. "Don't waste your time railing at me when you should be answering my question."

Nathanial's lip was bleeding where Spade had hit him. He swiped at it immediately, wiping the blood on a blanket, eyeing Spade with tension reeking out of every pore. Then Nathanial let out a short, unamused laugh.

"You're the first vampire in seventy years not to go after my blood. Even the guards, who were forbidden from tasting me, constantly snuck sips. I don't even know how to react to you ignoring it."

"React by telling me about the knife," Spade replied in an icy tone.

"Only weapons made from their own bones can kill a corporeal demon. Because of that, demon bones are almost impossible to come by. If a demon kills another demon, they destroy the bones. But a demon will keep one weapon as defense against other demons. I stole the bone knife from the demon who branded me when

I sent him back to the underworld. Just in case he ever returned."

Spade considered this. His knowledge of demons mostly consisted of information about the noncorporeal ones who possessed humans, so what Nathanial said could be true. But then again, it could be utter shite.

One way to be sure.

Spade grabbed Nathanial, pinning him to the wall. The man struggled with considerable strength considering his heartbeat, but he couldn't break Spade's hold. What he did do was snap his eyes shut at Spade's first move, however.

Clever sod. "I'm not going to hurt you. I only want to be sure what you're telling me is the truth. Open your eyes."

"No," Nathanial gasped. "You could make me do anything."

"For pity's sake, you have nothing I want except your knowledge," Spade replied curtly. "If that wasn't true, why would I bother mesmerizing you? Anything else I'd want, I'm strong enough to take without using my gaze."

Nathanial's pulse thundered like hoofbeats from a stampede and he stank like fear, but slowly his lids fluttered opened. Spade let his power blaze forth, seeking to dominate the will behind those hazel eyes.

The lad was stronger here, too, than Spade would have imagined. Then again, Nathanial would need an iron mental fortitude to endure Web's treatment the past several decades without going insane. Spade pushed that thought aside, because it led to a reluctant admiration that he couldn't afford to feel.

"Open your mind," Spade said, more power flowing from him.

He felt the snap of Nathanial's will as if breaking it had made an audible sound. Then he pushed through the trailing cobwebs of consciousness until he was sure anything he asked Nathanial would be answered with the truth.

"How do you kill a demon?"

Nathanial repeated the same answer as before in a monotone Spade was used to hearing from someone enthralled. The lad hadn't been lying. He must truly not know that revealing such information brought him closer to his own destruction.

"Why do you think I captured you?" Spade asked next, just to be sure.

"To save your girlfriend," Nathanial mumbled. "So I could help her control the power from the marks."

No, Nathanial had no idea what his fate was. Spade pushed back a flicker of remorse. He and Denise might not have a future together, but that didn't mean she couldn't have a future free from the demon's essence. Spade would make sure Denise returned to being human just as she wanted, with her family safe. Through his own fault, Nathanial was the cost of that.

"Who has the knife?" Spade asked, though he had already guessed the answer.

"Web. Keeps it close to him always. Afraid of the demon killing him to get me back."

No doubt Raum would indeed have tried to slaughter Web to regain Nathanial, if he'd known Web had him. But now Spade had him, and Web would know Nathanial would tell him about the knife.

Bloody hell, Web would be *expecting* Spade to try to take the knife. He'd know Spade needed it, just not for the same reasons Web had kept it.

Spade's mouth twisted. Looked like Web would get another chance to kill him, after all.

"You will never try to escape me," Spade said, looking deeply into Nathanial's eyes. "Say it."

"I will never try to escape you," Nathanial repeated dully.

Web had probably forced the same directive in Nathanial. The lad had fought with him as Spade dragged him out of Web's, but no matter. In Spade's case, he wasn't using the command to try and keep Nathanial with him indefinitely, but only a short while. Just until he gave him away to Raum, where, if all went well, he'd also be giving Denise away, too. Surrendering her back to her fragile, lethal humanity that would end up forever separating them.

The knowledge of that rose like bile within him, but he forced it back. *It's what she wants more than anything else. Even me.*

"Right, then. Wake up," Spade said, releasing Nathanial.

The other man blinked and shook his head as if to clear it. "Find out what you needed to know?"

Spade's jaw clenched. "Yes."

And he was staying the course regardless.

Chapter 31

Denise had stayed up, waiting for Spade's return. When she heard the front door slam, she hurried into the hall, hoping to catch Spade before he disappeared into one of the upper rooms. But though she waited, no one came up the stairs.

Maybe he went straight to the study again. Denise went downstairs and checked the room they'd had their fight in, but it was empty. Then she peeked inside the other rooms on the first floor. Nothing. Finally she went to the front of the house again, her heart leaping when she caught movement by the entrance.

As quickly as that optimism shot up, it flatlined when the dark figure in the shadows turned around and Denise saw it was Alten.

Bones was wrong. It was dawn, but Spade hadn't come back, after all.

"Oh, hi, Alten," she said lamely. "I was just…" *Obviously waiting for someone who wasn't going to show up.*

"If you're looking for Spade, he went downstairs," Alten said. "Still looked mad, too. I'd leave him be if I were you."

Just like that, Denise's mood switched again. He'd come back. He might be mad, yes, but Spade was back. Well, mad or no, they were going to talk. They had too many things to work out for Spade to be avoiding her.

"What's downstairs?"

Alten shrugged. "His breakfast."

That's right. This was a vampire household, which meant there was a living buffet beneath them. Maybe feeding would put Spade in a better mood before she talked to him. She could hope.

"Show me," she said, tightening her robe around her.

"I don't think that's a good idea—wait!"

Denise had already turned around and started walking away. She'd find it herself. The house was big, but if it was like every other vampire community home, the basement would be renovated into a cozy mass living area.

"Fine, I'll show you," Alten said, sounding frustrated.

She gave him a sweet smile. "How kind of you."

His look said kindness had nothing to do with it. Denise followed him to the back of the house and down the staircase that led to—she'd guessed it—a plushly redecorated basement. To her surprise, only two humans were on the large sectional couch, watching TV The pool table, computer area, kitchen, and exercise room seemed to be empty.

"Where is everyone?" Unless this was the smallest

vampire entourage she'd come across, several humans were missing.

The boy on the couch looked up. "It's dawn, so they're sleeping. No one usually comes to eat at dawn."

So where was Spade, then? "Where's the vampire who came down here a little bit ago?"

The boy grinned and pointed down a hallway. "Follow the sounds. Kristie's a screamer."

Anger erupted in Denise. Spade couldn't have replaced her with someone else so quickly, could he?

Look what happened the first night Rachel and Ross were "on a break," her inner voice taunted.

Denise growled, raising Alten's eyebrows. She shoved Alten's hand away when he went to grab her arm, shooting him a dangerous look.

"Ready to wrestle me to the ground? Because that's the only way you're stopping me from going down that hallway."

"It's not—"

"Not what?" Denise interrupted Alten. "Not any of my business? I'll be the judge of that!"

Denise stalked down the hall the young man had pointed to, growing even more livid as unmistakable loud groans met her ears. Spade had arrived less than fifteen minutes ago! Bastard!

Something stabbed her in the palms. Denise looked down, not surprised to see those hideous claws had replaced her nails and her fingers were stretching into impossibly long lengths. *His fault.* She curled her hands as best she could without jabbing herself again and then banged on the door the sounds emanated from, fury making her reckless.

"Open this door!"

A few seconds later, the door swung open to reveal Ian, totally naked, very erect, and highly annoyed.

"What the bloody hell is *your* problem?"

Denise could feel the heat scorch across her face. Behind Ian, a naked young woman also gave Denise an aggravated look while Alten let out something that might have been a stifled laugh.

"Um…never mind," Denise stammered, spinning around, hiding her hands, that heat in her cheeks growing even warmer.

Ian slammed the door, muttering something about rude interruptions. The feminine squeals from inside the room resumed almost immediately.

"I tried to tell you that it's not Spade in there," Alten said when Denise came back into the room. He didn't even attempt to hide his grin.

"You could have tried harder," Denise got out, still attempting without success to wipe her mind clean of what she'd seen. "I absolutely never needed to know that Ian was pierced *down there.*"

Alten let out another snicker that was cut off by Spade's voice behind them.

"What are *you* doing here?"

The guard had just let Spade out of Nathanial's cell when Denise's voice drifted down to him. Why was she down here? Was something wrong? Had Raum somehow found her while he was out?

Spade tore up the stairs into the basement just in time to witness Alten laugh. Denise was in front of Alten, red-faced, her hands behind her back.

"What are you doing here?" he demanded, grabbing her by the shoulders and taking in a deep sniff. No scent of the demon on her skin. Some of the red cleared from his vision.

Denise's mouth was open, her eyes wide. Spade forced himself to let go, take a step back, and otherwise not loom over her snarling. Looking at her, so lovely, was more than Spade thought he could bear. Ian's words rang in his head with all the sinful temptation of a snake holding out an apple. *Were I you, I'd change Denise over regardless of her objection...*

He snapped out of that treacherous line of thought when he noticed her hands were still behind her back. It wasn't her normal stance, and her shoulders were twitching like she was moving them.

Spade didn't grab her again; he moved behind her faster than she could whirl away. A curse escaped him when he saw the claws sticking out from her hands even though she tried to hide them.

She'd partially shifted again. *Selfish, foolish bastard*, Spade lashed himself. He should have considered this possibility. Yes, it had maddened him to realize Denise didn't intend for them to have a future together, but he should have stayed. After all, his shredded emotions wouldn't manifest in a horrible physical transformation, like hers could.

"Denise." Spade made his voice calmer than he felt as he continued to curse himself. "I apologize for snapping at you. What did you come down here for?"

Alten began to ease away. Denise flicked her gaze to him as if she wanted to follow him.

"I wanted to talk to you, but maybe we should wait until you've gotten some sleep," she muttered.

Not when waiting might mean another complete transformation for her. Even though being so close to

Denise was like pricking his heart with silver needles, Spade wasn't about to let that happen to her again.

"Tell me now, what was it you wanted to speak with me about?"

Her eyes became shiny and she blinked. "Everything's happening so fast," she almost whispered. "I mean, a month ago, I was still grieving for Randy, and now you've got me thinking about changing into a vampire so we can have countless years together, and I... sometimes, I don't know if I'm ready for what I feel for you."

She was thinking about changing over? Spade couldn't help but stroke her face while every nerve inside him went taut with anxious expectation. *Please, let it be that.* By Christ, he'd apologize on his knees for walking out earlier, if that was the case.

"Ready?" he asked softly, but also with irony. "Life never waits until you're *ready*. I wasn't ready to turn into a vampire, but I did. I wasn't ready to lose someone I loved a long time ago, but it happened. You weren't ready to have your husband murdered, but he was. You certainly weren't ready for a demon to brand you, but he did. And neither of us might be ready for what we feel for each other, but that doesn't make those feelings go away."

Spade leaned closer, his voice lowering. "Here we are, Denise. Ready or not."

She held his gaze, her eyes still shiny. "You're right. I don't care if I'm not ready; I need you. And I think I've come up with a compromise that'll work for both of us—"

Spade couldn't hold back the hunger and desire that slammed through him at hearing Denise say she needed him. His lips crushed over hers, his tongue claiming the dark, heady sweetness of her mouth. Her tongue was like wet, silky fire, stoking his need even further as, after a brief hesitation, she twisted it along his. Spade caught her wrists with one hand, keeping them behind her back. It wasn't out of fear or revulsion over the claws, but because it made her breasts press more fully against his chest.

Denise moaned when his free hand cupped one of those luscious breasts, the silk robe and nightgown he'd left out for her no real barrier against his touch. He caught her nipple between his fingers, already so hard, and gave it a slow, sensual pinch. Denise moaned into his mouth.

Her scent ripened to an addictive lushness with her desire. She seemed to sink into his arms even as she rubbed against him with a purposeful, sultry abandon. He'd been a fool to think he could ever let her go. She'd broken through the barriers he'd erected around his heart, making him feel more than anybody else ever had. Even if a few decades were all he'd have with her, it would have to be enough.

Denise ducked her head, breaking off their kiss, her breath hitting his neck in soft gasps.

"Spade...wait..."

That's right, they were in the basement with two humans gawking at their every move. Spade swept Denise up and walked swiftly out of the room, claiming her mouth in another kiss. Desire made her taste stronger and sweeter at the same time, inflaming him, making him unable to keep from stroking her hip and her breast as he carried her.

Denise made muffled sounds against his mouth

while her temperature seemed to shoot up a few degrees. Her heady scent grew stronger, too, entrancing him. He reached the landing of the first floor when she tore her mouth away with a strength and speed he hadn't expected of her. Something hot, wet, and unbelievably rich swirled down his tongue.

"Spade, I—"

He couldn't help it; he swallowed. His guttural moan made her stop speaking in mid sentence. Her hazel eyes settled on his mouth—and widened. Nothing short of his own death could have stopped Spade from licking his lips, and then hers, to catch the remaining traces of her blood from where she'd moved too quickly and scraped her bottom lip on his fang.

Spade could almost feel the intoxicating ambrosia stealing through his veins. His heart didn't beat, but he'd directed his blood south at their first kiss, circulating it there to keep him hard for her. Denise's blood seemed to race there as well, turning his already-boiling desire into a mindless flat hunger. *Now. All of her,* now.

As his last consideration to propriety, he staggered into the nearest room, not bothering to see if he'd managed to kick the door closed before he fell to the floor on top of her.

Denise's first thought on seeing her blood stain Spade's lips was *Oh shit*. Then the fire that leapt into his gaze and the way he dominated her mouth in his next kiss made her decide that self-preservation was overrated. Sure, she should be screaming to Bones for help, as it was clear Spade had no intention of letting her go until the effects from her blood ran their course. But despite her blood obviously affecting him, Spade hadn't tried to bite her. If Denise screamed for Bones, it would mean Spade would stop what he was doing—and she didn't want him to stop.

His tongue plunged repeatedly into her mouth, twining and twisting with such seductive intensity, Denise soon felt like breathing was overrated, too. Spade's one hand still contained hers behind her back, but the other…oh, the other ran over her body in the most erotic, merciless way, squeezing, stroking, and probing her flesh at all her most sensitive points. He tore away her nightgown and robe with a noise of impatience, his mouth at her breast before Denise could even gasp in air.

"So soft, hard, and hot, all at once," Spade muttered as he tongued her breast. A sudden strong suction at her nipple had her back arching, but even as she reveled in the sensations from that, his hand landed between her legs, palm pressing deeply against her clitoris.

Denise couldn't stop the cry that came out of her mouth. She looked at Spade's shirt in frustration, wanting to feel his skin on hers, not fabric. And his pants… had she ever hated anything as much as she hated his pants at this moment?

"Let me go," Denise gasped, tugging at her hands.

Spade's grip tightened on them. "No." A low growl against her breast that wasn't any less sensual for its refusal.

Of course. Her hands had ugly claws and nightmarish fingers. No wonder Spade didn't want her touching him with them; they were gross *and* dangerous.

Thinking about her hands was a douse of cold water on her ardor. Denise edged back, trying to sit up even though Spade's body was half covering hers.

"Spade, maybe we shouldn't—"

A bolt of pleasure shot through her breast, so sharp and fast, she couldn't breathe. When she did suck in a ragged breath, it ended on a moan as sudden, rapturous heat flamed in her nipple. She didn't have time to process what caused it before her other nipple flamed with the same incredible heat. *What had Spade done to her?*

Denise glanced down and another cry wrenched from her. Drops of blood pearled on her nipples next to two distinct puncture marks. They throbbed with the most astonishing pleasure in accordance with her pulse. Somehow, Spade rubbed between her legs with exactly the same intervals as that throbbing, almost bringing her to orgasm right then.

Even so, a sliver of fear made its way through Denise's haze of bliss. *He'd bitten her.* How much more of her blood could Spade drink before it threw him into a frenzy that would lead to him draining her, possibly even to death?

Spade's mouth was stained red as he rubbed it between her breasts, leaving a faint crimson smear. Then he brought her closer, brushing his lips over hers.

"Kiss me," he ordered in a thick voice.

Denise hesitated, torn between the urge to do just that and her instinctive aversion to tasting her blood on his mouth.

Spade's hand moved from between her legs to pinch her nipple. The blast of heat that followed had her jerking back so hard, her head thunked on the floor. When he did it the second time to her other nipple, she was almost crying from the pleasure.

More. More. Don't care if it kills me, just more.

"Kiss me."

Denise slanted her mouth across Spade's, licking

his lips, tasting their coppery tang, and then running her tongue inside to tangle with his. He made a rough noise of need and slid forward, his hips opening her legs wider, free hand yanking down his pants.

The hard stroke inside her was so sudden, deep, and forceful that Denise bit Spade's tongue in uncontrollable reflex. He groaned, thrusting again just as powerfully, sending a shudder of pleasure through her.

"So hot...*so good*."

His growl in her ear made her shiver with its vehemence. She arched her hips in anticipation of his next thrust—and felt his tongue flicking between her legs instead.

Her eyes flew open in shock that Spade had slid down her body before she'd even noticed. Now her thighs cradled his head instead of his hips, his black hair covering his face as he laved her with firm, impossibly fast strokes.

"I don't know what's more addictive, your blood or your honey here," his rough voice mused before another deep lick had her twisting in ecstasy.

Then a long, hard thrust made her cry out in the next heartbeat, Spade filling her so deeply, she choked back a sob. Another spine-bending stroke, then another, and then—

His mouth captured her below again, tongue lashing her flesh with the same hungry, sweet frenzy. Before she could cry out her passion, his hard flesh replaced his tongue, making her shudder at the powerful thrusts cleaving inside her.

Denise realized Spade had let go of her hands only when she found herself not knowing from one moment to the next if she'd be clutching his head or his hips.

He moved in a blink, seamlessly alternating between taking her with his mouth or with those deep, mind-blowing thrusts. Her breasts throbbed while her loins twisted with the varying sensations bombarding them.

Spade reared up onto his knees, pulling her with him, hands closing over her hips to hold her upright as he began to thrust so fast, so forcefully, that tears spilled out of her eyes. Still, Denise wanted more. She couldn't get enough of the wildness in him, how tightly he held her, or how his moans grew louder and more urgent. Her breasts bounced against his chest with every fervent, rapid stroke, nipples flaming from the friction of his shirt on the punctures. She was so close to coming. So close...

Fangs sank into her neck in the next instant. Before she could even be afraid, heat burst within her loins like a bomb going off, rocking her in wave after wave of ecstasy. Those spasms controlled her, made her oblivious to everything but the squeezing, throbbing sensations cascading from her center, filling her body with ripple after ripple of bliss. She didn't know if Spade still drank from her, and she didn't care. *If this is dying*, Denise thought, *I highly recommend it.*

Chapter 32

Don't swallow. Don't swallow.

Spade chanted it in his mind each time he bit Denise, stemming her bleeding from the shallow punctures with a pinch of his fingers. The pressure forced the juice from his fangs deeper into her, increasing the pleasurable heat, until she was unaware of him wiping her blood off his mouth instead of swallowing it.

Even still, his first ingestion when she cut her lip left him feeling drunk, causing him to take her harder than he had previously—and how she responded further shredded his control. He'd never been so aroused by a woman, never lost himself so much as he did when he was inside Denise. She took away his will and replaced it with raging need, turning him from a controlled sexual connoisseur into a feverish greenhorn who could barely hold his seed. Spade climaxed right after she did, with a roar of satisfaction.

He rolled over to lie on his back, Denise half draped across his chest. She was gasping, her beautiful body flushed, fingers almost absently stroking her nipple. Midway through their lovemaking, her hands had changed back, smooth skin and bitten nails replacing those talons and sharp claws.

"Now, tell me about your compromise," he said, knowing he'd agree no matter what it was.

"Give me a minute," Denise replied, still out of breath.

Spade let out a short laugh. "Take your time. I'm not going anywhere." And he wasn't. No matter how it might hurt later.

Her soft, warm hands touched his chest. "What do you—hey! My hands are back to normal. Lucky you; I'd probably have ripped up your back otherwise."

He took one of her hands and kissed it. "It would have been worth it."

She smiled, then her expression became serious. "When you walked out before, it *was* just because of our life spans being so out of whack once I get these brands off? Not that you have a problem with me being a different species than you?"

He could answer her question, but Spade knew another way to make Denise understand.

"I was in love in the eighteen hundreds. Giselda loved me, too, but she didn't want to become a vampire. I thought with time, she'd change her mind. A year into our relationship, my sire needed me and I had to leave. But when the time drew near for my return, Giselda sent a message that she'd meet me at my home. On her way, she was stranded with her driver. They weren't there long before the deserters came."

Spade paused, that old grief and rage still rippling through him at the memory. Denise curled her hand around his.

"Tell me the rest, Spade."

He pulled her to him, steadied by her nearness. "Giselda ran, trying to lose them in the forest, but they were faster. All five of them beat, raped, and sodomized her. Despite such a brutal assault, Giselda kept her wits about her. She pretended to be dead until she thought they'd gone. Then she dragged herself up and began to walk in the direction of my home. But the former captain came back to retrieve the sword he'd forgotten before in his haste to remove his trousers. He followed the trail of blood in the snow, and when he found Giselda, he cut her throat so deeply, he almost took her head off. Then he threw her body down a ravine. That's where I found her. She was so covered in blood, I didn't even recognize her at first glance."

Denise took in a slow breath. "And just yesterday, Web held a knife to my throat. Oh God, the memories that must have caused you—"

"Yes," Spade said tightly.

Her hands were warm balms on his shoulders. "You've leaving something out. Giselda wouldn't have been alive to tell you those kinds of details."

Spade's gaze didn't waver from hers. "We learned them after Crispin and I captured the bastards and forced them to describe everything they'd done to her."

Giselda had been avenged to the fullest, but as Denise would know all too well, revenge didn't take away the pain.

Spade touched her face. If this was his chance to make her understand, he wouldn't hold anything back.

"I managed to get through Giselda's death, but I wouldn't make it if I had to suffer through yours."

Her eyes brightened with tears. "As I said, I don't want to lose you, either. What if…I stayed human, but I didn't age and I was harder to kill?"

Only one thing could be responsible for such a state, but he had to be sure. "You'd be willing to drink my blood?"

His voice was calm, belying his raging emotions. Denise nodded, reaching out to touch his neck with a light stroke.

"Yes."

Spade couldn't help it—he clutched her to him, relief pouring through his veins in an almost tangible sensation. If Denise drank from him every day, even a small amount, it would be enough to extend her life indefinitely. She could still be killed with more ease than a vampire, but with his blood, she could also be raised as a ghoul, were she to meet an untimely end…

"Does this mean we're good?" Denise managed breathily.

He set her back, his relief turning to joy. "Yes. And I'm incredibly in love with you."

She heard those words as if they echoed all through her. *In love with you, in love with you, in love with you.* Happiness as she never thought she'd feel again swept over her, making Denise smile even as Spade's face became blurry through her tears.

"I love you, too," she whispered.

Her breath caught as Spade crushed her to him, rising and twirling her in a circle until her legs twining crazily. Denise laughed even though she could hardly breathe from his tight, possessive embrace.

"I never thought I'd feel this way again," he whispered in her ear. "Oh, darling, I feel like you've brought me back to life."

His words were so reminiscent of how she felt that she choked back a sob. She'd felt that terrible, deadening emptiness for only fifteen months. How had Spade stood it, feeling it for almost a hundred and fifty years?

Guilt wormed its way inside her immediately after that thought. Shouldn't it have taken her longer to love someone again? It had for Spade. Was she a bad person to feel this way so soon?

Spade set her back on her feet, gently smoothing her hair away from her face. "You'll always love him," he said, as if he'd read her mind. "That doesn't die just because he did, or because you now love me. Your love for him is part of who you are. It's a beautiful part, Denise. Don't be sad of it, and I will never be jealous of it."

Denise's eyes overflowed again. Spade was right. Randy and Giselda had made them who they were. Now they would leave the horror of their deaths behind, and, moving on, take only the best parts of them into the future...

"I want you to know if it was possible for me to change back to human, and that's what you asked of me, I would," Spade whispered. "There isn't anything I wouldn't do to be with you, Denise. I'm sorry I can't give you the normal life you wanted, but I promise to adore you every day for the rest of your new one."

"I love you," Denise choked, smiling when he kissed her with a passion and hunger that bent her spine back.

Three hard, loud bangs, followed by a bellow of

"Open this door!" had her jumping in the next second, startled.

"What the hell?" Spade muttered, letting her go to fling the door open with a scowl.

Ian stood on the other side.

"What is wrong with you, banging on like that?" Spade demanded.

Ian cast a wicked look at Spade, who wore only his shirt, and then one at Denise as she hastily closed her robe.

"Paybacks," Ian said succinctly. Then he walked away, whistling.

Spade watched Denise clear her plate, closing her eyes as she scraped off the last bite of banana cream pie. She had such a look of bliss on her face as she swallowed, Spade made a mental note to take a large slice upstairs with them later. And then spread it across his skin.

Crispin glanced up from his computer. "Mencheres is here."

Spade rose, not sensing him yet, but trusting that Crispin was correct. Since Mencheres had shared his power with Crispin almost a year and a half ago, his friend could feel the other vampire much sooner than anyone else.

After another minute or so, Spade felt the first sweep of energy in the air, faint at first, but distinctive, as Mencheres's power reached out and found him. Something inside Spade clicked, a form of acknowledgment he'd recognize anywhere, even if he were among thousands of vampires. It grew stronger as Mencheres neared, until Spade could sense the other vampire's emotions as well as the swirling, electrifying aura that distinguished Mencheres as one of the most powerful vampires in existence.

Such was the tie between Spade and Mencheres, the vampire who sired him.

Spade opened the door himself. In another minute, a silver Aston Martin rounded the corner of the driveway. When it stopped at the house, a black-haired Egyptian vampire climbed out with a grace that was impressive even for the undead.

"Spade," Mencheres said, a smile creasing features that looked younger than Spade's were, even though Mencheres was well over four thousand. "I can see you are happy again. I'm glad."

Spade enfolded Mencheres into an embrace, used to the sizzling vibration such close contact elicited. His sire always felt like a walking lightning bolt.

"I'm very happy," Spade replied, wishing the same for Mencheres. But sadness emanated from his sire, darkening his features with more melancholy than anyone who looked like he was in his early twenties should carry.

Denise hung back in the doorway. She'd been nervous about seeing Mencheres again. The last time had been that fateful New Year's Eve, but Spade needed his sire if he wanted to get the demon-bone knife with the least amount of danger.

"Hi," Denise said, looking so outwardly calm that if Mencheres couldn't scent her unease—or read her mind—he'd never know of it.

"How lovely to see you again, Denise," Mencheres greeted her, bowing.

Crispin welcomed his co-ruler more coolly than

Spade had. He still hadn't entirely forgiven Mencheres for his secrecy with Cat last year, but Crispin also knew how necessary Mencheres's presence was. Web would be expecting an attack, so he'd be prepared, but even Web's best defenses couldn't stop Mencheres's powers. The mega-Master vampire could freeze dozens of vampires into complete immobility with his telekinesis. With Mencheres's help, Spade could stroll up and take the knife from Web without the other vampire even being able to blink to stop him. The only reason Spade hadn't brought Mencheres on the raid to get Nathanial was that there wasn't time for his sire to arrive.

However, once proper hellos were exchanged and all of them were seated in the dining room, except for Fabian, who floated, Mencheres stunned him.

"I received a call from Web earlier," his sire stated. "He wondered if I knew the vampire I sired and my co-ruler had raided his home to steal his property. When I suggested that Web complain to the Law Guardians if he had an issue, he bade me to give you a message, Spade."

Denise's face paled, but Spade didn't let any of his emotions show. "And that message is?"

"Web said, 'I know what she is and what you want, so I propose a trade.'" Mencheres replied, his charcoal gaze flicking to Denise in interest.

Spade ground out a curse even as Crispin muttered, "How the hell did he find out? We sank the boat so none of her blood could be retrieved."

Spade replayed that awful moment in his mind when Web attacked the boat. He'd held Denise in front of him, but her gloves were on, so Web couldn't have seen the demon's brands. Then he'd stabbed her in the stomach, but Web hadn't put his bloody hand to his mouth—unless he did that later?

"He must have seen my hands," Denise said quietly. "They were changed when I grabbed his arm."

"That's right," Spade breathed, remembering the claws ripping through her gloves and the gouges she'd dug into Web's arms. "After holding Nathanial so long, he'd know what had caused that change in you."

Mencheres raised an inquiring black brow. "Am I to be let in on the secret?"

"Not here," Spade said, with a meaningful jerk of his head indicating the rest of the house. Everyone at this table knew what was in Denise's blood and all its effects, but that was as far as Spade wanted the information spread.

Though now Web knew, too. Spade stifled another curse. Whom had he told? Were there others, even now, gunning for the chance to snatch Denise away for their own sordid Red Dragon trade?

He could only hope Web's greed would keep him silent on the subject. After all, Web hadn't wanted to share news of what Nathanial was with others. Perhaps he still sought to corner the Red Dragon market by not revealing the other source of the drug.

Either way, there was no possibility Spade could let him live. Even after Denise got the brands off, Web might still pursue her in the hope that her blood was still somehow a drug. And if Web was successful in taking Denise and then realized her blood was normal…he'd have no reason to let her live.

A wooden hunk snapped off the table in front of him. Spade glanced down, realizing he'd unconsciously gripped the edge until it broke.

"Apologies," he said, though he couldn't care less about the table. "Did Web leave a number for me to ring him at?"

"He did," Mencheres replied. "You're going to call him?"

"Yes I am. Right now."

Mencheres raised his shoulder in an elegant half shrug, then punched a series of numbers into his mobile, holding it out to Spade when he was finished. At the second ring, Web's voice flowed over the line.

"Have you relayed my message to Spade?"

"He has," Spade said tightly. "What sort of trade do you propose?"

Web let out a false, pleasant laugh. "Spade, I must say, you surprise me. Killing my associate in Vegas. Murdering my guards. Stealing my property, all to take the source of my business from me—when you already *had* a source. If I'd realized you were so unscrupulous, greedy, and enterprising, I might have gotten to know you before this."

"I'm also impatient," Spade stated in a cold voice, "so get to your offer for a trade."

"Give me the girl, and you can have the knife. You'll still own half of the Red Dragon trade through Nathanial, which should be more than enough for you."

Spade swallowed back the murderous rage that made him want to list all the terrible ways he was going to kill Web into the other line. Instead, he forced his voice to remain cold and steady.

"I rather like the girl. What about trading Nathanial for the knife instead?"

Web laughed. "Because without the knife, Nathanial is a liability, as you must know by now. I don't know how the girl came by her marks, but Nathanial's demon, should he ever return, will seek him out with all the vengeance of hell. And we both know the girl's worth more than Nathanial. I'm being generous allowing you to keep what you stole from me, but if you don't give me something in return…well, I'll have nothing to lose by pursuing you all over the earth, will I?"

Spade was silent for a long moment, staring at Denise, who knew enough from hearing his side of the conversation for her to look sick.

"Fine," he said, holding out a hand when Denise gasped. "Where do you want to meet?"

"Right here in Monaco, of course," Web replied at once. "The Fontvieille pier. I'm sure you'll remember where it is."

The pier Web had under surveillance. Spade's jaw clenched. He would be walking into a trap where Web had home court advantage. His gaze flicked to Mencheres. *But I have a trap of my own.*

"Fine, then. Tomorrow at midnight."

"Looking forward to it," Web said lightly. "Oh, but you must understand that if I hear Mencheres is anywhere near Monaco, I'm going to assume you intend to double-cross me and our trade is off. And the hunt is on."

"You can't expect me to show up without protection," Spade snapped. "Come now. I'm a businessman, not a stupid one."

Web made a noise of exaggerated patience. "Fine. Bring your little firestarter friend, if it makes you feel better—though she had some trouble with that the other day, didn't she? Maybe the tales I've heard about her powers were exaggerated."

"Crispin would never allow his wife to go without him. You must know that, so your offer to have Cat come isn't real," Spade said, his tone hardening. "In that case, I assume your offer to trade the girl for the knife isn't real, either, so we have nothing else to say. Hunt me as much as you like."

"Wait!" Web shouted, just as Spade was about to snap his mobile shut. "Fine, bring the bounty hunter, too," Web said, sounding put out. "But only the two of them and the girl, or I'll think the worst."

Web must have a large amount of force at the ready, to agree so readily to both Cat and Crispin coming with him.

"A driver and Nathanial, too," Spade stated. "Else how will I know you've brought the right knife and not something you picked up at a hunting outfitter?"

Web let out another low laugh. "Smart and ruthless. We might have a very beneficial partnership ahead of us. Oh, and your driver has to be human. Can't let you sneak in another strong vampire, can I?"

Clever bastard. "Until tomorrow night."

He clicked the mobile shut, silently looking at the faces around the table. Everyone but Denise had heard the other end of the conversation. Mencheres looked grim.

"Why would you agree for me not to come, Spade? You know he intends to kill you, and he'll know if I'm near. Web has spies all over Monaco."

Spade stared at Mencheres. Then slowly, his gaze swung to Cat, the former half-breed who was now the only vampire in existence who derived sustenance from drinking nosferatu blood instead of human.

"Because your power will be there, Mencheres, even if you won't be."

Chapter 33

The SUV pulled into Fontvieille harbor, stacks of glamorous hotels behind them and luxury boats in front. The lights along the harbor were dark, however, the only consideration to the many hotel windows that would have a view of the parking lot. Since Denise could hardly see and she was down here, the cloak of darkness would be sufficient for concealing whatever would take place in the next few minutes from any high-rise onlookers.

Spade glanced back at her from his place in the passenger seat. He said nothing, but his face spoke volumes. Denise forced herself to smile. Spade shouldn't spend any of his energy worrying about her. He, Bones, and Cat had enough to deal with trying to stay alive tonight.

And once again, she'd be sequestered safely while

that was happening. Denise was *so sick* of being the person her loved ones fought for, instead of facing the danger herself. If she could have traded places with Spade, Cat, or Bones, she would have done it in a heartbeat. But of course, none of them would let her.

That will change, Denise promised herself. She knew the world she was committing herself to, so she'd learn the best way to live in it. It meant toughening up, but she was ready. In fact, though she hadn't told Spade, she wasn't ruling out becoming a vampire one day. Drinking Spade's blood on a regular basis would be her trial run. She wasn't the same person she'd been before, willing to wait on the sidelines. Or in the basement.

But first they all had to survive tonight.

Denise glanced at Cat. Her friend looked rattled, not that Denise blamed her. All their hopes for victory hinged on an ability Cat didn't fully know how to operate. Bones and Spade were confident that when the moment came, she would rise to it. Denise both feared and envied Cat for that awesome responsibility. When had Denise ever been the person trusted to lay it all on the line for those depending on her?

"All right," Spade said quietly. "Let's do this."

Oliver, the human driver for this event, stayed behind the wheel, keeping the SUV running, but Denise, Spade, Cat, Bones, and Nathanial got out. Denise looked around, not sensing the other vampires that she knew were there. Web's people. They were probably hidden behind every shadow.

The spot on Denise's palm itched even though the small wound healed after Spade rubbed his blood over it. Nothing was visible on the outside, but inside her palm was a minuscule transmitter capsule. Nathanial had one implanted in the same place, too. *Just in case we're separated, so Mencheres can track you*, Spade had said.

Denise knew the harsher reason behind the transmitter, even though Spade didn't say it. *In case Web wins and the rest of us are killed.* Web wouldn't kill her or Nathanial; they were too valuable. But she and Nathanial were the only ones Web intended to survive this evening.

She thought she'd throw up.

Spade's face cleared of all expression as he took her arm in one hand and Nathanial's in the other. Her relative hadn't spoken at all, either on the plane ride to Monaco or the car ride to the harbor. Denise knew Nathanial had been apprised of his role tonight, but she wondered at his silence. Was he afraid of being captured again by Web? She certainly would be, if she were he, though what she intended for Nathanial was so much worse than that…

Denise reminded herself that she had nothing to do with Nathanial making the bargain with Raum in the first place, but the rationalization felt hollow. She glanced at the tattoos covering the brands on her skin. If only there was another way to remove them.

Her attention was snapped away from that when Web appeared on the end of a pier. He must have been there the whole time; that was where Spade had been walking, but not until she was on the pier did she notice him. Web's tousled sandy hair was visible in the darkness, but those scary cobalt eyes were still too shadowed for her to see.

"Good evening," Web called out, as if this were a social call. Then he spoke into his phone. "Are we good, Vick?"

Denise didn't hear the reply, but when Web's casual stance relaxed even more, she could guess what it was. Yes, only the six of them had come to Monaco, just as agreed, which must be what Web's spies relayed to him.

"Don't you trust me?" Spade asked, a hint of amusement in his tone.

Denise didn't know how Spade could sound so coolly unaffected. She was almost quaking at the circumstances, and she was the safest person on the pier aside from Nathanial.

"Just being cautious," Web replied lightly. "You were a bit rude during our last encounter."

Spade chuckled at that, letting go of Denise's arm. "I'm sure you'd have acted the same way, were you me."

Now Denise was close enough to see the gleam in Web's eyes. "Very true."

She'd known it, of course, but seeing Web's eyes flick behind them with false nonchalance hammered home that this was a trap. Web had no intention of letting Spade, Bones, or Cat walk off this pier. Her heart started to beat faster. *What if this didn't work?*

"You see I've brought the girl," Spade said, not looking away from Web. "Now, show me the knife."

Web pulled out a thin black case from his jacket, similar to a jewelry box for a bracelet. Denise blinked. Was the knife really that small?

Web opened the box, revealing a pale blade that was all the same cream-colored substance from sharp tip to thicker etched handle. Demon bone.

"Slide it over," Spade commanded. "And then I'll send you the girl."

Web didn't argue, which made Denise even more nervous. They must really be surrounded for him to feel so confident. He closed the box and then slid it along the pier, watching them with a glinting smile.

Nathanial went and picked it up, taking the knife out and holding it up in the moonlight. He nodded.

"This is it."

"And now the girl," Web said silkily.

Denise cast one last look at Spade before she walked forward, slowly. Web's eyes slid over her in a way that felt like footsteps on her grave. *Package deals. Blood selling.* His plans for her would make her life a living hell, if he succeeded tonight.

Denise was almost within Web's reach when the smile slipped from his face. A hiss came out of him and his eyes turned green.

"What is this?" Web grated out. His hand slowly lifted from his side as if being pulled on by a great weight.

Behind her, Denise heard Cat grunt. She glanced back, seeing Cat's hands extended outward and green blazing from her eyes.

"Mencheres sends his regards," Cat growled.

"Run!" Spade snapped to Denise, drawing several knives from his sleeves.

Shouts erupted from the dark, and the empty-looking harbor was suddenly awash with movement. Denise grabbed Nathanial's arm and they ran down the pier, almost colliding with a vampire who appeared as if out of nowhere. When the vampire went to grab her, though, his reach slowed, like he was moving under water. Before he could touch her, Bones hacked a silver knife through his heart.

"Go," Bones ordered.

Several more vampires tried to stop her, but they swayed almost drunkenly, as if they'd lost coordination in their limbs. She and Nathanial managed to duck under their grasping arms and kept going, toward the parking lot and the SUV.

"Hurry," Cat called out, her voice sounding strained. "I can't hold them much longer."

Oliver appeared, running toward them, slashing and hacking with gruesome efficiency at every vampire he came across. With their movements reduced to that of a sluggish human and Oliver hyped up on vampire blood, Web's people were almost helpless.

"Quickly," Oliver said. The three of them ran to the parking lot, jumping into the SUV and speeding off before Denise caught her breath.

Web struggled to pull out a knife as Spade approached, but he couldn't move his hands to his jacket in time. *By Christ, she did it*, Spade thought. Cat hadn't absorbed Mencheres's power to immobilize people, or she didn't have time to learn to wield it like his sire did, but she'd gained enough from drinking Mencheres's blood to reduce Web and his men to slower than human speed. Thankfully, she'd managed to deflect it away from him, Crispin, Nathanial, Alten, and Denise, which had been their biggest concern. If none of them could move, the power would be useless. But with only Web's people affected, no matter how many of them there were, they didn't stand a chance.

He'd almost feel sorry about killing them when they were so hampered, except for what they'd intended with Denise.

Spade looked into Web's eyes as he held his knife to the other vampire's chest. And smiled.

"You will never use her," Spade said before ramming the knife into Web's chest. No Kevlar hindered its path as it sank to the hilt. Web truly had expected his trap to be sufficient.

"Don't," Web whispered.

Spade ignored that. With two hard jerks, he twisted the knife, shredding Web's heart. When he yanked it out, Web was lifeless on the pier, his skin starting to shrivel in the way that all vampires did once they experienced true death.

Cat was on her knees, her hands extended out, waves of Mencheres's borrowed power emanating from her to cast a net around the harbor. Her bright green gaze met Spade's.

"Hurry. I can't hold them much longer," she said.

Spade looked behind her, seeing Oliver, Denise, and Nathanial jumping into the SUV. Relief coursed through him. Oliver would take them out of the city, where Mencheres and Ian waited on the outskirts. Denise would be safe.

Spade joined Crispin to move lethally through Web's people, cutting them down with precise, swift slashes of his blade. He showed no mercy. Each vampire of Web's was a threat to Denise, if Web had revealed what was in her blood. Nathanial's words rang in his mind. *You don't know what normally happens when someone pounces on me while I'm asleep... Even the guards, who were forbidden from tasting me, constantly snuck sips.* That's what these vampires would have done to Denise. *All* of them deserved to die for it.

With a loud cry, Cat's power over the vampires

snapped. Roars of rage tore through the harbor as Web's remaining men fought back with all the speed and power of their vampire heritage. Spade's hands tightened on his knives as he released his own roar of rage into the night.

He didn't care if they were still outnumbered, he wasn't going to run. Let them try to take him down. He wouldn't stop fighting until all of them were dead.

Oliver drove at speeds that would have normally frightened Denise, but she said nothing. Master vampires could run better than sixty miles an hour. Some could fly that fast—or faster. Oliver had reason for hammering the pedal down on the accelerator.

"I think he killed him," Nathanial murmured. A smile lit his face, making him look heartbreakingly young, even though Denise knew he had to be decades older than she. "I think the fucker's finally dead!"

"I'm sure he did kill Web," she said, remembering the expression on Spade's face as he'd approached the other vampire. Denise repressed a shiver. If she ever saw that look on someone's face, she'd know death would soon follow.

"I've hated vampires for more than seventy years, but I love a few of them tonight," Nathanial said. His voice held such a savage satisfaction that it vibrated. "I hope he kills them all. Every last fucking one of them."

Denise didn't say anything stupid like, *Was it really that bad when Web had you?* Of course it was. If nothing else, at least Nathanial could feel avenged tonight.

But she couldn't help but ask one thing. "Why did you do it? Why did you make that deal with Raum?"

Oliver gave her a censuring glare in the rearview

mirror. "You shouldn't talk to him," he muttered. "Spade said he didn't want you to."

Nathanial stared at her, his face paling. "What did you say?"

"Why did you make that deal?" Denise repeated, ignoring what Oliver said about not talking to him.

Nathanial still stared at her like she'd somehow sprouted horns and a tail. His mouth opened and closed several times before he managed to speak.

"You know his name. I never told anyone the demon's name. *How do you know his name?*"

"Don't talk to her," Oliver all but growled from the front seat.

Denise drew in a deep breath, meeting Nathanial's shocked hazel gaze. As she stared, she could almost see the knowledge forming in his eyes. Could almost feel the horror emanating from him as he pieced together the answer to his question.

"He sent you after me," Nathanial whispered. "That's why your boyfriend stole me from Web's. Not to help you control the power in your brands, but to return me to *him*."

Chapter 34

The sound that came out of Nathanial's throat would haunt her. It was a cross between a sob and the most despairing laugh Denise had ever heard.

"I should have known," Nathanial said, still making that awful, keening cackle. "They never let me around you, which I thought was odd since I was supposed to be there to help you. Then they never asked me to tell you about the tricks I'd learned to stop the change, in addition to keeping the baser urges under control. There are meditations, certain herbs you steep together to drink... but none of that matters now, does it?"

Oliver slowed down enough to laser a glare on Nathanial. "Do *not* speak to her again," he said.

"Stop it!" Denise cried out. "Let him speak."

"Spade doesn't—"

"I know Spade doesn't want me talking to him," Denise interrupted. "But even condemned prisoners get to have their last words."

Then she gave Nathanial a steady look. "You never answered my question. Why did you do it? Do you have any idea what your decision ended up costing me? Raum *murdered* I don't know how many members of my family looking for you. He threatened to kill the few that were left and *branded* me to force me to find you. You deserve to talk, but I deserve to know why."

"I don't have a good reason. I was a dirt-poor farmer in the eighteen sixties who stumbled onto the occult after a feverish priest stayed at my home. While he was raving, he talked about demons. It didn't scare me; it fascinated me. I'd always dreamed of being more than I was, and the priest unwittingly gave me the tools to do that. When he got better, I tricked him into believing I wanted to aid his work, but I really sought to learn how to summon and trap a demon instead."

Nathanial paused and sighed. "I was nineteen. Young, stupid, and arrogant. After I summoned Raum and bargained for long life and power, I sent him back to where he came from. I thought no one would be hurt. But then I found out I couldn't control the effects of his brands. I'd wanted to be powerful, but I didn't want to change into monsters from my nightmares. I found the priest I'd deceived and begged him for help. Together we learned how to curb the triggers to transformation and how to control what I changed into, when that still wasn't enough. When he died, he left instructions for other priests to help me. It was one of them who told me about vampires, and how a vampire demonologist might be able to mute my brands in case Raum ever returned. I got the tattoos and I thought… I might be able to live a semi-normal life then. But the vampire who took me to the demonologists knew my blood was different. And after I got the tattoos, he sold me to Web."

"You bargained your soul to a demon," Oliver said without pity. "You deserve what you have coming to you."

"I know I deserve it!" Nathanial shouted. "You don't know how many times I've wished I could turn back the clock so I never made that bargain, but I did. All through the past seventy years with Web, through every awful, degrading thing that they did to me, the only thing that kept me sane was knowing it could always be worse." His voice broke with pain. "And now it will be, and I know it's no more than I deserve, but that doesn't make me any less afraid."

Denise thought of her murdered cousins and aunts, her parents, and Raum's howling threats that he'd kill the rest of her family if she didn't return the man sitting across the seat from her. Then she thought of Randy's brave smile before he went out that basement door, and the guilt and cowardice that had filled her ever since.

"If you could have anything you wanted, what would it be?" she asked Nathanial quietly.

"That's easy." His voice was a rasp. "I want to live without being afraid or used or ashamed. I want a second chance."

Denise closed her eyes briefly. When she opened them, she knew what she had to do.

"Oliver, pull over for a second," she said.

He gave her a measured glare. "I'm not letting him go, no matter what you say."

"I know," Denise replied. "I just want you to stop for a moment. I promise, I won't ask you to let him go."

Oliver gave her a wary look, but pulled over to the side. Nathanial let out a weary grunt.

"Don't worry. I couldn't make a run for it even if I wanted to—and believe me, I *want* to. But Spade must've done something to me when he tranced me. I can't make myself even grab the door handle to open it."

"Good," Oliver said shortly, glancing around before putting the car in park. He met Denise's gaze in the rear-view mirror. "It looks safe enough here for the moment, what do you want?"

Denise took a deep breath. "I'm sorry."

And then she whipped up the gun Spade had left for her in the backseat and smashed the butt of it against Oliver's head.

Spade prowled the docks, looking for any more of Web's people. The scent of death hung in the air, sharpened with the harsher aroma of undead blood. Spade savored it. It was the scent of Denise's safety.

The fighting had been brutal, but now most of Web's people were dead. A few had managed to run off completely. Cat and Crispin were busy stacking the bodies into one of the larger boats, where an explosion would give them a modern version of a Viking funeral. In Spade's opinion, it was more dignified than they deserved, but they couldn't leave them out in the open as they were for humans to find. Flames would burn off any paranormal evidence in their blood, leaving only a strange cache of charred corpses with varying ages in the boat to be found, no supernatural traces left behind. As for Web's monitors on the docks...they'd been found and destroyed.

Crispin already had to green-eye a few humans to forget the slaughter they'd stumbled onto. When the police didn't show up, Spade suspected Web had warned them away from the docks earlier. Web wouldn't have made Monaco his home without having an in with the local human authorities.

Spade felt a grim satisfaction as a search of the harbor and surrounding grounds of the hotels turned up no more vampires. As to the few that got away, he'd find them. They had no Master of their line to protect them now. It wouldn't take him long to track them, especially not with the bounty he intended to put out on them—preferably delivered dead instead of undead.

"Spade!"

His head jerked around as he recognized Oliver's voice, fear slithering up his spine. He wasn't supposed to be here. He was supposed to take Denise and Nathanial to Mencheres and *stay with them* until Spade rejoined them later.

Spade flew in the direction of Oliver's voice, seeing the other man had just reached the docks. On foot.

"Where's Denise?" he demanded, dropping out of the sky to grab Oliver. *"Why isn't she with you?"*

"She knocked me out," Oliver said thickly. "She'd been talking to Nathanial, and then she just clubbed me. I didn't even see her raise the gun, she was so fast. When I came to, she'd already gone. I searched for her, but I didn't find the SUV. I don't know how long I was out…"

Spade threw back his head and roared with pain. There was only one reason Denise would have done such a thing.

She was going after the demon herself.

* * *

"I don't think this is going to work," Nathanial muttered.

Denise threw him a quelling glare. Her palm still burned from where she'd cut the transmitter out after dumping Oliver's unconscious body on the shoulder of the road. That blow to the head wouldn't take too long to heal, with the vampire blood he'd drunk earlier. She'd cut Nathanial's transmitter out, too. She couldn't go through all this just for Mencheres to track them and stop her.

"You remember what the alternative is, right? If you like your soul and want to keep it awhile longer, you'll quit saying this isn't going to work and start brainstorming ways it *will*."

"Raum is an ancient, powerful demon. You're just a human. How do you think you can outfight Raum enough to stab him in the eyes? Call your boyfriend. He has a better chance of defeating Raum."

"If I do that, I may as well shoot you with this gun. It would be more merciful."

"You could shoot me all you want, it won't kill me," Nathanial said bleakly. "If it were that easy for me to die, I wouldn't be here. I tried every way to kill myself over the years. Hung myself. Shot myself. Stabbed myself. Jumped off a cliff. Blew myself up. Even had someone cut my head off—"

"No," Denise gasped. "You did *not* survive all that."

Nathanial gave her a weary, jaded look. "You don't get what these brands are, do you? If they'd let me speak to you before, I could have told you. They're extensions of Raum's power. *All* his power, including his regenerative power. So just like nothing but that bone knife can kill a demon, nothing but that bone knife can kill someone *branded* by a demon. Took me a while to figure that out, but by then, Thomas convinced me not to use the knife on myself."

"Who's Thomas?"

"Was. Thomas was the priest I tricked who later helped me."

Denise cast another glance at him while she drove. "You didn't really survive your head getting cut off, did you?"

"You know how vampires regrow a limb right away after it's cut off?" Nathanial made a slicing gesture across his throat. "New head, same look, within an hour. Made the person who decapitated me shit himself before he fainted."

Denise remembered Raum taunting her the day he'd branded her that she was now beyond mortal death. She didn't realize how *far* beyond he'd meant.

"But I bled when Web stabbed me. Spade had to heal me."

"Of course you bled. But he didn't have to heal you. You'd have healed soon enough on your own. Might have taken a day. You haven't been branded that long, you said. The longer you have the demon essence in you, the faster you'll heal."

This was all so hard to take in—and frightening. If she was successful, she'd be branded for the rest of her life…and that life might last longer than she could even conceive of.

Or it might end before the sun rose.

"We need Spade if you're going to try to kill Raum," Nathanial said for the tenth time.

Denise snapped out a reply without looking away

from the road. "Don't you get it? Spade won't risk my life for your soul. He'll offer you up to Raum in a heartbeat. I can't get him involved."

Nathanial was silent for a long moment. "Why are you doing this for me? Taking on a demon when you could just hand me over and get back to your life?"

She let out a long breath. Because she couldn't live with herself if she gave him over to the demon, knowing what would happen. Because she'd made up her mind that she was not the same person who'd stayed below in the basement that fateful New Year's Eve. It was time for her to stand tough. To face the monsters, instead of letting others fight them for her.

"You said you wanted a second chance? Well, Nathanial, so do I."

Chapter 35

Denise stood under the pier, the sand ending in waves a few feet behind her. The SUV had just sunk beneath the dark waters, filling quickly with all its windows rolled down and the doors open. Denise raised the gun, aiming it at Nathanial. She'd never shot anyone before in her life, but that was about to change.

"Are you sure this is necessary?"

Nathanial let out an impatient sigh. "You're determined to fight Raum on your own, so you'll need the element of surprise. If you summon him and I'm standing here calmly waiting for my doom, he'll be suspicious. You'll lose your element of surprise—and Denise, even with the element of surprise, and shifting into whatever you think is strong enough to beat a demon, your chances aren't that great."

"Aren't you the pep talker?" She was already nervous about facing and fighting the demon. Hearing his perception of her odds wasn't helping that.

Nathanial gave her a hard look. "You should call Spade."

"You've got such a death wish," she muttered. "For the last time, I'm not calling Spade. Period."

Denise wasn't telling Nathanial the other reason she was keeping Spade out of this, aside from the fact that he'd absolutely never let her do it. Raum had an ax to grind with Spade after those salt bombs. If Spade showed up anywhere near the demon, Denise had no doubt Raum would try to kill him. With her unheard-of capacity for injuries, she had more of a chance than Spade did.

And she'd be damned if she'd stand back once again and let the man she loved fight—and die—for her.

"So if Raum knows these bullets won't kill you, what's the point of me shooting you?"

"Because if I'm wounded enough, I can't shift. You wouldn't have been able to shift that day after your stab wound, except Spade healed you. That's why Web kept me drained of blood all the time, aside from selling it, of course. He knew otherwise I'd shift into something that could take him out. If Raum sees me wounded, unable to shift, he'll be a hell of a lot more inclined to think you're not double-crossing him."

Her palms were sweaty, making the gun feel slick in her grip. "Where, ah, do you want it?"

"If it's in the shoulder, it won't look convincing enough. In the heart might kill me if Raum removes the brands right away once he arrives...and we need him to remove the brands from me, by the way. That's your best chance to attack, when he's concentrating on pulling his power from me back into him. Aim for the middle. It'll take long enough to heal that Raum won't be suspicious, but should be healed enough that it won't kill me when I'm human again."

"But if I hit a major organ and you're still not healed enough when you become human again, it *might* kill you. I think I should just shoot you in the leg or something."

Nathanial waved his hand. "Look, we don't have a lot of time. Your boyfriend is probably scouring the area looking for you, so if you want to keep him out of this, you need to aim for the gut and shoot me already. If I end up dying from the gunshot wound, it's still a far better fate than what Raum has in mind."

Denise took one step forward, centered her attention on Nathanial's side around the navel level, and then pulled the trigger.

He stumbled back, holding his side, red leaking out from his fingers. "Mother*fucker*," he panted.

"Sorry," Denise said uselessly.

"It's all right." Nathanial's voice was hoarse from pain. "Now, hide the demon-bone knife in the sand by your feet. Then all you need to do is slice off those tattoos on your forearms. Once the protective spell is altered, Raum'll know it. He'll come running, believe me."

Denise tried to steady her nerves and then reminded herself that being wigged out would only help in this case. What prompted a transformation? Hunger, nerves, pain, stress, and horniness. She'd have four out of the five covered. It should be enough to prompt her to shift. Of course, Nathaniul thought there was nothing Denise could imagine strong enough or horrifying enough to defeat the demon.

Well, Nathanial hadn't been there that night on New Year's Eve. She'd seen one of the creatures that had killed dozens of powerful vampires, ghouls, and her husband. It burst into the basement and mauled Cat's mother. Only the spell that created such an abomination being broken seconds later, and a lot of vampire blood, had saved Justina.

Raum had no idea the kind of horror Denise had lurking in her nightmares, but she was about to show him.

"I'm ready," she said, tossing her cell phone farther up on the sand, but burying the demon knife a few inches from her feet.

Then she took one of the silver knives she'd stolen from Oliver and sliced it down her forearm, careful to only remove the skin and not bite into the tendons. Or arteries. It burned and throbbed with a terrible fire, making her break into a sweat and bite back a whimper. *Almost done. Almost...*

"God *damn* that hurts," she whispered when she was finished.

"Careful." Nathanial's voice was grimly amused. "Don't curse God now. We need all the help we can get."

Denise gave him a fleeting caricature of a smile but then swiped the blade down her other arm before she lost her nerve. It hurt just as much as the first one did, and was more difficult, with the blood slicking down the blade and her fingers shaking from pain. When she'd reached the last etching near her wrist, she was gasping, her fingernails starting to curve into those hideous claws that she now realized had always been those of the monster from her nightmares. The same one she intended to transform into shortly.

The knife fell from her fingers and Denise folded up her arms, holding them to her chest to stem the bleeding.

When she glanced back at Nathanial, someone stood in her line of vision.

"Why hello, Denise," Raum purred.

Spade circled the skies over Monaco, focusing his vision on every vehicle that even remotely resembled an SUV. He'd flown over the whole bloody principality twice and yet still hadn't found it.

What if Denise ditched the SUV and took another car? She had a gun, after all; it would be easy for her to force someone out of their vehicle. What if looking for the SUV was a waste of time that might cost Denise her life?

Crispin flew as well. Cat searched on the ground with Oliver, as neither of them was able to fly. It had been almost half an hour and there was no sign of Denise or Nathanial.

Could she have gotten out of Monaco that fast? Which direction would she have gone in? Dammit, *why* had she done this? That demon-dodging sod wasn't worth it!

"Mencheres!" Spade suddenly said out loud. He aimed for the nearest rooftop, dialing on his mobile on the way down.

"Did you find her?" were his sire's first words.

"No," Spade said shortly. "But can't you track her another way? A few months ago, your visions of the future weren't coming to you anymore, but have they returned since then? Or can you use your power to see where Denise is now?"

It sounded like Mencheres sighed. "My visions haven't returned. I see nothing anymore…and neither can I use my power to pinpoint Denise's location. That, too, is gone from me."

"Why the bloody hell haven't you found a way to fix that!" Spade almost shouted into the mobile, fear making him irrational. "I've never once asked you to use your power for me before. Why now, when I need you the most, are you of no use to me?"

He hung up before Mencheres could reply, wanting to keep his line free in case Denise called. She still had the mobile he'd given her. It had been in the backseat along with the gun. Spade tried to calm the rising panic in him as he took to the skies again. *Fate couldn't be so cruel as to do this to him twice, could it?*

Or perhaps Fate was *exactly* this cruel, letting him fall in love with another human, only to once again have death snatch her from him.

Raum faced Denise, his black eyes lit with red embers and his light brown hair blowing in the cold breeze coming off the water. He wore jeans and a T-shirt with "Got Brimstone?" emblazoned across the front of it. If she didn't know what he was, Raum's bizarrely normal appearance wouldn't make her look at him twice. But she did know what he was, and the smell of sulfur enveloped her like an unwanted embrace.

"You dare call me here, so close to salt water? You think that makes you safe? I'm very, very disappointed in you," Raum bit out, advancing a step toward her.

"You took advantage of my kindness, broke our agreement—"

"Raum," Denise interrupted. "Look behind you."

The demon did a slow circle and then his laugh echoed out. He bounded over to Nathanial and seized him in a gleeful grip, swinging him around with the same sort of uninhibited exuberance that Spade had twirled her with just the other night.

"Nathanial, my long lost protégé, how *happy* I am to see you again!" Raum exclaimed. He even kissed Nathanial full on the mouth, with a loud smacking sound. "Ah, you taste so despairingly sweet. I intend to have such fun with you, you know that."

Nathanial cried out at something the demon did. Denise couldn't see what it was through Raum's back, but whatever it had been, it was painful.

"You think that hurts?" Raum hissed, his tone changing from ringingly cheerful to something so low, Denise could barely hear him. "You have no idea what agony is, you deceitful little filth, but you will. *Forever.*"

No matter what happened later, right then, Denise was glad for everything she'd done in the past two hours. She *couldn't* have lived with sending anyone to what Raum had planned for Nathanial. Yes, Nathanial had made the bargain with the demon, but dammit, he'd already paid enough for that during his time with Web. He'd been a stupid kid who made a terrible mistake, but he shouldn't have to be eternally punished for it.

And if she lived through what she did next, she'd stop punishing herself, too. For letting Randy get killed, for the miscarriage…all of it. *It's time for both of us to be forgiven*, Denise realized. *More than time.*

"Raum," she said, raising her voice. "I want to get

out of here, but first I want you to prove that you can give me my payment."

The demon swung around, still cradling Nathanial in an embrace tighter than a lover would use. "Oh, really?" Raum drew out. "And how do you *think* you'll have me prove that?"

The dangerous challenge in the demon's voice would have made Denise back away shivering five weeks ago, but not tonight. She met that red-tinged gaze without blinking.

"You promised me if I brought Nathanial to you, you'd leave my family alone forever. And that you'd take these brands off and your essence out of me, returning me to a normal human. You might say I'm a little leery of you after everything I've been through, so why don't you show me first that I'll survive getting these brands off. Or I run as fast as I can back to the vampires, and you can try to chase me while toting Nathanial."

A smile played around Raum's lips. "Quite the little firecracker now, aren't you? I like this side of you, Denise. It's very attractive."

The way he emphasized that last word made Denise's flesh crawl, but she knew that was why he'd done it. Raum wanted her to be cowering and frightened, but if she let him rattle her even once, she wouldn't have the nerve to follow through on the rest of it.

"Take the brands off Nathanial. Let me see that he's normal again. Then take off mine and we can go our separate ways, me alone and you with him. Like you agreed."

"Don't do it, please," Nathanial begged. Tears leaked out of his eyes, and the desperation on his face was palpable. "That's too quick. Don't you want to torture me when I'll be able to heal over and over? Haven't you wanted to make me scream for a *long time*, Raum? You can't do that if I'm human!"

Clever ploy, Denise thought. The demon's expression had been skeptical when Denise finished talking, but after hearing Nathanial, he smiled with such malevolent anticipation that part of her wanted to run away from the mere sight of it. *Don't you dare*, she ordered herself. *You can beat him. He'll never expect you to fight back.*

"Why, Nathanial, you *have* smartened up these past long decades, haven't you? You know no matter what I do to you, it's better than what will happen once you're human and I can kill you. I did plan to take my time playing with you first, but—"

"Yes, yes, play with me!" Nathanial shouted. More tears poured. "I deserve it, you've earned it…"

"But this will be even more fun!" Raum said, his voice turning into a feral roar.

Then Raum seized Nathanial's forearms, the demon's hands covering those intricate tattoos, before he plunged his fingertips inside Nathanial's skin.

Nathanial screamed, high-pitched and piercing. That smell of sulfur increased while a hazy buzzing seemed to fill the air.

"Feel that?" Raum snarled. "It's the end of your immortality, boy!"

Now, Denise told herself.

She scratched gouges into her legs with her clawed hands, bringing a fresh spurt of pain. In her mind, she focused on the image of one of the creatures from that New Year's Eve. Creatures so foul, so powerful, they didn't exist anywhere but in the darkest realms of the most forbidden black magic.

That feeling of blind chaos spread through her body, the same one she'd felt when she transformed on the boat. This time, however, Denise didn't try to fight it. She fed the wildness, expanding it with all the horrible images from that night. Focusing on all the details of the creature that months of antidepressants, therapy, and distance from the undead world still hadn't let her forget.

Her skin felt like it burst, waves of pain and energy racking her entire body in lightning-fast blasts. Only a small part of her was aware that Raum turned around to give her almost a quizzical glance.

"What the hell?" he muttered.

A howl came out of her throat, as hideous and loud as the sounds that had haunted her nightmares. Then Denise bent and pulled the bone knife from the sand.

She'd show the demon *what the hell*.

With another unearthly bellow, Denise charged at Raum.

Chapter 36

Spade felt the vibration in his pocket even over the wind ruffling his clothes. He snatched out his mobile, hope leaping in him when he saw the call numbers.

"Denise!" he shouted as he answered it. "Where are you?"

An awful, bone-chilling howl came over the background before Spade heard Nathanial's weak voice.

"Hurry. I can't help her. I can't even tell which one she is…"

"Where is she?" Spade thundered. He'd kill that rotten sod if anything had happened to her. He'd rip the flesh from his bones—

"Under one of the two commercial piers in Vieux Port, Marseille. Hurry."

Spade cursed as he hung up. Marseille was more than an hour and a half away, even at his fastest speed. Could Denise hold off the demon that long?

He aimed his body like a bullet northward even as he dialed Crispin. He picked up on the first ring.

"She's under one of the two commercial piers in Vieux Port, Marseille. The demon is there. Where are you?"

"I'm still in La Condamine, almost two hours away," Crispin replied with open frustration.

And Mencheres was even farther away in Genoa. "Get there as quick as you can," Spade said, hanging up.

He channeled all his energy not into his body, but on a point southwest in the distance. He had to be there. Not here, there. Now. Denise needed him. *Go faster.*

Flashes of Giselda's crumpled body at the bottom of the ravine filled his mind—her hair reddened from blood, face frozen in pain, body still warmer than the snow around her. She'd been dead only a couple of hours before he arrived on that day. The knowledge of how short a time had elapsed between his arrival and her death had haunted him for over a century, but now would he lose Denise by mere minutes?

He would not fail. He could not. *Go. Faster.*

The ground blurred into nothingness beneath him. Only the expanse of the water on the horizon mattered, beckoning him with the whisper, *She is here.* If he concentrated enough, he thought he could almost feel Denise, could taste her struggles against the demon like acid on his tongue.

Go. Faster.

Time passed. That dark water in the distance became more than a hazy smudge low in the sky. Buildings lining the seashore crystallized into more than misshapen, indistinct lumps. After another few minutes, he could make out the basilica landmark, with its golden statue of the Virgin Mary as if she were peering over Marseille. He changed direction ever so slightly to hone in on Vieux Port. *Not much longer now. Come on, Denise. Keep fighting.*

A few minutes later, the outline of the piers came into view. Spade streamlined his body more, trying to avoid even the slightest resistance to the wind, his power capacity at its zenith. Still, he couldn't see what was underneath the piers. He wasn't at the right angle yet, he was still too high…

Spade dipped as low as he could go without risking crashing into any of the structures between him and his goal. Even with the wind roaring by, the first of the howls reached his acute hearing. They sounded like the baying of the damned. Were those the sounds of Denise still battling with the demon, or Raum chortling over his victory?

Go. FASTER.

He sighted the underbelly of the piers in the next several seconds, which seemed to stretch out like a warp in time. The sounds came from the one nearest him. Spade focused on that, seeing a male lump that had to be Nathanial lying on the sand. But ahead of him in knee-deep water, two forms clashed in violent combat.

Two forms. Spade's heart felt like it exploded in his chest. Denise was still alive.

And yet he knew his strength was deteriorating. Blood loss from the fight, combined with the expulsion of all his power to reach her as quickly as he had, left Spade almost dizzy from encroaching weakness. He'd arrived in time to fight the demon, but he had almost no energy left.

All I need to do is hold him off until Crispin gets here, Spade thought grimly. He only needed to keep Denise alive that long. He could do it. The demon might not have any silver, after all.

The figures locked in a death match became clearer with each passing second. Spade had never seen the demon before, but even this far away, it was obvious neither of them was in human form. Two equally horrendous monsters grappled each other in the surf.

Smart girl, the thought flashed across his mind. Denise must have dragged the demon into the salt water, knowing how it would hurt him. Another few seconds showed that one of the creatures held a pale, bony knife. Spade couldn't tell which was Denise. One of the creatures had bulbous muscles, an enormous, misshapen head, and a powerful body covered in skin that seemed to be blistered. The other was just as large, with an appearance that seemed to be derived from the most grotesque version of the grave—

Spade zeroed in on them, moving his arms in front to hold his fists out in a straight line. With the fierceness of their battle, neither was aware of his zooming approach. Their snarls and howls of fury rang in his ears, one of them now so very familiar.

He plowed into the enormous blistered-skinned creature with all his speed, knocking it away from the other one. Slamming both of them into the soft sand floor, covering the creature with seawater and his own body. The tremendous impact stunned Spade as well, but he forced his body to twist, holding the creature on top of him. His arms lashed around the struggling figure, fighting to keep its head locked into position. The creature bucked and flailed so powerfully, Spade knew that if he didn't let go soon, his arms would be ripped from their sockets.

"Denise, now!" he tried to scream, but salt water and sand filled his mouth. His entire head was under water. She couldn't hear him, or perhaps she was too far gone mentally to even understand.

The creature's claws bit into the arm Spade had fastened around its neck, tearing. Pulling. Pain and pressure built through Spade's body, but he didn't let go. It would have to tear him to pieces before he'd release that monstrosity back on Denise—

A shriek split through Spade's ears, unbearable even through the cocoon of water and sand. Then that heaving, thrashing creature in his grip began to shudder, its claws no longer ripping into Spade, but sliding off instead. The sea felt like it boiled around him, foam clouding what little vision he'd had, until he saw nothing but frothing white. And then the twenty-stone creature on top of him began to shrink…until it was pushed away and fresh claws dug into his skin.

Spade let the other creature pull him up, not batting away the monsterish hands that gripped him. He blinked, trying to get the sand out of his gaze, but could still make out the rapidly decomposing body at his feet. Its eye sockets were blackened holes with that bone knife still sticking out of one of them. Then Spade turned back to the hulking form of the large, ravenous zombie bending its head toward him.

"Get back, you don't know if that's her!" Nathanial shouted.

"Yes I do," Spade replied, gently grasping the warped arms and ignoring the needles of pain from the claws still stuck in him. "It's all right, darling. You can stop now. Look at him. You did it. He's gone."

And she had, as amazing as that was. Lovely, brave, gentle Denise. Demon slayer.

Those claws pulled out of his arms and that beastly head dropped, looking down as if ashamed. Spade didn't hesitate. He pulled her into his embrace, noting with irony that in the form she'd chosen, ripped straight from that awful New Year's Eve, they were now the same height.

"It's all right, darling," he repeated, stroking her. "It's finished. You can come back to me now, Denise, come back..."

During the several minutes it took Nathanial to crawl over, smelling strongly of blood, Raum's body had turned to bones in the surf and Denise had transformed back into herself. Spade kept one foot planted on the remains of the demon as he drew off his shirt and covered her with it. Most of her clothes had been torn beyond decency in her fight with Raum, or torn from her body expanding into a much larger size.

"Spade," she whispered at last, tears sparkling in her gaze. "You knew me. Even like that, you knew it was me."

"Of course I did," he responded, holding her tightly. Overwhelming relief coursed through him, mixing with joy as the panic from the past few hours released its hold. Denise was safe. She was whole. He'd ask for nothing more out of life.

"I couldn't do it," she said, voice soft. "I'm so sorry for worrying you, and for hitting Oliver, but I couldn't give Nathanial to him. It would have destroyed something in me that I refuse to lose, and I couldn't risk Raum getting revenge on you for those salt bombs, either."

"I don't want to talk about that now." Yes, he was still upset over how she'd risked herself so recklessly, but he didn't want to berate her at the moment. He was too damn glad that she was alive.

She took in a deep, ragged breath. "Spade...the brands are permanent now. Only Raum could remove them, and he's dead. I can't die as I am, unless you stab my eyes out with that demon knife, but I'll stay like this. If you can't deal with me being a—a shape-shifter, I'll understand—"

"Foolish girl," he cut her off, pulling back to look into her hazel eyes. "According to what you just said, you're safer now than you ever would be, even as a vampire. So I don't give a rot about you occasionally changing shape. You could transform into a zombie, a werewolf, or a cat again. Whatever you fancy. I'll still be there, and I'll still be madly in love with you."

She hugged him fiercely. "I love you so much," she choked.

Spade returned her embrace with equal passion, that feeling of joy and relief growing even deeper. He meant what he'd said. If Denise were a vampire, well, silver was easy to come by, but demon knives? The only one he knew of was still in the bony eye socket of Raum's corpse, and Spade would grind the demon's remains to dust so that no other weapons could be forged from him.

Even as she still clutched him to her, Denise started to laugh. "Nathanial can show me how to better control the changes, but even so, you never have to worry about me turning into a cat again. Didn't you know? I'm allergic to cats."

Epilogue

Denise placed the bouquet of flowers on the grave. They were mixed with pinecones. She knew he would've appreciated those more than the lilacs, tulips, and roses.

She cast a look around the cemetery. Spring was definitely in full swing, covering the bare branches of the trees back in their leafy coats. The ground underneath her felt soft. Warmed from the sun. Not hard and cold, as it had been the day she'd buried him.

"Hey," Denise said low, wiping away a tear as she touched the headstone engraved *Randolph MacGregor. Beloved son and husband.*

"I wanted to tell you that I'm with someone. You met him before. His name is Spade. Yeah, I know, a vampire, right? We haven't been together that long, but sometimes...you just *know.* I knew with you. I told you I'd love you forever, and I will,"

Denise paused to wipe away another tear. "I love him, too, and I know this is right. It might be soon, but it's right. And I know you would have hated what I did to myself since you died, so I wanted to tell you I've let go of the guilt and the fear. When I remember you, Randy, I'm going to smile, not cry. You're a part of me. One of the best parts. I just wanted to tell you that."

She stood up, brushing the headstone once more. "And if you meet someone named Giselda," she whispered, "tell her she's still part of Spade, too. A beautiful part. Please thank her for that."

Denise touched her fingers to her mouth, kissing them, and then placed them against his name.

"Goodbye."

Her eyes dried by the time she walked back to where Spade waited by the car, but they hadn't been tears of grief. They were of warm remembrance, and when Denise walked into Spade's arms, she was smiling.

"Ready to go, darling?" he asked, kissing the top of her head.

She didn't need to look back. "Yeah, I'm ready."

Nathanial rolled down the window of the backseat. "Now I get to meet my family?"

He asked the question with such hope that Denise's smile widened. After this, they were going to her parents' house, where Denise would introduce Nathanial to the remainder of his family, far removed though they might be.

And she'd be reintroducing Spade to her parents as their new son-in-law. They'd been married twice in the past two weeks. Once by a justice of the peace, and once vampire-style by slicing their palms and declaring themselves before Cat, Bones, Alten, Ian, Mencheres, and a ghost that Denise still couldn't see. That marriage might not be recognized by vampire society, as Denise could never change into one, but to Spade, it counted, which was all she cared about.

"Now you get to meet *our* family."

* * * * *

Dear Readers,

Hope you enjoyed *First Drop of Crimson*! The next "spin off" novel in the Night Huntress series, *Eternal Kiss of Darkness*, features one of the most powerful vampires in existence—Mencheres—as well as a new heroine with a complicated past of her own.

Kira dreams of being a detective, but because she testified against her former husband, a cop who was killed in prison, no police force will accept her. Her disastrous first marriage and all the cheating spouses she's tracked down as a private investigator have made Kira wary of relationships. When she comes home from an all-night stakeout, she interrupts what she believes is a gang-related attack of a handsome young man. But before she's knocked out, Kira sees things that are impossible— fangs, superhuman speed, and the "victim" killing his attackers without even touching them. Then when Kira regains consciousness, she discovers the man she tried to save isn't human—and neither were his attackers. Even worse, the charismatic vampire won't let her go, because now she knows about what lurks in the night.

Mencheres is a four-thousand-year-old Master vampire who lost his visions of the future, making him doubt his usefulness as a leader. On top of that, a former enemy is investigating Mencheres for breaches of vampire law, and Mencheres knows the ancient Master vampire won't stop until he destroys him. The last thing Mencheres needs is to be saddled with a human, but he couldn't just leave Kira to die after she tried to "save" him. His plans to heal Kira and erase her memory of what she'd seen backfire, however, once he discovers Kira is immune to mind control.

Kira presents Mencheres with a problem: He can't trance her to forget about her new knowledge of vampires and ghouls, but if he lets her go and she tells other people about the undead, the Law Guardian after him will have the proof he needs to annihilate Mencheres. As he spends time with Kira trying to convince her not to talk about the undead world, Mencheres recognizes a kindred spirit, and is torn. If he keeps her against her will, he's ruining his only chance to have a relationship with the first woman he's fallen for in thousands of years. If he lets her go, Kira may be responsible for giving his enemy all the tools he needs to bring Mencheres down.

Thanks so much, readers, for making it possible for me to extend the Night Huntress world with stories featuring side characters I've grown to love as much as Cat and Bones. Also your e-mails, comments, and continued support have been more than amazing. I hope you continue to enjoy your journey through the world of vampires, ghouls, ghosts, demons, and the occasional dark magic. I know I've enjoyed sharing my stories with you.

Jeaniene Frost

At Avon Books, we know your passion for romance—once you finish one of our novels, you find yourself wanting more.

May we tempt you with . . .

- **Excerpts** from our upcoming releases.
- Entertaining **extras**, including authors' personal photo albums and book lists.
- Behind-the-scenes **scoop** on your favorite characters and series.
- **Sweepstakes** for the chance to win free books, romantic getaways, and other fun prizes.
- Writing **tips** from our authors and editors.
- **Blogs** from our authors on why they love writing romance.
- **Exclusive content** that's not contained within the pages of our novels.

Join us at
www.avonbooks.com

AVON
An Imprint of HarperCollins*Publishers*
www.avonromance.com

Available wherever books are sold or please call 1-800-331-3761 to order.
AVON0815

*G*ive in to your Impulses!

These unforgettable stories only take a second to buy and give you hours of reading pleasure!

Go to *www.AvonImpulse.com* and see what we have to offer.

Available wherever e-books are sold.

AVON
IMPULSE

AVONIMP0815